THE TOURMALINE

ALSO BY PAUL PARK

A Princess of Roumania

Soldiers of Paradise
Sugar Rain
The Cult of Loving Kindness
Celestis
The Gospel of Corax
Three Marys
If Lions Could Speak and Other Stories
No Traveller Returns

THE TOURMALINE

Paul Park

A TOM DOHERTY ASSOCIATES BOOK
New York

This is a work of fiction. All the characters and events portrayed in this novel are either fictitious or are used fictitiously.

THE TOURMALINE

This book is printed on acid-free paper.

Edited by David G. Hartwell

A Tor Book
Published by Tom Doherty Associates, LLC
175 Fifth Avenue
New York, NY 10010

www.tor.com

Tor® is a registered trademark of Tom Doherty Associates, LLC.

Library of Congress Cataloging-in-Publication Data

Park, Paul, 1954–
    The tourmaline / Paul Park.
        p. cm.
    "A Tom Doherty Associates book."
    Sequel to: A princess of Roumania.
    ISBN-13: 978-0-765-31441-3 (acid-free paper)
    ISBN-10: 0-765-31441-X (acid-free paper)
    1. Teenage girls—Fiction. I. Title.
    PS3566.A6745T68 2006
    813'.54—dc22
                              2006011274

First Edition: July 2006

Printed in the United States of America

0 9 8 7 6 5 4 3 2 1

FOR MIRANDA, OF COURSE

1

Catching Up

1 The Hoosick River

ALL AFTERNOON THEY SEARCHED the riverbank. Peter went a mile in both directions, tramping through the high reeds next to the water. At intervals he called Miranda's name.

It was a bright, clear day. The reeds were golden in the winter sunlight, which dazzled him and blinded him when he stopped to catch his breath. But the light had no warmth in it. Past three, the shallow water in the hummocks and the roots were covered with a veiny skin of ice. Peter's feet were numb inside his running shoes. Hoarse and discouraged, he went back to the boat to search for woolen gloves.

Andromeda was no help. Since her transformation, she'd never been a barking kind of dog. She'd scarcely made a sound except for a breathless wheezing almost like speech. But now she ran in circles on the higher ground, yelping and howling. Sometimes she had her nose down, but there was nothing methodical in the way she sniffed and searched. She might just as well have chased her tail.

How much was left of her? Peter asked himself. Packed in her dog's narrow skull, how much was left of the girl he'd known? Raevsky—the old man—was better, more effective. He kept to the place in the high pines where they'd last seen Miranda, before she'd faded and vanished into the air. He went outward from the clearing in a spiral, his pistol in his hand.

In the morning he'd been stiff and lame, and in the afternoon he still moved slowly. He limped down the steep bank to meet Peter at the boat.

Six hours ago they'd pulled out of the current and stopped at this curved, sandy shore. Lured by—what? Peter had seen someone he thought he recognized, a woman in a long skirt. She'd called to them from the high ground. Then she'd come to greet them as they brought the boat to shore.

At that moment all of them had been waylaid by something separate, some illusion from the past. Miranda didn't even glance at the woman, the Condesa de Rougemont in her embroidered vest. She didn't wait for the boat to come to land. She'd thrown down her paddle and stepped out into the shallow water. She'd scrambled up the slope and disappeared into the woods and that was that.

What was she looking for in this empty forest, on this empty river? Now she was gone, and Peter stood with his hands in his pockets where Raevsky had drawn the boat onto the pebbles. Above him somewhere, Andromeda yipped and wailed.

"No reason to seek more," said Captain Raevsky with his sibilant Roumanian accent. His gun was in his pocket and he blew on his hands. He moved his weight from one boot to the other, because of the cold or because his feet were sore. "Now we make camping."

Peter was relieved to hear him say so. Stamping though the frozen reeds, Peter had already half-convinced himself it made more sense to leave. They must be close to where the Hoosick River joined the Hudson near Mechanicville. He remembered the distances from home. He and his parents had driven up to Saratoga more than once. But in this world there was no town before Albany, and even Albany was a tiny place with just a few thousand souls, as Raevsky called them. But there'd be food in Albany. Food was what they didn't have, except for some stale biscuits.

They could put in a couple of more hours on the river. Miranda had left them. There was no reason to stay. Yet when he saw Raevsky reach into the flat-bottomed boat and pull out one of the big canvas bags, Peter felt a shudder in his body that was like hope. With another part of his mind he told himself he never wanted to leave this Godforsaken shore. So he dragged the tent from the pirogue and then carried it up the slope to a flat place in the golden grass, while Raevsky pulled dead branches from the trees. Andromeda was nowhere to be seen.

In the morning on this trampled rise above the river, he had seen a woman or woman's ghost, dressed in a long skirt and embroidered vest. Even a name had come to him—Inez de Rougemont. Now all that seemed dreamlike and unreal, except for the scratches on his forearms, the bites on his shoulders where the woman had attacked him, diverted him, prevented him from following Miranda. Then she'd dissolved and disappeared just as Miranda had—Peter laid out the stiff canvas and slid the stakes into the sandy ground. Because the wind was stronger now, he found some rocks for the corners. It was a military pup tent. When it was up, he brought the blankets and sleeping bags from the boat. Of them, at least, there was no lack.

These were all supplies from Raevsky's journey up the river. He'd come from Roumania to kidnap Miranda for some woman named Ceausescu—Peter was unsure of the details. But in a series of catastrophes his men had all been lost, leaving blankets enough for six or seven, but food for none.

Raevsky made a fire-ring of river stones and dragged some logs to sit on. He built up a big fire and was heating water in a tin pot. Now he sat pulling off his boots, crooning over his damaged feet, which Peter could see were mottled and discolored in some places. With his clasp knife, Raevsky scraped away some skin.

He ripped a shirt to make clean bandages, which he smeared with ointment from a jar. Grimacing, he slid his feet into his woolen socks again. Squatting among the rocks, he pounded up some biscuits in a pot, then softened them with boiling water.

He was in his fifties. Under his knit cap his hair was gray. And his beard was rough and grizzled over his blotched, uneven cheeks. When he smiled, as now, holding out a bowl of sludge and a tin cup of ouzo, Peter could see his upper teeth were missing on one side.

"So. Eat. In the morning, then we see."

"I'll stay here," Peter said impulsively, idiotically.

Raevsky shrugged. "Is nothing. Why? She is not here."

Peter sat with his warm biscuits in his wooden bowl. Off in the woods, Andromeda yowled and was silent.

Raevsky stared at him. His eyebrows were coarse, his eyes sunken and bright. "What you saw?" he asked, finally.

Peter shrugged. It sounded stupid to say. "There was a woman. She called out to me. Rougemont or something—she was dressed, I don't know, like a Gypsy. Now I can't even remember. Look," he said. He put down his cup and bowl, then held up his hands. They were scabbed and torn.

"And so? I did not see this Gypsy."

Now it was getting dark. The sun was down behind the trees on the far bank.

"So?" Peter said.

Raevsky blew his nose on his fingers. Then he wiped them on his trousers. "When you saw Miss Popescu . . ."

He spat into the fire. In a moment he went on. "You smell burning smell? Fire burning and black powder? Then something, some ordure, and so? Murdarie—garbage?"

He sniffed to clear his nose again. "Is telling you, this murdarie of conjuring. Is like a conjure trick—no woman there. Me, I saw blackness, blindness, then you and the dog, fighting with nothing, only a spirit or shadow. Then Miss Popescu, all alone. Then nothing. She is gone."

"Yes," Peter muttered.

All afternoon he'd tried not to think about it. So he'd occupied his mind with searching and shouting and stumbling through the grass. All the time, though, he had known what Raevsky knew. She was gone. Peter could not bear to think she'd left him and gone home.

"Think!" Raevsky said. "What did you see?"

Peter felt tears in his eyes, and so he turned his face away. He sat watching the wide bend of the river below them, listening to the sound of the water. He couldn't bear to think that maybe right now she was back in Williamstown, the real Williamstown where he and she had got to know each other and had gone to school, and where his mother was buried and his father lived on White Oak Road. He couldn't bear to think that she had left him here in this new version of the world, where America was a deserted forest full of lunatics, and Roumania of all places was a great power, and he didn't know anyone at all.

"I saw her in the clearing," he said. "And above the trees I could see something, the outline of a building. Just for a moment—it was farther on. I was looking at Miranda, but I saw this other thing out of the corner of my eye, a stone building. Then she was gone, and when I looked up there was nothing."

"Make me this house." Raevsky sat forward on his log. He took a drink from his tin cup, then held his left hand out in front of him toward the fire. "Make me look."

Peter sighed. "It was big. A tall narrow building with a tower. Stone walls. Wooden shutters. And a copper roof—you know that green copper. Just the roof—I saw it above the trees. There was a steeple on the tower."

"Ah," Raevsky said. "You did not see this before?"

"No, but . . ."

"What did you smell? Did you smell this garbage . . . ?"

"No. But there was something. Salt, I think."

They sat staring at each other. "Again," Raevsky said. "Before you say 'No, but . . .' "

"I didn't think about it. Not till now. But Miranda told me about something like that, maybe in Romania. Roumania, whatever."

"Yes," Raevsky hissed. He gestured with his tin cup of liquor. "And you know nothing. But I tell you. This is her father's house, Prince Frederick Schenck von Schenck who sold us to the Germans. If not for Ceausescu—no, is not important. She is there! You will see. In Roumania. Salt, you were smelling at Constanta on the oceanside!"

Doubtful, Peter watched him across the fire. Though not a tall man, nevertheless he was impressive, because of his big chest and long arms. His legs, though, encased in dirty woolen trousers, were spindly and small. "What am I telling you?" he said now. "You understand this thing. You saw this house when Miss Popescu was little—little girl. You and Sasha Prochenko. Is it not so? You remember this somehow!"

Peter laid down his cup and bowl. The sweet, wet biscuits were uneasy in his stomach. "I've never been to Roumania," he murmured doggedly.

Raevsky took a sip of ouzo. Then he blew his cheeks out, whistled a low note. "So is true you have no memory? Pieter de Graz—you are a famous man! I myself saw you come from Adrianople when I was with the army. More than twenty years. When you beat the Turkish champion."

Peter didn't want to listen to this. In this new version of the world he had a past, but he didn't want to hear about it. "My name is Peter Gross," he said. "I live with my father on White Oak Road. In June I'll be eighteen. This year I had Mr. Langer for English composition."

"So, maybe that was true one time. I did not know of this Herr Langer. Now I say you are the Chevalier de Graz. You and Miranda Popescu, and Prochenko too, I think you are in a dream world like inchisoare . . . like a prison. Now you wake up and one half thinks is still dreaming. One half knows truth. Look at hands."

Peter imagined he would put his hands behind his back, or else roll them in the belly of his sweater to keep warm. Instead he found himself stretching them together toward the fire, his left hand as he remembered it and his huge, new, right hand, with its black hair and chipped nails.

"Look," Raevsky said, pointing at the bull's-head birthmark below his right thumb. "Is de Graz's mark. How do you explain?"

He had no explanation. He had been born with a birth defect, a stump that ended halfway down his forearm. There'd been a time when he'd said prayers at night, hoping he would wake up whole. But not like this, with a grown man's hand, a hand that was not his own.

"How do you think you know this name, de Rougemont, who was in the gazettes and rich magazines of Bucharest twenty years before?"

Peter shook his head. Unbidden, an image came to him, a woman in a silk dress, laughing as she danced with a man in an old-fashioned uniform, with gold braid and epaulettes. "How long?" he asked.

Raevsky rubbed his nose. "Prince Frederick killed in prison before Miranda Popescu is born. That is twenty years. Then she is in Constanta with her aunt Aegypta Schenck and that is seven or so. Then nothing—she and the others gone, Prochenko and de Graz. We said the empress put them to the wall because they were Prince Frederick's men. We said the girl is . . ." He put his fist to his throat. "Now I am glad it was not so!"

"How old was he—de Graz?"

Raevsky shrugged. "Twenty-five, twenty-six and so. Even then younger than me."

Peter didn't want to hear it. More than once his parents had told him about what had happened when he was five years old. It was as if he'd forgotten how to talk. They took him to a specialist in Boston. Then in a year he'd learned again. "But you were like a different child," his mother had said. Twenty-five minus twelve plus five, he calculated now.

"So I will guess about Prochenko," Raevsky went on. "I have heard this story when a man turns to a dog. Old conjuring from Carpathian Mountains. Transylvania. You will see. I know him one time with Prince Frederick at Havsa—I see his eyes. Who is this dog now with Lieutenant Prochenko's eyes? He will come back, I say. Body and soul. Little and little."

Peter did not find this reassuring. But maybe Andromeda had had a year like his when she was small, when something new had entered her. If so, what would she grow into now? What would he grow into, little and little?

"Sasha Prochenko," he muttered aloud. And it was true. The name seemed to mean something.

"Prince Frederick's aide-de-camp," murmured Raevsky. When Andromeda yelped again from where she cowered in the woods, he lifted up his forefinger and pointed at the sky. "I tell to you," he said, "there is this duhoare, a stink of conjuring."

Peter made an effort to unload this from his mind. What did it matter about the Chevalier de Graz, the other man? He was who he was, and Andromeda, and Miranda, too. They weren't some other people. "Miranda told me about the castle on the beach," he said.

Captain Raevsky slapped his knee. "And so that is dovada—evidence. I swear to you that this is so. Here she is gone. There—she wakes up in that place. You see the house. So she is in Constanta, nowhere more. I swear on the platosa—the breasts of Nicola Ceausescu. She is there, I know. I will go to find her in that place."

As he drank more, he lapsed more into Roumanian. With his thumb he brushed the small insignium embroidered on his woolen shirtfront, the red pig of Cluj.

This was his monomania, for which he had sacrificed his men and most of himself, as Peter understood. Not for one moment did he waver now. And Peter had heard it all before: He would go and find Miranda and deliver her to the Baroness Ceausescu's house in Bucharest and receive his pay, whatever that meant—money, a kiss, a pat on the head, or a kind word. "I will take steamboat to New York City," he said now, plotting his way. "But not fear," he continued, as if to reassure Peter with what he must know was a lie. "Nicola Ceausescu will make her happy in her house. In Saltpetre Street! Your friend will live there and be glad!"

Peter wondered if the old man had ever had a conversation with this woman, the Baroness Ceausescu. What had she said to him to command him so completely? Whereas Peter had been with Miranda for many days, and felt her arms around him when he was sick, and listened to her, and argued with her, and had good days and bad days—days they'd hardly spoken. He'd known her in two worlds, at school in Massachusetts and then here, where people treated her like a piece of property to fight over and steal.

The evening had closed around them. Peter couldn't see a moon.

"You must remember Nicola Ceausescu," Raevsky went on. "Is possible you saw her in the theater. So when the baron is inside government, but he is not a husband for her. Not good husband, too old and too much wounds from fighting. Now she is in her house, still growing like a . . . flower. Is true, oh you will see in Bucharest, when she is come home to her place. I tell you when she sent us from the Gara de Nord, I and my men, and my sister's son to Bremerhaven on a train. Then she touched my hand, each one! She is no aristocrat, no snob. Daughter from people, from Roumania. Body like boy's, but skin is soft and clear!"

Around them the darkness had settled in. Peter could still see the massed shadows of the trees across the river, and over there the sky gave a charred glow. On the other side of the fire Raevsky mumbled and muttered, and Peter didn't pay him much attention. But even as he let the words get lost in his own thoughts, still he was affected by the fervid tone, if not the sense. It was not Miranda that Raevsky was describing in increasingly precise detail. Still the description brought a picture of her in Peter's mind, her dark blue eyes and pale skin and dark brows, her habit of drawing a strand of her black hair out from her face and perching it behind her ear.

"She has a spot on umar—shoulder," murmured Raevsky. "Where the line falls to chest. Oh, and the line of neck, sharp, like . . ."—on and on. In his mind's eye Peter saw not features and details so much as moods and expressions: how Miranda's forehead would grow dark with anger, which before he'd met her he'd assumed was something that could only happen in a book. How a blush suffused her cheeks, etc. The way she chewed on her lips sometimes. Gestures also: In the morning, even in the cold cave they'd stayed in when he was sick, she would step outside and do some stretches in her T-shirt, always the same order, always the same ones. Habits: They had come here without toothbrushes, and she had found a way of flossing with long strands of grass.

"We'd started to be friends before," she'd told him once. "There's no reason that has to stop." He remembered her expression when she said this, at the same time that Raevsky was describing the small lines that curled around the edges of her lips, when Nicola Ceausescu smiled.

That was enough for Peter. He couldn't listen anymore. There was something useless about this, he thought, something that felt like masturbation, particularly if Miranda was in Roumania or wherever. Far away, but he would find her before Raevsky did. What else was he supposed to do? He would take Andromeda and find her, and one day they would wake from this.

Immediately he heard Andromeda's long howl, as if it had been conjured by her name. It was closer than before. She had come out of the pine trees and was standing on the bank above the river. Now he saw her silhouetted against the lighter distance, stopping on three legs with her foreleg curled, her muzzle raised.

2   *Saltpetre Street*

THAT SAME DAY, WHEN the Elector of Ratisbon collapsed on the marble stairway of his hotel in Bucharest, there was some limited pandemonium. He was helpless to prevent two junior officers and the ballroom manager from carrying him into the lobby and placing him on a settee. Unaware of his disgrace, they brought him water and smelling salts, while at the same time the hotel doctor chafed his wrists and loosened his cravat. The doctor was not able to suppress a sniff at his atrocious ugliness—even though his head was spinning, the elector noticed this, and it brought him to his senses quicker than the stink of the ammonia under his nose. Always he was braced and refreshed by the bad opinion of fools.

In any case the doctor was a quack, neither taking his pulse nor listening to his heart, where it was obvious the trouble lay. He wanted to remove the patient, as he called him, to Brancoveanu Hospital, which was out of the question. One Roumanian was bad enough, and the elector certainly would not permit himself to be touched by more than one. He would not be prodded by barbarians, who doubtless still used maggots and leeches in their operating rooms.

But he was able to prevail upon the natural chauvinism of the German officers. He had a ticket on the seven o'clock train to Munich. If he could send a telegram, he would have his personal physician meet him at the Bahnhof.

Lying on his back on the settee, even to himself he was not able to admit the truth: that General Stoessel was frog-marching him back home to answer charges of conjuring, prestidigitation, and reanimating a corpse. And the general, when he was summoned from his room, was not able to admit it either. An old-fashioned gentleman, he allowed the elector to retain a molecule of dignity. Or perhaps courtesy had nothing to do with it, and it was more a question of German prestige: The elector would be escorted to his suite to rest there and arrange his packing, until a diplomatic attaché arrived to take him to the train. Stoessel knelt beside him to murmur the details. He wouldn't place him under guard. In return he asked for a promise to go gracefully and not make any trouble.

From his place on the settee, the elector gave his solemn word, while at the same time he observed with contempt the gray hair in the general's ear, the flecks of dandruff on the collar of his uniform. The elector was a modern man, a man of science and a patriot. He would not be bound by idiotic conventions, and not just because these specific charges against him were false. Whatever ghost or spirit had appeared in Greuben's room, the elector had had nothing to do with it.

No, there was work to be done, and even in his weakened state the elector was the only man in Bucharest to do it. No, he would not break his sworn parole to benefit himself. But it was not by following social niceties that he could serve his country and its civilizing mission in Roumania—an antique martinet like Stoessel couldn't be expected to understand. Because of his prejudices, he could not even be depended on to see the threat, which came out of the hidden world.

The elector had lost consciousness for only a few moments. Now he was able to get up and walk to the elevator without incident. Doubtless Stoessel thought he'd lost his balance on the stair, light-headed from the turn of Fortune's wheel. Bashed his head on the marble balustrade—the general would have no sympathy for any illness, much less for the effect of any conspiracy or curse. So it was important for the elector to pretend nothing had happened, to walk alone, unaided, and to maintain his strength until he reached his own fifth-floor suite. Then he staggered to the armchair under the portrait of Inez de Rougemont—a society belle of the previous generation, painted in Gypsy costume. He was grateful for the warmth of the afternoon sun that spilled through the high windows. Gasping for breath, he lay back against the cushions while he pondered what to do.

He understood, or thought he understood, two things. First, that Miranda Popescu had disappeared out of his hands. And second, that the Baroness Ceausescu was implicated in her disappearance. At least she was involved in the attack on him—as he'd pitched onto the landing of the hotel stairs, he had smelled the aroma of pig shit and brimstone, too subtle for anyone but him to notice, and in any case it had dissipated by the time he'd woken up. The brimstone was the stink of conjuring, and the barnyard odor was the signature of the Ceausescu family—the red pigs of Cluj. And if Nicola Ceausescu was able to attack him, knock him to his knees in the middle of a crowded hotel, then it was clear the elector had misjudged her. His natural contempt for women had allowed him to underestimate her strength. Was it possible she had the Popescu girl?

Not content with stealing the tourmaline that was essential to his plans, had she been able to steal the girl also?

During his crisis on the stairs, the elector had been able to extract Miranda Popescu out of her American wilderness, a mental feat no less prodigious for having been unplanned—a product, he supposed, of his unconscious intellect. Now, seated in his armchair under the spring sun, with separate parts of his mind the elector was searching the Hoosick riverbank in North America, and at the same time the environs of Prince Frederick's castle in Roumania, where the girl should have arrived safe with all the other bric-a-brac he had transposed. But everywhere he looked, Miranda Popescu was not there. She was not among the tall pines where the boy and the dog and the gray-haired soldier searched along the river, and she was not among the scrub oaks and the overgrown roses of her father's garden on the Black Sea.

Yet when he brought his gaze in closer, and tried to penetrate the slate roof of the baroness's house near Elysian Fields not two kilometers from where he sat, he found himself baffled—repulsed by an active power. What had Stoessel said? He'd sent half a dozen soldiers to arrest her for complicity in Claude Spitz's murder. But the elector suspected the priority might be low or even nonexistent for the military commander of the city. Because he had no appreciation of the science of conjuring, Stoessel couldn't understand the kind of threat the baroness might pose, not just to the elector's life—which after all didn't concern him—but to the future of German interests in Roumania.

The elector pulled his watch from the pocket of his waistcoat. It was only five o'clock. He had more than an hour before Stoessel sent a car for him. At his elbow a bottle of Abyssinian whiskey stood on a low table, and he poured himself a small, restoring glass.

He had been on the edge of triumph when he'd suffered his little heart attack. Weakened by Greuben's accusation and the prospect of a trial in Germany, nevertheless he'd been about to rid the world of Miranda Popescu. She would no longer, by virtue of her nature and the superstitions of her people, pose a threat to Germany. The simulacrum of himself that he had animated in the Hoosick wilderness was reaching out its knife. But then the elector was struck on the hotel stairs, and the little world he had assembled on the riverbank to lure her from her boat—all of it had disappeared when he'd lost consciousness. Her childhood home in Constanta, which he'd managed to restore from his own memory of Prince Frederick's estate, had been sucked back across the ocean in a current of mnemonic aether, the model subsumed into the original again.

What a stupendous effort that had been! No wonder he was exhausted. With unprecedented mental skill he had made a thousand objects if not real, then at least substantial enough to fool the girl for twenty minutes, half an hour—though doubtless she'd been caught in her own trance of remembering. Stuck like a fly in a web of memory, but she'd escaped by the time the elector raised his head up from the marble stair.

And as all those imagined objects had come back across the ocean, had she come with them? But if so, where was she now? Neither on the riverbank nor in Constanta. Instead, what if the baroness had snatched her as if out of the air, by some new process of conjuring unknown to the elector? And if so, what use did Nicola Ceausescu have for the white tyger of Roumania, who held latent in her silly, girlish body the power to defeat him and the German army, as she'd already demonstrated on the day she was born?

He took another sip of Abyssinian whiskey, the finest in the world. No, this was a nexus of strength that could not be permitted, that must be challenged and destroyed. And not by General Stoessel, who'd think he was a foaming lunatic if he tried to explain—or worse, a criminal. No, by the elector himself, and there was no one else. Greuben and the others who used to do his work, now it was obvious he could no longer depend on them. And probably that was more of the baroness's cleverness. Doubtless it was she who had sent Spitz's corpse into Greuben's room. Who else but she could have guessed he was the murderer?

In his thoughts the elector was like the captain of a steamship, lulled to complacency by the flat sea and the warm weather, who too late sees the iceberg loom out of the fog. Under the whiskey's influence he gave the baroness more credit than she deserved. But at that moment she appeared to him a terrible and subtle adversary whose strength had been concealed by his own prejudice. So it was with a kind of gallantry that he decided to confront her in his weakened and exhausted state, and more than that to sacrifice everything, to leave everything behind, even his luggage and his clothes. General Stoessel would never forgive him. The foreign minister would never forgive him once he heard.

Nevertheless, the elector was happy as he struggled up out of his chair and slipped the bottle of whiskey into the pocket of his cutaway coat. A few hours before, he had dressed in formal clothes in order to receive a medal or a diplomatic appointment, he had guessed, because of his service to his country. Now he did not change his suit. There was no time for that. But over everything he put a raincoat, then he took his hat and cane. He wasn't naïve enough to think he could escape the hotel unnoticed. His smallpox-pitted face made that impossible. If stopped, he would say he was going for a stroll, or to the tobacconist in Trajan's Row, or to the pharmacist around the corner. It was true he had the makings of a headache.

He rode down through the elevator cage in the middle of its coil of stairs. And immediately the hotel manager skittered toward him across the tiles, wringing his hands and murmuring in his irritatingly proficient German—"Your grace, I am so sorry. . . ." And when the elector stammered his invented errands, the man begged to be allowed to send a messenger as well as a valet to help him pack. "Your train is not for seventy minutes. Is it not so?"

"Yes. I will be back directly. I would prefer some of the fresh air. . . ."—it was he, the elector, who sounded like a foreigner. What was wrong with him? His voice was like an echo in his own ears.

Once through the revolving doors and out into the Piata Revolutiei, he tried to lose himself among the crowds. But that was difficult because as always the unmannerly Roumanians drew back from him as if unwilling even to share a public street. Luckily, though, the sun was disappearing behind mottled clouds, and by the time he reached the smaller streets below the square, it had begun to rain. This allowed him to pull up the lapels of his coat, pull down the brim of his fedora; he glanced around. No one was following him. Stoessel was as good as his word.

Under a gray drizzle he wandered down the Calea Victoriei. He passed the turnip-domed temple of Artemis, where some kind of mumbo-jumbo celebration was taking place. He passed the tiled façade of the Greek baths, and the crenellated armory where the empress had last appeared in public. When was that—a week ago? Everything had happened so fast. Since then she'd escaped into the mountains were she'd joined some partisan irregulars. Stoessel's dragoons, of course, had entered the city without incident, after the collapse of the Roumanian army.

Now they patrolled the thoroughfares, mounted men in rubber capes, the rain sluicing from their high helmets. Proud of their discipline, the elector nevertheless concealed his face whenever they passed. He was afraid of being recognized, and so he stared instead into the plate-glass windows of the fancy shops. Always before he had taken a cab or a private carriage along this road. He had never noticed its magnificence.

Now the day was drawing in. In forty minutes he stood in Saltpetre Street outside the baroness's house, a tall, narrow mansion in a row of others. The new German authority had kept the gaslights burning in the streets, but the rain was heavier now. Cold in his damp coat, the elector studied the candlelight that burned in several windows. What should he do? Greuben had told him about the corridor under the street, which led to the garden of the building opposite. But recently that house had been sold to pay the baroness's debts. And even though it still looked empty, the elector was not the kind of man to slink and spy. No, he would walk up the front steps like a gentleman. In the pocket of his raincoat, he fingered his small silver derringer.

As it happened, the front door was ajar. He slipped inside, into a small square entrance hall between the street door and another door of clouded glass that led into the house. A dim light burned behind it, and the elector paused. Was this the spot where Nicola Ceausescu had cracked the head of Spitz the jeweler, brained him with a candlestick? Then her servant had dragged him out, abandoned him in his own carriage. Greuben had found him by the Targu Bridge and finished the job, although the jewel was gone. The tourmaline was gone.

Nicola Ceausescu had stolen it. And tonight the Elector of Ratisbon would take it back from her, by force if necessary. He'd take it back to Germany where it belonged—the inside door also was unlocked. He placed his cane in the stand, then hung up his hat and raincoat. He put his hand on the curiously carved brass lever and stepped into the house. The smell of pigs and conjuring was stronger here, though doubtless his was the only nose in Bucharest that was delicate enough to smell it, an acrid back-odor that competed with something else, a hint of soft perfume.

As quietly as he could, he fumbled down the darkened hall. Light came from an open doorway, and the sound of movement also, a quick light step. With the derringer in his hand he put his shoulder blades against the flowered wallpaper—no, nothing. There was silence for many minutes, until the elector crept down the hall again and peered inside the door.

Immediately he was aware of a ticking clock. Light came from a pair of candles in brass sticks on the mantelpiece. Was it one of those that she had used on Herr Spitz? Between them hung a portrait of the old baron, the star of Roumania glimmering at his throat. There was a time when he'd been deputy prime minister, after his perjured testimony against Prince Frederick Schenck von Schenck.

The widow stood with her back to him, looking toward the mirror on the opposite wall. He shrank against the door frame, but the glass was angled away. She did not turn around. Her narrow shoulders were hunched forward and she was hugging herself, her arms wrapped in a silk shawl. It was patterned in green paisley with golden threads that caught the light, and under it she wore dark riding breeches and high boots. Now she looked down. The elector watched her upper vertebrae, the nape of her long neck, her helmet of chestnut hair, cut at the same line as her jaw.

If he had followed more closely the artistic career of Nicola Ceausescu, perhaps he would have recognized the pose. It was from the third act of Florio Lucian's version of *Medea,* when the queen reveals that she has murdered her own children. There is no remorse or even melancholy in Lucian's piece, which the baroness had first performed in Moscow twenty years before. Medea rises fresh from the bath where she has drowned her young family, unclothed but for a shawl.

The orchestra is silent even when the queen begins to dance. From her body's eloquence, as if through a process of synesthesia, the audience can almost guess the musical accompaniment. Watching from the doorway of the baroness's room, the elector could almost hear it. Nicola Ceausescu raised her knee and made a small kicking motion standing on one leg—a plaintive gesture in the original performance when her legs and feet were bare. Now there was something ominous in her booted kick, something triumphant that was foreign to the opera but appropriate here.

The baroness had lost some of the innocence she'd shown at the premiere, or at least some of the pretended innocence—she had been homeless in the streets before the impresarios had found her. And though the elector had never been susceptible to female beauty, still he was astonished by what he felt in his damaged heart. He had the derringer in his hand, but he could not press the lever, even to extinguish a threat to Germany or to prevail against a woman who had tried to kill him not three hours before, and who would have shown him (he was sure) no mercy if their circumstances were reversed.

The baroness stripped away the shawl, revealing her bare shoulders. The light shone on her flawless skin. Under the shawl she was dressed in a yellow camisole. The elector was astonished by her beauty and the beauty also of the jewel she carried, the purple tourmaline that he now saw for the first time.

Entranced, he watched her slide it over her skin as if it were a bar of soap. Stolen from Claude Spitz the jeweler, nevertheless it was a piece of German property—Kepler's Eye, dug from the brain of the famous scientist. It contained a natural and verifiable power, which is why the elector craved it.

With the stone there was no limit to the good he could accomplish. Always up to now his plans and aspirations had been thwarted by prejudices of the mindless, sabotaged by his own ugliness, his cold and unlovable nature. Once he had the stone in his possession, he intended to make a scientific study of the phenomenon, how a lifeless mineral could ignite passions and emotions, love itself—now he understood the trick. This was not a real emotion he was feeling as he watched the movement of the baroness's naked arm. No, it was something artificial, motivated by the jewel. Nicola Ceausescu was a repellent, brutal slut, tonight as always.

He could see that now, too late, and could see also her face and her violet eyes in the looking glass, her triumphant, smiling mouth. She had darkened the glass, and now it cleared. Too late he understood that she'd been watching him all along. His hand, as he reached out with the derringer, felt leaden and crippled. Any second-degree adept could have recognized the language of her gestures, the hypnotic trance that now disabled him. The pistol fell to the floor.

"YOUR GRACE, I'M PLEASED TO see you," said the Baroness Ceausescu. "Soyez le bienvenu—be welcome, please."

She spoke in French, the language of the cultured classes in Roumania. She took one of the brass candlesticks from the mantelpiece. Squatting down, she held the burning taper beside his face. "Have you really come alone?" she said. "Your grace—you are a brave man."

What a difference a few hours made! When she had reached out to touch him on the hotel stairs, she had been afraid of the elector's strength. But now he knelt between her boots, his body under her authority. She let the light play on his seamed and pitted face, a chaos of broken features out from which peered two big, chocolate-colored eyes.

She put the candle down on the stone hearth. "Your grace," she said, "permit me." She had stripped one of the tasseled cords from the window curtains. The softness of her voice as she secured his hands was utterly unfeigned, as if she were inviting him to join her in some intimate refreshment.

It was her exploration of Medea's sympathy for Jason (the father of her slaughtered lambs, poor man!) that had made the Moscow performances into a triumph. And for the elector too she felt such pity, while at the same time she pulled the cord so tight it cut into his wrists. When she recalled the contemptuous and public way he had humiliated her in the pastry shop, she pitied him. How terrible to be at the mercy of someone you have wronged! Particularly someone who could not forgive you. Because forgiveness was the opposite of sympathy.

"I'm afraid you are not comfortable," she murmured. "Believe me, it is only for a little while."

The numbing curse, magnified and made more potent in the mirror, nevertheless would not affect him for long. That was the reason she was tying him so tight, with loops of rope around his ankles and his wrists, now joined behind his back. This was how she'd trussed Aegypta Schenck before she died. Daily she reminded herself, punished herself for that. Doubtless she had positioned the elector to remind herself again. She knew he could speak to her. "Speak to me," she murmured near his delicate, small ear.

"I have something you want," he mumbled, his lips numb.

It was true. He held her only child, her son, a prisoner in Germany. How unkind to have mentioned it!

"I could arrange for his return," he muttered.

How heartless to give her the choice! No, she would not be fooled. She would not bargain for her son. No, she could only hope he was well treated in Ratisbon, in a modern clinic or in her enemy's house. She could not care for him now, penniless as she was, running from the police. When she was established as the white tyger of Roumania in whatever form that took, then she would command him to be sent to her.

She did not deserve, in any case, to see her son—not yet. Just in these last days she had betrayed a boy in her care, used him and discarded him. Now he lay in prison if he was even still alive. Daily, hourly she thought of him to punish herself. But surely she could not allow his sacrifice to be for nothing. He'd been willing to die for her.

Now the man she'd wanted him to kill was in her hands. She could not let him go, not even for her own son's sake.

"I will put him on a train to Bucharest," said the elector. "Allow me to send a telegram. You have my word."

His word—what good was that? This was some new trick. "Your grace," she murmured near his ear. "You must not expect me to bargain like a shopkeeper."

The effect of her small conjuring was wearing off. She had pulled up his dress cuffs, and now she watched his slender forearms clench, his wrists turn as he searched for a looseness in the rope. She must be quick.

On the mantelpiece under the portrait of her husband stood a celadon jar, a gift from the Maharajah of Hokkaido, a Korean nobleman who long ago had come to hear her sing. Inside the jar was a blue apothecary's bottle with an eyedropper screwed into its top. Kept in its place of honor, the bottle contained the same quick poison—extract of castor beans—that her husband had used to take his own life eight years before. Depressed by his wife's coldness, his son's illness, but most of all by his betrayal of his only friend, he had put a single drop onto his tongue. Now the baroness wondered what another drop would do, when placed upon the liquid, trembling surface of the elector's eye.

Experimentation is the key to alchemical success. She stood up, aware as always of her body's language. In her light camisole she ran her fingers up and down her arms. She had studied the elector's face in the mirror when she'd done her little dance. From his expression she had guessed he had enjoyed it, though she had not thought he was that sort of man. Still it was kind to give him pleasure at the end.

"Tell me," he said, and she could tell by his enunciation that the numbness of his lips was wearing off. "Do you have the white tyger here?"

"Yes," she answered. In the mirror she watched his ruined face.

"Where is she? How did you bring her here?"

"She came in by the door the same as you." The baroness smiled, not for his benefit. "She is in this room."

And he must have been an idiot after all, because he actually moved his head to peer around, as if he expected the white tyger to appear among the armchairs and sofas of the small square room. Rain fell against the windows.

"I mean Miranda Popescu," he began.

The baroness watched him in the glass. Seen from that angle, she realized with surprise, his face showed a perverse beauty. Perhaps it was impending death that suddenly ennobled it, or else in the mirror she was able to forgo comparisons with other human faces, forgo also an instinctive horror of disease. Gratified by her own generosity, she saw how the spots and fissures of his face made a pattern that gave meaning to his eyes, as if they appeared at the center of a whirlpool. At the same time she was fumbling for the bottle in the celadon jar. There was a box of phaeton matches, a few graphite pencil ends, all the usual detritus that accrues in such places. But the poison was gone. Maybe Jean-Baptiste had moved it, worried the police might search the house.

And she was thinking about what the elector had said about Miranda Popescu, the daughter of Frederick Schenck and Clara Brancoveanu. The girl had occupied too much of her time over the past months. First she'd had to dig her out from the artificial world where her aunt Aegypta had hidden her, extract her like an escargot from an elaborate, conjured shell. Once free of it, the girl had reawakened in the North American wilderness, where the elector and the baroness had squabbled over her.

Now, evidently, she had disappeared. Nicola Ceausescu had sent someone to catch her, had sent that fool Raevsky, who had failed. Where was the girl now? And more than that—who cared? For as it turned out, she was not the white tyger after all, the savior of Roumania, who would throw out the potato-eating Germans. No, she was just another unlucky girl. The white tyger—as the baroness imagined she'd discovered in the last few hours—lived in this house in Saltpetre Street, stood in this room with her nicotine-stained fingers searching the bottom of the green jar, and was justified in any act of cruelty in the fight against her enemies, her country's enemies. But damnation, where had Jean-Baptiste hidden that little bottle?

All this time she had been watching the elector in the mirror while she fumbled with the jar. He knelt behind her and had let his face sink down so she could see the bald spot on the crown of his head in a circle of black hair. Now she looked away so she could search the mantelpiece. Immediately she heard a crash and felt herself dragged down.

The elector had freed his hands, had reached up to slide his hands under the waistband of her trousers. She could feel his hands on her bare skin. The cloth ripped and she felt his hands on her body as he pulled himself up. And when she turned to face him and hammer at his head with her palms' heels, she stumbled backward over the lip of the hearth. She fell on her back across the stones, while he dragged himself on top of her. She felt his weight on top of her.

His face was near her own as she scratched and pulled at his hair and ears—even now she could not bear to touch his face. Until the roaring in her head drowned out all blame, still she reproached herself for making such a sloppy knot. The gilded, satin rope had been too slippery. She understood that now. Under no circumstances should she ever have turned away from him. But mostly she was horrified to see his face so close, and smell his perfumed breath, and see his exquisite small teeth in his distorted mouth. She flailed at him to keep him at arm's length. But he had his hands on her throat, and she couldn't breathe. As her consciousness wavered, again she imagined his face as a sort of whirlpool or a drain.

THE ELECTOR OF RATISBON CLUTCHED her slender neck, tried to subdue her body underneath his own, though he was not a heavy man. He clutched her with his hands, but he could not bear to look at her, and as her mouth opened and her tongue came out, he turned away. He could no longer hear the ticking clock, and so he looked for it behind the armchair in the corner, watched the oscillating pendulum in the high case, the carved iron hands—how long would this take? Already he could not endure it. Lying across her body with his ankles tied together, he told himself that he would not have touched this hateful woman except in self-defense. He straightened his arms, raised himself so as to press with his entire weight. He stared at the golden clock face—what a waste this was! What a waste of time and effort, this last quarter of an hour!

This creature, he realized now, was no threat to Germany. In his hotel room he had given her too much credit. Now he regretted his missed train, his broken promise, his lost career, which made it even more essential to secure the jewel—frustrated, he knocked the back of her head against the stone tile. It was clear this woman knew nothing about Miranda Popescu. By God, where was the girl? She was not in this house, it was sure.

But the baroness's struggles were weaker now. The candles on the mantelpiece, out of sight from where he lay, flickered and made shadows in the little room. The old-fashioned horsehair furniture loomed above him. He was conscious of his own breathing as the baroness's breathing failed. His thumbs had found the ribbed tube of her windpipe. She no longer buffeted him around the head. She no longer tried to writhe away. Still the clock hands had not budged.

He couldn't look at her. Under his hands he could still feel her stubborn life. His fingers pressed into her neck—part of this was not a waste, he told himself. He would take Kepler's Eye from the baroness's body. Where had she hidden it in these small clothes? He would restore to Germany a piece of German property, and the stone would do for him what it had done for her. Johannes Kepler had been an ugly man.

He risked a glance at her and saw her eyelids were sealed shut. The job was done.

For a moment he relaxed his hands. But he'd been premature, and now her eyes stretched open. Horrified, he shouted out. Please God this was the death spasm, the last rage as the body gave up hope. Her face was red and mottled, her hands scratched at his wrists. Her back bent under him and lifted them together off the floor. Oh, he could not tolerate this. If not for his duty to his country and himself, even now he would release her, let her up, give her some brandy with his own hands, make her promise not to meddle in politics or conjuring—no, her promise was worth nothing.

This woman who twisted under him, whose back bent like a bow, who hurt his ears with her gurglings and gruntings that were worse than screams, her husband had been a powerful alchemist. After the creature died—gave up and died, for the sake of all the gods—he would explore the house and find the baron's laboratory. Maybe he had books the elector had not seen. He would climb the hall stair onto the second floor. . . . In his mind the elector began an exploration of the house. Room by room he wandered through it, a meditation technique that he had read about in Chinese manuscripts, and which he now hoped would lift him up above the horrifying present, where two animals were locked together in a struggle to the death—he the serpent, the symbol of his house, and she—he could see it now. Moments before he'd been afraid to look at her. Now he could not take his eyes away. He could not but stare at her, and he saw now there was something catlike in her face. If she'd deluded herself into thinking she was the white tyger, then that delusion had come out of the stone. He'd have to guard against megalomania when the jewel was in his power, but right now he could almost believe in what she said. He would make certain at the moment of her death, which was fast approaching—let it be soon, by the bowels of God! His fingers ached. He could not press any harder.

It was horrible, but even now her staring eyes and contorted face maintained a kind of beauty, her chestnut-colored hair lit by an oblique shaft of gaslight from the alley outside the tall window. Worst of all he sensed some pleasure in himself. There was pleasure in feeling this woman subside under his hands. He was conscious of his sweat and her sweat also on her slippery neck and breasts—her camisole had come undone. One strap was ripped away. Part of him could celebrate the natural dominance of men, which at the same time surprised and disgusted the other part—oh, he was eager to be gone! And he would snatch up the tourmaline, and maybe a few books, and stagger out into the night—just one moment more! He could feel the shuddering of his heart, the pounding of the blood through his body. From a medical point of view as well, it had been a mistake to come here, when all he needed now was to rest in the saloon car to Germany, or in his sleeper after the results of this terrible day. The blood was hammering in his brain, mixing with the sound of his own cries, mixing with another sound that now he heard for the first time, a stick or a fist on the front door, and men's voices shouting out in German: "Polizeistreife! Sicherheitspolizei!" etc. He had not thought he'd been loud enough to raise the watch.

No, but here were Stoessel's men, shown up too late. The baroness's throat was bruised under his hands. He tried to fall on her, add to the pressure there, because the slut was still alive, he could feel it. The long hand of the clock had scarcely shifted.

Now the police were here. He could let go and leave all this to them. He tried to move but found his ankles still tied stupidly together, found his fingers still locked around the baroness's throat. He could not budge them.

Besides, the policemen had found the door open and had already come in. He could hear their boots in the hall, and now they were surrounding him, helping him up. "Herr lieutenant," he gasped. "I'm glad to see you!"

In their exuberance they were a little rough. He counted six stalwart men in the brown uniforms of the Hanoverian Guard. The elector was out of breath, but he managed to gasp out as he was pulled across the room, "General Stoessel wants to examine her in the matter of Herr Spitz. If you search her you will find the jewel she stole from him. I am . . ."

But the lieutenant was squatting over the baroness's body. "I know who you are," he said. With what the elector supposed was commendable chivalry, he took the green shawl from where it lay on the carpet and used it to cover the woman's torn camisole and torn trousers. At the same time, with commendable professionalism he was attempting to revive her. "Madame la Baronne," he said, "Je vous en prie—are you all right?" And then in German to one of his men: "Get me some water. We are not too late."

It was true. After an episode of spasmodic coughs and gulping breaths, the baroness's limpid eyes crept open and she turned onto her side.

If he had been a better student of theatrical history, the elector would have recognized in her movements the beginning of the last act of *Ariadne in Love*, where the heroine is wakened by the rescuing god after a night of violent excess. On the beach in her ripped costume, Ariadne also turned onto her side, stretched out her naked arm, murmured, "Where am I—ah!"

"If you search her, you will find the evidence of the crime, which is a priceless piece of German heritage," said the elector, suddenly aware of his croaking, ugly voice and clumsy gestures. How embarrassing to be tied at the ankles like this! Two men supported him to keep him from falling over. "I am . . . ," but again the lieutenant interrupted.

"Thank heavens we were not too late," he murmured over the baroness's chestnut hair. Then in a moment: "I must tell you that Herr Luckacz wants to talk to you about the Spitz affair, at your convenience. When you've recovered."

"Captain, you have my word," whispered the baroness, her voice soft and bruised. Tears stood in her eyes.

The elector was seized by a desire to laugh. In the drafty room he felt the sweat slide down his arms. The lieutenant mumbled a few more words, too soft to hear. And then, "My father saw you at the Federal Theatre House in Hildesheim. Every night for a week, though he was just a student."

Nicola Ceausescu ventured a weak smile. "Captain, you are very kind. But you must come back and let me thank you properly. . . ."

All this time she had not raised her head. The elector stared at her until she lifted up her chin. Even then it was as if she were afraid to look at him. Her eyes made small attempts—he had to admit her skill was astonishing. She turned her face to him in profile, then shrank against the broad chest of her rescuer. She let her shawl slide down to reveal her naked shoulders.

She was at least a decade older than the officer, who now admired her with calf-struck eyes. The elector watched his nostrils flare as he admired her smell. He himself suppressed a bark of laughter. Then with the coarseness of defeat he said in German, "You will see she's not even an honest whore. She's no intention of paying you for what you've done."

He stood supported by two guardsmen in steel helmets. Hands under his armpits, they hoisted him onto his tiptoes as the lieutenant stood. "You are a disgrace," he said.

In Hanover the local government was run by peasants and factory workers, which meant that idiots had risen to all positions of authority. This man was typical, a handsome, empty-headed lout with yellow hair and a soft yellow mustache. Now he spoke to the baroness again. "Madame, you must see this fellow does not represent the best of Germany. He is a civilian first, a private citizen. The order has come down. The general will ship him home to answer a complaint. I must warn you—he's a conjurer."

Though her eyes showed astonishment, the baroness was still able to manage an adoring smile. "I didn't know. I was just lighting the candles when he broke in."

3   *After Five Years*

IN CEAUSESCU'S SERVICE YEARS before, once Captain Raevsky had visited Prince Frederick's castle on the beach. Then the prince was already dead,
his sister chased back to her cabin on the Brancoveanu lands in Mogosoaia
north of Bucharest.

Then the castle was already empty. Now, sitting on his log in the American
wilderness, it was easy for the captain to imagine Miranda Popescu waking
there, stretching herself awake in the March sun while he and Peter lingered on
the riverbank. She would yawn and wake up in the garden near the fountain.
The picture was as clear as if he'd seen it in a photograph.

But from his fifth-floor suite in the Athenée Palace Hotel, already that day
the Elector of Ratisbon had scanned the beach, the castle, and the grounds and
had discovered nothing.

Later, when he was again in his own house in Germany, he found himself
returning to his vice of clairvoyance, like an addict who can't acknowledge his
own danger. Disgraced, sequestered, but not in legal jeopardy—his family con-
nections had seen to that—he sat in his study in the schloss at Ratisbon, contemplating the Roumanian coast.

Miranda Popescu was not there—where was she? But if he'd been able to
turn his eye into the future, then he would have seen her.

When, to protect her niece, Aegypta Schenck had placed her in an artificial world, had invented the United States of America and the Romanian republic, and had written the book of their history, she'd worried that a seven-year-old child would not be easily adopted from the Constanta orphanage. Rachel and Stanley, the Americans she'd had in mind, were looking for a younger child, a girl no older than three. Thinking also that Miranda would be happier without her childhood memories, she'd tried hard to accommodate them.

In a moment, with just a few written words, she'd robbed her niece of five years—more than five. But when Miranda made her journey to the real world and Roumania, when she stumbled through the woods into her father's garden, all that lost time had come back. The place was as Raevsky pictured it. But on the Black Sea beach north of Constanta, Miranda was more isolated than she yet knew. Six thousand miles separated her from Peter and Andromeda, as well as five years and a few months.

Spring had come. There were flowers in the garden and the grass was high. From where she stood among the brambles and weeds, through a cut in the sand dunes she could see the water. The stone wall rose up, and she could see the steps to the terrace, but she didn't want to go that way, not yet. The sun came from behind a cloud. Drawn to the sunlight on the water, seeing no one, afraid of the empty house, she left it for a moment to trudge north along the shore. Maybe she thought for a moment she could escape the lost years the empty castle represented. From time to time she climbed up to the dunes.

"Peter!" she cried out once, but she knew he couldn't hear her. Birds passed overhead, and there were pelicans in the water. Inside a tidal inlet she found an abandoned boat. It was pulled onto the hard shingle and the bottom was broken out.

Since she'd arrived here, for half an hour she had been moving without thinking, observing things without talking about them in her mind. Now she stood staring at the broken boat, letting her anxiety build—there was no way to put it off any longer. In fact she was anxious to see the place; she turned back toward the spire of the castle. No, but she couldn't, not just yet. Midway where the pebbles were replaced by fifty yards of coarse yellow and black sand, she stopped.

And then suddenly a memory where there had been nothing before: She had come down here to go swimming in the old days. She'd come with Juliana and her family. Now she remembered the red and white pavilion where she used to change, the shape of the big rocks, the sweep of iron-encrusted sand. She remembered the light on the water and the feeling of sand on her toes—

this sand. And she sat down to unlace her boots and strip off her stinking socks. She rolled up her jeans and then stepped down into the small thin waves, and the water was warmer than she'd imagined, though still it was not warm.

Now she looked around again to make sure she was alone. The boulders would shelter her from someone in the dunes, someone in the tower. And because she was so dirty and filthy, and because she remembered this place, with trepidation she stripped off her dirty pants and stepped into the water, dressed only in her shirt and dirty underwear. The surf was gentle. It was a windless afternoon. The sun shone in the dark sky and the light felt good after so long in the snowy woods. The water was so clear.

At first she thought she'd splash her legs and leave it at that. But her hair was tangled and she wanted to get it wet. As one long wave receded, she took off her wool shirt and threw it behind her on the sand. With her arms crossed over her chest, she waded out until a bigger wave came and soaked her above the waist.

How glorious it would be to dive into the water and then climb up onto the beach and feel the heat of the sun! It would feed her hungry skin. Instead, the rocks banged around her feet. She was cold when she came out of the water, vulnerable, self-conscious. She didn't even wait till she was dry before she put on her scratchy shirt and chafing pants. With sandy feet she trudged back to the castle.

As she approached, she told herself she had to find some food. With food in her stomach she might have dared to take a proper swim. Now, as if the sun had thawed out part of her that had been numb with amazement, or as if the water had sobered part of her that had been drunk with memory, she realized how frightened she was and how alone. Knowing they were far away but not guessing how far, she called again for Peter and Andromeda. And when she found the path from the beach, again she hurried by the terrace of the castle without looking up. She hurried through the garden to the caretaker's cottage where she'd fought the man with the scarred face. He'd shown her breakfast on a long table. She climbed the steps into the room to look for some of those apples and rolls, but they had never been genuine and now they were long gone.

What had happened? She had seen the roof of the house. She'd been paddling down the river with Peter and Captain Raevsky, and she had seen the roof beyond the trees. Even when she'd found the place, she'd known it wasn't real, not in the ordinary sense. Objects shifted and lost substance when she touched them. And the man with the scarred, ruined face who had attacked her, he'd been more like a ghost than like a living creature. She had beaten him, disarmed him, knocked him to the ground here in this room. She'd darted through the door into the garden and then circled through the woods calling Peter's name. And when she'd given up and come back, the house was different, real this time. When she came up the steps again, the boards were real under her feet.

Had she been dreaming? Woken up? The cottage showed signs of an old struggle. There was broken crockery across the broken floorboards and the back door was off its hinges. It led to the pantry, Miranda now remembered, a low room off the back. In the old days there had been cabinets and ceramic vessels, a stone sink and a hand pump, a stove with a tin chimney. But the room was wrecked now. The outside wall was broken, and briars grew through the hole.

She found pots that were still intact but empty. The pump was dry. Once again Miranda turned, hoping to see Peter in the middle of the cottage's larger room, but there was no one.

Then she went out into the garden and lay in the rich warm grass. By the overgrown fountain she dug her hands down through the lily pads. Tiny frogs jumped through her fingers. She drank the water and she poured water from her cupped hands over her face and hair.

Around her there were birds and butterflies and hummingbirds. She lay down for a moment and put her arm over her face. She felt both languorous and desperate. She could lie in that warm place forever, and at the same time she must jump up. The sun was halfway down the sky.

At four o'clock in the afternoon she did what she'd been dreading, and climbed onto the terrace of the castle past the stone lion with the stone shield on its breast. Dressed in her black jeans and woolen shirt, she stepped over the octagonal, terra-cotta tiles toward the shattered French doors. Moss outlined each tile, and there was broken glass. She sat down on the balustrade to pull on her stiff socks and boots, which she had carried up the steps.

In this place, as in the cottage, every object seemed to liberate a new memory. Once free, they were gone. But by the dozens and the hundreds they receded into the air, leaving behind a sense of familiarity that was painful and exciting. This rough, convex, stone surface where she sat. These broken tiles. These curled brass door handles that were blackened now.

The doors sagged open. She slipped through them into the main entrance hall. Above her hung the big gas candelabrum whose ceremonial lighting was the sign her aunt was actually in residence. The candelabrum would mysteriously descend from the vaulted ceiling. A servant on a stepladder would reach up with a brass taper.

Across from Miranda stood the square-paned high windows that looked out over the sea. They were in shadow now. Facing them had been an area of comfortable furniture, big armchairs and settees, which were now ripped down to the springs. Miranda could see footprints of small animals in the dust. There was the inlaid table under which she'd run her wooden trains—a present from her aunt during the festival of Saturn. The threadbare oriental rug was gone.

Along one wall some of the bookshelves were intact, and under them there was a pile of leather-bound volumes. A book lay at her feet, and she picked it up. The plate on the inside cover showed a monkey holding a mirror. Below it a forceful signature. *Pieter de Graz.*

The Chevalier de Graz. The name gave her a shudder of recognition. And she found she could puzzle out some of the text as she opened the book, even without the French translation on the facing page. "Departe doara luna cea galbena . . ."—something about a moon over some icebergs. It was a book of love poems.

Now she was here, the language was coming back. In this place she'd been a child, not a baby. She understood that now. And maybe it was the language that was bringing back her memory now. Thoughts can't exist without words for them, Stanley had told her once.

Before her were the doors that led to the rest of the house. They hung drunkenly on their hinges, and some of the carved wooden panels had been smashed in. On the other side there was a stone-flagged hallway. Again the carpet was gone. To her left as she went in, a small and unpretentious staircase led to the second story, and straight ahead was the dining room and the kitchen. The hall she had just left, with its high windows over both the garden and the sea, was the largest in the house.

Most of the furniture downstairs had been carried away, and the rooms were empty except for broken glass and dishes and a few broken chairs. But when she gathered her courage to climb the wooden staircase, she found places on the second story that seemed undisturbed. There was a smell of bats in the stairwell, and some of the woodwork had been gnawed away. But the rooms were not wrecked, nor were the windows broken. The furniture was whole, and much of it was covered with thick, white, protective cloth. It was obvious no one had been here in some years. The curtains in the windows, particularly those overlooking the sea, were ripped and faded, and all the rooms had a strange, bad smell. Dust was everywhere. On the wooden floorboards Miranda's footprints left a mark.

The biggest room was on the east side of the house. It had a balcony overlooking the gray water. This was her aunt Aegypta's room, and she'd never been allowed to enter. Now with a furtive sense of transgression that wafted back across the years, she stepped over the threshold. There was a wicker dresser and a couple of wicker armchairs. There was a high, single bed with four carved posts, and on its dusty cover she laid down the book of poems while she stood looking around.

A line of photographs in tarnished silver frames stood on the dresser. Some were sepia prints and some were hand-tinted. Most showed ladies and gentlemen in formal clothes. Then there were several of the lady whom Miranda had only seen in dreams or in tara mortilor—the country of the dead—and even now no memories came back. But this is how she must have looked when Miranda lived in the house, her aunt Aegypta in a younger version. In one of the photographs she wore boots and trousers and carried a shotgun over her arm. In another she held a baby. With a sour, impatient expression, she pushed a lock of hair from the child's face.

Another photograph was larger than the rest. It showed a dark-haired girl of maybe seven or eight or nine, standing in the garden beside an ornamental plinth. Miranda took it to the long windows that led onto the balcony. With the sleeve of her shirt she cleaned the glass. The girl had small protruding ears.

It hurt Miranda to look into the girl's worried face. She couldn't put the feeling into words, but she found she could remember the circumstances of the portrait, the photographer in his dark coat, crouching behind his enormous apparatus. Lieutenant Prochenko had been there, the handsome guardsman who had been her father's aide. He'd been standing behind the photographer, making faces to make her smile as if she were a baby. He'd said something rude as usual when she was posing—called her his little lump-cat; always he refused to see that she was growing up. Her forlorn expression in the photograph, that was intended as his punishment.

But she couldn't yet begin to think about Pieter de Graz or Sasha Prochenko. It was hard enough to think of Peter and Andromeda. She pressed the glass face of the photograph against her chest, then placed it facedown on the dresser. Suddenly the room seemed airless, and she left it and ran up the stairs again; none of these rooms was particularly familiar. Or else only one at the top of the house where she was headed now. It was built into the base of the steeple, reached by a special half-landing off the third floor. It was Miranda's room, and she knew because she remembered suddenly how she had struggled to claim it. Her aunt had meant to use it as an upstairs study because the light was good. But Miranda had begged and begged.

She stayed in Juliana's cottage if the house was closed. But when the glow of the gas candelabrum spilled from the French windows over the garden, then Miranda would pack her clothes. As darkness fell, holding her little bag, Miranda would slip her hand into Juliana's hand. They would walk together up the garden path and in the small side door. They would climb the stairs together to Miranda's room.

The door was set into an odd high threshold that you had to step over. The silver doorknob was carved in the shape of a rose, one of the symbols of her father's family. And when she turned the knob and opened the door, she found the room as she remembered, an octagon of yellow walls set into the circle of the tower, and each wall held a high window. The windows were covered with wooden blinds, which she now pulled open. She fastened the cords onto their brass cleats.

There was her desk and bureau, there was her small bed. There was her full-length, gilt-framed mirror with the yellow shadow in the glass. Miranda had not seen a mirror since she'd been in Williamstown, and she stood staring at her reflection. Then without thinking she opened the top drawer of her bureau and drew out her silver and tortoiseshell brush and comb. They had belonged to her mother's mother. She sat on the edge of the small bed and began to comb the tangles from her hair, which was still damp.

But one big hank of it was hopeless. Toward the west the sun was going down behind the trees. After a few minutes, sick of staring at her ghostly face, she threw down the brush and stood in front of each window in turn, trying to remember each framed view. The trees had grown up, she saw immediately. There was the carriage road. The fenced-in fields were overgrown with briars and weeds and straggling, small oaks. In no direction could she see another house.

Beneath her feet there was the tessellated floor, an imitation of a Roman mosaic in Constanta. It showed the face of Diana in profile, surrounded by a pattern of running deer. Made of small squares of multicolored tile, it was quite crude— not nearly as fine as the original, which Miranda now remembered. It had been uncovered when they built the train station, and then put into the museum.

Miranda sat down on the bed again and looked at all the small details of the room, especially the imperfections—the cracks in the veneer, the place where she had scratched her name into the surface of her desk. She pulled out the drawers of her bureau and rummaged through the clothes, which were not numerous. Who was this girl who had lived here? Certainly it was not she who had folded these small frocks so neatly. Her room in Rachel and Stanley's house had been a mess.

She poked through the top drawer. There were pen nibs and dried-up ink bottles, some wax candles and some matches in a sealed tin candy box. There were some coins in a green glass jar. There was a small, leather-bound book—a diary, obviously, stamped with her name in gold and locked with a small clasp.

She held it, stroked its cover, then sat down in the chair before the desk. She pulled a lock of hair out of her face, perched it behind her ear, as if in preparation.

But she didn't want to break that seal or read that book, not yet. Though doubtless there'd be clues to help her, still she felt she couldn't bear it. So she laid the diary on the surface of the desk, lining it up neatly with the corners. Dizzy, suddenly, from hunger, she sprang up and went downstairs.

The diary was important, she told herself. But first things first, as her adoptive father would have said. For an instant Stanley's face came back to her, his long hands gesturing out of the past. But more important was her situation now, as he would have been the first to say: There must be something to eat here.

Again, there was nothing in the ransacked kitchen, but she found the cellar stair. She struck a match on a strip of carborundum and lit one of the pale candles, releasing a beeswax smell. The candle was as big as her wrist, and the light gave her a flickering comfort. First things first. She picked up a poker from beside the cast-iron stove. In the cellar there were bins of potatoes and things, she now remembered. The dark stairs led to a stone hall that stretched the length of the house. It had been looted, of course. She found broken crates. Some of them had once contained some vegetables.

In a bin on the far side of the hall there were bottles that had not been broken. She put down the poker and held one up to the candle. Inside the brown glass was a yellow liquid: Hungarian wine, as she deciphered from the handwritten label, from Tokaj.

But there was nothing to eat. In the kitchen, which she now searched for the third time, there was nothing. She found a corkscrew, and as the sun was going down she climbed up to the room under the spire. She put the lighted candle on the desk, then cut through the wax seal over the mouth of the bottle and opened it.

All day she'd tried not to think about Andromeda, Raevsky, and especially about Peter. She had tried not to wonder where they were, what they were doing, whether they were searching and calling along the cold banks of the Hoosick while she explored this house. Whenever she had seen her thoughts disappear along that path, she'd called them back. Now she indulged herself, raised the bottle, drank.

4   *The Water's Edge*

"LOOK," RAEVSKY HAD WHISPERED, five years and a few months earlier.

Night had come. There was no moon, and to the east the stars were hidden in a flock of clouds. To the west the sky was clear, and there was a gentle glow in that part of the heavens across the river, though the sun had long since set. It was like the glow over a town at night, but there was no town there, only swamplands punctured with dead trees and then the snowy, empty woods.

It was the aurora borealis, Peter decided, feeling suddenly happy, suddenly sad. More than once his father had taken him in the pickup to the top of Petersburg Pass. And once he'd taken a longer trip with both his parents to Quebec. They'd gone camping on a lake.

"Look," whispered Raevsky. Andromeda was silent, poised on three legs. The yellow fur was high along her back.

Peter had allowed himself a kind of relaxation by the fire. Hunched in his canvas jacket, hands held out, he did not care to look. He'd been thinking about the days when he'd lain sick and delusional inside the cave. Miranda had stayed with him. It was miraculous how he'd recovered when his fever broke. Raevsky had given him up for dead.

But when he was most contagious, that was when Miranda had been most kind. She had fed him and given him water, hugged him with her cool arms. She hadn't touched him after he'd recovered. When he was no risk to her, then she had left him and disappeared, just as the wild men who had taken them in out of the storm had run away, afraid of the infection. She'd left him on this pestilential bank, which under the northern lights had taken on a stark and eerie beauty. All day they had not seen a squirrel or a bird.

Now he turned his head. Below him down the slope, the boat was drawn up on the strand, out of the soft current. A flat-bottomed pirogue, heavily loaded with him and Miranda and Raevsky and the dog. Now it was empty.

An animal had come to it, a big animal. Making no noise, it stepped out of the shadows, a catamount or cougar of some sort. Its head was low along the ground, as if made heavy by the weight of two curved tusks that overlapped its chin.

"Ah, God," murmured Raevsky. And then he continued in Roumanian. Already Peter could make out some words. It was as if inside him there was someone who was rummaging and exploring, someone who could understand Raevsky's language, and he didn't want to think about that person.

Sometimes at moments of crisis over the past few days, it had been hard for Peter to recognize himself. Instead he'd been possessed by something new, pulled from his interior as if by his new hand. He'd listened to a new vocabulary of feeling that was like the half-understood Roumanian words—a sudden rage first of all, which nevertheless had a kind of calming, numbing, narcotic effect, and which was also mixed with joy. In this mood he had confronted the wooly mammoth in the snow. Later he could tell himself that he'd tried to save someone's life or else impress Miranda at the very least. Still he knew those reasons were a way of covering his joy, his guilty present to himself.

Now he felt it and the rage, too. Fleetingly, Peter wondered if the Chevalier de Graz had ever bothered to justify this feeling. Now he found himself rising, found a charred stick in his right hand.

Making no effort to be silent, he kicked through the dry stubble until he stood at the top of the bank, twelve feet or so above the water. Below him the slope was sandy and eroded down to the pebbly beach. A pink part of the sky was battling a green part along an undulating front. Big as a sheep, the animal had paused between the boat and the river. Under the glow its fur shone dirty pink, dirty green, and then a dirty white. It yawned as it stared up at him, displaying enormous ridged eyeteeth, each as long as his hand.

He found himself imagining a razor and brush set, made out of those teeth. Even though he'd never shaved but once, and then with aerosol cream and a disposable, he found himself coveting those teeth. Breathing slowly, he tested the strength of his stick against the ground. And then he would have flung himself down the bank, or else descended quietly step by step, except for a noise behind him.

The cat heard it, too. Almost imperceptibly it shifted its big, flat eyes from him to some other indeterminate place nearby. Peter also turned his head, intrigued by the new sound, one he hadn't heard through all the difficulties of the past few days.

Raevsky was weeping. With one hand pressed around his cup of ouzo, the other over his face, he rocked back and forth on his old log, a small shuddering movement.

Peter saw no tears in the uncertain light. But the sound was unmistakable. When he looked down the slope again, the cat was gone.

Feeling suddenly foolish, he threw down his stick. There was something about the sound of weeping, tearless or not, that washed away the rage, the calm, the joy. He felt no urge to comfort the old man, and didn't even know what he might do to comfort him. Or one thing: He stood looking away over the swamp and the dead trees until the noise subsided. Then he stumped back to the fire on his numb feet.

Raevsky was murmuring and muttering in Roumanian. When he switched to English, the sense came clear. "Oh, I will tell you I go to Constanta for the white tyger. She is waiting in her castle. So I bring her to Bucharest, to the Ceausescu house, as it was my promise—no. It is talking only. Never any more. Can you see I am on the river of my death? Carl and Ferenc, Gulka and the others, Alexandru, my sister's son. Near as we come down to the water, I think. The rest—brave talk. Not true. I will not see my lady's face again! Not her face again."

Peter stood with his hands in his pockets. As Raevsky spoke, he caught an image of Miranda on a terrace overlooking the beach. Listening to Raevsky's desolate snuffle, he took comfort in imagining her there, her golden bracelet on her wrist.

5   The Castle on the Beach

BUT AT THAT MOMENT Prince Frederick's castle stood deserted. A shutter had worked loose from one of the windows at the base of the tower and was beating itself to pieces in the March wind. Five years and a few months later, when Miranda stood looking out, no trace of it remained.

Now in her upstairs room she put down her bottle of sweet wine. Almost she felt like weeping from sheer loneliness. Alone in this house except for ghosts and clumsy memories, she also was alone in this strange world, a single light burning along this whole deserted coast.

When she thought of Peter and Andromeda, soon she left them in the snowy woods, the boy with the man's right hand, the yellow dog. Soon she brought them back in time with her, to before her aunt's history book had been destroyed in the bonfire on Christmas Hill. She'd brought them all the way back to Berkshire County where they'd been friends: Peter with his missing hand, and beautiful Andromeda whom she'd known since childhood. She remembered Peter's face as he'd shown her little places in the woods he'd loved. As for Andromeda, a hundred moments like a pack of photographs—her best friend on her mountain bike, or playing soccer, or walking together on hot summer evenings, the streetlights shining on her yellow hair.

These memories sharpened her solitude until it was intolerable. Now to take her mind away, she turned her small chair and set it toward the mirror. She sat down and studied her face again in the dark glass. The candle was behind her. But even in the uncertain light she could tell. In Williamstown she'd been fifteen years old.

She turned her face, lifted her chin, put her fingers to her upper lip. What was the difference? Peter had seen it right away. "What's wrong with your face?" he'd said on that first morning in the woods. Well, what was wrong with it? Something lost and gained. She did look older now. Peter had said so and it was true.

Was it a coarseness, a thickening? Everywhere and nowhere—rougher skin, a darkness around her eyes? Or else she'd put on weight. Maybe it was to avoid perceiving these things that she'd been thinking so insistently about her friends.

She touched her cheeks and forehead, touched her breasts. Stanley had once told her, only half joking, that if you felt really bad about something, then you should find some other painful thing to think about, because that was the only way you could distract yourself. You should find some thing that hurt you and excited you, because here in this room when she was a child, now she remembered wanting to grow older. Many times she had looked into this same mirror, desperate to grow older so that Lieutenant Prochenko might look at her. And sometimes in Williamstown for other reasons, but that was over now. Here she was in her own country, an unfamiliar world that was the only world. And she was home at last in Great Roumania, not Stanley's daughter but Prince Frederick Schenck von Schenck's. Prince Frederick, Princess Clara—strangers she had never known. And if that was true, then all of it was true. The white tyger, everything, all of it.

BUT THE WHITE TYGER—AS ALMOST everyone imagined—lived in Bucharest two hundred kilometers away. That was the title the Baroness Ceausescu had recently adopted, publicly, semiofficially, to correspond with her private hopes. That evening at sunset she was eating dinner in the Palace of the People, which had been the Empress Valeria's official residence. Under the protection of the German Occupational Authority, the white tyger had reopened and renamed it. Now in one of the small dining rooms her guests were the outgoing German ambassador and his wife, cloddish people on whom she nevertheless depended. Frau Behrens had been an admirer of hers when she was on the stage.

The Baroness Ceausescu sat forward on her chair. These days she kept early hours. Dessert and coffee were already being served. Her loyal steward, Jean-Baptiste, was at the sideboard, fussing with a bottle of Imperial Tokay. Surely this was the most delicious of all wines! But it was delicious also to refuse it, to hold up her hand as Jean-Baptiste poured the precious, honey-colored liquid into crystal goblets for these Germans. As he grasped the bottle, Nicola Ceausescu studied his fingers—old, wrinkled, but still strong. As he came close, she smiled, waved him away. Abstemiousness was a virtue now. When she was poor, it had felt like a vice.

Her guests sipped the wine, and she amused them with bright anecdotes. Exquisitely and virginally dressed, she touched her forearm to the tablecloth, while at the same time she told a story about the love affairs of a well-known Italian tenor. The words she used would have been vulgar in a man's mouth. But with the part of her that always judged, she appreciated their effect when spoken by a charming and beautiful woman, as all the world agreed. Frau Behrens didn't matter; she was besotted, starstruck, drunk. But on the ambassador's poised face there was a blush of happiness that seemed to coat his cheeks. With his napkin he dabbed gently at his white moustache. And there was something else inside him too, a tremor of condescension that gave the baroness a secret joy. Yes, it was important for him to condescend.

Yes, she'd discovered in her life—it was difficult to scrounge a living from the streets. But it was easy to be powerful. She had learned her skill upon the stage, to give each member of the audience what he wanted. The corrupt men, she would enrich them. The generals, she would give them armies and machines. The poor, she would bankrupt the country if only just to feed them for a day. Even in this small exercise she could feel her power—first, it was already something of a scandal to invite this elderly, old-fashioned couple to her private dining room: just herself, two women and a man. Second, she had dressed with great simplicity, had smoked no cigarettes and drunk no wine. Third, she had conversed lightly and agreeably on many subjects. Fourth, she had ended the evening with this story, using language that bordered the obscene. Looking into the eyes of the ambassador, she felt she could imagine his disdain, imagine also that on their way home in the carriage the old man would put his arm around his wife's doughy waist. And when they arrived he would suggest he might pay a visit to her bedroom. And she would lean against him and murmur, "Oh Gunther," or "Oh Gunnar," or whatever his potato-eating name might be. And the next day the ambassador would write in his dispatches without mentioning his wife: "I was honored by a private dinner with the 'white tyger,' as she calls herself. She is a delightful woman, but my dear . . . !'"

Yes, she'd done everything perfectly and could allow herself a little recklessness. She wanted something from these people after all. When dinner was complete, she brought them to the parlor on the first floor and made them sit in small uncomfortable chairs. She stood by the piano and in the hoarse small voice that nevertheless had entranced Europe, she sang without accompaniment from her new opera, or ballet, or oratorio (sometimes her thinking about it changed)—a major work, in any case, that she herself was now composing from the incidents of her life. Many of the songs were already complete. This one, from the first act, was both plaintive and chilling, because of the honesty with which she probed her own ambivalence after her husband's suicide—her guests were smiling and nodding.

She broke off in midword. Their reaction was not satisfactory. From the table she picked up the letter she had written to the German foreign minister. She glanced at the first paragraph and found herself dissatisfied by the dry diplomatic language. In no way did it do justice to her feelings. The words required an interpretation that she now found herself providing as she stared at Frau Behrens's gloved hands.

"Please deliver this," she said. "I'll tell you what I've written—I make no secrets of the truth! It has now been more than five years since my son was taken from me by Theodore von Geiss und Ratisbon, who assaulted me in my own house. You yourself assured me he'd be punished—that was a lie, and my son was not returned. Maybe at that time the decision was correct, because of the violence in my country, and I myself was forced to live in hiding. Because of you and your government, order is restored. On my knees I thank you and kiss your hands, though they are wet with blood. Do not think we will consent to live forever conquered and abased! But on my knees I am begging you for the return of my boy Felix Ceausescu, now held by a criminal, and I ask you to imagine my torment. How can you keep him from his mother's arms?"

It was a relief to speak so frankly. Nevertheless the baroness could detect a problem. In a single moment she had destroyed the entire effect of her dinner party. Part of her was glad—Frau Behrens had a shocked expression on her stupid face. And the ambassador nodded gravely.

"Please take this message," continued the baroness as she crushed the letter between her hands. "I'll send this after you tomorrow morning," she continued as she dropped the crumpled paper to the floor and stepped on it.

Wiping her eyes, she left them suddenly. She told the chamberlain to escort them out while she climbed the great stairs. She was trying to maintain her equilibrium.

At the mezzanine she turned and stood looking out over the long gallery. But her feelings were genuine, she thought, and she surrendered to them until her slender shoulders heaved with sobs. What had she done? She was incorrigible. Yet surely it was these Germans' fault to have hurt her and driven her to such extremes. And her own opera or oratorio was to blame, because the music never failed to bring her crudest emotions to the surface. Where was her son now? What was he doing now? Several times Behrens and the others had assured her he was well. But she'd had no response to any of her letters.

Jean-Baptiste now came to her. The gaunt old man was dressed in expensive clothes—the tyger's personal livery. Still he looked awkward and unkempt, and he spoke with his usual lack of ceremony. "We followed your instructions to put some kind of potato in every dish. Did you notice? The pastry dough was fluffy, wasn't it?"

He was trying to comfort her. She shook her head, smiling through tears. "Their bodies crave it," she sobbed into her handkerchief. "But we must not be too obvious. What about the sherbet?"

"Burnt potato dust. A sprinkle."

Cheeks wet, she laughed. "Potatoes have an aphrodisiac effect for them," she said. "That's what I've heard." Then she wiped her face and blew her nose. "Was there something else?"

"No."

"I'll go to Domnul Luckacz, then." She paused. "Thank you, my friend." Jean-Baptiste did not reply. He was already tottering down the stairs.

Or was it possible she was lying to herself? Sometimes days went by and she did not think about her son. Sometimes she couldn't even bring his face to mind. In which case she'd been reckless for no reason—no, she'd worry about that tomorrow. Now she was tired.

She continued up the stairs to the small sitting room. Always at the end of every evening she sat down for a minute with Radu Luckacz, chief of her police. As she entered the chamber, she saw him at the window looking out over the lights of the Piata Revolutiei. "Ma'am, are they gone?" he asked.

He was a fussy man. He wore his gray hair long, brushed from his forehead. His moustache was absurdly black, as if he'd smeared it with boot polish. He had not removed his overcoat or gloves. His hat was in his hands.

Often when she saw him Nicola Ceausescu felt a stroke of pity. He needed a woman to take him in her hand, to smooth away his nervousness. It was obvious his wife and daughter couldn't manage it—as always, he seemed anxious and depressed. He had been standing almost in darkness; now she moved to the table to turn up the lamp. He stood facing her, turning his hat in his hands, avoiding her eyes because he loved her.

In the days since she had first acquired Kepler's Eye, the baroness had come to be familiar with many kinds of love. This was not the small frisson of the German ambassador (if indeed she was right about that, and if indeed she had not ruined everything with her stupid recklessness), but a deep and desperate feeling. As she approached him, she could see him cringe. Always she took care to stand a little close.

He took refuge in officiousness. He listed his agenda for the following day. Then at the end he hesitated. "Ma'am, as you know I have kept several persons in the area of Constanta, among whose duties is the continued observation of the castle at Mamaia beach, which passed from Frederick Schenck to his sister. Tonight I have received a telegram from one of those men. He tells me he has seen a light burning in the tower, and so I have asked the provincial commissioner to investigate. This would not be worth mentioning except I know the local people are frightened of that place. Aegypta Schenck was a conjurer, as you know."

The baroness smiled. "You amaze me."

"Ma'am, there is no need to make fun. These phenomena are real. It is my duty to protect, but first you must believe there is a danger. We have not yet seen the victory of science over superstition."

"To be sure."

In fact it was easy for the baroness to think the worst. Part of her was as she seemed that night to Radu Luckacz, superficial and trusting, but there was another part. A blackness could come over her as sudden as a storm.

She listened to Luckacz a few minutes more. "A hailstorm destroyed the fruit trees outside Ploiesti," he was saying. "Also as you know there is continued drought in the Dobruja region—" It was too much. She scowled at him and clapped her hands.

Later she'd apologize. "That's enough," she said. "Don't bore me." And to efface his wounded expression, she gave him her hand to kiss. "Please," she said. "I have a headache."

Again, as with the Germans, she found herself eager to be gone. Full of an apprehension that was as sudden as an attack of nausea, she slipped out of the door, then climbed the steps to her own small apartment.

A light was burning on the side table. Beside it on a Chinese porcelain dish, a ham sandwich lay in wait. The light gleamed from the surface of the jeweled mustard pot, a gift to the former empress from the Sultan of Byzantium.

Nicola Ceausescu scarcely glanced at it, though she was hungry. She passed instead to the inner door that led to her private boudoir, a small, square, empty space, along one wall of which stood an iron bedstead. There she slept most nights. When she was powerless, she had been hungry for luxuries, had slept in silk sheets among silk pillows.

But that night she continued past the rice-paper screen. In a hidden corner of the room there was a hidden door that led to a garret underneath the eaves. The former empress had used the space for storage. But Nicola Ceausescu had furnished it secretly. She had had transported there in sealed boxes the contents of her dead husband's laboratory from the house on Saltpetre Street.

She lit a candle in the doorway. On her left hand there was a small altar assembled out of Valeria's bric-a-brac: some gilded Egyptian statuary on the flat surface of a carved and painted Russian box. A sphinx knelt with her hands outstretched, and on her palms she held the tourmaline, Kepler's Eye. Now the baroness lit the lamps on either side of it, and admired the green and purple surface of the gem.

Usually she liked to keep it hidden on her body, touching her skin. But the dress she'd worn that night had not allowed it. Now she reached out her forefinger and touched its surface. It was the source of the people's love for her, she knew. She took a dolorous, fierce pleasure in reminding herself. Without this jewel she was nothing, the most worthless and miserable of women.

Farther on in the garret she found her husband's ironwood table. With a piece of cloth she rubbed the dust from the surface of the four-sided adamantine pyramid. Now there was a tiny light that burned in it while she sat down and began her meditations.

A light in the tower window high above the beach. The image brought with it a frisson of unease as the baroness cast her mind abroad. Fingering an unlit Turkish cigarette, she lay back in her armchair with her eyes closed.

Often she was able to convince herself she was the guardian of her people, a bulwark of protection in these difficult times. Then it felt good to pinch the noses of the German oppressors, who rode through Bucharest as if they owned it, and managed the resources of the country like a private bank. Other times, as now, she understood how much she was dependent on her benefactors in Berlin, who had established her and kept her and would doubtless dispose of her if she offended them too much. She depended on them even more than her own people, and when she sat in her leather armchair thinking about that, in her bedroom in the center of her palace, she felt cold and vulnerable. Then she was disturbed by images of failure, and when she opened her eyes, she saw one of these was taking shape inside the pyramid, a figure of a girl.

She was sitting on a child's wooden chair, looking into the inner surface of the pyramid as if into a mirror. And she was weeping. Tears fell from her dark eyes. She leaned forward with her shoulders hunched, her arms clasped over her chest as if hugging herself or keeping herself warm, though it must have been a warm night in Constanta by the sea. A half-empty bottle stood upright by her foot.

It was Miranda Popescu, home at last. The baroness had seen her in a photograph taken years before. A girl then, now she was a woman. From what the baroness could see, she had some of her mother's shape, though her face recalled Prince Frederick: rather pale, with heavy, dark eyebrows and large eyes. Quite plain: Her mouth was too large, also, though her lips were thin. Her dark hair was on her shoulders, and she had small, protruding ears.

As the baroness watched, she pulled a lock of hair back from her face. The sleeve of her shirt slid down to reveal the golden bracelet that had belonged to Miranda Brancoveanu in the ancient days—just a trinket of worn beads, each carved in the shape of a tiger's head. But it was also the mark of the white tyger, the savior of Roumania, and the baroness coveted it.

Where had the girl been for these five years? She'd imagined her dead, or living her life out in the North American wilderness. But at the same time she had always known this day would come. Now here she was in Europe. Miranda Popescu was in Roumania itself, and immediately the baroness could see some complications.

As she sat in her small garret, she too felt tears come to her eyes, and she found herself weeping for this young woman, alone and in such danger.

SHE SAT WATCHING A LONG time. She watched Miranda make her bed and snuggle into it. Lulled from her loneliness by the sound of the waves, the girl fell asleep, and when she woke, the sun was high over the water. The light slanted from the east window.

Thirst and hunger made her rise. Her tongue was thick and sweet. She stood looking out the window at the water. Then she went downstairs.

In the garden she found herself walking back to the cottage where she'd first arrived. Or else where she'd returned, she had to keep reminding herself, in this place where everything seemed familiar and new at the same time. How had this miracle occurred? Just yesterday she had been floating on the Hoosick River with her friends.

The cottage on the riverbank had not been like this one. It had resembled it the way a dream resembles life. Now she had awoken in the real place, where doors and windows did not reform and disappear. But where were Peter and Andromeda? Where were they now?

Light-headed and weak, she climbed the steps of Juliana's house. In the dream she had remembered scrabbling at the floor, looking for the secret place under the boards where Umar kept his gun. She had not found it. In the dream it had not been there. But now she knelt and searched again through the dirt and accumulated leaves until she uncovered the little ring that Juliana's niece had shown her. Roxana, her name was, or had been—a fox-faced, slit-eyed girl.

And the ring twisted and the panel pulled up, and there was something underneath wrapped in an oiled rag. It was a gun, a revolver with a long, octagonal barrel. The handle was made of white bone.

The gun was familiar to her. Miranda's adoptive grandfather—Rachel's father—had something just like it in his house in Colorado Springs. It was the pride of his collection, and he'd unlocked his glass case and shown it to her every time she visited.

Miranda held it up, and it was heavy in her hand. There was something else, too, wrapped in the oiled rag—a tin box of soft-nosed bullets. And something else again, an embroidered bag with a leather drawstring.

There was money inside. She could feel the shape of the coins inside the cloth. This was good, because she'd lost her purse of silver beads. She'd left it in the pirogue. She hoped Peter would get some use out of it.

These gold coins, as she saw when she opened the bag and shook some of them out, weren't like the ones she had spent in tara mortilor. They were more recently minted, hard-edged, uniform, with double-headed eagles on one side, Cyrillic letters on the other. She looked for a date but could not find one.

And there was a piece of paper folded many times. As she unwrapped it she saw a worm had eaten a meandering hole. Then she was reading her aunt's minuscule handwriting. "My dear niece, it is my pleasure to present you with this weapon that belonged to your father and his father, and which I know you will use wisely. This is the first of the treasures I have left for you if there is a break in the rope and I am not there to guide your hands. First I tell you you must leave this place because it is not safe and full of robbers and murderers and spies. . . ."

Miranda sat back, looked up at the peaceful sky. She felt a wistful kind of irritation. How long had the letter lain under the floorboards? Robbers and murderers—there'd been no one here for years.

She read a few words more. "Here I must tell you what to do without delay. If the worst has happened and my enemies have buried me, then go to Insula Calia, where you will receive more precise directions. . . ."

She stopped reading. Why had she expected anything different? Why had she expected some piece of comfort, maybe, some acknowledgement of how hard this was? Or maybe some story or information from the years that had gone by, some tiny vision of her father or her mother or her life in this place? Maybe some answer to a question that Miranda didn't even know enough to ask, an answer that would come as a relief—nothing like that. More precise directions.

Part of her craved them, even though it was hard to imagine how they still could be of use to her, now so long out of date. But in her mind's eye she caught a glimpse of her aunt's unyielding and unsentimental face, whether a memory or a projection, Miranda couldn't tell. This much was clear: Even after death Aegypta Schenck was not yet done with guiding and criticizing Miranda's every step.

So what was wrong with that? Why did she resent it? Surely she could use a little direction now. Was it just the tone—you must do this, you must do that? That was part of it, but there was more.

Her aunt didn't trust her enough, obviously, to give her information rather than commands. She didn't trust her to come to the same conclusions as herself, and maybe there was a reason for that. Because when it came right down to it, Miranda didn't trust her, either. Nothing that had happened reassured Miranda that her aunt always had her best interests at heart.

Maybe it was true what the scar-faced, smallpox-pitted man had told her on the riverbank, and she was like a pawn on its last move, poised to become a queen. But she knew her aunt was trying to win the game and not protect her pieces. If Miranda's death would profit Great Roumania, she suspected what her aunt would choose.

Now, perched on a briar near the Magdalena fountain, a brandywine bird strutted and preened. Miranda had seen one like it in her dream of tara mortilor—the land of the dead. It was the spirit creature of Aegypta Schenck, though doubtless its presence here was a coincidence. Slowly, languidly, she picked up the revolver and pointed it. The gun was heavy in her hand. She pulled back the hammer, closed one eye in an exaggerated pantomime. The bird cocked its head, ruffled its feathers, and disappeared into the bush, leaving a single iridescent feather floating to the ground.

Miranda folded up the letter along the seams without reading the rest of it. She'd look at it later. The night before, desperate for anything, she would have pored over every word. No doubt tonight as darkness crept across the terrace she would feel the same; she put the letter off till then. In the meantime, some of these decisions were surely her own. The sun was warm, the grass was green, and the gun, now, she examined more carefully.

Most summers Rachel and Stanley had taken her out west to Colorado, to the suburban house where Rachel had grown up. Now Miranda wondered whether her aunt Aegypta had deliberately placed this gun in Rachel's father's collection so Miranda would be familiar with it now; it broke apart in a familiar way. But she was surprised to find it loaded. She shook out the bullets and felt suddenly safer. Stanley had always disapproved of guns in people's houses. He had always made fun of Rachel's parents.

That had been in the false America. Even now Miranda thought of it sometimes as the real America, with its shopping malls and nuclear bombs. For a moment the gun was like a bridge between the worlds. Miranda rubbed the steel with the greasy rag, seeing how the surface of the metal was inlaid with brass or bronze or gold, in any case a yellower metal that decorated the barrel and the drum with an ornate pattern of winding leaves and thorns. On each side the plate where the firing mechanism fit into the stock was incised with a yellow rose. In contrast with this pattern, the white bone of the stock was smooth and plain.

She slipped the purse of coins into her pocket and wrapped the gun, unloaded, into its rag. Stanley had always told her that guns by themselves caused more havoc than robbers or murderers or even spies, she supposed—statistics proved it! But the weight of the revolver reassured her. And the money would be useful, she told herself.

Standing up, she felt the blood rush from her head. It was obvious she must get food, and she could buy it now. Should she walk west along the carriage road to find a house or a town? Or should she walk among the dunes, north or south? North, she decided, because the abandoned boat in the inlet was the only sign of humanity she'd seen. Briars had overgrown parts of the garden and the back end of Juliana's house, but the berries were small and green and hard. In a month they would be ready.

She followed her tracks from the day before until she found the boat. It had been drawn up along the striped and pebbled sand among dried scraps of seaweed. And it was clear that something bad had happened recently. What, in fact, did her aunt have to say about enemies and spies? She'd read over the letter as soon as she got back to her room. With its help, she'd figure out a plan. And in the morning she'd get out of here—as soon as she had pushed the boat onto its keel, Miranda could see how the bottom had been broken out, either with a head-sized rock that now rolled against the front compartment, or with a rusted hammer that was stuck into the sand. There was a tangle of torn clothing. Amid pieces of a broken oar, brass shell casings were scattered along the high tide line. Above the line the sand was trampled, and there was a V-shaped trough as if something heavy had been dragged away.

Hungry as she was, she refused to think about what might have happened. Instead she rummaged for things she could use. The compartments underneath the bow and stern were latched with iron hooks. One was empty, but the other held a hot, stinking package of tarpaulin. Opened, it revealed a folded, circular net, weighted along its edge with pieces of lead. There was also a short, dull knife with a broken blade.

The inlet was a tidal pool. It backed onto a swamp of reeds and cattails where a tiny stream came down. The tide was rising now, flowing quickly over the bar that separated the pool from the sea. Coming that way, Miranda had seen the movement of small fish. They had knocked against her ankles as she'd waded through the inlet. Trapped by the rising waves and then sucked back over the bar, they had flashed their silver bellies in the brown water. She had not been able to catch them, but now she carried the net down to the bar. Standing on the collapsing shore a yard or so above the water, she could see the fish turn in a school, and she flung the net over them and hoped for the best.

More than once Stanley's father had taken her to fish for perch on a lake near his house in Westchester County. They'd used rods and reels of course, but the patience was the main thing. Brainless, the fish came back and back. After several empty casts she figured out how to spin the net, uncurl it in the air, and the weights opened it up flat.

Then she caught some fish. Holding the net like the bag, she swung them down against the dry sand. She spread the tarpaulin on the top of the dunes and laid out the stunned silver bodies in the bright air. They were small, two inches long at most. She hoped they would dry in the heat until they were like anchovies or kippered herring.

She went to the boat to find the knife. Already when she came back, flies had preceded her. She sat down on the tarpaulin with twenty or so fish between her outstretched knees. One by one she cut their heads off and dug out their small guts, which she dropped into a hole in the sand. Pausing sometimes to bat the flies away, she split the bodies down to their spines and laid them out with the flesh up. Then she waved her hands over them for twenty minutes or so, but when she picked one up it seemed unchanged, though the day was hot. How long did fish take to dry? Hours? Days? She remembered a picture in a social studies book, a woman in South India stooping over a pile of fish laid out in the street between two turquoise houses. Now that she thought about it, everything she had attempted with these fish was based on that picture, which of course referred to nothing and no place—not in this world. And of course her grandfather's house in Westchester, his rods and reels, all that was gone.

She scraped some flesh away from the silver skin and the weak spine, and ate it. She couldn't help herself. She ate seven fish for breakfast and then continued walking. The beach was straight and endless, and the waves were long and small. She searched her memory for impressions of this place, but there was nothing.

Long past noon she was worried she would find no water, and turned back. When she came to the fish again, they had achieved a rubbery hardness, though there were flies. The small hole with the guts and the fish heads was full of them.

None of this was satisfactory or gave her confidence for the future. Nevertheless it was a kind of preparation. Miranda forced herself to eat some more, and wrapped the rest of the fish in the net, which she carried over her shoulder with the tarpaulin. When she saw the spire of the castle again, she went into the garden and drank at the Magdalena fountain. She was hot and sweating. The night before, she'd slept in her dirty clothes and her damp underwear. The wool shirt was Blind Rodica's, but the jeans she'd worn all the way from Massachusetts. Her bra was too tight. Her underpants were stiff and gray and streaked with blood.

The next day, she thought, she would try the beach to the south. Perhaps Constanta lay that way.

Or maybe she'd try the carriage road inland. Yes, that was obviously the best choice. But why was it so hard for her to make up her mind what to do? The truth was, much as she missed Peter and Andromeda, much as she detested her isolation here, her sense of everything held in abeyance, still she found the silence restful. It was obvious she couldn't stay here. Even if there were food she couldn't stay. But she knew that if she took one step away, then everything would start again. Now for a moment she was like a girl on a high diving board, moving back and forth, taking a few practice jumps. One step, though, and she would feel the plunge. Along the carriage road, after a mile or a half a mile she would pass a house or a village or a town.

Try as she might, she remembered nothing of what lay over the western horizon, though she must have traveled that way many times. Past the house and Umar's house and the garden, the surrounding map was blank. Insula Calia—where was that?

This was her last night of preparation. Tomorrow she would walk straight out the road. She would read her aunt's letter, do what her aunt told her. More than that, she would use her influence to send a message to Peter somehow—no, maybe that wasn't such a great idea. Murderers and spies—at first she wouldn't tell people who she was, until she found out what it meant to them, to her. She'd keep her bracelet hidden. She'd invent a name for herself. She had some money now, and a way to protect herself if worse came to worst. She'd gotten food for herself. When it was first light she would go.

But she wanted new clothes. She wondered if there was something in her aunt's closets or drawers she could wear. She hadn't searched the bureau in her aunt's bedroom. The clothes in her own room were for a seven-year-old girl.

So she went back to the castle to her aunt's room, and then climbed to her room again. Once there, she stood in front of the glass, overcome with loneliness. Where was Peter now, right now? Surely he hadn't left her all alone. Surely he would look for her, would know or guess or feel where to look.

In time she lit the candle. She had brought some things from downstairs. Now she moved the candle to a stool beside her.

When she was younger, she had always tried to avoid looking at her own body. She was self-conscious about it, and had not kept a full-length mirror in her room. Andromeda had liked to parade around naked in the house if she was changing her clothes, or after a shower when her mother wasn't home. That was all right for her—she had the body for it. But Miranda had tended to slip into her clothes without looking, especially as she'd started to mature. She didn't have a bathroom of her own, and never spent much time in her parents' bathroom or the one on the ground floor. Once when she had taken a long shower, Stanley had walked in on her while she was staring glumly at her face and hair. She'd been wrapped in a towel. He'd laughed, then come to hug her.

Even now, with no one around, she found it hard to strip down to nothing and examine herself. She found it hard to strip out of the hateful clothes, the chafing underwear, stiff with salt from the previous day. And even when it was all off, she found herself looking at different parts in isolation. Close to the surface of the mirror, she examined her elbow, the seawater rash along the crease of her thigh.

Maybe she couldn't remember any more, but there was no individual part of her that seemed different when she looked at it alone. And maybe it wasn't just modesty that had made her hesitant, but a premonition. When finally, with a lump in her throat, she held up the candle and stepped away from the glass, and stared at her face and head and body all together, her first impression was she scarcely recognized herself. Something given, something stripped away— no, it wasn't true. For there she was after all, her pale skin and narrow nose, her ears that stuck out, and her nice, wide forehead. There she was after all, her thin lips, her long neck, and then the rest, and you might even say there was an improvement. Why was she even worrying about her childhood, what she remembered? Look at her—her childhood was gone.

How many people could recall more than just a couple of things from when they were five or six or seven? So what difference did it make? What did it mean to say your childhood made you what you were? She'd asked Peter once and he'd just stared at her.

Now, standing nude before the mirror, the thought of Peter filled her with embarrassment; she looked for a small moment more, and then she put the candle down. And as the sun set, she tried to lose herself in new details. Among the clothes that she had brought from her aunt's drawers, she selected some silk underwear, made without elastic. Then she slipped on some men's clothes that she had found in a back bedroom—a dress shirt, collarless, with French cuffs that she rolled up. The shirt was a pale yellow. With it she wore pleated linen trousers, lighter and more comfortable than her jeans.

The shirt and trousers, she wondered if they were Lieutenant Prochenko's clothes. They weren't exactly clean, because they'd lain there a long time. The shirt had a peculiar smell. But everything was much more comfortable; she combed her hair out with the tortoiseshell comb. There was still a terrible tangle and she yanked at it. She caught a glimpse of herself in the mirror, made a face, put her tongue out.

She had found some silver scissors in the drawer, part of the same set. If she was going to be different, she wanted a difference she could see. With a sudden impulse she began to cut her hair above the tangle at about the level of her jaw. She was skilled at this. She and Andromeda had often cut their hair together, in Andromeda's mother's house on Syndicate Road.

In back of her the door was open to the landing. She was concentrating on what she did, working carefully with the scissors and the comb. There was a hand mirror that sometimes she held up behind her. The candle cast an uncertain light now the windows were dark.

When she looked up finally, the scissors in her hand, she was shocked to see that she was not alone. There was someone standing in the doorway. The candle was between her and the mirror. She had seen a flicker of movement in the shadows, heard the rattle of a chain. But when she turned, the door was empty.

At first Miranda had no fear. Instead she felt a flicker of anger, part of her previous mood. Someone was spying on her. She put down the comb, and snatched up from her desk the long, unloaded revolver. It was heavy in her hand. She stepped to the door. It was dark on the landing and she could see nothing.

"Hai, nu te mai ascunde acum—come out now, show yourself," she said. She threw the scissors onto the desk, then seized the candle and stepped out over the threshold. "Come out," she said, and lifted up the light. There in a corner of the landing crouched a girl.

She also was barefoot and was wearing a long dress. An ankle bracelet jingled on her instep. Her shirt was embroidered in red thread. Her face was hidden in a mass of tangled, coarse brown hair, which she now parted with her fingers.

Miranda pointed the unloaded gun at her and held up the candle. She was excited by her first words of Roumanian, which had come out of her unasked. She felt a thrill of strength.

"Who are you? Show your face."

"Nu ma rani—please don't hurt me," said the girl. "I saw the light, and then my father sent me. No, I begged to go. Please, you are the one. The vampire knows it."

Miranda struggled to understand. Again she felt a swell of anger. "What are you talking about? Don't use these words." She felt both liberated and confused by this new language, which she used with the facility of an eight-year-old.

Once again there was a lot she didn't understand. But she wouldn't be intimidated in her father's house. She took a step forward. "Show me. What's your name?"

The girl pulled her hair back from her face, revealing a lumpy nose and high cheekbones, and almond-shaped black eyes. Miranda had been confused by her small size, and now saw she was older than she first had seemed, perhaps sixteen years old. Her lips were thick, and her face was chapped and rough. She scrambled to her knees and put her hands out. "Miss, I saw the lamp, I had to come. My father spoke a summoning. You must know it is not safe here. The vampire is on the road from Murfatlar. You'll see torches."

The light had changed in the little room behind Miranda. She stepped back as the girl got to her feet. She knelt on her bed and looked out toward the west, where there were lights among the trees along the carriage road.

"Usurper's soldiers," said the girl. "Please come with me." Already she was halfway down the tower stairs. Miranda snatched her things up from the desktop.

"Miss, put out the light."

There was no reason to keep it. Miranda blew out the flame. Torchlight was coming through the windows on the garden side. There were men in the carriage road by Juliana's house. She could see their torches, though they made no noise. And there were torches on the dunes.

The girl led her across the big hall, then pushed out through the windows to the terrace overlooking the sea. Stone steps led down to the water beside a wooden pier. The girl leaped from stone to stone until she was standing in the surf, and Miranda followed her. Suddenly terrified, she jumped down into the water, cold and dark. She followed the girl straight out underneath the pier, pulling herself among the seaweed and barnacle-encrusted pilings into the deeper water. The girl had flopped out of her skirt, which she held bunched in her hand as she pointed straight out toward the east. "Porpoise Rock," she whispered. "See the light." There was a red light over the water. It gleamed for a moment, then went out.

"Can you swim?" she whispered. Miranda pushed forward through the small waves. The light had not seemed so very far away. But the girl held her back—"No, they will see. Hide here. I will show you."

The water was to their necks. They clung to the second-to-the-last piling and waited. There were men with torches on the beach to the north side. And there were lights in the house now. After several minutes, some men came onto the terrace and stood looking out over the sea.

"Nosferatu," murmured the girl.

It was clear the one she meant. He stood with his hands on the stone balustrade. He looked to be in his early thirties, with curling black hair and pale skin. His white shirt was unbuttoned, loose. He peered up and down the beach and then over the water.

It seemed impossible he would not notice them: two heads clumped together between the seventh and eighth strut of the jetty, perhaps thirty yards away. Miranda found herself cursing her new clothes. She had her gun and her money and her diary in a nest of rags, and the whole thing was done up in the oilskin like a kind of a package. She had hoped to keep it dry, but now she let it sink into the water. She crouched down until only her head was above the surface, moving with the waves as they sucked in and out. She was aware of the girl whispering a chant or a prayer as the man on the terrace strode toward them down the steps to the jetty. A soldier followed him, carrying a torch.

How was it possible he did not see them? The boards creaked under his boots. Light spilled down through the boards onto the water as he walked the length of the jetty and stood above them. Another soldier followed him. "There is a trail of footprints," he said, "leading toward Mamaia Sat."

"Take the horsemen," said the vampire.

"What about the house? Shall we . . . ?"

"No. She might return."

"We found her clothes," said the soldier.

They were standing at the jetty's end. Miranda clung to the piling, her feet unsteady on the shifting stones. This girl, she decided—there was no reason to trust her. There was no reason to allow her to clutch hold of her as she was doing. There was no reason to allow her to pull her down into the water. "Trust me," the girl murmured, and pulled her down until she was submerged, looking up through the water at the torch at the end of the jetty and at the vampire's face as he peered over the edge. Her lungs were burning, but the girl forced her down among the tumbled rocks at the bottom of the piling, gripping her despite her struggles. The vampire's face hovered moonlike above them, distorted by the intervening water, and Miranda was aware of black eyebrows, even of soft eyelashes, because he was so close.

And when she came up for air, the face was gone, and the footsteps were receding down the planks. She and the girl clung to each other, bobbing in the waves until the torches were gone along the beach, out of sight among the dunes. Then Miranda tried to pull away. "Go," said the girl. "Swim out to where you saw the light."

The water glistened here and there with phosphorescence. Miranda tried to hold her bundle above the water. The waves were not heavy and there was no undertow. Behind her there were torches on the beach. Miranda could see the girl's head as she struggled after her.

There was a current of cold water, and then another warmer current. The moon was rising over the sea. She swam into the path of the moon until she saw a low rock break the surface of the water in front of her. She was swimming over a sand bar, gleaming white beneath her. The water, which had been deep, now grew shallow again, and she heard it gurgling and sucking at the sides of the rock, a long, misshapen ridge, higher at the north end. Seaweed clung to it.

A voice spoke: "Is that Ludu?"

"Father." This was from the girl.

"You have her?"

In the light of the moon, newly revealed from behind a cloud, Miranda saw the outline of a long, low boat. Held into a crevice in the rock's far side, now it came away slowly and pulled around the head of Porpoise Rock. It cleaved between the girl and Miranda, who caught some strands of kelp and let the slow waves push her up and down against the rock. When the waves were at their lowest point, she found she could touch bottom.

She was full of apprehension and relief. There were three men in the boat—two oarsmen, each with a pair of oars. In the stern huddled the man who had spoken, and who now helped the girl to clamber over the side. "Where is she?" he said.

"There."

The man uncovered his lantern and held it up. Blinded on three sides, it spread a garish red light between the boat and the rock.

"There," repeated Ludu. With the red light in her eyes, Miranda could no longer see the men.

"Bring it in," said the voice, and the boat backed toward her, trapping her against the rock. "Don't be afraid."

Letting go of the weeds, Miranda shielded her face with her hand. "Put out the light," she said, and the man obeyed her. Now in a moment she could see him in the flat stern, holding the tiller. He had a wide beard and his head was tied in a bandana.

There was nothing to be done. Miranda swam the few strokes to the boat. Ignoring the old man's hand, she deposited her oilcloth bundle, then pulled herself over the side. Immediately the boat was underway, the two oarsmen making long, slow strokes. The oarlocks were wrapped in rags, but even so they jingled.

6 A Ribbon of Moonlight

FIVE YEARS AND A few months earlier, Peter had gone down to the pirogue and examined the footprints of the animal in the wet sand. He told himself that in the darkness he could not have seen how large it was. How could he have been so crazy as to think of fighting it, attacking it? He'd found the charred stick where he'd thrown it down, and it broke as he was using it to scratch away the prints.

He didn't mention the incident and neither did Raevsky. There was no reason to remind him, particularly since he had lost his melancholy from the night before. Chipper and excited in the morning light, he tended to his feet. Then with mock exclamations of pain he slid them into his boots and hobbled in a circle around camp. Peter stowed the tent and gear while he relit the fire and made their porridge of sweet German crackers.

"Double food today," he said. "Tonight we find the place, a few houses for the Africans." Then he described two long portages.

The night before, Andromeda had run away, as usual when there was explicit danger. Now she picked her way back over the stones as if her feet were also sore. Careful of her dignity, Peter put some biscuits into a tin plate. Even so she growled as he came close, wrinkling her delicate muzzle, showing her teeth.

Before they left, Peter walked along the shore again, calling Miranda's name. He stood on a promontory above the stream and cupped his hands around his lips. He wasn't hoping for a reply. Instead, there was something valedictory about the sound and then the intervals of silence. After a few minutes, though, he'd had enough and he came back. Andromeda was already in the boat.

He didn't want Raevsky to have to take off his boots. So he was the one who, barefoot, pushed the pirogue out, and later, barefoot, brought it in beside a downed tree. The portage cut off a wide bend of the water and some rapids. Whistling and singing songs, Raevsky pulled the canvas bags ashore while Peter took the boat on his back. He was surprised how light it was.

Or it was light at first. Because of its width, he had to stretch his arms out to support it. There was a special stick like a yoke that fit between the gunnels and over his back. Sometimes he lost his balance, and most of the time he couldn't see where he was going. The path led through birch trees and the swamp. Luckily, many feet had widened it; he walked with his back bent, the boat perched like a turtle's shell. He looked straight downward at his shoes and wet jeans, and at the boot marks in the frozen mud.

Many times he had to stop and rest. Away from the river, again Peter was struck by the silence of the woods. It was another cold clear morning, though he was sweating and his heart was pounding. Inside his woolen socks, woolen gloves, his hands and feet were cold.

Raevsky had gone ahead. Peter heard him cry out, heard the dog bark. He flipped the boat into the frozen grass and ran to join them.

A boy lay among the saplings beside the path. Maybe six years old, he lay curled up on his side. Someone had put a deerskin over the uncertain ground and wrapped him in a ragged blanket, which he'd kicked away. And though his feet and lower legs were bare, still he'd torn open his woolen shirt to reveal his ribs, his gaunt body and swollen stomach. His skin was dry and crusty, with patches of eczema on his neck and arms. His hair was cut close to his scalp.

Peter could see he was sick. His own memories of the cave, of lying listless in his own sweat, were too immediate. He remembered the vacant feeling and could taste again the bitter saliva in his mouth. The boy looked up at them with big, stupid eyes, too big for his emaciated face.

There was sweat on his high forehead, and even in the cold small wind his body stank. Andromeda was growling, scratching at the stones. Her yellow fur rose in a sharp ridge between her shoulder blades. Raevsky was on his knees, had pulled his gloves off. He'd thrown down the canvas bags and had produced a rag of cloth, which he reached out toward the boy as if to wipe his face. Or he made wiping gestures in the air without touching the boy's skin; now doubtless aware of his futility, he seized the canteen that Peter found in the outer pocket of the larger bag. He unscrewed the top, poured in some water that he held to the boy's lips, all the time muttering and crooning over him in a mixture of English and Roumanian. Peter understood the English part, which was a repetition of something he had said the night before: "Dead river, dead. Gulka, Ferenc, Alex . . ."

Peter stood light-headed, sucking in the cold air. The boy had been abandoned—not without love, not without regret. The deerskin and the blanket were proof of that. The water slid from his lips over his chin. He stared up at them, making no attempt to swallow.

Peter found the sight of him intolerable—his skin dry as paper, stretched over sharp bones. He wondered if this kid was just the bait in a trap, and he looked back down the path to where the boat lay on its side, propped against a broken stump. He studied the woods on either side of them, partly from caution, partly because he could not endure that wasted face.

"What should we do?" he asked.

Raevsky held a lump of snow against the boy's forehead. "You go on. Africans not far. African will help."

Peter looked at the boat. Then he bent to pick up one of the canvas bags. "No," Raevsky said. "Leave with me. Find help. Africans—"

Africans, Peter thought. It was hard to imagine what Raevsky was talking about. The old man had taken off his coat and rolled up his shirtsleeves, uncovering, as he worked over the boy, his corded, liver-spotted arms. Peter saw he had some blood on the collar of his checked shirt and on the cloth around his neck. He had taken off his cap. His hair stuck out like wire.

Something now occurred to Peter, irrelevant words his mother had taught him about six months before she died. Often now they came back to him, snippets of poems. ". . . you and I are old," he thought. "Death closes all. . . ." It was from Lord Tennyson's "Ulysses," a poem (his mother had said) that should not necessarily be taken at face value.

"No time! You come back!"

What did he mean? Already Andromeda had disappeared up the trail. Peter stared after her. His mind was moving slowly, but to tell the truth, he thought, he couldn't bear to stay here with the boy, his sharp dry face.

"Go!" Raevsky shouted. "Go, go!" Then he relented. His face lost some of its exasperated look. He even smiled, showing the toothless gap in his upper jaw. "Dead river—no! Is chance for us. Conjure and death. Always we fight it, now to end."

He shook his head. "Go!" and Peter went. He ran and walked along the path by the Hoosick riverbank. He ran and walked, ran and walked along the path. Sometimes Andromeda raced on ahead. Sometimes she stayed with him.

"Africans not far," Raevsky had said, but it was far. Out of breath, the cold air sharp in his lungs and in his teeth, Peter had time for useless thoughts. What was he doing here, running by himself along this trail through the woods? Miranda was gone and now Raevsky was behind him. Only Andromeda was left, someone who had always laughed at him all the way through school. Even now she was making fun of him as best she could, mocking his slowness. She would wait for him in the middle of the path, yawning and stretching as he came close, pushing at the leaves and snow with her stiff forelegs while her tongue curled out.

Sometimes in high school she had stood in the middle of the west corridor with her hands on her hips, wearing a T-shirt and short skirt or something—she'd never seemed to carry any books to class. Her short yellow hair, dark eyebrows, and gray eyes. Now she pricked her ears, sniffing at the air, running back and forth through the woods parallel to the trail. As apprehensive as he felt—always he had to wonder whether he projected feelings onto her, and whether there was anything left inside her of the girl he had known in Williamstown. Sometimes, looking into her gray-and-blue-flecked eyes, he thought he saw . . . something, some remnant of a complicated thought.

In the transformation to this world, at the moment, Peter supposed, when he'd gained his new right hand, the girl had changed her shape. That first morning Miranda and Peter had found her on Christmas Hill, curled up in a nest of fancy underwear.

And maybe what had happened was even stranger than that. Maybe there was something else in her besides the girl and the dog, some connection to a Roumanian officer named Sasha Prochenko, a blob of connection that grew inside her like a tumor.

Peter stopped running. He put his arms over his stomach and bent over. He had a stitch in his side, and besides that he felt sick, and it wasn't just because the phrase he'd put together in his mind recalled his mother and the disease she'd died of. He wiped his mouth with his left hand, which still ached from carrying the boat. But his big right hand was strong and serviceable, horribly so.

Now Andromeda came running and whining. They had joined the river again, and Peter could see the wide, still water through the tree trunks. When he looked up, the light was glittering in the trees. Andromeda snarled at him to get him moving; after half a mile they left the stream and turned south again into heavier woods and bigger trees, birches and evergreens. They climbed up-hill for ten minutes, and then the ground leveled out, and they came into a clearing against a low cliff face. The houses were there, bark-covered, dome-shaped wooden huts, and also some scaffolding against the cliff. Smoke rose from three of the huts. The ground was dry and chalky under crusts of snow.

Cold and exhausted, Peter bent down with his hands on his knees. Why was he so weak? It was because he'd eaten nothing but biscuits these past days, nothing nourishing since they'd killed the wendigo. With his hands on his knees, smelling the smoke from the settlement, he found himself bombarded with fantasies of food. Wordless smells and tastes overwhelmed him, phantoms of past meals. Memories of Snickers bars. His mouth filled with thick drool.

At the same time he thought about the boy Raevsky had found, the mother or father who'd abandoned him. Feelings were sifted over with questions— what was Peter doing here? What would he do in Albany? Where would he go? Who was the African that could help him—were there Africans here? Why Africans? Andromeda ran into the space between the houses. Poised on three legs, she lifted her forepaw above the snow.

Now suddenly Peter imagined enormous superhuman figures with black skin who would stride out of these tiny huts and tell him what to do, how this strange world worked and where to find Miranda in it. So it was with more disappointment than fear that he watched someone approach out of the scaf-folding and the tent in front of it, an ominous small person in a turban and sur-gical mask, brandishing a short-barreled rifle.

Andromeda made the high snuffling whimper that sufficed her for a bark. But she didn't budge. She stayed with her foreleg curled.

"Hello," Peter called out. Light-headed, he stood up straight, raised both hands.

Someone was in the flapping doorway of the tent, a small person who said something and the woman with the gun relented—Peter saw she was a woman now. Red hair hung down her back, and under her unbuttoned quilted coat she wore a dress, a shapeless dirty garment of bleached cotton. Her mask also, looped behind her ears, was streaked with dirt.

She put up her gun. "Death closes all, but something ere the end. . . ."

thought Peter. Tennyson, and with the words of the poem Peter found himself remembering his mother's cancer smell. He caught a whiff of it, mixed with her perfume—he'd thought about his mother a lot today. Or else memories of her had gotten stuck to whatever he was thinking, words and images with hooks like burdocks, burrs—a simile she might have liked, though not the way he was expressing it, the proclivity, the prolixity—was that the word? Was it even a word? She was the one who told him that memory and perception were part of the same thing. She'd audited some courses at the college—what was wrong with him? He stood with his head whirling, his mouth full of saliva, his stomach and intestines like a dirty engine, and all he could think about were scraps of color (Raevsky's checked shirt-collar with blood on it, his rolled-up sleeves, spotted arms), scraps of memory. He found himself staring at the red-haired woman's surgical mask, while at the same time he realized all these stupid thoughts were not just the result of hunger and exhaustion. But he was trying to hide something from himself. He could hear a roaring in his ears, feel a twitch in his right hand. He had an impulse to drag the woman down, bat her gun away. She was no match for him. None of these people were any match for him. "Not unbecoming men that strove with Gods." Where was Miranda now?

He felt a hand on his elbow and he pulled away. Someone was talking. "You may rest here. Come."

He couldn't look into the person's face. "Come," she said. Peter saw the black hand on his arm, the small plump fingers underneath his elbow guiding him back toward the tent while the guard in the mask made threatening gestures at the trees.

"Where is Miranda now?" he asked himself. "Right now?"

"NOW" IN THAT CONTEXT HAD no meaning. Five years later there were cotton blankets in the bottom of the boat. Miranda wrapped herself in one of them. She sat beside the man on the stern plank while the girl Ludu sat at his feet. His heavy hand was on the tiller and he said nothing to Miranda as he steered the boat out to sea. With his other hand he pushed his daughter's wet, knotted hair back from her forehead while she spoke to him. "You saw him on the dock. He was this close. But I said a prayer to Saint Lucia with no eyes. We were covered in the blackness. Oh, but I was frightened!" It was true—her teeth were chattering. She seized hold of her father's hand and held it near her cheek.

"You've done it," he said.

"You see she is the answer to our prayers," continued the girl. "It's the face we saw in the glass. You begged for this and God heard you. Oh, but the vampire said he was to send the soldiers to Mamaia Sat. . . ."

What was she talking about—the glass? The mirror? Saint Lucia? There were torches among the dunes. "Hush now," said the bearded man. He had a bulbous, porous nose and a thick chest. He was dressed in patched black clothes. "Miss," he said, and smiled. His teeth were crooked, widely spaced. Miranda expected him to say something. But when she looked him in the face he dropped his eyes.

Soon he turned the boat north, parallel to the coast. The sea was calm and still. The two boys rowed with long quiet strokes, and they stared back at Miranda. Their long faces were expressionless. "Miss," said the bearded man, trying again. "You won't remember me. I saw you at Vama Veche when you were on holiday. On horseback with your aunt—a little sorrel mare. I gave your horse an apple. You won't remember. My name is Dinu Fishbelly and these are my sons. You understand me?"

Why did he ask that? It was because he spoke Roumanian instead of French, the language of the rich. "I understand," she said. She wanted him to go on talking. She wanted information, a clue to the role she was to play.

Sitting in the boat, listening to the jingle of the locks, she tried to think about what had gone wrong so far. When she'd imagined walking out the carriage road, she had prepared herself for a new beginning, for the vulnerability that comes from ignorance, at least at the very start. That was why she'd put off her departure a full day. Even so she had imagined herself holding back, traveling incognito perhaps to Insula Calia and perhaps to Bucharest, where no doubt she could learn a lot just from newspapers. She would wait and try to send a message across the ocean, and choose the moment when she could initiate events, either her aunt's plan, which she'd ponder at her leisure (if, come to think of it, the message hadn't gotten soaked in the water—no, it was still wrapped up in the oilcloth, so that was all right), or her own. But now these people had barged in and dragged her out into a game that had already started. In the stillness of the boat, listening to the sweep of the oars, she found herself irritated by their deference, which seemed insincere. Irritated by their questions, which she was afraid she couldn't answer. What could she do for them? Now already she was in their debt.

More than that, there was no longer any opportunity to hide, to pretend to be someone different than she was. But even your own self can be a role. Once

Andromeda had gotten her to try out for a play at school, and she'd had nightmares about forgetting her lines, learning the wrong part. Now she stripped the blanket from around her shoulders and rubbed her arms in the rough cloth. She heard Ludu whisper, "There it is," and knew she was talking about the bracelet, Miranda Brancoveanu's golden bracelet.

It was a mistake to even wear it. These people were staring at her as if she had two heads. She sat up straight, then turned her face in profile. Aware of her wet shirt, she folded her arms over her chest. If she was going to play the white tyger among these people, even in the dark, she needed a new bra and some dry clothes.

"Where are we?" she asked.

She knew enough to know that Dinu Fishbelly was a Gypsy nickname. How did that work in? Blind Rodica had been a Gypsy, and she had died to save Miranda's life.

"We'll be coming in near Lake Tasaul," said the bearded man, "That's where my house is."

They pulled toward shore. They had passed a small headland and were sliding in now toward the gravel beach. In shallow water the boys shipped their oars and jumped over the side, as did Ludu. The three of them pulled the boat up till it crunched ashore. With her oilcloth bundle under her arm, Miranda stepped onto the stones.

Fishbelly hadn't moved. Miranda was surprised to see the older boy step into the surf until he stood at the boat's stern. He took his father onto his back, and for the first time Miranda noticed that the man had no legs below his knees. The boy carried him up onto the beach, while Ludu and the other pulled the boat up to the dunes. There was a stake above the high water mark, and they tied the painter to it and then flipped the boat over with the oars underneath. Ludu had slipped back into her wet skirt.

"Warn them at Mamaia Sat," the old man said, and the younger boy ran away south on the packed sand near the water's edge. He had no shoes, and Miranda wondered how long he could run like that—as fast as he could go. She lost sight of him among the larger rocks of the headland, then turned to follow Ludu and the man on piggyback.

They took a path through the dunes and through the bushes and flat grass upon the other side. They crossed a larger road that ran in back of the dunes, then continued through the dry reeds on the other side until they reached the shores of a small lake. Among the reeds a house on stilts was built over the water, or at least the lakebed where the water had receded. The mud underneath the house was cracked and dry.

Dry clothes first of all, Miranda thought, and she would pay these people. She had her purse in her oilcloth package. It would be important to pay them, to reestablish her authority, and then sit down and ask them questions. She would buy some food from them before she fainted from hunger. With her aunt's letter to guide her, and some basic answers, she could make some choices—what did these people want from her? Was it safe even to be with them? Let alone to spend the night.

In front of her, Fishbelly reached down to slap his son on the rump as if he were a pony. If she paid them, Miranda thought, they could guide her to Insula Calia. Now she regretted not having pressed her aunt for information when she'd seen her in tara mortilor. That way she could have asked the questions she wanted to have answered now. Obviously there was much to learn, but no chance now except by keeping her eyes open until she could read her aunt's letter in privacy, in its entirety: There was a deck covered with traps and fishing weirs. There was a ramp of gray planks that led to the deck, and the boy staggered along it with his burden while Miranda followed Ludu up a ladder. The door was open and led into a single room. The walls were made of weathered, unpainted boards. The windows were covered with big shutters. There was a fire in the iron stove, a kerosene lantern on the long table.

"Get her some things," said the man as his son, panting, slid him down into a chair. Ludu led Miranda back into a corner of the room, set off by curtains around a straw pallet on the floor. "You'll sleep here," she murmured.

"No, she won't," called the man. "Codreanu will be burning the houses in Mamaia Sat—it doesn't take much in this weather. The fire will spread. We'll run for it when Gheorghe comes. Just a few things and we run. You—get us the horses," he said, and the other boy went out.

Ludu pulled some clothes from a line of four wooden crates against the wall. She stripped off her wet things and rubbed her body with a piece of cloth. Chilled, Miranda turned to face the curtain, which was made of printed cotton in a pattern of red flowers. Through it she could see the old man leaning his meaty forearms on the table, poring over something that was hidden from her. She supposed the curtain, transparent to her, would be opaque to him because the lamp was on his side. She unbuttoned her shirt. He did not look up.

"I'm taking you to the woods near Casimcea," he called out. "Please," he said, as Miranda was pulling on a loose, coarse shirt and undershirt, and heavy trousers. A few things that she'd taken from her desk in her father's house—a silver-handled toothbrush, a tortoiseshell comb—she now transferred to her new pockets. "We have to ride," murmured Ludu at the same time. She gave her woolen socks. "You'll wear my brother's boots."

"I tell you this because we must move quickly," called the man on the other side of the curtain. "We are your servants. Anything you want, then we will do. We have wished and prayed."

It didn't seem the right time to ask for food. Anything she wanted—a sandwich and a bed. Miranda didn't want to tell them things or talk at all. She wanted to listen. She didn't want to demonstrate how much she didn't know.

Also, she was worried about the horses. But if the man had seen her on a little sorrel mare in Vama Veche, then it must follow she knew how to ride. He didn't say the little sorrel mare had thrown her into a ditch. She sat down on the pallet to dry her hair while Ludu went to fetch the boots for her. She felt more confident when she was wearing them. She got up, stamped her feet, then strode out from behind the curtain. She had the oilcloth bundle in her hands.

Gratefully she unwrapped it and unwrapped the gun, the box of bullets. Inside the rags they were almost dry. The diary was almost dry. She rubbed it and the gun with the cloth around her neck, which she had used to dry her hair. She was pleased at the man's response: His eyes grew wide. "I saw that in your father's hand. Blessed on St. Sebastian's altar."

But the bag of money had gotten soaked. She untied it, put in her fingers and pulled out the saturated wad of paper that had been her aunt's letter. The words were illegible, and the paper ripped along its seams as she tried to unfold it. "This is great," Miranda said.

But inside she was cursing herself. How stupid she had been! The letter was a gift to her and she had spurned it, thrown it away. How long would it have taken her to read it completely? Already her aunt had been proved right. Apparently she was indeed surrounded by murderers and spies.

Maybe if she dried the paper out, something could be salvaged. Maybe she'd already read the most important part—she'd find something at Insula Calia.

And maybe her first instinct had been true, and there'd been nothing in the letter she could use. Surely it was better to think so now. Nothing could be accomplished if she had to depend on her dead aunt for everything. There was no reason to despair, not over a stupid piece of paper.

Still she was sickened by her own carelessness. Inside her empty stomach she felt a sudden surge of dread. It turned rapidly to irritation. She found herself irritated by the way the man with the beard was staring at her as if everything about her was important. She didn't deserve that kind of deference, not now, not yet. "So you might tell me what you want," she said. As far as she could tell looking around, there wasn't a crumb of food in the whole place.

The man sat in the only chair. Elsewhere there were stools and wooden crates and fishing gear. Nets hung from the rafters on one side. There was sand on the bare floorboards. It crunched under her leather soles. The place stank of the sea.

In the lantern light she could see the man's face, his protruding brow and sunken eyes, his cracked lips and red nose, his thick, gray beard. The red scarf around his head was gone now, revealing a bald scalp. His forehead had a mottled, bluish look. "I don't understand," he said, and for a moment Miranda wondered whether she had gotten the words right.

"What do I want?" he asked. His face was anything but friendly.

Miranda squeezed the water from the purse. Now she felt it would be a mistake to offer him money. Instead, conscious of effect, she loaded the gun and slipped the box of bullets into her shirt. Once in Colorado Springs, Rachel's father had shown her how to load and fire this kind of gun.

"Things have happened since that day in Vama Veche," she said portentously.

Not that she remembered anything about it; the man made an abrupt gesture with his hand. "What do I want? Please, miss, it is no mystery! I want to be free in my own country. I want rain in the Dobruja. I want the Germans out of Bucovina and Transylvania. I want Nicola Ceausescu dead and a Brancoveanu on the throne of Great Roumania. I want the vampire sealed up in hell or breaking stones upon the Brasov road. I want revenge on the men who maimed me."

He glared up at her. Ludu, who had been packing clothes into a canvas bag, now broke in. "My father was wounded in the fighting. The German horses were on the bridge, and my father stepped on a grenade. That was five years ago. Last month we went to the oracle at Insula Calia and he heard Mother Egypt's voice. She told him the prayers to say. Please, miss—now you are here."

"I've been away," Miranda said, uncertain. But some things she was beginning to understand. Nicola Ceausescu was the woman who had sent Captain Raevsky to kidnap her. And of course she had almost the same name as the former Communist Party chief who had been murdered in 1989, and whose exploits had been carefully described in her aunt's book, burned on Christmas Hill. Insula Calia was the place her aunt had mentioned in her letter. Doubtless she would have explained about all of this, only . . .

And if Miranda went to Insula Calia now, maybe she could talk to her aunt again—hear her voice. "I've been away," she repeated. Now her own irritation had flagged, and she sensed a growing anger in the man. "Nicola Ceausescu—tell me about her."

She watched Dinu Fishbelly squeeze his knotted red bandana in his fist. He leaned onto the surface of the table and thrust his head into the circle of lantern light. He spoke slowly, as if explaining to a child. "What are you saying? German soldiers are in Transylvania, in the oil fields. Ceausescu's widow calls herself the white tyger, and where she goes the people kiss her hands. Here on the coast whole villages stand empty. Now don't tell me we have risked our lives for the sake of a girl who knows none of these things. I tell you all the fields between here and Saraiu lie fallow except where our bones have been plowed under—don't you know this? Tell me you have heard our prayer!"

Miranda swallowed, looked down at her boots. This was a question that could not be answered. Still, she thought, an answer must be found. Clenching her teeth, she raised her head, forced herself to look at him until he turned his eyes away. Why should she be bullied by a man she didn't know? She had her father's gun in her hand.

Outside there was a clattering and snorting, and a pounding on the door. The boy who had gone for horses threw it open. "They are burning the trees," he said. "We have to go."

"We wait for Gheorghe," said the man. But he did not resist when his son and daughter came to lift him from his chair. He clambered onto the boy's back. Outside there was a fire behind the hill, and they stood watching for a moment from the deck. Then the boy carried his father down the ramp to where four horses stood among the trampled reeds. They were snorting and blowing. A little boy held two of them. The reins were wrapped around his forearms. Now he surrendered them to Ludu, who had the canvas bag over her shoulder.

Spooked, one of the horses pulled up. Ludu grabbed it by its cheek plate and led it forward while the old man climbed astride from his son's back. He had a special saddle, Miranda could see. He had no stirrups but his thighs were strapped in place with leather straps. The boy pulled them tight, and then the small red horse was stamping in a circle while the others drew back among the reeds. The ground was soft underfoot. Miranda looked into the lake beyond the house. It was a small sad puddle in the middle of the dry mud. Even so she saw the reddened sky reflected in the water.

The vampire was at Mamaia Sat, she thought, and in her mind she could picture some cottages huddled against the dunes. Was it Nicola Ceausescu who had sent him, the way she'd sent Raevsky? If so, was all this Miranda's fault already? She had been stung by the Gypsy's words to her, which had sounded like an accusation. Where was the boy who had run away?

"We wait for Gheorghe," said Dinu Fishbelly.

But the littlest boy burst into tears. And the other boy and Ludu were preparing to go. Barefoot, they swung themselves into their saddles. Ludu tied her skirt in front of her around the saddle horn, so that her legs were bare against the horse's side.

This is horrible, Miranda thought. She had a lump in her throat, and to distract herself, to reestablish some control, she tried to notice little things: the smell of burning in the air. In contrast with the people, these horses looked glossy and well cared for. The leather was new, and the metal jingled and shone. There was one horse left, a big shuffling gray—the biggest of the four, Miranda noticed. The others were waiting; she put her foot in the stirrup and pulled herself up. She'd ridden a horse a couple of times. Once she and Andromeda had visited some of Andromeda's cousins in New Jersey. Everyone agreed she'd done well, almost as if she knew what she was doing.

"Where now?" she asked.

"We must wait for Gheorghe," repeated the man.

But now the crying boy had disappeared into the reeds. Dinu's son bent his horse in a circle. It was black with lots of silver in its coat. Ludu followed him down the path onto the road. Then the two of them set off north between the lakeshore and the sea, in a running walk that soon turned faster. The surface of the road was hard-packed sand with a strip of beach grass down the middle.

"Stop," said the man. He held the reins of his red horse in his left hand close to its neck. Past his hand they were braided together in a long tail, and Miranda could see that with his right hand he was flicking the reins back and forth over the saddle horn, not striking the horse so much as caressing its shoulders on both sides, while his left hand moved back and forth and up and down as if anticipating the horse's head. Miranda studied him, searching for clues. He drew the horse around in a full circle while Miranda sat up straight.

Her stirrups seemed too high. The old man had a big saddle with a high, curved back. Hers was just a scrap of leather over a square of wool.

Back and forth flicked the braided reins. Miranda was also conscious of a clicking sound. The man was clicking his tongue and mumbling in a low voice. Then he must have come to a decision, because suddenly his horse pressed forward, and he released it and went up the road in a hard, immediate gallop.

She knew enough to know you held on with your thighs and not your hands, that you pointed your feet in and kept your heels down, that you moved with the horse and not against it, which was easier said than done. Inspired, she supposed, by the others, she blundered forward into a walk. She knew you weren't supposed to kick with your heels, but after a moment she found herself drumming on the horse's sides as it continued its slow amble. And when it finally changed its gait, she found herself tugging downward on the reins.

The red horse was much smaller than her gray one, but it was already out of sight. Unfamiliar stars shone through a veil of clouds—only the brightest, because it was not dark. A fire burned over the hill behind her, and she smelled smoke. On her left hand, now, the lake had gone away, replaced by a flat field of grasses over a broken wooden fence. There were some pine trees, more and more as she went on.

She had a lump in her throat and she couldn't get rid of it. So she tried to think about the horse and find a way to make it go faster. In a little bit she thought she was doing better. She relaxed her hands, relaxed her legs. The road ran straight and there was no opportunity to swerve or change direction.

Still confounded by the high stirrups, Miranda shifted her weight around, eased the pressure of her thighs and tightened up again. She raised her hands and lowered them. She had an idea she wanted to keep the horse's head up, its nose low. She experimented with a light hand, even let go the reins entirely at one point.

At moments she felt stabs of danger and urgency. At other moments she felt brief, furtive sensations: the loaded gun inside her shirt, chafing at her skin. It was good to feel it there. On her right hand, sometimes she saw the black sea through the dunes. The moon was out of sight behind her, but still she could not help but remember a poem she had read when she was in eighth grade and which Peter knew by heart. "The road was a ribbon of moonlight, over the purple moor. . . ." She remembered Peter Gross reciting the whole thing, and remembered wondering if it was his way to make a pass at her—not that she'd wanted that.

Then suddenly she heard hoofbeats up ahead, and the red horse was coming toward her down the road. "What are you doing?" shouted the old man. "Come," he said. "Stupid . . ."

The word was like a slap.

"Miss, come!"

The man had passed her coming back, and then pulled up his horse. He'd turned immediately behind her and was now chasing her up the road. Embarrassed, she supposed, her horse was now making a better effort. The man was close on the near side, and she could hear him mumbling and clicking.

On Miranda's left the grass had turned to scrubby bushes and a few low pines. The man came up beside her, and Miranda looked at him, or rather at his horse—its neck stretched out, its determined, staring eyes. The bit was loose in its mouth, she saw. She relaxed her own hands and her horse sprang forward.

Now they came to three big pine trees bunched together on the other side of a gray fence. Miranda looked over the red horse's neck, because she saw a movement in the trees. She saw the flash of a gun, white with a center of red and black. She heard the shot, and then the red horse was stumbling across the road. Her own horse veered to the far side. Blocked by the dunes, it pulled up suddenly. Miranda yanked backward on the reins and tried to come around, but the horse wouldn't budge. It pulled its head away from her and stamped its feet, moving sideways across the road.

She slipped from the saddle and let the horse go, while she ran back the way she'd come. She saw the lump of the fallen horse and some movement too, where Dinu Fishbelly was sprawled out on the sand. One of the straps around his legs had given way. But he was still caught by the other one and tangled in his long reins. His eyes were closed. His lips were split and bleeding.

She fumbled for the buckle on his leg, and he opened his eyes. "What are you doing? Get away! Leave me, for God's sake!"

Under the weak moon, the sky a burnt magenta to the south, she saw everything clearly. The inert horse, dead as a rock, its neck stretched out, its tail splashed across the road. The man where he had fallen in a crust of mud. His black shirt was made of patches sewn together with a scarlet thread. Miranda saw a patch of corduroy.

She found she'd pulled out her revolver. She looked down the road but could see nothing, no movement, nobody coming. She thrust the gun into her waist again and knelt down over Dinu Fishbelly, trying to see where he was hurt, wondering if she could carry him as his son had. She would find the gray horse farther on. It would wait for them. She knelt in the cool breeze from the sea, and she could smell the salt.

"What are you doing? Get away! Oh, miss," murmured the man. One eye was open, but the other was bashed shut.

Now there was a man in the road, strolling toward them. Miranda had expected him somehow; she wouldn't run away, not again. She was the daughter of Prince Frederick Schenck von Schenck, she told herself. And the man was—what? What kind of thing was he? Miranda heard him whistling a complicated tune.

The old man looked with his one eye, and instead of cursing at Miranda and pushing her away, now he grabbed her hands in his strong hands. And his voice had the respectful, pleading tone of earlier: "Miss, you promise now? By Jesus Christ and Mary Magdalene, who once lived in this place. I'm a drunken cripple and my daughter is a slut, and my sons are simpleminded. It is not for our sake I'm begging you—don't let us be cut down like dogs. Remember your own people who brought you back to Great Roumania."

There was something in his words that calmed her, took away her fear. She would indeed remember her own people. And it wouldn't be for nothing that men like Dinu Fishbelly had faith in her. You could decide things like that and they'd be true. She looked up and she knew what she was going to see. The vampire stood above them on the road, dressed in his black boots and white silk shirt. His black hair curled over his ears. His elegance did not dispel the sense of menace that clung to him. His hands were in his pockets. Miranda saw the moving bulge in the cloth as he searched for something with his right hand. Then he drew it out, a fishing knife with a wooden handle and a stained blade.

He squatted down fastidiously and plucked at the seams of his pants. Miranda tried to pull away, tried to find her gun again, but the old man held her. "Promise me!" he whispered. The vampire smiled.

"Let me help," he said.

Close as he was, Miranda couldn't tell whether she was seeing an apparition or a real human being. Though she could see every detail of his delicate face, still there was something ghostlike in the way he moved, quietly and without effort. Certainly Miranda was aware of the difference between him and the man who grasped her hands with such desperation. The man's breath was hoarse and choking, and a stink came from his body. His arms were shuddering and trembling as the vampire put the knife under his black shirt. "Watch me gut this fish," he said to Miranda, smiling, his dark lips close.

Blood dripped from the saturated shirt. The stink was overpowering. Fishbelly opened his mashed eye, and both his eyes were staring at her, only at her. He seemed scarcely aware of his attacker, who was moving the knife up his stomach through his clothes. But under the vampire's hands, he also seemed tinged now with unreality. His grip on her hands was failing, and she was able sprawl backwards and pull away and pull the gun out of her shirt—her father's gun which felt so heavy and so light—and pull the hammer back with her greasy hands. Surely her aunt, who had left her this gun, and who kept duck-hunting photographs on her bureau, would not have neglected to teach her how to shoot.

With her elbows locked in front of her she pressed the trigger and fired once into the vampire's smiling face. The noise of the gun was terrific, and her hands jerked back. Then she jumped up with the hammer cocked again; there was no vampire, no person there. But she stood shaking in the moonlight, terrified now, suddenly terrified to be alone, aware suddenly of the noise of the surf on her left. In front of her there was the empty road and a fire burning on the hill. Her ears were ringing and her hands ached. Below her lay a dead horse. But the dead man, also, had disappeared.

In this world, as now, there were unreal moments mixed in with the real, moments when all natural laws were suspended; it had been that way since the book of her past life had caught fire on Christmas Hill. Conjuring, people called it here, magic, she supposed. But how did it work, and how could she make it work for her, for Dinu Fishbelly? She stepped back a few yards and lifted the gun's warm muzzle to the sky. Above her was a veil of clouds. She listened to the sound of the surf on the shingle beach, and in time she heard the clink of a horse's bridle and the clump of its hoofs on the dry sand. Or rather two horses, because when she turned she saw the girl Ludu astride her pony, leading the big gray. She slipped out of the saddle and pulled down her skirt. "It was the man from the dock," Miranda stammered. "And your father—now they're gone."

The girl stood where her father had been. With one hand she pushed the hair back from her face. Miranda took a few steps down the road, peering into the reeds on either side. She expected the girl to say something, to ask her questions, but she stood without speaking.

Then finally, matter-of-factly: "He used to beat me," she said.

"We'll go back. We'll look for him. I don't know—he must be somewhere. It wasn't real."

Ludu shook her head. She stood gnawing on her lips and rubbing her mouth, and then she shrugged. She moved to the dead horse, unstrapped a rolled-up cloth that hung across its saddle bow. "You take the pony. She'll be easy now."

Miranda looked down. A small fat toad hopped across the sand into the grass.

7 | *The African*

"HOW DO YOU FEEL?"

The African had a soft, sweet voice. She swallowed her words sometimes, or looked away from Peter when she talked. Though of all the people he had met in this country, she spoke the most fluent English, still sometimes he had to strain to understand because she spoke so softly.

He lay on a rough bed frame, nailed together out of sticks of gray birch. There was no mattress, but he was wrapped in feather comforters and pillows stuffed with straw. A blanket roll supported his back so he could sit up.

She sat beside him on a low stool, also made of raw sticks with the bark left on. She was just a girl, maybe eight or nine. She'd brought him dinner, and now she was holding the tin plate. He had only managed to eat half of it. A mixture of corn bread and beans, it filled his stomach like a pouch of sand.

She had taken his temperature with an ordinary mercury thermometer. She had checked his pulse against the second hand of her wristwatch. Nor did she seem reassured when he told her he had already been sick, already recovered, and the disease had left no trace.

Altogether he was surprised by her competence. But more than that, the sureness of her gestures, a language of grown-up movement, though her voice was hesitant and shy. "All right," he said, in answer to her question.

Heat came from an iron stove in the middle of the tent. There was no wind, and the canvas walls hung flat, encompassing a square of softened mud twenty feet on a side. Other cots were in the tent. A half dozen people lay unmoving, covered in blankets.

"Where are your parents?" Peter asked.

"They're dead." The girl spoke gravely, simply, but without a hint of sadness: "Oh, how queer you are! They've been dead a long time."

She was a beautiful child, with fluffy black hair around her head, dark eyebrows, and pink lips. Her eyes were a dusty green color, accented (Peter saw) with makeup—a drawn line around her eyelids and her mouth. Her cheeks were paler than the backs of her hands, because of some white cosmetic powder. She wore a pale denim dress past her knees. Above it was a heavy brown sweater in a complicated pattern, buttoned down her front with wooden buttons. All of her clothes looked like hand-me-downs from another, older child. Her shoes, especially, were too big for her.

She put the plate aside, then reached out and took hold of Peter's hand. His right hand was tangled in the blankets, but his left lay open on the counterpane. She put her small palm against his as if measuring the difference. It was a charming gesture, he thought, and he allowed her to stroke his hand—she was an orphan, after all. At the same time he listened to her soft, serious voice as she explained how workers from the archeology dig had stayed here, mostly women. "Now," she said, "we've made the camp into a hospital."

But she felt a bit like a fraud, she said, because she hadn't any medical training. It didn't matter. There was no real treatment. People got better or they didn't. Their skin broke into lesions. For several days, since the illness had first spread among a tribe of English savages, she had treated some of the workers here and sent the rest away. Two people had already died. They were buried in the woods.

"Savages" was her word. She had been vaccinated when she was a child, she said. But she didn't know if vaccinations worked against this strain, whose incubation she had measured in hours instead of days or weeks. It was a long time since she'd been immunized. Smallpox had been eradicated in Africa, along with polio and many other scourges.

When Peter first had stumbled into the camp he had been weak and dazed. Things around him had swum in and out of focus as he sat in bed and tried to eat. He'd accepted a lot of crazy thoughts and crazy feelings, but now he wondered if he'd understood her soft, sweet whisper. Sometimes she talked like a grown-up, sometimes like a child. Now she turned her face away. Other small figures were moving among the sickbeds.

"Where are you from?" Peter asked, to distract himself from his bad stomach.

She squeezed his fingers and turned toward him. "Abyssinia. Eritrea. Have you heard of it?"

"I—I think so."

"What's your name?"

He told her. "I'm Waile," she said. "Waile Bizunesh. Eritrea is south of the Aegyptian Sudan. I thought I would escape, lead a healthy life. And not die young." She shook her head.

Peter wondered if he'd understood her. "You're here by yourself?"

"Of course." She smiled. "You must think I am mysterious. But you are the mysterious one. What has brought you to my excavation here? You are not like these savages or the Roumanian. You said some strange things while you were sleeping."

She didn't tell him what it was he'd said. She was talking about herself. "I confess it's true I've made a strange discovery. And I'll share it with you. My work here is a kind of dissertation. I was working in the valley of the kings near Heliopolis."

She'd turned away from him. On the other side of the tent someone moved and shifted on his cot. It was the little boy Raevsky had brought in. The girl—Waile—paid no attention. "I don't understand," said Peter.

"Of course you don't," she said. "For someone with my training it is also difficult to understand. We were excavating a chamber in the tomb. Nothing special at the bottom, just some interesting hieroglyphs from the twenty-sixth dynasty. But in Eritrea we'd heard about a place with similar inscriptions here at the world's edge. I received an academic grant—I came the normal way, I can assure you. I took the boat from Alexandria and then the packet steamer from New York."

She giggled. "I confess I spoke to the Roumanian. So I know you have a secret, too." Then suddenly she was staring at him, eyes wide, face serious. "I've had to shift the focus of my research. I am curious to see which parts of child-hood are learned, which are innate. I mean the behavior of children, and I've made some interesting discoveries. For example, I would never have told you any of this before—it is a secret, really. But I want to confide in you—isn't that so silly?" She gave his hand a squeeze. "You're not like these primitives who are attacking us."

Peter didn't know what to make of this. The boy rolled over to face them on his cot. Peter could see his big, listless eyes, his face covered with sores. One of the women sat beside him, then brought him a tin cup of water from a bucket by the stove.

"How is he?" whispered the girl—Waile. But the woman heard her. She came hurrying, her arms outstretched, and then knelt down in the mud. Because of her mask, Peter couldn't see her face.

"How is he, Fiona?"

"Ma'am, he'll live."

The girl shrugged her shoulders. "If we all live through till morning . . ."

Peter knew what she was talking about. He'd heard about it from Raevsky when he'd brought in the boy and laid him down. The night before, men had come out of the forest and attacked the camp. No one had been hurt.

"You see, I'm different each time I come up from the well," said the girl, squeezing his hand. Now she looked at him again, her face wide with surprise at her own story. "I climb up the ladder, and each time the rungs are bigger in my hands. Each time the spaces are wider, the well deeper—all these people see me leave on the boat to New York City. West to east over the ocean—oh, they waved and laughed the first time I went. Then in a few months here I am again! It's happened several times! And I don't come in a boat or through the woods. No, I climb out from underneath the earth—they won't go down into the well now. I could tell them a treasure was down there. I'd be right, but don't you see? Now they think I am a great magician, just like a Roumanian! Like a Roumanian conjurer on the Lido in Alexandria, making people disappear! A shilling a pop! But unfortunately they blame me also for this fever—that's enough!"

She paid no attention to Fiona, who hadn't moved, who was struggling to say more. A woman older than Peter, she had colorless light hair that poked out under her cap. Her eyes were blue and bloodshot.

Waile's ears especially were beautiful, dark rims and pink whorls. She wore a pair of gold studs. After Fiona had touched her forehead and shuffled away, Waile studied Peter's face with a grave, childlike intensity until, embarrassed, he looked down. He too had been staring. Now he looked into his lap—often he had found a way, lately, to hide his right hand from other people and himself, to allow the sleeve of his overcoat to cover it, or to twist it in the waist of his sweater, or in a blanket, as now.

But she had hold of his left hand and was squeezing and caressing it. Conscious of her green eyes on him, conscious of her smile, he studied her plump, tapered fingers and then, lying back against the bedroll, the bleached canvas ceiling of the tent.

"I've been talking about my troubles," she whispered. "But what I want to know is you. I come back over and over, younger each time, you see. Three times so far. And the tribes just get wilder and wilder, these people who live here." She laughed.

Peter had learned some of this history in dribs and drabs. The British Isles had been destroyed by an earthquake. Many had survived, had migrated into Europe and America—Peter had seen some of these Englishmen in the cave where he'd been sick. Now he wondered if he'd passed on his disease to them. A flick of a thought. Then it was gone.

"I asked the Roumanian about you," continued Waile. "But I can't understand. Like all his people he's a superstitious man."

"It's hard to understand."

Waile giggled. "So you see. It's just like me. I knew it!"

Peter didn't want to explain. He was trying to avoid thinking about Miranda, picturing Miranda, wondering where Miranda was.

But now the girl looked cross. "Tell me," she said. "It's not fair—I told you something. Now it's your turn."

At this moment she seemed artless and as innocent as her apparent age. So he found himself talking as a means of sidling away from the memory of the cave, the old English man with the white beard who quoted William Blake and poked at the bare skin of his stomach, which was just beginning to break out in hard white lumps. And Miranda with her arms around him—he told the girl how he'd been born and brought up in a different place, a modern town along the Hoosick River, a place with streets and houses and computers and electricity, where he had gone to high school, and where his father lived. But here on that stretch of the river there was not even a clearing or a break in the trees, or a rock or a stone or a brick left over from any of that.

"Where did it all go?" she asked, holding his hand.

So then Peter told her about Kevin Markasev, and how he'd come to school from the Ukraine or Romania or someplace, and how Miranda had a history book her aunt had given her, a book that summarized the history of every country in that vanished world. And how a woman named Ceausescu had sent Kevin Markasev to steal the book, destroy it, and how he'd caught up with them on Christmas Hill, and how he'd dropped the book into the fire, and when they'd woken up the town was gone, and Markasev was gone, and Miranda's friend Andromeda had turned into a dog. . . .

"Where is your friend now—Miranda Popescu? Why is that name familiar to me?"

"I don't know," said Peter miserably. "Captain Raevsky says she's in Roumania. But how can that be true? Yesterday morning is when I saw her."

The girl gave his hand a sympathetic squeeze. Now he was conscious of a smell from her, a sweet perfume that reminded him . . .

They sat companionably for some minutes before she spoke. "A world inside a book. Now the book is gone. You must not think I am laughing at you."

Peter had thought no such thing. "I know it sounds ridiculous," he admitted humbly.

Her soft small voice: "It is ridiculous. Why are you telling me these lies? After all you are a superstitious person just like the Roumanian. Dogs turn into people, like the fairy stories from central Europe. Do you want to impress me by telling me these silly things?"

She hesitated, then went on in an irritated tone. "The Roumanian told me something about this. But like you it was magic this, magic that, strange phenomena that cannot be believed. From him I expect this kind of thing. Roumania is famous for this silliness and everyone makes fun of Europeans of this type. They tell fortunes in the marketplace or work as clairvoyants in the theater. But I think there is some reason why we cannot travel to Bucharest and see things for ourselves, some danger. The restrictions are on our side—you understand? You talk in this silly way, but somewhere here there is a scientific fact, something that can be tested and studied. I know this from experience. I know what my former colleagues would say about what I've found at the bottom of my well, and how my government would ban all access even if I could find an explanation. Please tell me that you understand me!"

Still she rubbed his hand. He stared down at her fingers and made no move to pull away. And he did understand a little bit. Maybe there was another way of thinking about what happened that didn't involve werewolves and the supernatural. He was curious about that, but at the same time he was wondering why he was letting Waile touch him so easily. Then he remembered something.

When his mother had been sick, at the very end he had sat with her at the hospital. And she stank from the cancers that broke open on her skin, and she'd tried to cover them with makeup and sweet perfume, and because of the medication she had railed at him in a soft whisper, and he'd been both disgusted and brokenhearted, because he was missing her already.

Now he thought about his father working in the nursing home or sitting by himself in the house on White Oak Road. He thought about Miranda standing alone on the beach of the Black Sea, her golden bracelet around her wrist.

"But I seem to remember reading something about a bracelet," said Waile Bizunesh as if she'd read his mind. "And Popescu, Ceausescu—all these names ending with 'u.' I read about it in a magazine or else the *Cairo Mail*. You understand Roumania is closed to travel from my country. The Germans have a client government in Bucharest. Some kind of tiger. It is a ceremonial title, I believe. But a beautiful woman, so everybody says."

Peter felt his heart ascend, then climb back down. "What did you hear about it?"

The girl laughed. "I think it is five years from now. Always five years, at least on that side. A scientific constant, these little jumps in time."

Once, visiting his mother in the hospital, Peter had walked through the pediatric ward. Now he remembered a girl he'd met there who also had seemed older than she was. Suffering had made her older. She'd worn makeup, too. Because her hair was thin, Peter had been able to see the shape of her head under her curls.

Now he looked across the tent, over at the sick boy. Still he was staring back at them, though too far away to listen. "I describe it in my dissertation," said Waile Bizunesh. "But I want an explanation—is that too much to ask? That's for the real scientists, I suppose. I'm interested in what you say because I didn't think the labyrinth could stretch that far along the river—where did you say you were? But perhaps your friend discovered a new entrance to the well. Was there some kind of excavation where you stopped? Tomorrow if we live, maybe you and I could go upstream again, visit the place where your friend disappeared. And you could chase after her if you don't believe me. Maybe tonight I will be forced to show you the way if those men come again, though it is not my preferred direction, naturally! Do you know, there is no trace of me in Aegypt now. I'm an archeologist who came back after five years in America, got sick and died. It's not true—it's not true! I came back through the dig, east to west. Twice more, five years and five years. What would become of me—no, I'm joking. That would be quite an adventure, to live beyond my birth!"

"You read something in the newspaper?" interrupted Peter.

"Yes, last time I was in Heliopolis. News out of Roumania—don't look so stern! You know I trust you and I know you'll help me—isn't that odd? Another sign of childhood, and I'm not used to it. It's just a few months I've been like this."

Peter unwrapped his right hand, and with his dark, big fingers he pulled her fingers away. "What do you mean?"

"I mean I was in Aegypt four months ago. And I was in disguise, you see. Big, flopping hats, though I need not have worried. They think I'm dead, you see. Died of cancer. The problem is, why is there a child in the excavation? I have to sneak in past the guard at night. The next time I shall take Fiona as a nurse!"

Peter sat up. "And this was . . . ?"

All trace of giggling or girlishness now left her. Waile was almost sullen as she murmured, "Five years from now. Almost . . ."

What was this new bullshit? Was she laughing at him? Is this what she'd been trying to say all this time? He sat up and swung his bare feet over the side of his wooden cot.

"What's wrong, Peter?" asked the girl. "I've hurt you."

Nauseated suddenly, he crossed his arms over his cramping stomach. "I told Raevsky I would find him when I had something to eat."

"I have hurt you," she repeated as he fumbled with the new wool socks she had put out for him, the leather boots only slightly worn. "Is it what I said about Roumania? You know it is a superstitious country. I read these stories in the newspaper about the vampire there. It is just a story. But I didn't . . ."

Queasy, bowels in rebellion, Peter stumbled to the canvas door. "I've got to go to the latrine," he told her truthfully. But once outside he was unsure where to find it, though she had described the place.

Round huts flanked the tent, three on one side, four on the other. Behind, a rough scaffolding rose against the cliff face, and Peter could see there were petroglyphs carved into the rock, large winged shapes. Between the tent and the scaffolding the ground had been excavated to reveal low stone walls.

In the middle of the dig there was a circular wire fence. Peter headed toward it and unhooked the gate. There was a rough wooden ladder to the bottom of the pit, and he was halfway down before he realized this was stupid. No one would build a latrine down here in the middle of where they were working, and to get there you had to climb a ladder, nailed together and reinforced with twine. This was another part of the dig. The well was lined with beautiful blue tiles. Some were decorated with a pattern of what looked like hiero-glyphs. What was it that Waile Bizunesh had said? Altogether the well looked out of place in those woods, along that shore, as out of place as a modern bath-room with flush toilets.

He paused on the ladder about halfway down. He looked up and saw Raevsky's head silhouetted against the light. It was the middle of the afternoon.

"Get up!" he said. "Get up! Come out of that!"

"Why?"

"You do not smell garbage smell? Toilet smell? Conjuring? Pah!"

Later, after Peter had gone to squat in the woods, Raevsky showed him the defenses of the camp. On the other side of the low cliff, the rocks dropped to the water. There was a stone bridge down there. From the clifftop they could see it and the guard, a woman standing among the trees, holding one of the old man's guns.

"Is where they came across," he said.

He meant the wild men, the Englishmen. Afraid of smallpox, they'd at-tacked the camp, which they imagined was the source of the infection. "Stronger tonight," Raevsky said. "Leave to Albany is better."

They climbed down a narrow cleft in the rock, a hundred feet until they reached the riverbank. The stream was loud and narrow here. Among tall pine trees the bridge crossed into the woods on the opposite side. The stones looked old and solid, yellow sandstone, Peter guessed, and not the local granite.

"No dynamite," Raevsky said. He shrugged, spit over the bridge.

But it was probably all bullshit, Peter thought. Why would anyone attack a hospital, a bunch of women and kids?

"I told her, but . . ." The old man shrugged. "A respinge."

"Refused," Peter muttered.

"She refuse. She not leave this place."

"Why not?"

"Is her temple. Is her work. She pay much money to these people. I hear stories of a room of gold."

And a little later, grudgingly: "It is her conjure place."

They stood looking over the parapet. Over the sound of the rushing stream, Peter listened to the old man, one of his muttering monologues. And Peter substituted words he couldn't hear or couldn't understand: "Is enough, I think. One boy, sick, I put in bed. I stand here with my gun. They will not take that boy away. I am with Pieter de Graz—that's all—simple thing for an old soldier.

Bored with life, and so I say my lady I can find this girl, daughter of von Schenck the traitor. I tell them, Gulka and the others, is a simple thing and good money, though it was not so important, not with me. I am Ceausescu's man in the old days! So I tell them, Gulka and my sister's son—a little thing to find this girl. Now they swim in the dead river and that girl is gone! And I cannot go home! Not see my beauty, smell that smell. I cannot fail like that. And so one more little thing, de Graz and me—is not so much, I think. Is not so much . . . ," on and on.

Whenever he said that name, "de Graz," Peter felt a lurching in his stomach. After a few minutes he turned away, climbed the path again and Raevsky followed him. When they got up to the top, he saw a woman gesture to them from the doorway of one of the huts. Inside, a second woman tended the fire while the first opened a can of soup and put a pot on the stove.

They were in a raw wooden building about twelve feet in diameter. Waile Bizunesh came in the door as they sat at the trestle table and took off their coats.

She sat beside Peter and picked up a wooden spoon. A little girl with grown-up gestures—"I apologize," she said. "I want you to believe me. I don't want you to run away. Let me explain from the beginning," she whispered shyly. "There is a building in the desert outside Heliopolis. And there is a carved frieze along the pediment on each side of the square. Each frieze represents a line of worshipers before an altar, which is piled with animal sacrifices, and in fact there is a marble table in each corner of the building.

"Because of the inscriptions, we know that each procession represents a different historical moment. There is a coronation festival along the north façade. Opposite, a wedding ceremony. East and west, the military triumphs of Psamtik and his son Necho, pharaohs of the twenty-sixth dynasty."

Because the windows in the hut were obscured with canvas shades, light came from a carbide lantern in the middle of the table. The red-haired woman who had challenged Peter as he came into the camp had put her mask aside, revealing an unpleasant, misshapen face. Now she laid out wooden bowls and served. The soup was some kind of beef stew. It smelled good.

"But in another sense, each procession is carved precisely to resemble all the others—the clothes, the faces, the gestures, the offerings. So you see a single line of celebrants around the entire building. No, a repeating line. The illusion is that all these things occurred on the same day."

Peter was eating slowly, savoring each bite. Andromeda slumbered underneath the table. Raevsky finished two bowls of soup, and now he put down his spoon. As Peter watched, he lowered his head onto his forearms, crossed together on the surface of the table.

It was warm in the little room. Peter watched the old man settle down, watched his thin grizzled cheeks, his jaw clench and unclench. His neck was covered with red spots, an irritation or a rash. When he yawned, you could see where his teeth were missing.

"But from the inscriptions we know the sequence covers twenty years at approximately five-year intervals. There, you see? When we arrived, the building was entirely submerged in sand. There's also been some flooding long before. It wasn't until the second year that we discovered the tiled shaft, again, that led us to four chambers. Three of them were broken in—you see? Here also there are many rooms we must dig out."

Peter listened to her carefully, but he told himself he still had no idea what she was talking about. And still he found himself disgusted for reasons he didn't understand. Why should this bother him, out of all the crazy things that had happened this past week? Andromeda was a dog, for God's sake. She was sleeping underneath the table.

"My mother was in a survivor group," he said, louder than he'd intended. "Weren't you sick before?"

It was because of the girl in the cancer ward. And because of something Waile had said. She stared at him a moment. She raised her hands, displaying her pink palms. "Aren't you a clever boy?" she murmured, then smiled and clapped her hands together. "I tell you as a last resort," she said. "Why I don't want to use it."

She spoke softly, swallowing her words, so Peter had to look at her. "I told you I went back from here, west to east when I first found the way. Five years older and I almost died. I had to find my way back from the hospital, back into the dig."

This was something Peter felt he knew about. "Pancreas cancer," the girl said. "In Asmara we have a department of chronology. It is still in its beginning. I have heard a lecture on this topic—this we know. Why is it, for example, that in one country enormous changes can occur all in a moment? While in another place time is silent for a thousand years and nothing happens there. Evolutionists see big changes in morphology, then nothing more. In our own experience, one day can last a minute or a week. For young girls and old women time is not the same. That I know."

She sat beside him on her stool. She reached for his left hand and he allowed her to touch him. He could feel time begin to slow. She spoke: "Now in
this place we see woolly mammoths and sword-tooth cats, animals not seen in
Europe for millennia. West across the Henry Hudson, the map is blank. Also
east of Edo in the deserts of Japan. A bald spot in the world. People go there
and they don't come back. Large expeditions, all are lost."

"I could draw you a map," Peter murmured. He'd been to Denver. "We
drove along 1-70," he said. His father had taken him camping in Black
Canyon. Where was his father now?

The girl ignored him. "So there are a lot of theories. None of them make
sense. Maybe there are currents of time that shift over the world. Last night we
saw the northern lights. Did you see them?"

This question irritated Peter, and he moved his hand away from her. "It's
not the same thing. Time is something you can measure."

The girl shrugged. "Maybe there are different kinds of time," she whispered. "Clocks are one." Her brown hand was near his hand on the surface of
the table. He was keeping his other one, de Graz's hand, rolled into the belly of
his flannel shirt.

"Or you can think of it like an archeological dig," she said. "You have your
own system of tunnels. Then you break through into another system from the
past. It was like that when they excavated the Knossos maze."

Raevsky snored with his cheek on the coarse, raw wood. It was a soft, liquid sound. His mouth was open, his lips pushed out of shape. "West to east
when I went through," said Waile, "that first time I could feel my sickness
grow. East to west it left me. But I'm afraid if I stay here it will catch up. It will
chase me back. So when I think I feel it, then I take the boat to Alexandria.
And I come through again—it is five years each time. I measure—sometimes
less, sometimes more. It is a pattern. So last time I read in a magazine about this
name, Miranda Popescu. She had shot a man in Braila, I think. Along the
Danube river. And she was hiding from the police. That's where she is, I
think."

"It can't be the same."

"A policeman, yes."

"It can't be the same," said Peter. But now he knew what the girl was talking about: the shaft in the middle of the dig. "Why are you telling me?" he
asked.

She clapped her hands again, a small soft noise. "I want to know about the book that burned up in the fire! I want to know about your silly story!"

Then in a moment her voice had changed, and she was serious and grave. "And I want you to know our option to go back. To retreat, you call it—the captain will not listen. He makes the sign of the evil eye. So I'll tell you. A final resort, you understand. If you come back here, I will have gone. The cancer, I will have to risk it."

She put her fingers down. Beside his splayed left hand, they moved. They caressed the table's surface. Peter watched them from the corner of his eye. "We have six patients here with that young boy. All resting. And they will survive the smallpox. So you see it is important."

Peter felt a bead of sweat run down his ribs under his shirt. "Why me?"

The girl smiled. But in her face there was some hint of embarrassment or sadness—"Last night three men crossed the bridge with torches. They are frightened of this place, so Anna and Fiona scared them off. But I have never fired a gun. I have no training. Anna says more will come tonight."

"Why me?" Peter repeated, but he knew why. His stomach, which had been quiet, now felt sour again.

Waile's hand moved near his own. "The captain says you are a famous soldier in your country. So young! But I also am young for my accomplishments—perhaps we are the same! This is not your fight, I know."

But it was. These wild men had been with Peter in the cave. He'd been crazy with fever. But he remembered them pulling up his shirt, poking at the hard bumps along his stomach, which had cleared up the next day.

Now Peter clenched his left hand into a fist. "I see you are injured," the girl said, nodding at his right hand, twisted in his sweater, invisible in his lap.

"No."

She smiled. How many times had she gone through the tunnel from the Egyptian side to here? Three times, had she said? Crawling back in time away from her disease . . .

The air was hot and pungent in the hut. He couldn't wait to get outside. He shook Raevsky's shoulder, kicked at Andromeda and listened to her growl. But they followed him out.

In the late afternoon the weather had turned cold again. There was a crust on the surface of the shallow snow. They climbed down through the rocks to the bridge, where Fiona was standing guard.

Rested from his nap, Raevsky was in a good mood. "Is like old time! Old time in Nova Zagora when we fight the Jews. I am with Baron Ceausescu and Ninth Hussars. You and Prince Frederick in middle. Dead river—fight with dead. No one can touch."

"I don't remember," Peter said. It was the truth. But all day his body had felt strange to him. Faint with hunger, carrying the boat, maybe he hadn't noticed. But now he watched his feet punch through the snow. His walk, his gait seemed unfamiliar, splay-footed, swaggering. He let his arms swing at his sides.

Raevsky had one of the long guns. They crossed the bridge and poked around on the other side. Andromeda ran off into the woods over there among the outcroppings of rocks.

You didn't have to be a soldier, Peter thought, to see it was an easy place to defend. The bridge was narrow. It came down to a flat place among the pine trees and dead golden stubble, an open space below the cliff where once there'd been a house. Peter could see old foundations poking through the snow.

And was it true, he thought, that time sometimes grows quickly as a tumor? Pancreatic cancer was one of the fast ones. His mother had been sick for over a year.

Maybe that's what happened when the book was destroyed—they'd come unstuck in time. And if he could just catch up, maybe there was still a place where his mother was alive—lung cancer, hers had been. When she was sick he'd read to her, trying to repay in one year all the nights he'd lain in bed with her beside him and the soft buzz of the TV downstairs. In those days she'd paid him a dollar for every page of poetry he'd memorized, regardless of quality: *The Congo, Ulysses, Horatius at the Bridge.* He had been drawn to long war epics. " 'Lars Porsena of Clusium,' " he quoted now, eyes wet, " 'By the nine gods he swore, that the great house of Tarquin would suffer wrong no more.' " Raevsky gave him a blank look.

The bridge ran straight across to the rocks on the other side. About fifty feet long, it was supported in the middle by an immense stone pillar that rose out of the stream. What was its purpose, a footbridge from nowhere to nowhere in the middle of the wilderness? What had Raevsky said about dynamite?

" 'In yon straight path a thousand may well be stopped by three,' " Peter quoted, eyes wet, tongue lumpy. " 'Now who will stand on either hand and keep the bridge with me?' "

Again the captain shook his head. They were standing on the south shore below the cliff. Above them the rock trail led to the camp. But there was another more roundabout way beside the river, through the pine trees and then up.

So Waile Bizunesh had discovered a kind of time machine, Peter guessed. She'd gone back and back. And the last time she'd been in her own country, she'd read about the white tyger. And a woman named Miranda, who had murdered a policeman—well, it was interesting. Hard to imagine, but interesting. A last resort—no one would try to cross the bridge tonight. And tomorrow they'd go on to Albany. They would look for Ion Dreyfoos in the fish market, as Blind Rodica had explained when they had first come to this country. And he would make them passports and bring them to Roumania over the ocean. That was the plan Blind Rodica had made on the first day and evening before she died. It seemed like months ago.

As darkness fell, they sent Fiona back with the others. They had brought supplies—cheese and sausage, canteens of water, and the long guns. There was a natural bastion at the bottom of the cliff where they could crouch behind the rocks and aim down on the bridge.

"Aunus from green Tifernum, lord of the hill of vines, and Seius, whose eight hundred slaves sicken in Ilva's mines," thought Peter. Names to conjure with. In several trips they had piled up blankets and bearskins, which they laid upon the rocks. In the last light Captain Raevsky showed him how to load the guns—the black powder cartridge, the lead bullet in its paper wad. They had five guns, and they set the copper priming caps and laid them out.

"No one will come," Peter said. "If we light a fire, they'll see the bridge cannot be crossed." So they pulled down some dead pine boughs, which soon crackled up. It was a small fire just to show there was a guard. If a fight came, they'd put it out.

Peter sat with his back against the rock, looking up at the cliff's head with the bridge behind him. Shadows jumped and postured on the rocks. Raevsky was smoking a cigar. It had Egyptian hieroglyphics on the band. He had gotten it from the girl up above.

Andromeda was across the bridge. She jumped onto the parapet and ran back and forth. The roar of the water had become familiar, and Peter scarcely heard it anymore.

"What if they come from the other side?" he asked.

"Girl shoot. We hear." He pointed with his chin. "This side, Lieutenant Prochenko warns us. Bark."

He gave a grumbling sort of guffaw, and Peter wondered if he'd ever heard him laugh before. And of course it was a little ridiculous, when you could relax and think about it. Peter smelled the tobacco smoke, the hot pine pitch. He took his hands from his gloves and held them to the fire. "What was he like, Sasha Prochenko?" he asked, and then listened as the handsome young guardsman took shape out of Raevsky's words.

"Not so tall, but thin," murmured the captain. "Small bones. Yellow hair. No beard. Cold eyes—blue. Rich clothes also—what you say? Expensive. Very sure. Women love, but no man trust. What you say—charming, fascinant? Some days, then you will see."

"What do you mean?"

"Is conjure only for a little while. Heart of a man, it grows inside. Like a carcinom. Then he come back in the night time, you will see. Cry at moon in a man's voice. Dog shape sometime and then man."

Something to look forward to. "When I knew him he was a girl," muttered Peter.

"Girl also grow inside. Cold eyes, maybe her, too. You will see."

But Peter didn't want to see. Gray eyes flecked with blue, he thought, as he remembered the girl he'd known. "What did you say about Transylvania? Before, I mean. Something about the Carpathian Mountains. Wasn't that where Dracula was from?" Vampires—that's what Peter knew about Roumania. That was the only thing, except for one stupid poem.

"I do not know this Dracula."

In his mind Peter saw a young man with the girl's face he remembered— not that Andromeda had ever been his friend. Not that she'd ever been nice to him, exactly. She'd been too proud and too stuck up. But in a moment he decided he'd be happy to see her, happy to see anybody who knew about the life he'd left behind. She'd be someone to talk to about home, about Miranda.

"I do not know this name," Raevsky murmured. Then he smiled. Peter saw the gap in his back teeth.

"Howling at the moon," Peter said, and he smiled, too. Sasha Prochenko, if it came to that—he and Sasha Prochenko would have things to talk about. Prochenko would have stories about Miranda, not the same Miranda but a different one, someone who had spent her childhood in Roumania and now returned to it. Someone different and new who had shot a policeman maybe, or might shoot one in five years—what bullshit that was! Waile Bizunesh had clearly lost her mind, alone here in this forest. Or she was just a little girl making up stories. . . .

But maybe as a last resort he would climb down into her tunnel or whatever it was. Sitting back against the rocks, Peter found it easy to imagine, even fun. The wild men wouldn't come, he told himself. He would sit here by Raevsky with his hands out to the fire, and feel the food in his stomach. In a few hours they would go to bed. In the meantime it was pleasant here. And yes, there was something about this moment that seemed familiar, this kind of waiting. And yes, he'd liked the feel of the long guns, the smooth rubbed stocks with just a little old carving, the smell of powder and oiled steel. Raevsky had slipped them from their leather bags. Peter had asked him how to handle them. But he knew it all already, the taste of the cartridge in his teeth, the crunch of the rod inside the barrel, the satisfying weight, and not just because his Tennessee cousins had once taken him shooting for tin cans, to see if he could do anything with just the one hand.

Behind the cliff there was a section of orange sky, streaked with colors of the sunset. Peter found himself listening to Raevsky, who was cutting sausage into coins with his clasp knife. The old man was talking to himself, but in English so Peter could understand. In his sibilant, chaotic way he was telling stories of past wars, like someone in a restaurant remembering old meals—a habit of Peter's father during car trips, and his mother had often laughed at him.

Raevsky rubbed his cracked lips. He was muttering names of places, Nova Zagora, Havsa, Adrianople, etc. What had happened in those places? Blood and more blood, yet here Peter was, munching sausage by the fire as the shadows played over the rocks.

As the captain talked, Peter found himself thinking one more time about the tunnel to the future. "A little older," he murmured, part of a longer phrase that was itself part of a godless prayer he'd used to say in front of the mirror back in Williamstown. "I would like to be a little older," he murmured now, something he'd always felt in school, where gym class had been a nightmare, and every day was full of urgent things he couldn't do. In the adult world, he'd imagined, hoped, his disability would disable him less.

Now, with two uneven hands, he grasped at some of the same hopes. Miranda had left him behind. In high school she'd been a couple of years younger, which had felt good to him. But as soon as they'd arrived here he had seen the change in her. Now he wanted to catch up.

But it was all bullshit, naturally. In the morning, he and Raevsky would continue on to Albany, where they would find Ion Dreyfoos. . . .

Raevsky was talking about someplace in Bulgaria where he'd fought the Turks. Peter wasn't listening. Among the sheltering rocks he turned and looked out toward the bridge. He'd heard something, a shout, a whistling bark. And in the last light he could see Andromeda on the parapet, standing on three legs.

There was a light. There was another. Raevsky got up to stand beside him, and together they watched the torches through the trees. Men gathered on the opposite riverbank. Now Peter listened to another sound, a low and muffled drumbeat that seemed to come out of the crest of rocks above the torches.

"Is law not buy guns in Albany," said Captain Raevsky. "Not for English. Still . . . arrows will have." He threw his cigar into the fire.

There was a clump of torches at the far end of the bridge, where there were big steps and heavy stonework. Andromeda was gone. Raevsky picked up one of the long guns. "Shoot into the trees," Peter said. "Above their heads."

All the time the sun was setting, he'd been surprised by his own calmness. For minutes at a time he'd given no thought to the wild men. He knew that they'd been scared away the night before. Now here they were again, and he felt a sudden pressure in his bowels, though he had once more used the latrine before they'd climbed down from the camp. But even that wasn't a sign of fear. Or if it was, then he was afraid of something inside himself, some greasy, knotted feeling that he couldn't control.

The drum seemed to affect it. He felt a shudder in his stomach and then lower down. "Shoot into the trees," he said again, his voice strange to him. Surely if the men heard gunshots, they would run. Last night a woman had chased them away.

From where they stood they had an unobstructed view of the near half of the bridge, which reached the shore below them about a hundred feet away. You couldn't get a clear shot at the far end, though, because of the trees. The sound of the gun, the bullet rattling in the dry limbs would be enough, Peter thought.

Raevsky shrugged. He raised the gun and fired without aiming, the stock braced against his thigh.

Now the light was almost gone. But the sky retained a pearly luminescence, reflected in the hard crust of snow. Peter could see the horizontal line of the bridge, the perpendicular dead pines by the water's edge. He could see the torchlight on the stream. Behind him, Raevsky was scattering the fire, which made the bridge easier to see. They wouldn't need torchlight to pick the men off as they crossed.

But the lights hadn't moved. The men were clustered at the far end of the bridge. Where was Andromeda? With the gunshot the drum stopped, and in the silence after the loud noise, Peter heard the running of the stream.

He stood up among the rocks, cupped his hands around his lips. "Hey!" he shouted. Raevsky was reloading. The best plan was to stay hidden, to pick the men off when they ventured past the midpoint of the bridge.

But Peter couldn't tolerate the thought of that. The greasy knotted feeling was inside of him. He couldn't stay still; he jumped down out of the rocks, then slid in a shower of pebbles to the flat clear snow between the cliff face and the bridge.

He heard Raevsky curse behind him, and felt a sudden urge to defecate. His feet punched through the snow. He felt a grinding, dirty engine in his body that could not be stopped, as if a car slipped into gear and lurched downhill. With part of his mind he thought maybe he could talk to the wild men, explain things. But at the same time he understood how he must look, running like a madman across the snow, clambering up the stone steps of the bridge, then running down the narrow way, his hands above his head, and he could hear his voice crying out. Most likely they would shoot him down.

But as he reached the middle of the bridge, he could see the faces of the men under the torches. There were some he recognized, the big man dressed in skins, a quartz-headed club in his hand, the light glinting on his yellow hair. Peter had seen him in the cave when he was sick. Andromeda was beside him now, the stone footbridge scarcely wide enough for them to run together. The parapets rose to his waist on either side. Peter was shouting at them, and maybe they thought he was still sick, but obviously they recognized him. They pulled back from the stone pillars and then scattered down the steps, down into the woods below the rocks.

"Was none who would be foremost to lead such dire attack," Peter thought. "But those behind cried 'Forward!' And those before cried 'Back!'"

Now he understood what he was doing. And it filled him with sick fear to realize how little his body was under his control. Here he was, Horatius at the bridge, inspired by stupid poems about people who'd never existed in this world or any world. Maybe that would not have been enough to make him budge out of the rocks where he'd been safe, except for this grim, erratic force that he could feel in his belly and his guts, and that had led him out into the open here between the stone balustrades. The force had a name, a Roumanian name that was like his. Pieter de Graz. He stood with his left hand splayed on one capstone, his big right hand clenched into a fist, and he had to admit it felt good to see the English savages break and run and stagger back, regroup under the rocks.

He counted over a dozen. None of them had bows. The light shone on their fierce, dirty faces, their long hair tied with feathers or bits of shell. "Stay away!" Peter shouted, and then, idiotically, "It's all right. We're fine."

He meant they shouldn't worry about the smallpox. But now he imagined how he must appear to them, the feverish embodiment of the disease. Three men came forward armed with stone-headed clubs. One climbed up the steps onto the bridge, a red-haired brute with white stripes painted on his forehead and his cheeks. Peter saw the whites of his eyes, the firelight flashing on his teeth, and took a step backward. Andromeda was behind him. She hadn't gone past the middle of the bridge.

"Guts fer garters," sneered the man, his accent wild and uncouth. Above him the drum had started to thud again. To its rhythm, the men took up a ragged tune. The words were mangled and mispronounced, but Peter knew the proper ones:

And did those feet in ancient time
Walk upon England's mountains green?
And was the holy lamb of God
In England's pleasant pastures seen?

He fell back step by step. Posturing and feinting, the red-haired man came forward. He had a wolf skin over his shoulders, and his chest was bare. He whirled his club above his head and then came on. But at the middle of the bridge, where Andromeda stayed, Peter heard a boom from behind him and the man fell. Peter didn't know where he was hit, but the man groaned and cried out, his body wedged into the narrow way. Then snarling and with teeth bared, Andromeda flung herself over his head and leaped upon the man who was next in line, a black-haired man in a knitted cap, who dropped his torch and fell screaming. The dog was at his face, biting at his nose and lips. Two more shots passed overhead.

"At Pictus brave Horatius darted one fiery thrust," Peter thought. "And the proud Umbrian's gilded arms . . ." Goaded by the poem, Peter knelt to tug the club away from the red-haired man. So close, he could see the wound now and smell it. The man was shot in the body above the groin, and Peter smelled the stink of his ruptured intestines. Blood came from his mouth.

But he wasn't dead, and he grabbed hold of Peter's ear. He wouldn't let go of the club. Peter took the shaft in his left hand, but now he put his right hand under the man's chin, his dark right hand that never failed in its strength. Both of them were muttering and shouting, but the red-haired man subsided and let go. His club came free.

Andromeda held the other men at bay. In that tight space there was no room for more than one to face her. Peter had never seen her like this, slavering and furious. One man brought his torch down to burn her. But she darted underneath the fire and ripped into his crotch.

Peter went to help her. The man in the wool cap was screaming with his face in his hands. But the red-haired man grabbed hold of Peter's foot as he stepped over him. Peter turned to batter him with the club, and as he did he saw some other men behind him at Raevsky's end of the bridge. He hadn't heard any more gunshots.

And there were torches in the trees. Under the pearly sky, Peter could see Raevsky's pirogue, which they'd abandoned upstream where they'd found the sick boy. It was drawn up among the pine trees. The wild men were on both sides of the river now. Maybe they were even at the camp.

Shouting for Andromeda, Peter shifted the club to his right hand. He let his right hand lead him back. Now there was nothing in his mind that was separate from the hand, the big hairy forearm that led him back along the bridge. And while the red-haired man had given him such trouble, these others gave way quickly. He wasn't even aware of their faces as he pounded them with his club. One dropped his torch into the water. The other threw his crossbow down and ran. The dog was at his heels.

Still his right hand led him, the club upraised. Looking back, he could see men clustered at the middle of the bridge. He could see others in the trees beside the boat on the near shore. But there were none on the rocky cliff. At its base he found Raevsky.

Two guns were with him, flung down in the snow. The old man lay on his back. The ends of two short, heavy arrows protruded from his chest.

There was froth on his lips, which Peter wiped away. Then with a strong hand and a weak one, he took Raevsky up into the cradle of his arms. The old man seemed little, light.

Peter scrambled up the slope. In the rock niche he laid Raevsky down to change his grip. Three loaded guns were there, and he stopped to shoot them one by one into the knot of men below him at the bottom of the cliff.

They would have been safe here, Peter thought. The wild men would have given up and slunk away. Raevsky must have come down from his perch when he saw the men at both sides of the bridge. Now he lay among the rocks, and he said a few words in broken English. Then he continued in Roumanian: "The river of my death—I knew it! Now I join the others. But I saved one little boy, who would have died. And tonight I fought with the famous Chevalier de Graz!"

Peter shook his head. Below, the men started to climb the slope, while some with torches moved along the stream. Andromeda had already scampered up the trail, and now Peter followed her. He had the old man in his arms, and he was pulling him up, the left hand clutching and failing. Out of breath, he staggered up, his right hand under Raevsky's shoulder, and sometimes he dragged the old man through the pebbly chute. The whole way he recited to himself, over and over:

Then out spake brave Horatius, the Captain of the Gate:
"To every man upon this earth death cometh soon or late;
And how can man die better than facing fearful odds. . . ."

There was no comfort in the words. But the rhythm was something to fill his mind as he dragged the old man over the stones. Then he was at the top, and from the clifftop he could see the camp was dark. There was no light in any of the windows of the huts. The tent was black. Only a single carbide lantern shone. It was in the middle of the dig beyond the scaffolding, at the lip of the tiled well. As he watched, Andromeda ran into the circle of the light.

"But when you see Nicola Ceausescu," murmured the old man, "you'll tell her what I tried to do?"

"I'll tell her."

"Oh, you are a lucky man! The house is in Saltpetre Street. You will tell her how I spoke of her?"

"I'll tell her."

The way down was easier, and Peter could support him. With his arm underneath Raevsky's arm, he led him down the trail. The ladder would be the trick, though, and so it proved. But Andromeda had managed it. When Peter staggered with his burden through the circle of wire, he found the place dark. Andromeda had knocked over the lantern and then pissed on it, though it still flickered.

Hadn't he done this before? He remembered the snowstorm, and Miranda, and carrying Gregor Splaa through the snow. The man had died and then they'd left the body. That night he'd gotten sick.

Now, at the top of the well, still horrified by the violence of the last hour, he let the captain down onto the snow. He couldn't let him die, not now. He shouted out for help but no one answered. Where were they all? He thought he knew.

He saw lights through the trees and on the clifftop. He climbed partway down the ladder, then tried to pull Raevsky into his arms. Step by step he let him down. He must not leave him as he'd left Gregor Splaa. Peter would drag him thought the hole in the world, and he would find Miranda, and everything would be all right.

The ladder groaned and shifted along the top of the well. Peter climbed into the quiet dark. Murmuring, Raevsky slid down the ladder after him. Another carbide lantern, similarly upset, lay beyond an inner threshold at the bottom of the well. And the dog hadn't been able to squeeze out any more piss. The light guttered and flared along the rich blue tile.

He was at the bottom now. Reaching down with his right hand, he pulled Raevsky to his feet. He tried to get him to stand up, but he wouldn't, and so Peter had to carry him. Four passageways converged, but he stumbled over the threshold, following the light. Inside a square chamber painted with hieroglyphs and animals, he saw the body of one of the English women, Fiona or the other one, workers in the dig. She lay on her side, curled up, mask in place. Her gun was gone.

When would this stop? Were there wild men in the dig? As if to answer his question, Peter heard some shouting up ahead. The chamber he was in, again, had doors on all four sides. He stood in the middle, Raevsky in his arms, the old man's face near his own. His head lolled back. His eyes were closed.

Peter shuffled in a circle, peering into each of the dark doors. Shouting came from one, though it was muffled, far away—he couldn't understand the words. Maybe the wild men had torches there, out of sight around the turning of the labyrinth. Closer to hand, on the other side came Andromeda's soft bark, and as he peered through that doorway, he thought he detected some small light, a small blue glow. So he shuffled through that door, the old man clasped in the circle of his arms. His left hand was numb and tired, but his right hand grasped his wrist and would never let go. He could depend on that. And anyway it seemed as if the burden in his arms grew less and smaller. In the blackness of the farther room he paused, waiting for the soft, snuffling bark that would be his thread of light, and at the same time he felt the old man stir in his arms, and with a surge of hope he heard his whispering voice. "You will tell my lady how I saved that boy on the dead river when I set my boat downstream. He would have died there in the snow. . . ." Then on and on in a language that was not English or Roumanian, and that grew harsher and stranger with every word, while at the same time Raevsky lurched and twisted in his arms, a chattering, furry creature that dug its nails through Peter's sweater and hoisted itself onto his shoulder while Peter grasped it. He had the quick impression of a tail, and a fierce head beside his jaw, before the animal left him, leaped away. Peter clutched at it but it was gone, and he could hear its nails on the smooth tile—he knew what was happening. Raevsky had saved the little boy. But Peter had not managed to save Raevsky, who had come down from his safe place in the rocks to fight. Now he was dead, his spirit animal scurrying away into the utter darkness.

Or not so utter when he heard Andromeda's small bark. In that direction, beyond that doorway there was something, some tiny intermittent gleam. A beacon like a firefly or else the glowing end of a stick, drawn quickly against the surface of the dark. Numb and disappointed, Peter turned that way. How could he have failed, how could he have let the old man drop? All the time he had been carrying him, he had imagined walking through these rooms until he found the doorway that would let him out into the dazzling light of Egypt. Maybe they could take a taxi to the hospital. Raevsky's wounds, he told himself, were not life-threatening. His quilted coat had protected him.

A soft, snuffling sound, and then a yelp. A sound of nails scratching at the tile. Raevsky wasn't dead, Peter was sure of it. He was a tough old bird, or tough old monkey, or whatever he was—Peter could see some movement up ahead, through the doors where it wasn't so dark. And if he could chase the animal through the tunnel, then he would chase him out the other side, and chase him over the ocean out of this terrible version of America, away from the shores of the dead river. He would chase him back to Europe, and Roumania, and Saltpetre Street, and the woman Ceausescu would take care of him and heal him—just a touch from her was all he needed. And Peter would be older, and he would find Miranda on the Black Sea coast—he staggered through the doors and found a place where he could see a little better. He was in a different section of the dig, and the tile had given way to stone, and the air wasn't as cold, and he could smell bats and smoke and garbage up ahead. Then he saw the entrance to the old part of the dig, a long narrow passage of stone blocks, and the door in the middle, its posts and lintel carved with figures from Egyptian mythology. Men and women with the heads of animals, but Peter did not pause to admire them or reflect. Because in the half-light he had seen the creature scurrying up the steps, and it didn't look like a monkey anymore. It was longer, heavier, he thought, although he'd just caught a glimpse of it out of the corner of his eye as it disappeared into the blackness. The next room was black again, black and without light.

He stood in the doorway and peered into the dark. Then he heard movement again, the scratching of the creature's claws. And even though he felt weak now, and sick and discouraged, still he had enough strength to stumble forward toward the sound of that scratching, and stumble against the animal in the dark. He grabbed its tail, seized it by the base of its tail, and though it turned and growled and tried to bite him, still he was able to keep hold, even when it twisted to scratch him. But he had Raevsky now, and he wouldn't let go, and even though he felt nauseated and weak, he could feel the creature was weaker and slower also. He dug his hands into its fur, then changed his grip until he could embrace it around the ribs and crush it down into the stones; he twisted it with his whole weight and wrestled it to the ground. How could he have been mistaken about its size? It was bigger than he had thought—no, it was growing under his hands, under his body, changing its shape again, and he had won. He had wrestled the old man back from the brink of death, and with his strong right hand he had him pinned, and he could feel the human shape turn under him. He could feel the joint of the old man's shoulder, smooth and hot and naked under his hands, and feel the soft hair of his head, and the long smooth muscles of his back.

Raevsky had stopped moving, stopped resisting. But he was alive; Peter knew he was alive. Peter could feel the slow pulse of air through the old man's chest. Oh, but he felt sick, sick and weak! And there was no light anywhere, and no noise but a roaring sound like water. And his joints ached, and his right hand, and his knees and face. If it had not been for the smooth body under him, he would have thought he had lost consciousness in the dark. He put his cheek against Raevsky's burning flank, and then maybe he did sleep awhile.

When he awoke, the darkness was a little less. He lay on his back, and

Raevsky had escaped him, and the walls were painted with a frieze of figures. Men and women carried offerings to an altar. This was where the archeologists had broken through.

There was a hole in the stonework, and light broke in from the other side. Peter sat up and looked around at the relief carving, the painted stones. Because he was hot, he took his coat and sweater off. Then he crawled forward on his hands and knees, and he could smell the dust and oil and the warm air. He wedged himself into the hole in the stone wall, following the naked footprints in the dust. Naked footprints had led him from where he'd struggled with Raevsky. He had to get away, had to continue on, and so he dragged himself through. And on the other side the lines of painted people were identical, and the chamber was identical except for the sunlight that cut through the door in the opposite wall. And except for the woman on the floor, the naked woman who lay on her back and then turned toward him as he crawled in, making no effort to hide her nakedness beyond pulling up one long, slender leg. Sunlight from the door slashed across her face and her short blond hair. The light was full of dust motes.

"Andromeda?" he asked. Almost he didn't recognize her, although she'd scarcely changed out of the girl he'd known at school—years before, it suddenly seemed. Embarrassed now, he glanced away. But in a moment he looked back, fascinated (or so he told himself) by how she'd aged: a woman, he supposed. Five years. Was this what getting older meant, this sudden vertigo, this aching in his head?

Again he turned away. Andromeda's pale, flecked eyes were open, and her voice was full of disdain as she murmured, "What are you looking at?"

11

The Salt Throne

8 Prisoners in Ratisbon

BEFORE MIDNIGHT NICOLA CEAUSESCU walked alone though the streets of Bucharest in the Floreasca district. It would be hours before she heard what had happened at Prince Frederick's castle, and whether the Popescu girl was in her hands. Already she was sick of waiting. Already she had thought of a way to avenge herself upon the German ambassador, to punish him and his country for the humiliation she had suffered in her own house, in her own mind. Because the range of her official duties was so small, she was able to find time for passionate intrigue.

In the evenings, especially when Luckacz was gone from town, she often walked alone among the streets, visiting the clubs and public houses, impregnable in her disguise. Like Haroun al-Rashid, the Jewish caliph in the slums of Baghdad, sometimes she walked all night.

This evening past eight o'clock she had returned from visiting a private house in the Strada Spatarul. It was where she kept Kevin Markasev in luxury he didn't deserve—toward eleven she left the palace again. Without escort she slipped from one of the service entrances. From her mother she had learned a spell to draw attention, another spell to make men look away.

On nights like these she would go over in her mind the melodies and lyrics of the opera she was inventing, the story of her life set to music: how she'd been born in poverty with nothing but her talent and her beauty and ambition to sustain her. How she'd come to Bucharest and made her way onto the stage. How she'd married the Baron Ceausescu, who'd died and left her with a son and a roomful of debts. How the Elector of Ratisbon had stolen the boy away. And because the music in her mind was leading her now into a new, dark, poisonous, E-flat minor motif of revenge, as she paced the streets she brooded on the treachery of the potato eaters who still kept her son a prisoner in Germany.

On the stairway of a small hotel in Floreasca she removed her hat. The door was ajar on the third landing, and she knocked. She was shown into the sitting room of an expensive suite—a pink-and-gold affair with delicate French furniture. The lamp was turned down low on a low table, so it was hard for her to make a clear impression of her hosts, two sepulchral, dark men in business suits. They were Abyssinian arms dealers, known to her as Colonel Ouibika and Colonel Memlis.

Their country did not allow the export of advanced technology to Europe. Unofficially, much could be done. The Baroness Ceausescu had had a correspondence with these gentlemen. Now finally she had wanted to meet them and see their faces. She had confidence in her ability to read men's characters. In this room, though, she was thwarted by the uncertain light.

Negotiations had been handled by her steward, Jean-Baptiste, who was to have brought the final documents. If the colonels were surprised to see her in his place, if they even recognized her, they gave no sign. "Please, would you like some tea?" one of them—Memlis? Ouibika?—said in French. He gestured to the table, where there were three tall steaming glasses and a bowl of coarse brown lumps.

"No, thank you. I am here just for the moment. Arrangements will be made with the Central Bank. I wanted to know that I could trust you. When may I expect to hear?"

The two men looked at each other. The baroness could see their teeth. "Your office will be notified. Shipment will come by rail through Constantinople, as was agreed."

"Yes, of course."

Then she couldn't stop herself. "It is a great sum of money to expend on what is after all a natural metallic ore. I want your personal assurance it will be effective, as you represented to my steward."

"The cost of extraction is very high," said one of the dark men. "The element exists in a ratio of one part per three million. And the pitchblende must be imported from a laboratory in the Congo. You have asked for very large amounts for your experiments."

"And it is . . . dangerous," the baroness continued breathlessly. "Poisonous . . ."

"We will pack it in lead canisters. We will send a technician to instruct you. We believe you will be satisfied."

She was not satisfied. Still she had to justify herself. "You must think this is a strange sort of weapon for a woman like me. This is a political matter—you understand it is not possible to allow these people to bully us. These republics, these democracies—maybe one day such a thing is possible in Roumania. But until then we will not allow it. Who is next—Spain, Russia? The armies are already at the border. You must be concerned! And is it wrong to use these tactics against people so heartless, they are willing to keep a mother from her son? No doubt they find it useful to keep him locked up in prison to insure my good behavior!"

If the colonels understood what she was talking about, they gave no sign. In fact she scarcely knew herself—these men could not be expected to imagine the torments of her only child. Always in her calculations, the white tyger combined personal and public motives. Several times a week, working in her laboratory, she tried to penetrate the fog of darkness over Ratisbon. Of course she feared the worst.

BUT THERE WERE LIMITS TO her imagination, limits to her power, and she could not see how at that moment in a big, stucco house in a park above the town, a middle-aged woman and a teenaged boy were sitting together in a compartment without windows. The woman was Clara Schenck von Schenck, née Brancoveanu, and the boy was Nicola Ceausescu's only child.

Beautiful in her youth, Princess Clara looked brittle now after so many years under artificial lights. Her skin was shiny and she bruised easily. Her once clear features had softened and grown indistinct, as if the bones beneath them had grown weaker, or as if after all this time she was no longer her original self, but rather an unskillful imitation.

The boy, by contrast, had been raised indoors and he was used to it. Slender and rosy, he had his mother's purple eyes. Now he was laughing as he remembered some witticism from a book he had been reading two days before. They sat together at the breakfast table. Though elsewhere in central Europe it was late at night, in that room it was not yet noon. The single timepiece in the apartment, a double-keyed, ormolu clock above the fireplace, ran slightly fast. Though the boy wound it every third day, still its defect had not been corrected.

The woman and the boy had not the opportunity to notice without access to the world. Their host, too, had not disabused them. On the table lay the remains of toast and coffee, delivered by dumbwaiter when they'd rung the bell.

"Mother," cried the boy. He called all women "mother" and all men "father," a childhood trait that now had lasted into adolescence. "Let me tell you a secret. I dreamed last night I was swimming underwater. I could breathe perfectly well, and I swam over a reef where there were hundreds of little fish."

He took a sip of cold coffee. This was a game they played in the mornings. He would confide his dreams. And she with mock-seriousness would pick up the book that lay under the lamp, as she did now: *Madame Desostro's Guide to Slumber.* She put on her reading glasses, searched the index, and announced, "What good luck. To dream of swimming underwater means that we are going on a trip! Tell me, have you ever been to the seashore? My husband used to have a place in Dobruja on the beach. Near Constanta—I would love to see it again."

Both of them, the boy and the graying widow, shared a sense of enthusiasm at these moments, in which there was something artificial. In the same way, the lamplight on the tablecloth could only imitate the sun.

Before the boy had come to Ratisbon, the princess had lived in a different apartment with a window overlooking the town. She had received guests. She had taken newspapers and magazines. But several years before, her host had moved her to this suite of rooms and introduced her to her new companion, who was to take the place of any outside stimulus. There was a bedroom for each of them, a music room, a parlor, a drawing room, a library, all furnished with luxury and taste.

But there were no windows, and the only door fit cunningly into the wall so that it disappeared when closed. Fresh air came through a system of iron grates set into the floor. Food and supplies were delivered by the dumbwaiter. All the princess would have to say, in the middle of what she thought was the afternoon, was, "Oh, I should like some trout tonight. And perhaps a bottle of Orvieto. And perhaps some drawing paper and a tube of cadmium." In a few hours the bell would ring.

From this they knew that they were under observation. Sometimes when they were talking nonsense they would speak quite loudly in order to be overheard. At other times they forgot entirely and lived as kings or gods, only having to express their wants to have them met, within a certain range. Over the years Princess Clara had stopped thinking about her captor as a human being, imagining instead a soulless, overseeing presence. Otherwise she would have died of shame every time she undressed to take a bath or go to bed.

SHE NEEDN'T HAVE WORRIED. Only in the parlor, cunningly hidden in the pattern of the wallpaper, was there a pair of small holes. That night or morning, as Miranda was pulling herself up into the saddle of her horse, a man stepped away from the holes that oversaw the room. Or rather not a man but an automaton, one of the mental projections that the master of the house could make as real as flesh. And this one Miranda would have recognized, a handsome blond man with a small moustache.

Dr. Theodore climbed down a stepladder, for the spy-hole to the parlor was set far up on the wall. He found himself in the narrow corridor that described the perimeter of the entire suite of rooms and kept it separate from the rest of the house. It was a dusty, moldy place with uncovered lath on both sides. It was unlit, but Dr. Theodore needed no illumination. Following an internal summons, he turned the corner and the next, and then opened the hidden door that led him into an anonymous reception hall.

He strode across the polished floor, then out into the gallery. At one end was the small staircase that led to the elector's apartment. Without breath he climbed until he reached the upper landing, then knocked inside the open door.

In its spareness and simplicity, the room at the top of the house contrasted with most other sections of the building, but especially with the ornate and overstuffed abundance of Princess Clara's parlor. Sometimes as Dr. Theodore mounted the last steps, he contemplated briefly the nesting circles of contradiction that made up this last place of refuge. At first glance the room seemed as plain as a peasant's cottage. The furniture was unupholstered. The mattress on the bed was small and thin. There were no pictures on the walls.

A closer look would have revealed there were no ugly objects in the room. There were no objects, in fact, that were not of a tremendous rarity. The stools and tables were from China. They were made of purple elmwood and were hundreds of years old. There was a Chinese vase, a Roman statue of Apollo, and an inlaid suit of armor that had belonged to the founder of the house of Ratisbon. There was a paper screen from Abyssinia, decorated with the abstract calligraphy that distinguishes that country.

On the table stood a Japanese basket of plaited bamboo and grapevine, out of which grew a spray of tiny yellow orchids. They trembled in the warm night air. The glass door to the balcony was open, and the master of the room stood with his hand on the frame, looking out over the dark city. He was dressed, as always, in tight, formal clothes, which when he turned made an ironic display of his distorted features.

Dr. Theodore passed him and continued on into a corner of the room, where he opened a closet door. On an upper shelf there stood a line of notebooks, written in the automaton's elegant, clear hand. At intervals during the day he set down everything he'd seen and heard.

But now he turned, looking back over his shoulder toward where his master stood. The elector seemed scarcely aware of his presence. No doubt he imagined he could now control his simulacra without effort. Dr. Theodore was not the only servant in the building.

Sighing, the elector stepped from the window and sat down at his calligraphy table. Light came from a glowing bulb on a bronze stand—a piece of new technology from Africa. There was a book of maps on the table in front of him, and he ran his manicured, small hand along the one that was open before him. Supernaturally adept, Dr. Theodore squinted to see. He watched his master run his little finger up the Dobruja coast, past Mamaia, past Mamaia Sat. On a high, wooded hill above Lake Sinoie, the finger paused.

9 *Ludu Rat-tooth*

THEY CAME TO THE place in the middle of the night, a bald patch on a hill overlooking the lake. They were helped by the illumination of the fires to the south and then later to the north. The girl, Ludu, went in front. "My brother went on to Istria, to my uncle's house," she said. "I was right. I thought the vampire would look there."

So the road turned inland above Lake Tasaul, and they'd left it and continued north through the grasslands. They'd walked the horses and followed a rough track that sometimes gave out into sand. But when the land was higher, there were trees. Then suddenly they found themselves in a wooded dell, rising on the far side to a high, gorse-strewn ridge over the south edge of the delta. It was too dark to see, and Miranda was too tired, too hungry. She slid off the pony's back into the coarse grass, then sat hugging herself while the girl attended to everything, the horses first of all. She had some oats in her saddlebag. Then she stripped off the saddles and the bridles and rubbed the animals down, talking to them in an odd language that was full of grunts and moans. The air was humid. Miranda sat cross-legged on a boulder while Ludu lit a fire in a circle of dry earth. "Isn't it dangerous?"

Ludu rubbed her big, lumpy nose with the flat of her hand. "He won't come here. He was beaten here and almost died."

"Who beat him?" Miranda yawned.

For an answer Ludu took from her bag some carved wooden images and placed them in an alcove of the rock above the fire. Then when she was laying out the tarpaulin and blankets, she told a story that put Miranda to sleep as she pulled her boots off and rolled into her bed. It was a love story, lovers separated by their enemies. And the words must have flowed into her dreams, which were full of indistinct figures struggling on grassy hilltops. When she awoke she climbed barefoot in the warm day, up to where she could see the black-and-golden reed beds to the horizon, the barrier islands, and the great, bitten circle of the lagoon. It was the south edge of the Danube delta. Her face was bumpy with mosquito bites. The girl was still asleep.

Miranda had a crick in her neck, and so she stretched and did some exercises. She flossed her teeth with the sharp end of a reed, then took out her toothbrush and returned to camp. She stirred the coals of the fire and put on some dry sticks. She saw a metal pot with the remnants of some wet cereal and another pot of water. She remembered nothing of that, though it must have been the first real food she'd had in days.

Now she examined the two statues in the niche of the rock. At their feet was a small bowl of the wet food, sprinkled with some dry grains of rice, and surmounted with a lump of brown sugar. Behind her the girl lay on her stomach, her face hidden in a tangle of curly hair.

Miranda examined the statues as she brushed her teeth—a king and a queen, their faces long and solemn and dark with smoke and grease. They were dressed in dolls' clothes—scraps and snips of expensive fabric. Crowns of yellow wire twisted around their wooden brows.

She'd thought she'd wait for Ludu to wake up before she ate something more, but she was too hungry. So she sat down with the pot in her lap, and with her fingers she ate lumps of peppery, cold oatmeal while she looked up at the statues. "King Jesus and Queen Mary Magdalene," said the girl presently. "You've heard of them?"

Lying on her stomach, she had raised herself on thick forearms, shaken the hair out of her face. "Sure," Miranda said. Different stories though, she guessed. "Tell me."

The girl looked fierce for an instant. Then she relented. "Mary Magdalene fought the vampire in this place when Jesus sent her to Roumania. She brought the Gypsies with her out of Egypt."

"Well, now you see that's already a little different," said Miranda, putting down her pot. A bug was biting her.

Ludu got up. She walked down into the dell where the horses were tethered. Then she came back and packed up the blankets, and turned the tarpaulin over to dry. At the same time she told the story of Jesus of Nazareth, how he led the slaves to revolution on the banks of the Nile. Afterward he led his armies into Italy. He crucified the captured generals before the walls of Rome.

She went away and came back with a pot of brimming water. Gone were the deferential gestures and phrases of the previous night. In simple language she explained how Jesus in the underworld had stormed the devil's palace and the gates of Mount Olympus. He threw the devil from a cliff into the world. But the pieces came alive and hid themselves. So Jesus sent his generals through the earth, and to Roumania he sent his queen. "People say she was pregnant when she came to Mogosoaia. People say that's where the Brancoveanus come from."

Miranda had been interested in the first part of this recitation. She was always looking for ways to understand the difference between this world and the world where she'd grown up. But at the end, finally, she felt her spirits sink. So many of these stories found a way to involve her, weigh her down with expectations.

So she shrugged. "I've heard something different."

"Stories are like leaves," agreed the girl, setting the pot into the coals.

Miranda stared into the pale flames. Here she was alone without her friends. In America along the river, finally, some measure of control had come to her, a succession of small tasks. Now she had to start again.

"I thought a vampire was someone who sucked your blood," she grumbled. In the humid, breezy air the statement seemed absurd.

"I never heard that." Ludu scratched her hands, which were covered with small red spots. Then she continued. "This time his name is Codreanu. Sometimes maybe he's in prison or a poor man. But when evil people come to power in Roumania, then he comes. Now he is commissioner for Dobruja Province. That's how my father knew we had to fight. Codreanu hates all Gypsies for Queen Mary's sake."

She sniffed, wiped her nose. "My father took me to Insula Calia. Then to the temple where they have a piece of King Jesus's spear. Maybe he thought you'd be a warrior, a hero. Maybe that's why he was disappointed."

Maybe so. "You take what King Jesus gives you," advised Miranda silently.

"My father prayed and prayed before the altar. Mother Egypt told him in a dream the words to say. How to bring you out of the past time where you were."

Just a few days before, Miranda had lost herself in the woods in the American wilderness, then found herself outside Constanta on the beach. There was some information here: "I was in America," she said. "It wasn't the past time."

But even as she said this, she realized what she'd known before and not tried to explain—it was springtime here. Almost summer. When she'd last seen Peter and Andromeda, it was in the freezing snow.

"Every day on the anniversary of Mother Egypt's death . . . ," the girl went on. Miranda let her talk some more about her father's hopes and prayers before she pulled her back.

"How long ago did my aunt die?" she interrupted.

"More than five years."

Miranda heard a buzzing in her ears that was like the roaring of the sea. Then she swallowed and went on. Step by step. "For me it was last week," she said. "Last week—I don't know—the empress sent a letter."

Ludu shrugged. "There's no empress anymore. Valeria Dragonesti is in the mountains with Antonescu and his men—no friends of ours, except they fight the Germans. Nicola Ceausescu is in Bucharest, calling herself the white tyger."

The water boiled. Ludu stared it without doing anything. Then suddenly she was in tears, a raw, desperate sobbing that took Miranda by surprise.

Especially since it was Miranda who'd been sitting with a pain in her stomach—five years! Where was Peter now? Where was he in this world, and where was anyone who knew her? Step by step: "I'm afraid for my brothers," the girl said when she could speak. "I'm afraid for my father! He's strong, but he can't walk. Today you are safe here. Many have lost everything—I don't want to be like that. Now tell me please, where should we go? It can't be for nothing that my father brought you to Roumania."

"No, it can't be for nothing," Miranda repeated to herself. She put her hands out to the fire, although the air was warm. What comfort was there for this girl, who felt so isolated and alone, and who now continued, "Here in this place Queen Mary came upon the vampire while he was asleep. She came up by those little oaks. On this stone she grabbed hold of his leg and twisted so he screamed for mercy. Then she put him in a prison for a thousand years—can you do that? This morning they are burying the bodies at Mamaia Sat and Istria. My poor father . . ."

There was nothing to say to this. Miranda held her hands out to the fire. Always in the last few days she'd had a mental image of Peter and Andromeda running through the snow along the river, calling her name. She'd imagined trying to send a message—where to? Now she'd have to give that up, the image and the plan.

In Berkshire County her adoptive mother had always cried when she was punishing her. The Gypsy girl was crying now, rubbing the tears away—Miranda had been paddling down the river with her friend Peter Gross. Before that she'd been living in America. She'd been fifteen years old. She hadn't asked for any of this. "Listen, Ludu—"

"Don't call me that!"

"All right!" Miranda cried, frustrated. Then in a moment: "Maybe it's too dangerous for you to stay with me. Maybe you should go look for your brothers now and leave me."

The girl stared at her. Her face was red, her complexion bad. She held her hand over her face to hide her mouth.

Sea birds flew overhead. The air smelled of the marshland and the sea. As soon as she saw the girl's face, Miranda regretted having said what she'd been thinking. "All right, let's forget it. Can you take me to Insula Calia?" she asked.

Stanley, her American father, had taught her to focus on practical solutions to small problems. Step by step for the Gypsy girl. Step by step for her. First of all she had to stop being a baby. None of this was just her trouble. Last night she'd been a little dazed. Everything that happened, she could wake up from it as if from a dream. But in the morning light she had responsibilities. People had already died. And even if there was something dreamlike about the disappearance of Ludu's father, this much was clear to Miranda in the light of day: The vampire—Codreanu—was setting fire to the coast to find her.

The girl sat hugging her knees, rubbing her face with the heel of her hand, and Miranda felt a stab of guilt. For a moment she remembered her self-indulgence of the day before, the way she'd lolled around the castle as if she were alone in the world. Well, she was alone, more alone than she'd imagined then, and the girl, too.

She pulled the sleeve back from her wrist to show the golden bracelet of tiger-head beads, the bracelet of Miranda Brancoveanu in the ancient days. She also had come of out nowhere, started with nothing—the girl was staring at Miranda's wrist. She'd stopped crying and was sullen now.

The first of the Brancoveanus had defeated armies, founded a great nation. Here in the grassy dell, Miranda said, "I want to know if you will take me where I need to go, tell me what I need to understand."

Sullen, the girl stared at her.

"I want to know if you can help me." She almost added, "For your father's sake," but then she bit her tongue.

"And I want to know what I should call you," she continued after a moment. "Ludu—"

"—is my saint's name. You call me 'Rat-tooth.'"

For a moment Miranda thought she hadn't understood, though the phrase was simple enough. But then the girl smiled a joyless smile, and her teeth were thin and sharp. One of her eyeteeth was especially long, and fitted into a gap in her lower lip.

"Well, so can you get me breakfast?"

It was a good idea to give the girl something to do. She made some sweet tea with the water, and laid out a meal of bread and dried sausage. This she sliced with a hook-shaped knife while she was talking. The oracle was in the marshland north and west, three days away. They had enough food to get them there if they found forage for the horses. After that they needed some supplies.

Miranda shrugged. "I have money."

"Yes, I saw. Moldovan gold rubles. You are rich."

Miranda shrugged. "What about Codreanu? You said . . ."

"You are safe here. And Queen Mary's hermitage where we spend the night. In the daytime he is weak. So we must be there before darkness."

As she washed the pot, she answered Miranda's questions. She had answers to everything. "When the Germans came, Nicola Ceausescu was homeless in the streets of Bucharest. She was the baron's widow, but she had no money. But there were people in the German high command who'd seen her on the stage. The white tyger, it's a part for her to play. And they keep her son a hostage to control her—it was perfect, see? She was always a whore, and now she spreads for them."

"A hostage?"

"Yes, in a castle in Germany. In Ratisbon."

This was a surprise. Miranda's birth-mother, whom she'd never met, was a prisoner there. Raevsky had said so, and her aunt.

Nicola Ceausescu was the one who had sent Captain Raevsky to America, Miranda knew. And if he hadn't managed to kidnap her, it was mostly bad luck that had prevented him. To the end, to the last day she'd seen him, still he was always trying to persuade her to come willingly, telling her what a grand time she'd have in Bucharest as Nicola Ceausescu's guest—a beautiful lady, he had called her, much misjudged.

Now Miranda wondered if there were not some hidden reason why Nicola Ceausescu wanted her, something that might involve her mother and the baroness's son. "This man Codreanu. Why is he chasing me?"

Ludu Rat-tooth grimaced. "Isn't it obvious? It's your bracelet. People see you, they'll know Nicola Ceausescu is a fake."

"Don't they know already?"

"Yes, they know. But they're not sure. And there's nothing else, no one for them to love. Nothing to believe in. Valeria Dragonesti was no better. No— one thing. She kept the Germans out."

The sun had not shown its face all day. A high gray mist covered the sky. The girl packed up the camp. "The generals put her on the throne when you were a baby," she said. "Your father was half German, but he was a man, a friend of the Gypsies with his sister. Baron Ceausescu betrayed him and he died in prison. Then your mother ran to Ratisbon where you were born, and sent you back with Mother Egypt and the invasion plan from Germany—you see you saved us once before!"

Miranda was glad to hear this story of her aunt's confirmed, and she asked many questions about it. "How is it possible you do not know these things?" said Ludu Rat-tooth, not for the first time. "Your mother, no one knows. People say she is locked up in Ratisbon. Still now after more than twenty years."

Hearing this repeated, Miranda wondered why it made so little impression on her. Obviously she should be rushing off to Ratisbon, wherever that might be. Obviously—or at least it should have occurred to her to do so. And maybe she was a bad, unnatural daughter, but when she tried to imagine her mother's face, all she ever saw was Rachel in the Massachusetts house, the picture in Miranda's locket notwithstanding. Clara Brancoveanu was a prisoner in Germany. It was just words.

And anyway, how could her mother have given her up, surrendered her after one day when she was just a baby? Miranda pondered this as in the afternoon she and Ludu Rat-tooth walked their horses away from the water. Below the ridge they crossed northwest into an older forest of oak trees and beeches. There was no path, but the trees were widely spaced. Miranda's pony followed the gray horse, and Miranda did nothing except duck under the limbs of trees. Then they came to a dirt road through the forest and could make better time.

They saw no one on the road. The branches arched overhead. The dirt of the road was rutted and moist, and the horses' hooves made a soft, stamping noise. Miranda experimented with her pony, trying to turn it subtly, or make it slow down or speed up. She shifted her weight on its back, and increased the pressure of her right knee or her left. But the horses went hour after hour at a fast walk, and nothing she did made much difference, which was just as well. She was hungry by the time the girl pulled up the gray horse, and the pony stopped, too.

"Here is the place," said Rat-tooth.

She slipped out of the saddle. Taking hold of the horse's mouth, she turned aside under the trees, and Miranda followed her straight in under the beech trees on the left-hand side. Her whole body ached. She was grateful to be on the ground again, although her feet were hot, her leather boots uncomfortable. She stepped carefully over the fallen leaves, trying not to leave a mark.

In time they came to a clearing in the woods, and a small, round pool of water. There was high, soft grass, and some kind of ruined structure. "Queen Mary lived here for a day and a night," murmured the girl, as Miranda looked up at the darkening sky. "We should be safe."

Then immediately she would have started on her round of tasks with the horses and the camp, only Miranda held her arm. Miranda had been thinking long, gloomy thoughts. "Tell me," she said—Ludu Rat-tooth knew a lot. It was conceivable she might have heard, conceivable that in five years . . . "Tell me," Miranda said. "Have you ever heard the name de Graz, Pieter de Graz, or maybe Sasha Prochenko? Have you heard those names?" she asked. The girl shook her head, pulled her arm away.

BUT PETER LIFTED HIS HEAD as if he'd heard Miranda's question in the night air. In time and space he was much closer than she feared.

She would have been shocked to see him as he stood under the bridge. When she had left him his right hand had been thick and heavy on his boy's arm. Now his body matched it. He'd put on muscle and height, but less flesh than he needed. Even so he was a more handsome man than he'd ever been a boy. His brown hair, brown eyes, and crooked teeth were still the same. And she would have recognized many of his gestures and mannerisms.

Now he stood cursing in the dark, his lips twisted into a scowl. Photographs of the Chevalier de Graz, taken before his disappearance, would have shown this same expression. They would have shown him riding with his regiment or hunting bears in the Carpathians, or standing with his brothers and sisters and their dogs outside the Schloss de Graz in Satu Mares. They would have shown him with his parents, bluff, hard-drinking Roumanian aristocrats—whatever filter his character had passed through, it had not yet allowed any of those memories. Toward dawn, standing in the mud under the Kanuni bridge in Adrianopole, cursing after the lost dog, Peter Gross had no recollection of the place, even though the Chevalier de Graz had driven over the same road with Frederick Schenck von Schenck after the battle of Havsa on his way to meet the Turkish generals.

Part of this was an effort of will. He wouldn't give up his own mother and his father for a couple of battered sepia photographs. Peter's memory was much stronger, much more subtle than the chevalier's, and he had used it to protect his childhood, everything he was. Since he'd climbed out of the pit in Heliopolis, at free moments he'd gone back into the past, unearthing memories that were sometimes painful or touched with pain; it didn't matter. He had no desire to grow into something else.

And he associated de Graz with a dark part of his mind, an unreflective part that led him into violence and chaos. Raevsky had died, his spirit animal had scampered away. The man on the snowy bridge had grabbed hold of Peter's ear. Some memories he could not tolerate.

Certain skills had come back to him. He could speak Roumanian and French. A little Turkish might have come in handy, though. He pulled his boot out of the mud and strode down the slope under this other bridge. Beggars lived there in wooden packing crates and under oilcloth tarpaulins. This was the poorest section of the town, full of Bulgar refugees.

In the moneyless life he and Andromeda had led since they'd come out of the tiled well in Heliopolis, they'd passed months in neighborhoods like this, in Tunis, Alexandria, and Jerusalem. Though in his short life he had spent huge sums, the Chevalier de Graz had had no skill at generating cash. Neither did Peter Gross—his livelihood depended on the dog.

In the sophisticated cities of North Africa, he and Andromeda had been protected by people's ignorance, their lack of superstition. Even in Constantinople no one had glanced at the beast. But now finally they had reached the borders of Europe. These Bulgars, Hebrews, and Gypsies had a ruder knowledge. Sometimes as the dog passed, Peter had seen them make the sign of the evil eye.

Andromeda had been away for hours and he was worried. He'd been searching all afternoon. He stumbled down the embankment onto level ground, a wet stretch of cobblestones between the Tunca River and the pilings of the bridge. Overhead, the night traffic had almost ceased along the line of Byzantine stone arches, though occasionally a bullock cart still rumbled toward the city gates.

In the evening it rained. Along the black, quiet river, traffic had almost ceased. Under the bridge, though, a crowd of men had gathered. Some carried torches. The span closest to the water had been bricked up on the downstream side so that it formed a high-arched cave. Fifteen or twenty men stood in the entrance to that cave, swearing and shouting, and some laughed. Peter saw Andromeda's footprints in the wet mud.

He couldn't understand what the men were saying. But some of them had picked up stones. One of them held a pistol, an old, double flint-lock affair. He was a squat, evil-looking brute, dressed in a brown leather jacket (though it was a hot night), on which still hung some fragments of fur. Instinctively Peter selected him as the leader of this group and made his way toward him over the uneven ground. As he brought the gun down, Peter came behind him and seized hold of his wrist. One of the plates flashed and misfired.

Some Turkish might have been useful, though there was no time to talk. No time even to think what he was doing—Peter brought his right arm over the man's shoulder and pushed his forearm into the man's thick throat. At moments like this he gave himself into the hands of the Chevalier de Graz. He pulled the gun down as the man tried to stamp on his foot. Others had dropped their stones and come around now, a ragged, drunken, broken-toothed bunch of losers, Peter told himself. Some had their knives out, but Peter had the upper hand. They yelled at him; he didn't know what they were saying. He had their leader, though, and was hurting his windpipe as the man struggled and flailed. Then he found the second trigger, and his pistol fired.

There was a smell of smoke and powder. The shot resounded in the arch. Peter put his back against the wall and turned the man's body from side to side; he knew he'd won. The other men were worried now because the noise might draw down the janissaries from the guardhouse on the bridge. Some were already staggering away. The squat little man was struggling, and Peter used his body as a buckler, turning it from side to side as the others came closer with their knives. He was waiting for the sound of the policemen's whistle, and when it came, most of those who faced him turned and ran. He adjusted his arm so the little man could breathe, and then he threw him down completely on the muddy stones. Grimacing and roaring, he made a half-run toward the men who still remained in the entrance to the cave, then turned and ducked inside against the bricked-up wall, a distance of perhaps twenty feet.

The damned dog was in the cul-de-sac, crouching over a capon she had stolen, and she growled as Peter approached. In their journey from America she'd changed as he had, growing bigger and more fierce. Now she yawned, stretched her tongue out and then picked up the capon by it broken neck. Its viscera hung in the mud.

Again Peter heard the shrill whistle of the night janissaries. At the entrance to the cave the fat man lay groaning. But Andromeda wanted to play. She thrust her forelegs out, then bounded past him with the capon in her mouth. Peter was able to get a hand on the bird, whose head tore away. Then Andromeda was gone, disappearing out the open archway.

The bird was still warm, stolen from the henhouse of some citizen. Peter tucked it into his coat. He slipped under the arch and into the small space between the piling and the embankment. It was partly blocked with rubble, but he managed to climb through without making any noise, and then he followed the riverbank into a thicket of small trees.

The police were at the bridge now, and he waited in the thicket to make sure they wouldn't follow him. Night came. While he waited, as was his custom, he ran over some poetry in his mind, then checked in with his father in the house on White Oak Road. Flexing the muscles of his memory, he recalled many things—small words of his mother and then something Miranda had said to him in high school when he was in ninth grade. It was in the corridor by Ms. McDonald's classroom. She hadn't really known him then. But he knew who she was.

This was a way of subduing the Chevalier de Graz, whom he had allowed to possess him in the fight. Now he shivered in his wet coat. When everything was still, he walked downstream for a couple of miles before turning in a circle to the road again. Two hours later he crossed the bridge without incident and reached his hotel before dawn.

It was a waystation for impoverished travelers called the Dardanelles. Far from that body of water, it sagged on its foundations in a dirty, unpaved part of town. Peter and Andromeda's room was on the third story in the back, with a single, glassless window overlooking a bricked-up court. The floor was muddy and the plaster walls streaked with red where lodgers had crushed centipedes and other vermin. There was no furniture except a single, sagging bed, on which Andromeda lay sleeping when Peter came in.

It was dark in the room, except for the light that shone in from the court. Peter sat down on the bed and laid the capon on the floor, then fumbled for a bottle of water standing upright. He drew the cork out with his teeth and dropped it into his cupped palm. He was listening for a sound of movement from the bed. Soon it came.

There was the stub of a candle in a pool of hardened wax on the iron bed frame. When the water was finished, he broke the candle off and jammed it into the neck of the bottle, which he stood next to his boot. Pulling a box of phaetons from his pocket, he struck one of them and lit the wick, keeping the bottle low upon the ground. He did this out of a sense of modesty. He did not want to see Andromeda as she rose from the bed. He did not want to see her muscled body covered with a layer of fine hair. He didn't want to see her long, naked legs as she swung them off her side of the bed.

None of this, he thought, was intended to provoke him. She was oblivious. She showed no longer, for example, any trace of the way she had teased and flirted with him on Christmas Hill. So maybe he'd been wrong about that after all; he began to tear the feathers off the bird and drop them underfoot. Caught in a swirl of air, they scattered to the corner of the room or underneath the bed.

Peter was hungry. Without looking he could tell Andromeda was standing in the glow from the window, outside the light cast by the candle onto his boot and his hands and the bird and a circle of the floor. She was looking into the triangular fragment of a mirror, fixed to the wall beside the door. "So where the Christ have I been?" she said cheerfully. He knew from experience she would be touching streaks of blood and dirt, chuckling over her bruises. Her feet, especially, would be filthy and sore.

"You don't want to know."

He glanced up as he pulled the capon's breast feathers against the grain, and in the gathering dawn he saw her back as she shrugged off her linen shirt—she always dressed like a dandy, while he made do with rags. But it was true what she said. If she was to be let into card games and betting parlors, she had to look as if she had some money to lose.

She was rubbing her teeth, picking at them with her long fingernails.

Something dislodged, and she inspected the ball of her thumb. "Must have been a hard night," she said. "So what is it today?"

"A chicken."

"Ugh."

"I'll give it to the kitchen. Though I see you've had your breakfast."

"Yuck." She turned to face him, hands on her hips, and he looked down. One of the small feathers blew into the candle flame, emitting a singed smell.

"So what's our plan today?" she said.

He shrugged. "Still the same. We need a hundred fifty piastres each for new papers and visas. Plus what we owe for the room."

Andromeda smelled her fingers. "I'm not paying for this."

The creature who was dressing now in front of him bore little resemblance to the girl he and Miranda had known. There was nothing female about her as she pulled on her silk shirt, except of course for the obvious things, which now he glanced at furtively. It wasn't that she was sexless now, but rather double-sexed, moving back and forth continually over a line—she'd always been flat-chested. She'd always been athletic and strong. That wasn't it.

He had to admit that there was nothing sexual in the way she teased him. If anything, those feelings came from him, and sometimes at night he had lain sleepless beside her, thinking about Miranda, about kissing her and touching her body—it was useless. Where was she?

And there were moments also, in a certain light, when he knew Andromeda had changed less than he had. Certainly she was still beautiful, and not just to him. When she stalked the streets in her long boots, men and women turned their heads.

"I'm off to the Ali Pasa Carsisi," she said—the covered bazaar in the Hurriyet Meydani. Which meant she'd spend the morning pickpocketing, a special skill. Pilfered merchants would forget their losses, abashed by her self-confidence. Surely she'd adapted to her triple nature—girl, dog, Roumanian staff officer—better than he'd adapted to his new right hand. Much about her made him jealous and disgusted him. When they slept in the big, sagging bed, here and in fleabags across North Africa, he was the one who kept all his clothes on, though he was a normal man.

"I think I'm sleeping in," he said, looking up finally into her delicate, strange face, in which her animal nature now seemed to predominate. Sphinx-like, she smiled, though her pale eyes were wide and innocent.

"I need a cup of coffee, I swear to God," she said, and licked her lips.

She was teasing him. Always she wasted money on luxuries—coffee and cigarettes, ice cream and liquor, while he counted every copper penny. Because she was the one who brought in money, it was impossible for him to complain except to himself. But if she would just bear down and concentrate, they could cross the border into Europe, into Roumania. The line was at Gobrovo in the mountains, a hundred miles north—not far away. Of course he still did not remember, but he had fought with Prince Frederick on the outskirts of this same city.

Sometimes it seemed as if she were happy with the life they had. She didn't seem in any hurry to return home. She spoke Turkish and Aegyptian. She could even write in hieroglyphs. It was her fault they had wasted all this time. Once in Alexandria he'd seen her win enough at dice to buy them passage all the way and pay for food as well. Then four hours later she had lost it all, except for a thousand dinars that she'd spent on a gold ring. She'd done it just to goad him, he was sure. She'd laughed and shrugged her shoulders, winked at him with every losing cast.

And maybe he'd have been able to get her moving, then and now, if he hadn't been so sick. He'd caught a fever in the dig at Heliopolis, caught a fever from her, he'd thought, and he remembered how hot she'd felt when he'd grabbed her in the dark, in Waile Bizunesh's archeological dig. "Chicken? I don't think so," she said now. "I think some almond gazelles' horns, or those pistachio bird's nests. Maybe a shot of grappa, or who knows? I know the sun's not up, but you've been out all night. Come and have a drink with me. I'll read you the newspapers."

She was dressed, as always, like a man—tight pants and riding boots, a loose, cream-colored shirt unbuttoned down the front to show a gold chain. In her right hand she carried a pair of leather gloves, which she knocked now against her left palm.

Her chin and chest glistened with the merest shadow of soft, yellow hair, which completed the illusion. She smiled at him, then shrugged as he bent stubbornly over the bird. She reached for her embroidered jacket, which she'd wear over her shoulder in the marketplace among the covered stalls. It had a secret panel in the lining.

Her smile never faded as they listened to the thump of footsteps coming toward them down the hall. Then there was a pounding on the door and a voice shouting in Turkish. In an instant Andromeda was at the window with her leg over the sill, then she was gone. He dropped the bird and rushed to follow her; she had slipped onto the roof of an adjoining shed and was now running over the tiles toward the outer wall, which gave onto an alley. Maybe the dog had managed to climb up that way, but Peter was afraid he'd fall, afraid the tin roof would not support his weight. When the janissaries broke the door he was still in the room, and they arrested him.

10 *De Witte*

IT WAS CLOSE TO dawn. Near the west wall of the ruined hermitage, Miranda lay without sleeping. An hour before, the brightest stars had shown through a black mist. Now, though the mist was lighter, the stars had lost their brilliance, which was a relief, Miranda thought. Some of her clearest memories of home were of those nights in her backyard or in the field behind Garfield House, rolled up in a blanket while Stanley talked about the stars. Sometimes he had brought a small telescope, but most of all she enjoyed lying on her back to see the whole arc of the sky. During the various meteor showers, he and she had always gone out if it was clear. She knew all the constellations of the northern hemisphere. So in this place it was disconcerting to look up and recognize nothing.

She lay with her elbows wide, her fingers interlaced behind her head. She listened to the horses by the little pool. When they first arrived in the clearing, Ludu Rat-tooth had prevented them from drinking as much as they had wanted, had chased them away after a few swallows of water. But now they lay peaceably in the trampled grass, and sometimes Miranda could hear the sound of them snorting or shaking out their lips.

Ludu was asleep beside her. The hair had fallen away from her face. The previous day she'd seemed much older than her age, especially in the matter-of-fact, unsentimental way she had accepted catastrophe and loss. But now her toughness was like a mask that had fallen away, uncovering a softer and more childlike face. Her fist was at her mouth and she was sucking on her thumb. Under her upper lip on the left-hand side, Miranda could see the sharp end of her tooth.

Miranda had awoken with a sense of purpose, however, and when she looked up at the stars, when she thought about home, when she listened to the horses, when she examined the face of the sleeping girl, it was to prolong a moment of delay. Whatever dangers waited for her, she was comfortable here, lying with her hands behind her head. Now she sat up, put on her belt and boots.

If she was to function here, she needed to know about guns and horses, riding and shooting, which so far seemed to be the most important skills in this place. Her father was a general, her aunt had hunted ducks, and she too must have learned something when she was young—the language had come back, after all. In her dreams she had been riding, riding all night on the gray horse.

The most important thing was to be confident. And if she couldn't manage that, at least she could make her mistakes away from Ludu Rat-tooth. So she strode down to the pool and found the gray horse standing docile under the trees. The bridle hung from a branch. She put the snaffle into the horse's mouth, pulled the headstall over her ears, and buckled the strap under her cheeks. Miranda had studied all this carefully, had watched the girl the day before, and now she pulled on the saddle and tightened the girth, all the time whispering and talking. She let the horse smell her and then tugged her by the mouth, away under the trees.

When she tried to mount up, the horse walked a few steps forward. For a moment Miranda hopped awkwardly on one foot, but then she managed to drag herself into the saddle. The trees were big and widely spaced, but again the horse resisted. She found herself kicking at its sides. And then it broke away from the track they'd followed the evening before, and made its own big circle through the trees. She tried to pull it back in the direction she had chosen, and found herself yanking on its mouth, trying to muscle its head around without success. It was a matter of willpower, she remembered from her dream, and she found herself whispering and cursing. But the horse led her around in a big circle, and in a few minutes she saw the clearing up ahead.

She kicked its sides and it moved forward into the track again. "This time," Miranda told herself. At the same place as before, the horse turned under the trees, and in a few minutes they were back at the clearing, and there was a new horse.

Now it was lighter in the wood. Miranda could see the animal under the beech trees, a black horse even larger than the gray. Miranda pulled on her reins and her horse stopped short, while the black lifted his head and showed his teeth. He was a beautiful beast, but quite obviously exhausted: streaked with dust, and his eyes were bloodshot, staring. As she watched, the horse blew out his lips, then let his head sink down again. His tail and mane were long and tangled. There was an empty leather holster at his saddlebow where a rider might keep a long gun.

Miranda slipped out of her saddle and walked back, away from the two animals. Then she turned at the edge of the clearing. Under the dawn sky, beside the old stone wall there was a man standing over Ludu Rat-tooth. He was dressed in a dark uniform, and in his hand he held a short repeating rifle, pointed down.

The girl was awake. She lay on her stomach without moving and the muzzle of the gun was by her cheek.

Miranda had left her bag of money in her blankets, rolled in the shirt she'd used as a pillow. Now she saw it in the man's hand. As she watched, he slipped the purse into the leather pouch on his belt.

Guns and horses—Miranda hadn't been so stupid as to leave her pistol with her money. She'd slipped it into her belt as she got up. Now she pulled it from inside her shirt, pulled off the trigger lock. She checked the bullet in the chamber, while at the same time she was thinking about the vampire. She was remembering the stiff action of the trigger and the way the heavy gun had recoiled in her hand. She was remembering the smell of gunpowder, the ringing in her ears.

And maybe this was some kind of magic gun, and she could just point it at someone and they would disappear into a dream. That was what had happened on the moonlit road, and in the light of day it helped her to imagine the same thing: the soldier gone, the rest unchanged. He had his back to her, and she came forward as quietly as she could. She watched him push the muzzle of the rifle into Ludu's cheek, and make her roll onto her back. She watched him press the mouth of the rifle into the soft skin of her neck; he also was exhausted. His blue uniform was dirty, and one of the sleeves was ripped. He had a knot of silver braid on one shoulder, silver stripes on both his cuffs. He wore wire-rimmed spectacles and was wounded on his scalp. His short yellow hair was stiff with blood behind his ear. He had no hat.

All this Miranda saw as she came closer through the grass, her pistol out in front of her. The man didn't hear her, wasn't listening. He was distracted. He moved the rifle down the girl's long throat. Miranda could see her shirt was unbuttoned, and the man moved the rifle down her chest, pushing away the cloth flaps. Miranda saw him sway a little on his feet. His boots were black and scuffed.

He hadn't spoken. He stood with the mouth of his gun on Ludu's breastbone, as if uncertain what to do. But now the girl opened her mouth and turned her head, and then she saw Miranda. And her expression changed, and Miranda saw it change, and so doubtless the man would see it, too. Something had to be done right now, although in a sense the entire situation was idiotic, like something in a Western movie. What was Miranda supposed to say—"Hands up?"

"Hands up," she said. It didn't sound so foolish in Roumanian. The man turned his head.

Two nights before she had fired on the vampire in the dark. But that had been an unreal moment with unreal consequences, and it did not make this moment easier. Then she had fired in a panic at a grotesque, alien thing. This was a human being, even if he was a thief and worse, and it was horrible the way he'd touched Ludu Rat-tooth, caressed her with the muzzle of his gun.

She aimed for the middle of his chest, then raised her hands couple of inches. She would shoot him through the shoulder and disarm him. But she didn't, found she couldn't, though she could feel her hands shake with rage. She glanced into the man's face, glanced at Ludu's face, and watched the opinion solidify in each—she was not capable of this.

Why didn't the man bring up his gun? She wondered if it was even loaded. She had a lot of time to wonder as the man began to smile. But then he dropped his rifle and leaped for her, grabbed for the muzzle of her revolver. She pulled the trigger and her hands jolted back. Birds in the ruined hermitage, disturbed by the noise, rose suddenly into the sky.

Ludu rolled away, jumped to her feet. Then she knelt over the soldier and picked up his rifle. "Stop," Miranda said.

"German pig!"

The girl was suddenly in tears. She threw the rifle away into the grass. Then she sat back on her knees and she was crying, her hands hiding her face.

The soldier lay without moving. His blue eyes were distorted by the lenses of his spectacles, one of which was cracked. Miranda had shot him through the shoulder under his collarbone. It was where she'd aimed. The cloth of his uniform was singed over a neat dry hole.

Miranda stood above him. She herself had no intention of crying. "He's got my money in that leather pouch."

The girl wiped her nose with her forearm. Her eyes were fierce, glinting with tears. "Finish it. He's a German."

"No."

"Let me get out of the way."

"No."

Miranda could still hear, ringing in her ears, the report the gun had made. She stood with its muzzle pointed up. "Please, miss," said the girl.

"We'll take his horse. We'll leave him here."

"Oh, stupid!" said Ludu Rat-tooth. "A German officer. You think he's alone? He saw us and the horses."

When Miranda said nothing, she went on. "Miss—don't make me do your filthy work. It will be gone in a second—so!"

She spat, and the moisture sprayed across the soldier's face. His eyes, which he had closed momentarily, now opened again.

Again Miranda imagined a scene from a movie or a book. It was useless to talk about this. Miranda knew she couldn't kill this man or else allow him to be killed. She could be angry, too. "Get up," she said.

Now the soldier struggled to speak. His lips were dry and chapped. "Give me water," he murmured.

The girl spat across his open mouth. "Don't let him talk," she said, but it was too late.

"Please," murmured the soldier.

He spoke in Roumanian but with a strange, soft accent. "Leave is worse than dying, if you leave. Already they have found me gone the last three days. From this headquarters in Dobric. Give me to drink. I am not German."

The hole in his shoulder was wet now, and the frayed cloth around it was red. "Liar," hissed the girl.

Miranda knelt. She squatted over the man as he struggled to sit up. When he reached for the gun she shoved him back again with her left hand, so he lay flat.

"Dead," he muttered, "dead is better."

In a little while he went on. "You will open my shirt. There is an envelope. Take it out now. You will see."

Holding the gun up, muzzle pointed to the sky, Miranda slipped her hand into his jacket. Some of the silver buttons were undone. He had some ribbons on his chest, which was thin and frail. "I tell you, dead is better," he murmured again.

"Do you two know each other?" asked Miranda in English, between her teeth. "You seem to have this all worked out."

She meant they both wanted her to shoot him. There was a rip in the silk lining of his jacket, and Miranda could feel the outline of an envelope. She drew it out and stood to look at it. Stepping back, she lowered her pistol, then drew out several sheets of crisp, official stationery. They were covered with smeared, minuscule typescript, in German.

Her words brought a new response from the wounded man. His English was better than his Roumanian, though he spoke with the same soft accent: "I am begging for your help if you are enemies of Germany. Not for myself, although I meant no harm and what I did you is repaid. Take the money back—I cannot stay here where my enemies will catch me. This is information I must bring to my own country. I was riding to Tulcea Crossing in the delta so to come to my own place. If I had not the strength, I must find the Russian attachée at Braila at the trade negotiation there. Her name is Djourek, and if you say you have a message from Alexci de Witte . . ."

"Why would I say that?" Miranda was studying the typescript as if it meant something to her.

"Please—my own life, it is gone. But I must bring these papers home. If you are a soldier in this war then you must help me, for this will mean a victory or a terrible defeat. I should have taken that bay pony and left my gelding, though he is worth ten times as much. I pay for that mistake. You have horses, and so take this document and do what I have said. It is cruel to leave me to be tortured in Bucharest or Berlin while you do nothing with this information. Cruel and stupid. If my country comes into this war . . . Please, give me some water."

Miranda shuffled the papers while the man turned his head toward Ludu Rat-tooth. "I know what side you are. She hates me when she sees the German uniform. I tell you if you take these documents, many Germans will die. Otherwise . . ." He broke off. "Ah, can't you see that I myself am a dead man? Promise you will do this thing. Anna Djourek, in Braila. Say the name! Ah, God, it's scarcely one day's ride. Will you promise? I am a desperate man!"

"What am I looking at?" asked Miranda.

"I must tell you. It is the order of the march. On June eleventh German infantry will cross the border into the Ukraine. So, in ten days' time. I was in headquarters of the Third Army Corps. They will go north from Focsani with two divisions. They will cross the river at the Cosmesti bridge. Everything is in those papers. I will go . . . ," and then he lapsed into a foreign language that Miranda supposed was Russian. He had raised himself onto his elbow and the grass under his back was touched with red. But he was in pretty good shape under the circumstances. He spoke for a long time. There was spit on his lips. "Please," he said finally. "Give me water."

Miranda slipped her pistol into her shirt, along with the letter in its envelope, and knelt over him again. She picked up Ludu's water bottle from the grass. What should she do? It was easy enough to give him water. But she could not forget the sight of him, swaying on his feet, opening Ludu Rat-tooth's shirt with the muzzle of a rifle.

She had the bottle in her hand. When she came close, he grabbed her. He was stronger than she'd anticipated, and he pulled her down onto the ground while he was fumbling for the gun. Because of her surprise, he almost had it when she caught hold of his wrist. It was thin in her hand. De Witte was a small man. She rolled onto his wounded shoulder, and she could hear him grunt.

But he had seized hold of her left hand with a grip she couldn't break. And she could hear his voice murmuring in her ear. "When you see her you must say I am not dead. And you must ask her to remember the May festival at Oberammergau when she came from the university. And if she asks how she can trust you, tell her she was wearing a blue dress, embroidered like a peasant. And give her this."

Miranda felt her left hand close on something sharp. At any moment she expected Ludu Rat-tooth to come and help her. But she looked up and couldn't see her. Instead she saw another pair of boots.

She let out her breath. And there were more pairs of boots, and other men in dark blue uniforms. One dragged de Witte away and held him down.

Miranda rolled onto her knees. She hunched her back, making her shirt billow out as she pushed the gun under her belt, the letter with it. She kept her left hand closed on the sharp thing. She was looking down, examining the long grass. There were some ants.

Now everything was quiet. Miranda watched the toes of a pair of black boots in front of her. The leather was worn, carefully polished.

When she raised her head, she found herself looking up into the face of a tall soldier. His hair was black, and he wore a small black moustache and beard.

His face was long and showed his bones. The shape of his black eyes showed some Asian ancestry. "We came in time," he said, smiling, in Roumanian. "You are not hurt?"

"No."

"That is good." He spoke fluently, without an accent. "We were looking for this criminal. You have my thanks."

Behind the soldier, to Miranda's surprise, two others were kneeling over Alexei de Witte, and one was carrying the water bottle. The other had stripped off his jacket and was bandaging his shoulder with strips of gauze that were already wet with blood. A third stood at a distance near the crushed place in the grass where Miranda had spent the night. He was carrying the rifle.

"Now I am here to give you the thanks of my government and to ask if you've been harmed. What is your name?"

"Miranda."

"Ah, like the queen from your history books—Brancoveanu, is it not? Surely you are as beautiful as she was to have been. Did this man say anything to you?'

Miranda wished she'd thought to have invented a new name. Anna? No, that was the woman she was supposed to find.

"No," she said. "He attacked us as we slept."

"Who?"

"Me and my friend." Another soldier now appeared at the edge of the clearing, leading a subdued Ludu Rat-tooth.

The Eurasian man—an officer, Miranda supposed, though she couldn't tell it by his uniform—spoke a crisp command in German and the soldier took his hand from the girl's elbow. Smiling again, he reached down to help Miranda to her feet. She brushed his hand away as she got up.

"He did not say anything to you, or give anything to you?"

"No. We were asleep."

"And so the gunshot that we heard . . . ?"

He glanced down at her belt, where the butt of her pistol was protruding. Miranda said nothing—"This must have surprised him!" continued the man. "Please!"

He reached out his gloved hand. Miranda laid the gun into it. He raised it up, inspected it, spun the barrel so the bullets dropped into the grass. "Where did you come from? Why are you sleeping here?"

Miranda thought a plaintive tone was best. "Mamaia Sat. Two nights ago our house was burned. This was my father's gun. My uncle lives in . . ."

"Where?"

"In Carcaliu," said Miranda. The name rose from a hidden place.

One of the soldiers stood beside them, and the man asked him questions in German. He answered in the same language, and Miranda caught some proper names. Mamaia Sat. Zelea Codreanu.

The man with the moustache had been smiling all this time. But now he grimaced and screwed up his mouth. He snapped the revolver closed, then raised his hand, and the soldier broke off in midword. Behind him, the two others were still kneeling over Alexei de Witte, who was not conscious.

"Ah, I am sorry," said the man with the moustache. "On behalf of my government—these men are criminals. Believe me, you will not suffer long under their hands. In Bucovina we have thrown these scoundrels out."

Plaintive and defiant was the attitude Miranda wanted. She stared up at the moustached man, and he stared back. "My name is Arslan Lubomyr. He did not give you anything?"

"When?"

"After you shot him? Ah, I see. It is a joke."

The man grimaced, and turned to look at the black horse. A soldier—the one who had brought Ludu back—had stripped off the saddle and bridle. The horse stepped back. His head dipped down, and Miranda could see he was lame in his back foot.

With a pocketknife the soldier was ripping into the back of the saddle, splitting all its seams. He cut into the seat from underneath and ripped the small blanket in half. At the same time the two other soldiers tore the lining from de Witte's jacket, stripped off his boots, undid his pants.

Miranda wondered if the last time de Witte had grabbed her, wrestled with her, it was because he knew the noise of the gunshot would draw these men. He wanted them to think she was his enemy. Maybe the robbery, all of it was just his playacting—was it possible? So Lubomyr wouldn't search her. So he would let her go.

The soldier beside Miranda was talking again. Lubomyr raised his hand. "Where was she running?" he commanded, nodding at the girl.

"She was afraid."

The man frowned. "She was leading two horses and Telemonian Ajax. Ah, of course—she is a Gypsy! That explains it! You should be careful with your friends."

He strode over to where she stood and spoke to her for a few minutes. Miranda couldn't hear what they were saying. She watched the two men search under de Witte's clothes, while he lay unresponsive. She watched them rip the heels off his boots.

Then the man with the moustache was at her side again. "She says she lost her father. Is that true?"

"Yes."

He clicked his teeth, then shook his head. "So you give me your word— Miranda," he said. "I do not allow my men to touch the women, and I will not allow them to touch you." He stared at her for a long time.

"I myself do not believe," he went on. "And if so, why give it to a girl from Mamaia Sat? He is a dangerous man. Anything he told you is a lie."

Sulky and defiant, Miranda shook her head. One of the soldiers spoke in German.

"He says maybe you took it," said the moustached man. "This was why you were fighting. But why take something of no value when you leave his money?" He held up the leather pouch from de Witte's belt.

"We can ask him," he continued. And as if listening to him, the soldier who had bandaged de Witte's shoulder now splashed water in his face and pulled open his eyes. He struggled, but they held him down. Now, weakly, he started talking in Roumanian, words Miranda didn't recognize, though she assumed they were obscenities when she saw Lubomyr smile.

"No," he said. "This is as you told us." He nodded at Ludu Rat-tooth. "You, she, he all say the same."

Then in a moment he continued. "I am sorry for this. And we must take your strawberry pony to carry this man. In return I will give you the black horse—keep him." He raised his hand when the soldier beside him started to speak. "He belongs to Captain Richter, who sits like a sack of apples. Now this man has ridden him to death—he was a valuable horse. But you'll get a few drachmae—here," he said. "Money means nothing to us. We do not rob or harm you, though if your soldiers were in Germany I would not say as much for them. You understand this—tell your friends. Maybe one day I will come see you in Carcaliu."

He threw the leather pouch into the grass.

11   *Irony and Luck*

TWO DAYS AFTER HIS arrest, Peter received a message. He stood in the courtyard of the Eski Seray in Adrianopole—a huge, square, crumbling structure, a fortress in the old Roumanian wars, and mostly ruined in the bombardment that had preceded the Peace of Havsa.

Portions of three stories had fallen in. Peter sat against a rock in the hot sun. The fortress was now used for prisoners awaiting questioning. Conditions were not good. Peter had no money. There was nothing to eat.

But now the guard brought him a hunk of bread and a bowl of cold soup, and as he ate, he found a scrap of paper in his mouth. He spat it out into his palm and then unfolded it. In Andromeda's slashing and elaborate handwriting, it read: *Upper West Window Before Dawn.*

Not very precise. But there was a window that was higher than the rest among the ruined galleries on the west side of the building. A little after midnight Peter climbed the choked stairs. The window was barred with an iron grille set into a deep embrasure. In the darkness he climbed into the dusty space. Balanced on the narrow, sloping shelf, he did not sleep.

He put his arm through one of the rusted squares and held himself against the grille. All was in darkness inside the fort. Rats, lizards, and men crept among the rubble. Outside there was a little light, though the moon itself was not visible. Peter looked down to the wire fence, and after many hours he saw the dog come out of the small wood and dig a hole under it. Then he saw her cross the bare ground to the bottom of the wall a hundred feet beneath. A tree of ivy grew there.

Peter wondered if it was possible for Andromeda to climb so high. But in time he heard a rattling, and near his window the leaves trembled. Then there was a movement, a shadow clinging to the larger trunk that grew against the wall.

"Are you there?" she whispered. Peter could see her fingers on the window ledge. Then she jumped and he leaned back suddenly, almost tumbling out of the embrasure. The ledge was narrow on her side and she clung to the bars. She squatted on the ledge with her knees splayed. With both hands she had grabbed hold of the grille in front of his face. All was in darkness. She was naked, Peter knew.

"I've got something for you," she mumbled, because her mouth was full. She had hidden something in her mouth, and now she was spitting it out. Something was hanging down her naked chest. He hesitated, then reached his left hand through the bars. He felt her mouth on his palm, felt her disgorging something from her throat. Then he drew back a greasy package: coins wrapped in sausage casing. Then there was a tiny, slippery bottle—the size they use on airlines—covered in the same substance, and finally a slab of meat, slightly chewed. "It's not as disgusting as it seems," Andromeda whispered. "Trust me." Her voice was clearer now.

Peter said nothing. Wedging the crook of his right arm into the grille, he began to eat with his left hand. He couldn't help himself, he was so hungry.

He was close to her. Her face was close against his face, separated only by the rusted bars. He heard her long, low, whistle in his ear. "Boy," she said. "You're all banged up."

It was true. Peter's face was scabbed and puffy.

"People don't have anything good to say about this place," Andromeda whispered. "Don't eat too fast—you'll choke. There, that's the good stuff," she went on, as he uncorked the tear-shaped bottle with his teeth. "Twenty years old. Finest of the fine."

He couldn't answer her. There was no reason to describe how he'd had to fight for the watery tepid soup that was his breakfast. And it hadn't been a fair fight. Eyes wet, he shook his head. Trying to chew, drinking little burning sips, he pulled himself closer to the bars where she clung like a monkey. He pressed his cheek against the rusted iron near her hand, and examined her long, dirty fingers. Then they were gone; she had jumped back, settled back out of sight, and the leaves and branches shook and rattled. He was afraid she would leave him. Then he saw a glow and smelled her cigarette.

Over the months he'd gotten used to her physical peculiarities. But at that moment she appeared to him like a magical being, a kind of angel, almost. How could she have carried all that stuff up in her mouth and throat—and then a cigarette and matches, too! Had there been some pouch around her neck he hadn't seen? Or did she have powers that could help him? He couldn't speak. He sat watching the orange glow, which came and went. Then he heard Andromeda's voice. "It's not so bad."

It was as if these words gave him a kind of permission. The tears were on his cheeks. His mouth was full, and he tried to keep himself from making any noise. He was afraid someone might come and try to take away his scrap of meat, his little brandy bottle, his eleven silver piastres. He didn't want to fight, although he knew he would. He'd kill someone before he let them take these things away.

There was too much meat in his mouth and now he coughed some of it out; he couldn't help it. He thought he'd never been so miserable. All night before Andromeda had come, he had been murmuring poetry to himself. But then he'd thought about his mother in the hospital and when she came home to die. His father was a nurse's aide, and he knew what to do with medications and to keep her comfortable. But one night he'd fallen asleep on the cot in the guest bedroom where she was staying.

Some of these poems he had not spoken since then, since he had sat beside the bed during the late night. His father lay asleep with his mouth open, and Peter was not sure whether his mother could even hear him or even understand him. Too late he regretted learning so many long poems about wars and fighting—"The Congo," "The Revenge," and so few of the sixteenth- and seventeenth-century English love poems that were her favorites. They flee from me that sometime did me seek.

Intent on his misery and his remembered misery, at first Peter didn't notice that Andromeda had started talking. Even after he began to listen, it took him several moments to begin to understand the words, whispered at the limit of his hearing. ". . . But you must understand the knowledge is in you someplace in your heart. So you must trust me when I tell you that these things are true. And you must let me tell you about the Chevalier de Graz, how he won the Star of Hercules at Nova Zagora, not by going back to burn the bridge. But when the Ninth Hussars were broken in the woods, and the Jews chased us all day through the rain until we crossed the river—fifty men were drowned and a hundred horses. I tell you when the prince came riding through the camp looking for you, then I was glad. My friend Dionysus Lopatari was shot through the jaw, and that night I hated you. When we were out with the pickets I saw you climb out of the mud. And you had a calf clasped in your arms, a little Bulgar calf you'd rescued from somewhere. I saw the prince's face, and I tell you I cursed God. You were an arrogant fool, eighteen years old, and the next year you were a captain in the guard—what was their motto? 'Loyalty and Iron'? How we would laugh at you and your parades! I had a drinking club in Floreasca."

Peter watched the end of the cigarette glow bright and then subside. Then the voice came, low and rough. "My friend, it's loyalty and iron after all. When the prince was dying and he called us in, and he asked us to fight for Clara Brancoveanu and her unborn child, I knew he was thinking about that morning when he watched you drag that calf out of the mud. It was wounded in the eye, and we could hear it bleating from half a kilometer. There was a broken rail fence and you clambered over. What the prince was thinking in my case, I have no idea. I had no desire to babysit that little snot-faced girl for those years in Mamaia. That little lump-cat with her horses and her schoolgirl crush. But when we failed with Princess Clara, we could not fail with her."

How had she brought the cigarette up dry? Peter asked himself. He was watching the orange glow. Still he said nothing.

"But this is what I wanted to tell you," continued Andromeda. Her voice seemed to speak to him out of the past: "When I saw de Graz drag himself out of the mud, and he was wounded in the head after that stupid defeat, and he was lifting the calf up, and I could see into his eyes, and he was glad of it. Wet with joy. Not just glad to be alive, but happy in that place. All night I had nursed Dionysus Lopatari and damned God and wept for home."

Peter watched the end of Andromeda's cigarette. He didn't speak for a long time. "Last night I was dreaming about home," he said at last. "Then when I woke up, I was thinking about my dad, what he's doing now. And I was thinking about the ice house, and Christmas Hill."

He watched the glow of the cigarette. "I don't expect you to understand," said Andromeda. "You're just a weak American boy in part of you. It's your choice to live with dreams, but the man I knew," she said, "would have been happy here. In two days the guards would have been begging him to let them keep some of their pay for the sake of their wives and children. Let me tell you one more story: You think I've been lazy. Drinking and gambling—I tell you it wasn't time. We came early to Aegypt through that spider hole. We were following Miranda Popescu, but we must have passed her on the way—that girl was not in Great Roumania. Not yet. What was there to talk about?

"Now, I think the world has changed. Last night I saw the prince's sister in a dream—Mother Egypt as the Gypsies called her. She showed me Mamaia Castle all abandoned. She showed me Miranda Popescu on a black gelding. She told me another game had started—listen to me! I tell you this because you have to know it is important to get free. Loyalty and iron, my friend. Do you remember after the prince's death, and Clara Brancoveanu was locked in Ratisbon, and Antonescu sent his men to clean out Mamaia once for all, and put down the traitor's sister as he called her, and the traitor's child? We brought the people from the village to block the way, and kept them twisting for six days while old Aegypta got the order reversed—just us and our fists and my stupid arguments, while the nurse kept the baby in her arms—not one man was killed. Remember that. Tomorrow night I'll come again."

Below the window, the sentry was crossing the perimeter. He disappeared around the edge of the building. Then there was a rattle in the branches of the ivy tree. Andromeda was gone.

But she would come again at nighttime. The day seemed to stretch out like a desert until then; already in the east the sky was turning pale. But Andromeda would come and tell him stories that were not exactly comforting.

These were the stories men told each other before battle, Peter thought. No comfort, but loyalty and iron. Maybe he'd have something to tell Andromeda. One thing he promised himself: He would not let them take his soup away.

Leaning into the embrasure, his cheek against the bars, he looked away north where the clouds were bruised and dark. Unlike Andromeda, he'd had no dream, no vision of the future or the past. He scarcely knew which way to look.

NOR, PERHAPS, WOULD HE HAVE recognized her at first if he had seen her, a short-haired woman on a black horse, two hundred and fifty miles north-northeast, cantering uphill into the town of Braila as the sun rose.

This is what had happened. The horse was not lame. But Ludu Rat-tooth had wedged a stone into his hoof and picked it out when the Germans were gone.

All that day and the next morning, she and Miranda had argued and rested in the forest clearing. At the same time she taught Miranda how to care for the animals. Together they had combed the gelding's tail and mane and rubbed his body down, while he drank from the pond and rolled in the sweet grass. "Why should they give us this, and money, to do what? We don't know these people. They owe us nothing."

"Please be quiet. The money was my own."

"Then wait for the oracle to tell you. Mother Egypt will tell you. . . ."

"Yes, I know. But there's no time to waste. Ten days, he said. I must go now if I'm to be in time. Then we can go to Insula Calia. And for once I'll tell her what I've done already."

Still she found a little time to waste. Sitting against the stone wall of the hermitage, Miranda had broken open the leather diary she'd taken from Mamaia Castle. It was written in French in a careful, childish hand. One of the last entries was this:

Saturday, 18 Thermidor. Captain de Graz took me to Murtfatlar to show the little Turkish mare my aunt has given me. I do not like Captain de Graz or any man who talks about my father. But the mare is a sorrel roan of fifteen hands very flexible and light in the bridle—small head long neck—I shall enjoy taking her over the big stile! I shall call her Daisy or perhaps not. My aunt says I shall take her when I go away to school. Until then she will be stabled in the village and I'll go every day. . . .

Miranda's French was good, due to the efforts of Mr. Donati when she was in seventh and eighth grade. Sitting in the grass, she puzzled over these small, serious, entries:

Wednesday, 6 Brumaire. It is hard for me to write this, because the lieutenant was cruel to me today. I think he must have no idea how I feel. He took me riding as he promised, but all day he was pressing forward until poor Aramis was out of breath and I had to stop—it's been so hot for so late in the year. He led me over the hedgerows as if to prove I couldn't follow. So I put the spur to Aramis, though he really is too small. It didn't matter. He got over, and I'll make it up to him. But the lieutenant was gone and I couldn't even catch him on the way home. Later I told Juliana and she laughed at me. She told me Lt. Prochenko has a woman in the village, it is a scandal she says. That must have been where he was and left me to ride home. I know I am young, too young. But I'll be eight years old this spring and I can grow up fast without a father and a mother. Anyway it's only sixteen years difference, which will not seem like anything when I am his age. I used the whip on Aramis all the way home. But he went lame and pulled away from me, and then I had to get help from some farmer. My aunt was furious and took my books away because of my cruelty. She did not understand. But she understands I hate her, because I told her. . . .

Miranda rubbed her nose. It embarrassed her to overhear the feelings of this young girl. "Last night I wet my bed again. . . ." Miranda would have liked to think that if she'd ever kept a diary in Massachusetts, she would not have filled it with such stuff. She felt like a snoop to read about it. More than that, she felt a residue of shame—what a brat she'd been! What a selfish and precocious brat! Though maybe diaries didn't always show you at your best.

Still, it made you think there was a reason you forgot most of your childhood. You might be too ashamed to go on. But people could change, luckily, and there were things to be learned here: stories about her aunt, and things her aunt had said about her mother, held prisoner in Ratisbon. One winter, twenty-seven porpoises had beached themselves and died.

Most of all she read about horses. Obviously she'd been obsessed with horses, feeding them, caring for them, naming them, analyzing their habits, and of course riding them. Just this one fact gave her confidence. Besides, the big gelding proved easier to manage than either the pony or the gray. In the morning she combed him and rubbed him. Ludu showed her, but she knew already.

Because the Germans had taken his saddle, she first climbed onto him bareback. She didn't touch the reins. He was gentle, and she found she didn't have to turn her body to turn him. It was enough to turn her head.

Ludu Rat-tooth was astonished as she went around the clearing. She doubled back, then made a figure-eight, and then another. On the fifteenth time around, bored already, she had come to a decision. "If you won't go with me," she said, "will you wait?"

Subdued, Ludu began packing their things. Miranda sat on the horse for a few minutes, and then slipped down to help her.

The wood where they'd slept was in the high ground between the Danube and the coast as the river flowed north into the delta. At noon they came out of the trees above the village of Dorobantu. They'd gone slowly, for Miranda was riding bareback and the girl was leading the pony. They'd seen no one on the road, and the rutted streets of the town were also deserted. The girl found some women sulking in the narrow houses, who nevertheless were eager to sell them bread and fish paste and raspberry syrup in thick glass bottles. The horses drank at the well, while Ludu negotiated for a saddle.

They spent the night in Macin, and in the morning Miranda caught the ferry before dawn. Ludu Rat-tooth was inconsolable as they stood upon the dock. "You will not leave me here?" she cried. "Last night I saw my father. He was in the branches of the death tree and the blood was on his face."

"I promise I won't leave you. I'll see you in an hour."

Why had she come? Why had she chosen this detour? First, it was because every choice now seemed like a detour, and she was searching in the past for a pattern that made sense. And she was grasping at the story she had first heard from her mother's letter—how when she was just a few days old, she had smuggled out the plans for an invasion near the town of Kaposvar. Her aunt had hidden them in her diaper. What condition were they in when General Antonescu unfolded them upon his table?

Second, she had a mental picture of Anna Djourek, the Russian attachée. She imagined a yellow-haired, dark-eyed girl, dressed in an embroidered smock in Oberammergau, which in her mind was not a town at all, but a pasture full of wildflowers, and Anna Djourek appeared in the middle of it like Julie Andrews in *The Sound of Music*—no, that was not it. That was an illusion, conjured out of nothing and maintained over another picture to cover it.

Miranda had shot a man. The moment it had happened, she had scarcely paused to notice, because of all the chaos of that day. But in the night she lay awake and thought about it, how the man had flailed his arms and staggered backward and collapsed, how he had dropped his gun and fallen. His knees had given way. He had lain flat on his back with a small, dry, singed, neat hole through his shoulder. Later, the hole had filled with blood.

And perhaps that shot had killed him. What had he said, that he would rather die than be brought back and tortured in Berlin or Bucharest? Maybe that was happening to him now. Miranda could not think of that.

"You won't leave me?" said Ludu Rat-tooth.

Miranda had woken with a headache. And she felt no better when she stepped aboard the boat. The ferry had a small, uncertain, internal-combustion motor, which gave out clouds of greasy smoke and a sound like the firing of a gun. Packed in with people and animals, Miranda saw nothing of the trip across the water—the sky was still dark. In any case, alone among Roumanians, she was too nervous to pay attention to her surroundings. She was afraid of being recognized, even though she'd taken off her bracelet and put it in her pocket. Still, she kept her head down; it was not until she'd reached the other side, and coaxed the black horse up the ramp onto the dock, and swung herself into the new, high saddle, that she looked properly around. Ludu had told her the way. She took the river road into Braila, which was scarcely more than a village at that time, and one of the prettiest places in all Roumania.

Built near the confluence of several rivers, it stood over a great system of marshland. Flights of water birds passed overhead. On Miranda's right hand stood a line of shooting lodges—tin-roofed, gaily painted, so she now leaned back and slapped her horse upon his croup—not that he needed urging. Raising his head, he pounded up the slope into the village.

There Miranda had to pull him back, because of the chickens pecking in the dirt. The road was lined on either side with wooden duckboards. Well-dressed men and women promenaded. Braila was the headquarters of the Black Sea Fleet, and there were many naval officers. The women wore long dresses and carried parasols. Up ahead was a bronze statue of the naked Venus rising from the shell. Bronze dolphins played.

In this quaint border town, delegates had gathered to resolve a trade dispute. For most of the past month, Crimean fishing boats and gunships had blocked the entrance to the Danube, in violation of the Treaty of Alibej. The Roumanian government had been slow to respond. The German maritime commissioner had asked for caution.

Zelea Codreanu was there for the Roumanians. Miranda saw him take the air in front of the town offices, surrounded by his secretaries. The street was crowded now with horses and carriages. Miranda turned her head as she walked the horse past. There was no reason, she hoped, for him to recognize her in the daylight. He himself looked heavier, more solid as he peered over the tops of his half-moon spectacles at a small man in uniform. He wore a silk top hat. He carried a sheaf of papers under his arm.

She did not see him turn around to stare at her retreating back.

Miranda walked her horse through the jostling traffic. She didn't know what she was looking for. But up ahead she saw a narrow wooden house set back from the road. A flag hung breathless from the roof of the porch, a double-headed eagle, which was also stamped on Miranda's gold coins.

What was she to do with the horse? In Western movies, in front of the saloon there was always a wooden rail. Or there had been a courtyard to the hotel at Macin, and Ludu had arranged everything with a couple of barefoot grooms. Here on one side of the house was a cobblestone alley where the horse didn't want to go. Instead Miranda slid out of the saddle and led him through the wrought-iron gate into the garden, and left him to eat the tallest flowers. She'd only be a few minutes, she thought.

She had with her Alexei de Witte's insignium. He'd pressed it into her hand. It was a simple agate brooch, set in a ring of carved silver. As she came onto the porch, she slipped it from her pocket and gave it to the woman at the desk inside the front door. She asked for Anna Djourek, and then waited as the secretary disappeared into the back of the house.

After a few minutes a woman came down the staircase. Dressed in a blue gown, she was holding the brooch in her palm. Her hair and skin were dark. Miranda was surprised to see she was quite fat.

She blinked as she approached, as if she'd come out of a closet into the bright light of the hall. Her eyes were slightly crossed. "S'il vous plait?" she asked.

"I have a letter from a friend of yours," Miranda said in English, while the woman blinked at her. She seemed baffled, so Miranda repeated herself in French.

"Ah, a friend?"

"Yes. He wants to say he's safe. Please, is there a place for us to speak?" Miranda turned her shoulder to the secretary, who had reappeared now at her desk by the door. She was staring out the window at the horse in the garden.

Miranda held the letter out, but the woman in the blue gown did not take it. "Please?" she said again.

Miranda gave the three pages of typescript a suggestive waggle. "Alexei de Witte gave me that brooch. He said you'd . . ."

Anna Djourek interrupted. "Ah, I do not know this name."

Again Miranda made a gesture with the letter. "Please, he said it would all be clear if you would read this. He said it was a message for your government. . . ."

"My government?"

Miranda clenched her teeth. She had not anticipated that the woman would be an idiot. "Follow me," she said, and walked into the house toward the staircase, away from the secretary by the door.

"Please, you cannot go there," said Mlle. Djourek.

Miranda turned back. "He gave me that brooch and said you'd recognize it. He gave me this letter, which is a message for your government. I know you will find it interesting."

Now, finally, the woman took the three typescript pages and held them up.

"It is in German?" she asked. "I do not have my glasses." She peered briefly at the embossed seal of the German Republic, and read a few words before looking up. " 'Streng Geheim . . .' What is this, please?"

Miranda came close to her. "It is the order of march for the Third Army Corps," she murmured. "They will cross the Russian border at the Cosmesti Bridge."

Anna Djourek smiled at her and wrinkled her nose, as if these words meant nothing. In fact they meant little enough to Miranda, who was losing patience. She was here for the sake of the man she had shot. "Alexei de Witte," she said. "He told me to tell you you were in a blue embroidered dress in Oberammergau, when you came from the university. . . ." And there was Julie Andrews in her mind.

But in Braila, in the house of the Russian delegation, Anna Djourek screwed up her face. She raised her hand and pushed Miranda in the chest, pushed her away so that she staggered back against the wall, which was covered in green-and-white flowered paper. "Quel salaud—what a disgusting pig!"

The brooch was in her hand, and now she threw it down. "And you also. Who are you to know these things? Who are you—his lover, eh? What is your name?"

She raised the typescript pages to a few inches from her nose, glared at them for a few seconds, and then crushed them into a ball. "What are you telling me? He is disgusting, I tell you—what do you know of these ridiculous accusations? The Cosmesti bridge? It is absurd. In any case I have no military function. Oh, who are you, who are you? Oberammergau, how can you say this word? What does it mean to you? Irina"—this to the secretary at the desk—"you summon the police."

But the police were already on their way. Codreanu had dispatched them.

THAT SAME MORNING, IN GERMANY, the Elector of Ratisbon received a message. He sat in his apartment at the top of his house. His delicate, small hand followed an ancient crack in the surface of his table. Over the centuries the grain had receded into the wood, leaving a marbled and uneven texture that gave him pleasure.

On the table was a square of mirrored glass. Now as he watched, slow, printed letters appeared on its smooth face, one after another. Impatient, he looked away, forcing himself to examine an arrangement of columbine and wheat stalks in a heavy, stoneware vase. He counted to five hundred. Then he looked back.

MY FRIEND I LOOKED WHERE YOU TOLD ME AND I FOUND HER NOT FAR AWAY. SHE EVEN SAID HER NAME. I GAVE HER A HORSE AND SENT HER ON HER WAY BUT YOU WILL NOT BE DISAPPOINTED. IN THIS WORLD THERE IS IRONIC COIN-CIDENCE AND LUCK. YOU WILL BE VINDICATED I THINK. SHE WAS THERE WHEN POOR OLD ALEXEI DE WITTE REACHED THE END OF HIS RACE. BUT I THINK HE DID NOT FUMBLE THE BATON.

After a few moments the letters faded and the surface of the looking glass was clear. The elector sat staring at the image of his face, where the words had been.

There was a time when he had avoided the sight of it, had lived in a world without reflection. Managers of the great European hotels, when he had booked a suite of rooms, had had the looking glass removed even in the bath. But he had not been abroad in many years. Nor had he attended many of the social and political gatherings where once he'd been ubiquitous.

When he had last come out of Roumania, he had been brought before a court of inquiry, accused of conjuring and prestidigitation. But because his father had been a high-ranking diplomat, and because he was related through his mother to an influential French family, the legal process had not gone further. His passport had been revoked and he'd returned home.

Since then he'd scarcely left the confines of his house. As a matter of patri-otism and convenience, with all his strength he'd tried to break himself of dangerous mental habits. He had pursued a new physical regimen and a course of study in literature, philosophy, and art. But because he spent so much time alone—his parents were dead, and he had no wife or children—all mental paths inexorably led back to the source of his disgrace: the hidden world, which after all exists, although his government had tried to subjugate all knowledge of it as a matter of national will.

They were fools. They left themselves vulnerable and unguarded. The democratic traditions of the country, though they had led to prosperity and strength, also had this disadvantage: the suppression of superior men such as himself, who had been maimed and rendered worthless in the public eye. Yet surely there was still a way for an intelligent and modern man, a citizen of the future, so to say, unencumbered by vain social and religious constraints, to offer service to his country.

He sat staring at himself in the mirrored glass. The childhood disease that had broken his face into chaotic lumps and splotches—it was not the enemy. Often now through hours of staring he had come almost to love himself, love the way he looked. Sometimes the entire house of his ancestors, vast as it was, was still not big enough to contain his love.

BY THE CLOCK ON HIS wall it was almost noon. But in her private suite of rooms, Clara Brancoveanu was enjoying a late supper. All day the princess, as she sometimes did, had fasted, taking nourishment from lemon water and the appetite of her young friend. Now she was eating crackers, while he finished a salad of asparagus spears.

He stopped and wiped his mouth. Distressed by something in her face, he cocked his head to the side. He smiled, then frowned, then tried to amuse her with a series of absurd expressions until she burst into tears. Then, "Oh my mother," he said. He came around the table to her side and went down on his knees before her chair. He pressed his cheek against her hands.

Light came from tall, yellow candles. It flickered on the crystal and the intricate silk tablecloth. The princess tried to smile. "I am a foolish woman, Felix. Don't mind me—the fancies of a foolish woman. I'm afraid I will not leave this place."

Her hair, coiled in soft braids, was gray. Her face was soft and wrinkled. "I think I've been a prisoner for half my life. At first it didn't matter after the prince was dead. And when Aegypta took the baby, where would I go? Only she was brave enough to stay at home. Always I'd expect this man to let me live someplace in Paris or in Alexandria—it didn't matter. Now I think he must have lost his mind. What purpose does this serve after these years? Or maybe he has died and they've forgotten us."

The boy looked up at her. "Mother, will you give me my piano lesson tonight?" Then in a moment, "Did you have any children besides me?"

She tried to smile. "Haven't you been listening? She was living in Mamaia with my sister. She'd be a woman now if she were still alive. Where is she lost in the wide world? I saw her only once when she was one day old. Aegypta said it would hurt less, but she was wrong. We smuggled the paper in her nappy!

Oh, how we tweaked him by the nose! In all my life it was one thing to be proud of—haven't you heard this story? Haven't I told you this?"

"No, mother." Felix pressed his cheek against her hands.

"Now I wake up and I cannot breathe. Buried alive, that's what I am. And I think I'd give up everything if I could find my way to Great Roumania again. If I could see the lake at Mogosoaia or smell the salt air. My family had a hunting lodge outside Braila—oh, it was beautiful in the old days. And then of course the house in Kronstadt—Brasov—in the mountains. That's where I saw my husband for the first time, when he had come back from the military college in Berlin."

After a moment Felix squeezed her hands. "Mother, will you give me my lesson now?"

Princess Clara smiled. Pulling away, she dried her eyes with her thin knuckles. "Yes, I'd like that—never mind about me. Aegypta said I'd have to be the bravest, but it's never felt so brave to me. Just that I am dying, and I'm afraid I will die here. You won't let that happen, will you, child?"

THAT DAY THERE WERE OTHERS who were thinking of Roumania, if only as an image of freedom or a place far away. They coveted the sights and smells and sounds. In Adrianopole in the courtyard of the Eski Seray, Peter Gross backed slowly from a big man who was dangling a chain. Across town, not far away, in a restaurant with covered windows, Andromeda sat back against the wall. Sick to her stomach, she examined the dealer's jeweled hands as he laid a line of cards upon a green baize surface. Her pale eyes were closed to slits.

But in Roumania itself, there were some who wanted to be elsewhere. In a room at Third Army headquarters in Dobric, Lieutenant-Major Arslan Lubomyr, dressed in the dark blue uniform of the German general staff, stood holding a square of mirrored glass. By this means he had sent his message to the elector, but now the words had faded. The reflection showed his thin, ascetic, Tartar features; he put his hand over the glass as if to block them out. Then he raised his eyes to the map on the wall, where the Cosmesti bridge north of Focsani was circled in red ink. From there his gaze slid up the Russian border a thousand kilometers to the town of Sestokai in Lithuania. That crossing was also marked in red.

12 *Insula Calia*

IN ADRIANOPOLE, IN THE justice house on Sarayici Island, Peter stood in a line of prisoners. His hands were tied behind him. Men shuffled forward one at a time to stand before the cadis, the judges in their cubicles at the front of the high room. Peter thought briefly of the line in the airport terminal, once when he'd flown with his father from Albany to Raleigh-Durham.

At the front of the line he had to wait. In front of him three wooden cubicles protruded into the hall—the offices of the three judges who decided these cases. Around the perimeter, next to the open doors and glassless windows on the north and west sides of the hall, stood old men in brown uniforms. They wore bandoliers of cartridges and carried old-fashioned muskets. Veterans of Roumanian wars, Peter imagined. Maybe a generation ago they had fought against the Chevalier de Graz. Peter found himself staring at one, a thick-jowled man with a gray crew-cut and a bristling gray moustache. He had a belly, and between the stretching buttons of his tunic Peter could see patches of his undershirt.

It was a sweltering morning. Drops of sweat ran down Peter's sides. Before dawn he had been brought here with a dozen others in a covered, horse-drawn cart. He had been happy to leave the prison, and that happiness had lasted to the front of the line.

In the days of his imprisonment, no one yet had told him of the charge against him. Always he had reassured himself it must be something minor—stealing a chicken, improper documents. Or they'd question him about Andromeda. Already he had had his punishment. No sane judge could disagree.

So he was optimistic as he waited, and it was only as he approached the front of the line that he began to worry. Who knew what was going to happen, after all? In his mind, to soak up nervousness, he had been going over a long poem he had learned when he was young. But he couldn't quite remember the final verse. A thought occurred to him—was he the only person in this world who knew this poem? And was the end of it now gone for good? And if he fudged the ending, and wrote down the poem, and tried to sell it as his own, would he make enough money to cross the border to Roumania? If so, why stop at Tennyson? He could do Shakespeare, e. e. cummings, Yeats.

The guard beckoned. Squaring his shoulders, Peter crossed to the middle of the three rooms. Under his breath he was reciting:

Half their ships to the right and half to the left were seen,
And the little Revenge ran on down the long sea lane in between.

His hands were tied behind him with three strands of chafing twine. Peter imagined he could break them or twist his wrists so that they fell away. He stood now at the door to the cubicle and looked in.

Thousands of their sailors looked down from their decks and laughed,
Thousands of their soldiers made mock at the mad little craft,
Running on and on till delayed,
By the mountain-like San Philip of fifteen-hundred tons,
Up towering above us with her yawning tiers of guns . . .

There was a big man sitting at a large carved wooden desk. The room was lined with bookcases and leather-bound books. In one corner on a table stood a statue of Moses carrying the tablets of the law.

The big man looked up. He had enormous, powerful, sloping shoulders, on which his bald round head seemed to perch without the disadvantage of a neck. He wore thick, wire-rimmed spectacles that made his eyes seem huge. In spite of this, and in spite of his fatness, he gave an impression of energy and power. He leaned forward in his chair, his pencil like a toothpick in his huge fist. There were no books or files on his desk, but just a folded newspaper on the blotter, held down by a brass paperweight. A small current of air disturbed the pages. Peter looked up and saw a fan, previously unnoticed, hanging from the faraway vault. It turned slowly, whether by hand or by machine, Peter couldn't guess.

The cadi stared at him for a long time. "Why is it that I recognize your face?" he said finally, in English. "Do you know me? I am Aristophanes Turkkan."

"No, sir."

"I could swear," murmured the cadi, and he stood up so suddenly his chair almost fell over backward. He came out from behind his desk to peer into Peter's face. He had big arms and a big chest.

"Peter Gross—you are Roumanian, no?"

The cadi was dressed in a loose red jacket and military pants, brown with a red stripe. A red tarbush stood upon a stool in the corner. "I was just reading what has happened in your country. Now you come back with a face out of my dreams—where is it? Here, look, let me read it—do you know my language?"

"No, sir."

"Yes—let me read it. It is from this morning, see!" He snatched up the newspaper and shook it open with one hand. "Now let me tell you what this says. It is a story from Braila on the coast—two days old already. No one cares about it here. No one cares about Roumania since our German friends are there. But that is a mistake. These people are not beaten yet, I tell you."

He kept his pencil in one hand, brandishing it like a tiny weapon. He shook out the paper and folded it back, creasing it against his chest while at the same time standing close to Peter, who could smell liquor on his breath.

The newsprint was so thin it was almost transparent. The paper was called *The English World Tribune,* and its pages were ornamented with black woodblock illustrations set slightly askew. On the top of every page was a portrait of a Roman orator in a toga.

For a long time since Miranda's disappearance and especially since his arrest, Peter had felt vacant and unoccupied except for small, scurrying presences: loneliness or worry, vermin in an empty room. Except when taken with the small tasks of survival he would sit by himself, clasping and unclasping his hands.

Waiting for what? For this newspaper article? Waile Bizunesh had mentioned a story in a newspaper or a magazine. Certainly as Peter stood listening, arms tied, he felt a door open and slam. He imagined himself grabbing hold of the newspaper and snatching it away. And if the cadi objected he would shake him till his teeth chattered.

"Let me see now—here it is. Here it is. Braila—you know that is headquarters of the fleet. 'A legend came to life in these past weeks, and now this picturesque little town is all abuzz.'—what does that mean? 'From the waterfront to the pagan statue in the square, people are talking about events that have left a policeman dead. Dressed in Gypsy clothes she rode her horse into the town, and went immediately to the house of the Russian consul, where she gave her name as Miranda Popescu. The office of the governor has issued this description that has spread throughout the province. Everyone is looking, whether to arrest her for murder or to crown her queen, for there are feelings on both sides. The Baroness Ceausescu has dispatched an investigator who arrived in Braila last night. . . .' I tell you it is all the same with these people. Always the same. It was like this in Kara Suliman's time, when Miranda Brancoveanu came out of the hills. God willing, they will find her. Look, there she is!"

The cadi pushed the folded newspaper in front of Peter's nose. He could see the illustration—the black hair and protruding ears, the straight nose and heavy eyebrows. The artist had made her more beautiful than she was, which irritated Peter. "Let me see," he said.

"No. There is nothing more of substance. Innuendoes and rumors—it is always violence with these people—"

"Please."

The cadi stared at him. Under his spectacles his big, distorted eyes were oddly penetrating. "It is not your place to give me orders. You will not give your orders to Aristophanes Turkkan. It is the same with you as well—I know your case. It is because you have no law to guide you. You pray to false gods and they give you violence—what are the details? You killed a man under the Kanuni bridge."

When Peter was arrested, the officers had spoken Turkish, which was no help. Until this present moment he'd assumed that they'd been looking for Andromeda. She was the one who'd robbed the market stalls, cheated at cards, raided the hencoops. He'd been prepared to answer the judge's questions, pay for the dead capon.

Now, excited by the newspaper story, his mind moved quickly—he was innocent. The man under the bridge was not dead—how could he have died? Peter had not harmed him. There'd been a struggle, and a gun had misfired, and everyone had run away. That's the way it was; Miranda also couldn't have killed anyone. She was also innocent, falsely charged.

All this time he had been testing the knots of twine behind his back. "Please let me see the paper," he said, but the judge held it up. Again he had come close, and there was sweet wine on his breath. He was a tall man, taller than Peter—"Who are you?" he murmured. "I have seen your face."

Then he continued in a different tone. "You're accused of shooting Jacob Golcuk to his death. I saw the report of seven witnesses who all agree. You tried to rob this man. So let me ask—are you a race of devils? They say it was this woman who shot this policeman in Braila. And do you know who her father was? The devil himself—General Frederick Schenck von Schenck."

Peter tried to pull his hands apart. "I'm not a thief," he said. "I was looking for my dog under the bridge."

"Your dog!" The judge was in high fury now. "And that makes it all good, to shoot a Turkish citizen in cold blood? 'Yes, certainly,' says Domnul Gross, if he was searching for his dog! But let me ask, where did you dispose your gun? We searched your room."

"I didn't have a gun. I tell you the man was still alive." Peter raised his head, shook his shoulders, and the judge stepped back. "It was his gun and he fired it."

For a moment the judge seemed disoriented. He stood against his desk, his eyes wide under his spectacles. Peter seized the time to tell his story of that night. When the men came to attack him he took hold of one of them—he had a leather coat with patches of rabbit fur. And when the watch had come the men had scattered, leaving their friend still groaning when Peter ran away.

He tried to tell this story as convincingly as possible, as if to a reasonable man. "Why would I attack eight men under a bridge in the middle of the night? Jacob Golcuk—was he rich?" But the cadi stared at him, shaking his head as if distracted, though he did not interrupt. Peter wondered if he was listening. Above their heads the fan turned slowly. Surely he could get his hands free from this stupid twine. What then?

But as the great San Philip hung above us like a cloud,
Whence the thunderbolt would fall, long and loud,
Four galleons drew away from the Spanish fleet that day . . .

"Tell me where I've seen you," murmured Aristophanes Turkkan. "Is it on the wrestling ground?"

Then he continued in a different voice. "You say you're not a thief, yet you share a room with a known pickpocket. You are here with forged papers, and this name Peter Gross is evidently false. It is true what you say about Golcuk, but I think maybe this is a disagreement between criminals, which does not excuse you. I have spoken to the governor of the Eski Seray, and he says you are fighting all the time these past two days over money and illegal contraband."

This was unfair. Tired of being beaten, he had tried to defend himself, that's all. He'd let Pieter de Graz out of his cage for a few minutes, that was all. With Andromeda's piastres he'd attracted a new class of tormentors.

Behind his back, now he yanked at the twine and felt it give. "I swear the man was breathing when I left. Isn't it more likely that these other men attacked him and then blamed me when the guard arrived—a penniless Roumanian? Show me the witnesses' reports. I have a right to see them—"

But the cadi shook his head. His eyes were huge. "It is not for you to bully Aristophanes Turkkan, as you bullied these poor prisoners in the Eski Seray. It is up to me to judge the credibility of these accounts, and I have done so. Penniless, you say. But in prison you've been drinking liquor and eating chocolates. As for your dog, where is your dog? No one has seen this dog—where is it now? What kind of dog is it?"

He had stood up again, approached Peter again. But now abruptly he turned away behind his desk. As he was sitting down, as he was pulling out a wooden drawer and rummaging through the papers, Peter found himself staring at a brass cup on the bookshelf behind him, carefully polished, and engraved with the outline of two struggling, naked men.

"You are barbarians," muttered Aristophanes Turkkan. "What do you know of justice? It is obvious we do our job here, and we decide both sides. 'Where is your dog?' I ask him and he says nothing. What can he say? He knows this case is finished, yet still he wants to argue."

The cadi lapsed into another language as he pulled out a slip of parchment filled with calligraphy and carrying an impressive wax seal. Still muttering, he pulled out a pen, a brush, a jar of ink. He was asking himself questions in Turkish. Peter didn't try to understand. He had an idea. The man had laid out his paint pot, and was beginning to sketch out an ornate signature. "For your official document," said Peter, "maybe you'd be interested in my real name."

The cadi looked up, goggling at him with his huge, blinking eyes.

"It's true I offered you an English version of my name. Perhaps you would be interested. . . ."

More goggling. Then, "No, no. This is sufficient. The place is already filled in."

The cadi bent once more over his signature. Peter noticed there was sweat on his bald head. It gathered in the V-shaped creases on his forehead.

"Pieter de Graz. The Chevalier de Graz."

The scratching of the pen nib on the parchment slowed and stopped. The cadi glanced at him and Peter imagined that he saw a look of fury cross his broad face, before it crinkled up and he began to laugh. This also was short-lived, and changed almost immediately into scowls. "De Graz! Another lunatic! And now I am an old man. Do not trouble to lie. De Graz died long ago."

After a moment he replaced his pen on the pink blotter. "The resemblance is true," he said. "What of it? If you are the son of such a father, you have shamed him."

He shouted out in Turkish and a guard looked in the door. It was the bristling man with the gray moustache, the double-barreled gun, and the white undershirt.

But anon the great San Philip, she bethought herself and went,
Having that within her womb that had left her ill content.
But the rest they came aboard us, and they fought us hand to hand. . . .

The words came unbidden into Peter's thoughts. Aristophanes Turkkan was still muttering as he folded up his papers. "Who should know this better than I do? The Chevalier de Graz had a birthmark on his hand. All the world knows—do you have a birthmark on your hand? Hah, I did not think so."

Peter yanked and twisted at the twine behind his back. He turned his wrists into the knot and the twine parted. The cadi kicked over his chair and came out from behind his desk. He was eager to fight. The guard raised his gun up by the barrel like a club, but Peter's hands were free. He reached out his right hand, and shoved it in the cadi's face so that he could not help but see the discolored birthmark in the shape of a bull's head, in the lap of muscle between his thumb and forefinger.

For a dozen times they came, with their pikes and musketeers,
And a dozen times we shook 'em off, as a dog that shakes his ears . . .

Other guards, other men now came into the open door. Peter felt a blow on the back of his neck, just at the moment when the cadi seized hold of his hand and bit him on the thumb.

IN ROUMANIA, IN THE MOUNTAINS north of Bucharest, the Baroness Ceausescu sat reading in her summer pavilion. She had come up from the city to escape from the hot weather in her favorite provincial residence, built by the former empress near the village of Vadu Oii. Above her rose the forested slopes of Penteleu, still with a cap of snow upon its crest.

The pavilion was a simple, rustic, wooden structure, which suited the white tyger's present tastes. The roof was thatched, the walls were unpainted cedar boards. On the three sides away from the sun, the glassless windows were un-shuttered, covered only with copper screens that let the breezes in.

The furniture was also simple: wooden couches and chairs, softened with embroidered pillows. The tyger perched diminutively in the corner of the largest armchair, her high-arched, naked feet curled up beneath her. Though in her previous life she had often affected men's clothing and military uniforms, now she only used them for purposes of disguise when she walked the streets at night. At home, at her leisure, she dressed in delicate and girlish clothes, made by expensive dressmakers in Paris and Berlin. Today especially, in a flimsy elegant frock of flowered silk, she shone like a jewel in a rough wooden box. And the simile was completed by the stone she held in her left hand, which as she read she rubbed and stroked over her long neck and uncovered shoulders. It was a large and perfect tourmaline, rough-cut in the rondelle style, gleaming as if it were itself a source of light. The purple color served to emphasize her violet eyes. She was reading a book of plays.

Annoyed now by a stupidity in the text, she knotted her dark brows. In her own opera she would avoid these mistakes. Raising her eyes, she looked out over the garden that led downhill toward the shore of a small artificial lake. Then she threw down the book. Leaving the jewel in her lap, she reached instead toward a bundle of dirty clothes on the table beside her, stiff black trousers and a woolen shirt. But she was interested especially in the underclothes, which she now held up and examined not for the first time. She plucked at the elastic and the acetate, then brought the whole mess up to her nose to sniff.

Jean-Baptiste came into the room without knocking and gave her a tired look. He stepped disdainfully over the wide planks of the floor as she threw down the clothes. He carried a brass teapot on a brass tray.

"Domnul Luckacz is here."

The baroness picked up the book again so she could snap it shut. She said nothing to the steward as he came and went, but smiled as Luckacz entered— "My dear friend. You'll like some tea?"

She didn't get up. She didn't move her right arm, languidly posed over the top of the chair. With her left hand she hid the jewel under the cushions and sat against it, comforted by its hardness in the small of her back.

Radu Luckacz came forward until he stood in the middle of the rug. As always, he tried to hide his awkwardness by immediate and officious talk. He stood in his drab suit, holding his hat and a brown envelope, and at first the baroness couldn't bring herself to listen, because she was examining his hair. Always before she had imagined his moustache to be grotesquely dyed, glossy black while his hair was gray. But now she noticed some new streaks of black over his ears. Though for her benefit, she was sure, they could only enhance his drab and crowlike appearance—these last few years had been hard on him. As his responsibilities had increased, he had become more frail and diminished.

And as she looked at him, the baroness felt herself suffused with tender feelings that impeded her from listening to what he said. So she turned away and reached for her glass of tea on the low table. Then his harsh, accented voice came clear.

". . . As you know, I was in Braila until two days ago. This was during the investigation of events to which I will return. But first of all I wanted to protest to you and tell you something that might serve to explain the extraordinary reaction of the rural population in that area. Everywhere our policemen and inquisitors have been met with noncooperation when they attempt to carry out their normal duties. The simplest questions are met with noncompliance. It is a poisonous atmosphere, and it is the commissioner of the region who is responsible—I am referring to Domnul Codreanu, whom I have not liked or trusted. In interview after interview I heard complaints about him, accusations of corruption and bloodthirstiness, most of which I was not able to believe. It is clear that people suffer from the lack of rainfall in that area. In my estimate they have received not more than twenty percent of the drought relief that we have solicited from Berlin. This is the result: Whole sections of the coast have been depopulated. And even if one tenth of what I learned is justified, still this man Codreanu is culpable of terrible crimes. The chief of the German water board—you know they are drilling for oil in that area—also made high-handed and arrogant complaints, and if the Germans make these accusations, as you know it is like wolves complaining about lions. I tell you these things because of your soft heart when ordinary people are suffering for no reason. Nevertheless, the chief of the water board made the most blatant allegation of sorcery, conjuring, and prestidigitation, none of which conflicts with what the others have said, though that area is full of superstition."

Radu Luckacz paused here to draw breath.

"What about the girl?" the baroness asked.

The policeman made an impatient and dismissive gesture with his hat, which he was holding by its crown. "I sent you the clothes that were discovered in the castle at Mamaia. Surely you'll agree that nothing like these fabrics has been seen before. She had an accomplice, a Gypsy in Macin. This man Codreanu has sworn to find her, which must not be allowed. He has no sense of the process of the law. Let me show you the photographs the Germans gave me. You will agree they are appalling."

Holding his hat crushed under his elbow, he pulled two photographic prints out of the envelope and held them out.

Both involved crowds and were full of blurred images. Both were shot in darkness by the light of a bonfire, so that many details were lost. But in both of them the vampire's face was clear.

"You see he has organized a private company of soldiers he calls the Legion of Aphrodite. He claims to be protecting the rights of all Roumanians, and to protect them from foreign influence. In this he is inspired by the policies of your late husband, which he has taken to criminal extremes. The baron never would have allowed this. You see he is speaking under the gallows. Two Gypsies and a Turk."

The white tyger turned the prints into the light so she could study the vampire's handsome, pale, insolent face. Oh, God—"This is the man? Zelea Codreanu—you are sure?"

Impatient, Radu Luckacz waggled his hat. "He is comissioner for the Dobruja district under your authority."

"My God, I had not seen his face."

When Luckacz raised his eyebrows, she protested. "The potato-eaters suggested the appointments there because the border is close by. They gave me a list of names."

"I tell you he's too much even for them. I was taken to a place outside the town of Babadag, where I was shown ten men in an unmarked grave—"

The baroness stood up. Leaving the tourmaline hidden in the pillows, she walked to the window overlooking the lake. "But this is terrible!"

"Ma'am, your compassion is well known."

Clasping her hands together, the baroness turned back into the room. "Oh, my friend, but this is terrible! You must tell me everything."

It was not compassion that had touched her. Though it was difficult to imagine the death of innocents, still, what could be expected from that man? Commissioner for the Dobruja—this was not her fault. She would not have permitted this if she had known. She would not have allowed such a challenge to herself.

In the photograph she'd recognized him. The vampire was a creature of darkness that must be imprisoned or destroyed, a sickness in the body of Great Roumania. Radu Luckacz was talking and she interrupted, proposing to dismiss the man immediately. She would write the letter as they spoke.

"Ma'am, I can tell you he would not obey. He would laugh at you just as he laughed at me. He told me he would be president in Bucharest one day. Democratically elected—that was the phrase he used. I cannot tell you his impudence—he said he would marry you. I must tell you he is like a president in that place, and with a private army."

Then would it be possible to send troops or soldiers? She made the suggestion to Luckacz but did not listen to his reply, which had to do with talking to the German ambassador—she would not talk to the German ambassador! She had no need to beg from the potato-eaters. All that would take time—a president in Bucharest! If the vampire were to be defeated, it would not be through normal means or channels.

The potato-eaters were the last people to understand this crisis. What did they know about vampires? What did Luckacz know? This was not a matter for talking or deciding, but for action. In these matters of public policy there was a straight way and a hidden way. Radu Luckacz was the master of the straight way. But he knew nothing of her skills and strategies.

Listening to the policeman, she ran her finger across the photograph of the vampire's face, his pouting lips. Her own husband had told her the story, had shown her an engraving from a hundred years before. Then the vampire had been some kind of count or grand duke, and after that a silversmith in

Brasov—how was it possible? Commissioner for the Dobruja district—how had she been taken unaware? She must return immediately to town or else to Brasov, better yet. Luckacz must not go with her.

These thoughts preoccupied her as she listened. Radu Luckacz was talking about the girl again, about whom he knew nothing. Miranda Popescu had disappeared into the marshland, and he was unable to predict where she had gone.

PERHAPS ANOTHER KIND OF investigator—less of an atheist, less of a free thinker—would have guessed the significance of the Insula Calia shrine near where the Brancoveanu family had kept a boathouse and a shooting blind. This was fewer than twenty kilometers south of Braila, where the police were asking questions.

And no doubt the baroness would have guessed, if she'd been able to think clearly now about the girl. If she had been able to remember her fears of half an hour previous, before she'd known about Zelea Codreanu—(No, it was intolerable! But she would defeat this monster! She would not rest. . . .)—if she'd been able to remember, she might have found a way of telling Luckacz what she knew, that Aegypta Schenck von Schenck had hunted ducks and snipe at Insula Calia in the marsh.

Mother Egypt had been laid to rest in Mogosoaia five years before. Her grave there was a place of pilgrimage. It was guarded and tended by the monkey-people she had done so much to protect, and who lived in a preserve nearby. At all times there were crowds of pilgrims at the raised mound near the Venus pool, dinning her dead ears with supplications. By contrast Insula Calia was a rude site, known only to a few. Aegypta Schenck had camped there every fall until the year of her disgrace. Duck-hunting had been her favorite sport.

On the first anniversary of her death, a fisherman had seen a fire burning in the reeds. Now among the small and vanishing community of Gypsies, the island was a place of healing. The ghost of Mother Egypt sometimes visited the place. Nor was she shy with her opinions.

This was where Dinu Fishbelly had come to pray for the return of the white tyger. The island was on a salt dome in the marsh, the Balta Brailei between the old and new stream of the Danube. It was a long, snakelike piece of ground. But on the north end of the island was a plug of rock salt and a mine that had been dug out many hundreds of years before. Stone steps led into a cavern where the oracle was kept.

A more astute investigator than Radu Luckacz—or one like the baroness, or, for that matter, like Domnul Codreanu, with access to the hidden world—might have predicted how the Gypsy girl would lead Miranda there to the oracle of Mother Egypt in the salt cave. A fisherman brought them in the afternoon, poling his flat-bottomed boat through the shifting beds of reeds.

That day Miranda was moody and upset. She sat without talking at the front of the boat. When they landed on the low, grass-covered island, she left Ludu Rat-tooth to do everything. She stood looking west over the broad stretch of the river.

Since the events at the Russian consulate, the Gypsy girl had become her faithful servant. Care and flattery that at other times would have made her feel uncomfortable, now Miranda welcomed in her current mood of doubt and self-doubt. While the girl gathered food and supplies out of the boat, she climbed into the trees above the ruins of some stone foundations. She sat down on a chunk of quarried stone.

Her hair was cut, and she was dressed in a peasant shirt, expensive riding pants and boots, bought with some of her Moldovan rubles. She sat sweating in the stubborn heat, her mind fixed upon nothing but the gold horizon. They had hours to wait. The ghost rarely came before dark.

There were shifting masses of dry reeds, gold and black as far as they could see. This year was different from most years because of the drought. Nevertheless, this north part of the island was still covered with a mass of vegetation. It was as if all plants and animals had managed to escape to the high ground here after a terrifying flood. In the space of a single acre grew a jungle, with vines and bushes reaching up to drag the treetops down. As she sat, Miranda listened to the buzz and flicker of insects and birds. The treetops were full of ospreys' nests. Trumpet-shaped flowers hung down from the vines, and the leaves were so green they were almost blue.

"He's gone," said Ludu, carrying up the baskets and the rugs. She was talking about the boatman. "He'll come tomorrow morning. He asked for your blessing so he could tell his children."

Miranda groaned. Everywhere she'd gone the past few days, men and women wanted to touch her, grasp her hand, finger her bracelet, stare into her eyes. They'd asked her to pray for rain—what for? Because she'd killed a man.

"Please, miss, we are uncovered here. Will you come on?" The girl had fallen back into the respectful tones of their first meeting, before her father's death. "Miss, come," she said, putting her head down and carrying all the baggage up the slope. There was a path hacked through the undergrowth, a tunnel through the leaves. Miranda followed her more slowly. Her legs were stiff.

The path came out on the lip of a small dell on the high point of the island. The view was eastward over the rivers of grass, the golden reeds. Above them rose some high, puffy clouds. Near where they stood some old cedar timbers had been pounded into the ground, now supporting a crown of wild grape vines. Underneath there was a place to sit and sleep, a square of sandy ground amid outcroppings of rock.

The shrine itself was at the bottom of the dell. Nothing grew where the salt came to the surface. Halfway down, a hole was cut into the slope. This entrance was surrounded by a dozen wooden crosses set at different angles; some leaned perilously, and some had fallen to the bottom of the dell where there was a garbage dump of crutches and broken glass.

Ludu laid out their blanket rolls. "We want to go down for a look before it gets too dark," she said. "So you'll see the place. We'll put the lantern there," she said, unwrapping an oil lamp with a glass chimney.

She laid out some of the food the villagers had given them and covered it in cheesecloth. A faint, astringent smell rose from the dell, growing stronger as they climbed among the rocks down toward the entrance to the mine.

The girl carried the lamp and lit it in the shelter of one of the crosses, though there was no wind. Miranda put her hand out to touch the wooden surface, still covered with bark. In Roumania this was also a symbol of King Jesus. What was the story Ludu had told her? The king had used this punishment on others. Maybe the devil himself had hung on such a cross.

They entered. They had to stoop. Their footsteps crunched over a bed of pebbles and the lamplight shone on the dirty walls. Almost immediately they came into a cavern, an uneven cube hacked out of the rock. The Gypsy put the lamp down on the gleaming floor.

"This is the place," she said. "Oh, can't you feel that it is ancient? People say Miranda Brancoveanu came here once when she was young, before she freed us from the Turks."

Was the white tyger always there before her? "I might have known," Miranda muttered in English.

"Miss?"

The walls were mottled black and white. Everywhere they showed the mark of hammers and adzes. "There is the throne," Ludu continued, indicating a rough stone seat that protruded in one block out of the floor and the far wall. "That's where I'll be when you will chain me up."

This was a nasty surprise, although now Miranda saw the lengths of chain protruding from the rock, attached to leather cuffs. "Why?" she said.

The girl shrugged. "Please, miss, the spirit will come. This is the way she likes to come. Don't you know?"

Miranda was no longer shy about confessing ignorance. She shook her head.

"Well, when those first groups came here after Mother Egypt died, there was always one who went into a trance. Sometimes she would hurt herself or else some others, which is why . . . But these are old chains from the ancient days."

None of this was reassuring to Miranda. Why was everything so complicated?

"I sat here when my father chained me up. Oh, my wrists were sore!"

None of this was reassuring. Because of some stray words on a letter she'd neglected to even read, Insula Calia had been Miranda's sole objective for many days. Now she was here, she felt a trepidation. On the one hand she imagined telling her aunt about de Witte and Anna Djourek, receiving her congratulations. One the other she imagined having to confess the death of the policeman, and it was almost worse to think her aunt would have no interest, wouldn't care. Instead she'd load Miranda down with some new task or burden, and Miranda wouldn't be able to tell her that she wasn't the right person to accomplish whatever it was—the policeman in Braila had shown her that if nothing else before he died.

Or there was a third alternative. Nothing could happen at all. Then what would she do?

Outside in the open air, when they climbed up to their camp, Ludu seemed happy, cheerful, excited, unconcerned. She opened a bottle of wine that the villagers had packed in ice. They sat in the long shadows over the grass sea, punctured at intervals by forested islands. They drank wine from earthenware cups, and ate big strawberries and Turkish peaches. Later there was black bread, mustard, onions, and potted ham. The air was cooler as the evening came.

Miranda felt her heart grow lighter as the sun sank behind the trees. Above them spread the burning sunset. If she'd learned anything since Christmas Hill, it was to take each moment separately. The policemen had come into the garden of the Russian consulate in Braila and she had fired her gun at them—what else could she have done? And she'd hit one, and the black horse had taken her away. Later she had crossed the river and arrived back at Macin.

Away from the towns, everywhere she was a hero. That first night Ludu Rat-tooth had taken her into a Gypsy encampment where the word had already spread. They didn't care about de Witte and the German plans, and Miranda hadn't told them. For them it was enough she was Miranda Popescu, and she had killed a man.

That first night the old men and women drank her health around the fire, while she sat in a daze. For some of them and for Ludu Rat-tooth, the war was already won, the Germans driven home, Antonescu and his partisans, Ceausescu and the vampire all defeated. "You'll remember me when you are living in the Winter Keep," she said now, raising her cup. "Please, maybe you will take me with you. You'll remember the Gypsies when you are queen?"

Her words reminded Miranda unpleasantly of things that Gregor Splaa and Blind Rodica had said. In back of that, because she was trying to maintain her mood, they reminded her of a game her American father and mother had played on long trips in the car, driving north during the vacations or out to Colorado the summer she was twelve. Stanley had invented the game, which was called, "If I were king."

"If I were king," he'd say, "no one in the state of Maine would be allowed to make any kind of representation, painted, carved, or otherwise, of a lobster. They wouldn't even be allowed to say the word. They couldn't even say 'lob' if they were talking about throwing a ball. I'd fine them—just a few dollars a time, but it would take the place of these damn tolls."

Or Rachel, once on the beltway around Indianapolis: "If I were king, I'd get rid of this entire state. I mean, who would miss it? What's the point?"

Or Miranda: "If I were king, I wouldn't allow anyone to advertise a restaurant with pictures of a pig in a chef's hat eating sausages. It's just too disgusting. What kind of psychotic pig eats sausages?"

"Don't blame the pig," said Rachel. "The pig's a victim."

Or Ludu Rat-tooth: "I want you to promise you will let us go to school and own land like other people. We won't be punished for talking our own language. That was my father's dream—you'll promise me?"

Or Miranda again: "If I were king, no one could use the word 'nitely,' on pain of death."

Or Ludu: "And you must promise me you'll let us worship our King Jesus without shame. That you'll close the temples with their false gods no one believes in. And the corrupt officials, and the policemen . . ."

Miranda had fired her gun at a policeman. He'd had a black moustache and a raspberry birthmark on his cheek. He'd fallen over, crumpled up around a wound in his stomach while she climbed onto her black horse. He'd been wearing a helmet and a blue uniform. Later people had told her he was one of Codreanu's thugs, that he deserved death a dozen times—what did that mean?

In these villages, where the men brought out their weapons to show her and the women kissed her hands, now in a few days it was as if she had a power at her back pushing her forward. And there was a role in the lives of these people that someone could definitely play. All of them had stories to tell, bitter stories of oppression and harassment.

But was this the role for her? She found she wanted an assurance from Aegypta Schenck. Some sort of reassurance about the dead man—legionaries, people called them in the villages, and told stories about their cruelty. She had fired almost without looking. He'd had a black moustache just beginning to turn gray, and he'd worn a helmet with a metal shield above his eyes. He had crumpled up around his wound, and she had turned away, climbed onto her horse. Later details she had learned from others as the rumors grew.

She sat here eating her sandwich. Sometimes she missed Peter so much she found it hard to breathe. Andromeda as well. The sensation of missing them came in waves.

Ludu Rat-tooth had taken out her statues. As the sky grew dark she arranged them underneath the arbor and held small pieces of saturated bread to their lips. Miranda had stood up to watch the sunset, and when she turned back, the girl was smiling and holding out an unlit candle. She pushed her hair from her face, which in the last light seemed beautiful for a moment, animated and bright-eyed. She looked happy, and Miranda felt a corresponding happiness.

This place was magic to the Gypsy girl. Through her, Miranda could feel some of its magic. With the part of her that thought in words, she thought: Maybe one day I'll see Peter and Andromeda again. Maybe one day I'll see Stanley and Rachel and the rest.

When it was almost dark, she followed Ludu down the slope into the mine, unused since Aegypta Schenck had bought the property in the old days. The lamp was burning in the salt chamber. They lit their candles and put them in the entrance of the tunnel to the outside air, "to call the ghost," Ludu said. Then she sat down on the salt throne and laid her forearms on the salt rests. She showed Miranda how to cuff her wrists and lock the rusted chains. All the time she was prattling happily. "Don't worry about me. The last time I was here, my father locked the chains on me and then I fell asleep. I just fell asleep and had the strangest dreams. I dreamed there was a pit dug in the earth, and I was bringing the wooden bucket. But Gheorghe caught my arm—he wouldn't let go. 'Look,' he said, and I could see something moving in the pit. At first I thought it was just worms and bugs. But then the more I looked, the more I saw all kinds of animals. That was when my father brought you to Mamaia Castle."

"Do you miss your father?" Miranda asked.

"Yes." Then she shook her head. "He used to beat me."

There must have been some kind of airshaft at the top of the chamber, because the lamplight flickered. It shone on a wall that looked greasy and wet, though it was dry. Seams of dark rock alternated with the coarse, gray salt, which had a cleansing smell. It was pleasant at first. But after a few minutes you could taste it in your throat.

The strangest thing about this girl, Miranda decided, was that it didn't bother her to talk about the past. Cut off from her family, it didn't hurt her to look back. But was there a difference, she now thought, between Ludu's situation and her own? The girl was smiling as she spoke, and Miranda could see the rat-tooth and the rest of her sharp mouth. Ordinarily she took pains to hide it, and hid her mouth under her hand whenever she smiled or laughed. Now her hands were fastened down.

Miranda walked to the door again and stooped to look out. The little valley was now darker than the cave. When she turned, the ghost was there.

Ludu had leaned forward so her coarse, curling hair was in her face. Now she sat back and shook her head. In the lamplight her almond-shaped eyes had a yellowish cast. She turned away from Miranda. She pressed her shoulders and her cheek into the salt wall that formed the back of the chair. "I remember," the ghost murmured.

After a moment Miranda stepped forward into the center of the chamber. Aegypta Schenck didn't move her head, but still peered at her sideways, her chapped, spotted cheek against the rock. Miranda saw the strain in her arms and legs as she tried to press herself into the wall.

"Yes," she murmured, "you will do."

She spoke in English, a language the Gypsy didn't know. Miranda stood listening to the hiss of exhaling air, watching the sudden, jerky expansion of her aunt's chest as if she breathed through an effort of memory and will—a grudging concession to her host.

Miranda closed her eyes. She had something rehearsed. "I know I disappointed you when I saw you before. Peter was my friend," she said. "He was sick, and I couldn't let him die. Not for you and not for anyone. I'm sorry. . . ." There was more, but the words gave out, and she listened to the rasping breath.

"Oh, that," whispered her aunt. There was a hiss and a rattle, and then, "Oh, child, that is old news—indeed."

The important thing, Miranda thought, was to speak normally as if to a normal person. The wine she'd drunk was helping. "So you're not mad?"

A pause. "I am not angry. Much time is gone."

The important thing, Miranda decided, was to avoid long gaps in the conversation. "It wasn't such a bad place," she pleaded, "where you were."

Silence, and the hiss and breath. "I have yet to thank you. For setting the bird—free."

She meant the brandywine bird, her aunt's spirit animal, which Miranda had liberated from its cage in tara mortilor. Was that why her ghost was free now, why it appeared to people in places like this? It had never occurred to Miranda. "I saw your bird," she blundered on. "In the castle garden. Were you watching me?"

All this time her aunt had pressed away from her as if she wanted to escape. But now she turned her head. Miranda listened to the hiss, and then her coarse whisper. Nor did she deign to answer Miranda's question: "That was a long time—ago. When I last saw you. In those days I was—scarcely cold. I was at the—border. Now I have crossed Elysium—from end to end. In five years I have—seen such things. No, child—I am not angry."

Miranda wiped her mouth. Remembering the way her aunt had hugged her in tara mortilor, she wondered if she should approach closer. She wondered if there was a way to generate some human warmth inside this creature, who now said, "Don't touch me!" as if she sensed the impulse.

Miranda didn't need to be told twice. She stepped back, held her hands up. She listened to the hiss and breath, and told herself there was no reason to be afraid. Her aunt would never hurt her, maybe. "I want to tell you something," she said. "Something I did for you. I stole the German plans. They will cross the river at the Cosmesti Bridge on June eleventh. But the Russians know about it now and they'll be warned. . . ."

Miranda let her voice trail away. The ghost looked anything but gratified. Her face was stiff with strain, her cheeks were wet. Her breath came hissing out.

"Why did you think—I would be pleased?"

"Because of what you did!" Miranda cried. "Didn't you tell me the story about me and the diapers?"

The ghost wasn't able to speak more than a few words without swallowing, after which she took a breath. She squeezed out a hiss and a rattle between each phrase. "Did I say that? I don't remember—asking you—to fight a war. I thought I told you to bring peace—to Great Roumania. I thought you might—provide a voice. I thought you might—help us. Schenck von Schenck was my name. Your father's name. We are not enemies—of Germany."

This was disconcerting to Miranda. Abruptly, it got worse. "What is the date—today?"

"The seventh."

"I thought so. You will not have heard. At dawn this morning—German infantry—attacked the Russian lines in Lithuania—along a ninety-kilometer front. The defenses were weak. Fourteen regiments—were pulled back from the line—yesterday night. They were packed in rail cars—to be transported south to Cosmesti and the Roumanian—frontier."

The words came rough and slow. "I tell you—there are crowds of German boys today—dazed and wandering the Elysian Fields. But there are twice—as many Russians. One hundred thousand men—surrendered without fighting. Among them was—Felipe Romanov, the tsar's only son. Today the Reichstag met—in special session—to declare a celebration—in Berlin."

There was nothing to say to this. Miranda found herself examining Ludu Rat-tooth's hands, knotted into fists. The chains were tight around the leather cuffs. "Do not blame yourself," the ghost continued. "The Russian generals—considered many pieces—of information. The letter you delivered—was just one. There were arguments—concerning authenticity.

"So you were not—the only person fooled. And yes, the cause goes back—to Kaposvar. The officer who planned this scheme—was Arslan Lubomyr—a friend of my old enemy—who holds your mother prisoner. Who sent the illness to America—that almost killed the Chevalier de Graz."

What a relief, thought Miranda savagely, not to be the only person fooled! "How do you know these things?" she cried. "How do you know?"

"Rumors fly fast . . . among the dead."

In a war, thought Miranda, they must spread very fast.

The air in the salt chamber was oppressive, though there must have been some draft from somewhere, because the flame trembled in the lamp. It shone on the black and mottled walls whose surfaces looked wet but were dry. Above Miranda the vault was hacked away in chunks.

Forward progress seemed to have stopped in that small room. She found she couldn't look the creature in the face. The silence was intolerable. "So," she murmured. "What should I do now?"

"Are you—asking me?"

Miranda said nothing.

"I want to know—child—because you have—rejected me before."

After each phrase Mother Egypt took a swallow, then a hissing breath. "I want to know—child. I had a plan—that I had built—for many years. You were to bring me—out of death—and I would help you. Instead—you left me here—in pain. I had gifts for you—letters—you didn't read. So are you—asking me?"

"I want to know what's going to happen!" Miranda said. "I want to know what I am going to do."

"I cannot—know the future."

A new kind of oracle, thought Miranda bitterly. The future seemed to stretch out in front of her, trackless and empty. And the past, shredded and trackless, too.

Stanley had once told her when she was complaining about a history paper: "It's the past that gives the world its shape." Robbed of whole years, woken from a dream, was it any wonder she made such mistakes?

"I'm sorry," she said again. "Peter was my friend. I couldn't let him die."

She listened to the hiss and rattle. "Are you—asking me?"

"What?"

"Always there is—something—in you. Something to be—broken down. I remember when you were a—child. When was the last time—you asked me or anyone—for help?"

The light flickered in the glass chimney. Her aunt now made a low coughing sound, and it took Miranda a moment to realize she was laughing. The Gypsy's head had fallen forward. "Child—I remember that—expression on your face—when you were—six years old. You were always—stubborn."

"Then don't ask me!"

"Say it again. Do you think—the white tyger—is just words? No, it is something—that you are. Or you become. Or you are not, without my—help."

"I didn't ask for this," Miranda said after a pause.

"No one asks—child."

"Please don't call me that," Miranda said. "I'm not a child. Why should I believe you? What are you saying? That I can't be anything without your help?"

"I'm saying you must—offer me—an empty cup."

"Oh, that's fine," Miranda cried, indignant. "And I should trust you? What have you given me so far? A gun. Fine, thanks. A man is dead who never did me any harm."

"You are the daughter—of a soldier."

"A dead soldier. Anyway, I threw the gun into the water. I don't need it."

"No—you don't. I did not mean for you to use it—as you have."

Miranda looked into the girl's face. She could almost see her aunt there, lurking behind the red, pimpled skin. The slitted eyes, high cheekbones, lumpy nose. The Gypsy's eyes were shining in the light. They had a yellow tint. Her lips were pulled back, showing her sharp teeth.

The two candles in the doorway flickered and went out.

"You have—rejected everything—and ask why you have nothing. But you must just—open your palm."

Tears in her eyes, Miranda looked into her open hand. "Show it to the Gypsy girl," whispered the ghost. "She reads fortunes. Not like me."

Hesitantly, Miranda stepped forward.

"Show me!" said the ghost. Miranda reached out gingerly, expecting to be slapped. And in an instant she knew why: Rachel had never punished her like that. Stanley had never punished her. But her aunt sometimes had rapped her across the fingers after she'd asked her to stretch out her palm.

Miranda saw the strain in the girl's body as she pulled against the leather restraints. The chains pulled from the wall in a sudden eruption of salt powder that burst into Miranda's mouth and nose. The ghost was free. She threw her back against a corner of the wall, forcing her into the rock. The glass chimney of the lamp tottered and broke, and the flame went out, and they were in darkness.

Miranda felt herself pressed down into the gravel floor, her cheek against the floor. She felt the blood on her cheek, the stinging salt. The ghost's voice was in her ear. Miranda recognized the hoarse, rough whisper of her dreams. "Say it now! Admit it! Stubborn child!"

Terrified, Miranda twisted her head and tried to scratch at the hands that held her down. She heard her aunt's throaty laugh: "You cannot hurt me. Only a Gypsy girl who never did you—any harm."

Miranda struggled for a moment more. Then she relaxed her body and lay still.

"Good. That's better. Now. I want you to—say it. Say what you must say."

As soon as she stopped struggling, the ghost relaxed its grip. But there it was if she tried to move.

"Say it! Beg for it! When the first white tyger—begged for help in this same room . . ."

Miranda set her lips together. Cramped and aching, she lay still for several moments. Then she relented. "What I need . . ."

Again there came a soft flutter of laughter in her ear. "Is that the best—you can do? I remember when the farmer—brought you white asparagus in Mamaia. Such rudeness! You refused to eat it. You sat until midnight with your plate—in front of you. Until Juliana . . ."

"Help," Miranda whispered, and the world shuddered to life.

The darkness fled. The Gypsy girl was gone. Miranda was alone in the salt cave. Light came from a new source, a clay lamp in the center of the floor.

From where she lay, her cheek against the floor, Miranda had a good view of it. Once when her adoptive parents had taken her to New York, she had seen a lamp just like it in an exhibition of artifacts from Pompeii. A flame protruded from the spout, and it shone on a chamber that was like an ideal version of the old one, a perfect cube cut out of the white rock. The salt throne had disappeared. Air came from the black entrance where the candles had stood.

Miranda saw these things as she raised her head. Now the relief she felt at the ghost's departure was troubled by a new thought: Where was she now? The walls and floor were smooth. The stone was not pure white but a dull, mixed, dusty color like the sand on a beach. Here and there the surface glinted with darker flecks and veins. Miranda stumbled to her feet.

She was in a new version of the cave. And if she stumbled out the entrance into the dark night, what would she find? Would she have changed again? Would everything have changed again?

She sat down on the floor next to the lamp. She sat cross-legged and put her face into her hands. In her ears there was a roaring sound and something else. A little bird was caught above her in the vault, and she listened to the beating of its wings.

This was not tara mortilor, she knew. She had no sense of moving through a dream. Nor was it the world of her childhood in Massachusetts. One more time would she have to start from nothing? She absolutely couldn't bear it.

Still, first things first. There was an object on the floor next to the lamp. It was a disk of some yellowish metal, gold or brass or bronze, or else a mixture. The rim was carved in a pattern of roses that surrounded a flat, smooth, polished, unfigured circle. It had a handle of carved briars. Picking it up, Miranda knew she was holding a mirror, an ancient mirror from the days before silvered or mercury-coated glass. The metal was stained and tarnished so she could not see more than a shadow of her face.

The back of the mirror was also carved, incised with a scene Miranda remembered from Greek myth. Circe the magician, sitting in a low chair. She stretched out her arm, and with a long reed she was tickling the heads of Odysseus's men. Some had already turned to pigs.

There were letters carved in a circle around this scene, and Miranda could just make them out. GNOSESAUTON. This meant nothing to her. But she glanced at the clasp of her gold bracelet with its own circle of minute, indecipherable words. Then with her cuff she tried to rub some of the tarnish from the mirror's face. But the metal wouldn't come clean.

She heard a fluttering in the corner and the bird was there, beating its iridescent wings against the surface of the wall until it found the dark hole to the outside air. It was a brandywine bird. Then it was gone, and Miranda heard another noise. A little, brown-furred mouse was trapped along the base of the far wall, squeaking with terror. It was caught in a kind of snare. And when Miranda put the mirror down and came toward it, she thought it might expire from fright. Shivering and trembling, it turned to face her. It was a dear little thing, though when it pulled its lips back, Miranda could see the sharp rat's teeth.

AFTER LUNCHEON THE BARONESS CEAUSESCU started back toward Bucharest. She rode in a closed carriage with eight horses and four postillions. But in the evening she had not gone farther than Brasov, where she'd arranged to spend the night. Soldiers had ridden ahead.

She came into the walled city by the Trumpeter's Door. At the state accommodations in the Piata Sfatului, she was met by representatives of the jeweler's guild who had prepared a public dinner. There was music and a reception in the town hall. It was not until almost midnight that she made her excuses and returned to her room to change her clothes. Her train to the capital left at dawn.

She disliked women and had no women in her household. Using a charm of misdirection, she managed to give Jean-Baptiste the slip when he was turning down the bed. She found the servant's stairs, the servant's door, and she was in the street, walking under the gaslights of the central town. The moon was almost full, which helped her after she'd left the circle of lit streets. She was looking for a house that had been famous once. Now it was abandoned—the residence of Lucas Hirscher the silversmith, who had been the vampire's previous incarnation.

She found it in the Strada Eroilor, a cul-de-sac off the boulevard. A tall mansion in the style of the previous century, now its windows and doors were boarded up and covered with graffiti. A sheet of pressed tin had been pulled back to reveal an entrance used by criminals, lovers, and thrill-seekers, though on that night the house was empty. The baroness uncovered her lantern in the great hall.

Lucas Hirscher had been notorious in Transylvania. From his youth he'd cultivated vice with the sensitivity of an artist, and it was only his proximity to wealth that had kept him out of prison or away from the gallows tree. Finally his own wife and daughter had forced him to justice and murdered him in his own bed. Later the girl had drowned herself.

There was a scurrying in the wall. The house was overrun with vermin and stray cats. In the dining room the baroness discovered what she was looking for, a painted portrait of the vampire mounted on a wall above a rubble of broken plaster. She lit the face within the circle of the lantern's eye. There he was. He had the same face as Zelea Codreanu, the same lustrous eyes and fat red lips.

The house was now a shrine for the worship of Hecate, banned by the order of the German government. The baroness herself had signed the order, forwarded from the Committee for Roumanian Affairs. The locations of the cult had now withdrawn from public view. There was a witch's circle drawn in chalk on the bare floorboards underneath the painting. There were stubs of candles and the stiff body of a rat, hung from a piece of lath thrust through the wall. Its desiccated belly was full of coins and nails.

The baroness had brought some of her own paraphernalia, including the tourmaline, which she gripped against her chest. "Gnose sauton," she began, and then continued for a long time in the Greek language. The air was dense and thick. No draft or current threatened the lantern or disturbed the flames from the candle stubs that she now stooped to light.

Always the waiting was tedious as she murmured her charms and listened to the scratching in the walls. Not having eaten much at dinner, she was hungry and her throat was dry. It was long past midnight when she heard a creak outside the door and caught a glimpse of a girlish shadow. She addressed her in the language of the dead. "Oh, my dear—please come. Livia—is that your name? Your father has told me how beautiful you are. Please let me see. I've brought a gift for you."

In the center of the witch's circle, surrounded by candlelight, she had laid the presentation necklace of the jeweler's guild, given to her that evening after a series of brief speeches. It was made of feldspar and yellow diamonds, woven together on a platinum chain.

ALSO PAST MIDNIGHT, WHILE THE baroness enticed Livia Hirscher under the light, the vampire came to Insula Calia with his men. With muffled oarlocks they had rowed upstream from the village of Chiscani on the western bank. When he'd felt the presence of the ghost in the salt chamber, then he'd guessed what he would find.

Under the fat yellow moon the four boats pulled out of the main current and around to the stone landing on the east side of the island. They came ashore at the stone dock where they tied the boats up to the iron rings. Zelea Codreanu was the first ashore.

Above him rose the crest of the small hill. All was in darkness. While the men waited for his signal, he raised his delicate nose into the night air. That night they were hunting the white tyger. They had brought nets and spears because they wanted to capture her alive.

The vampire never slept. By day he pored and fussed over dry papers, wearing his gray civil-service uniform. But at night he allowed himself more elegant fabrics. He wore a black silk shirt and leather pants. A strip of cloth was knotted around his upper arm, bearing the insignium of his political party, the Legion of Aphrodite: a phoenix rising from the ashes of its nest.

And he had brought his legionaries, the usual mix of unemployed stevedores and fishermen from the port of Galati. They had accompanied him before on various raids. Now they climbed ashore, nineteen ragged barefoot men and boys. Some carried torches, bundles of kerosene-saturated burlap on the tops of poles, which he now lit with his cigarette lighter as they clustered around, despite the risk of fire in the dry reeds. "Men," he whispered, "I know you would not hesitate to shed your blood for Great Roumania and what is right. We're here to apprehend a criminal. Have a care, but she is only a girl, doubtless asleep, one of a parasitic race of so-called aristocrats who have sucked the life of our dear country, kept us all in poverty and shame. . . ."

BUT MIRANDA WAS NOT ASLEEP. She was in the white salt chamber with the seven-metal mirror in her hands.

Then she let it drop. In a moment she felt too confined in that small space. And the lamp burned too bright for her new eyes. She'd lost sight of the rat and couldn't hear its squeaking. Had it escaped as well?

Miranda ducked her head into the low tunnel and scrambled out into the night. Above her was the golden moon. She climbed out of the dell onto the ridge and looked down to see the torchlight gathered at the dock. She was no longer afraid. Now I have lost everything, she thought. And so she came walking down the forest path, alive to every birdsong and whisper until she stood on the dry slope above the legionaries as they came ashore. Her eyes had settled into a different kind of vision. She saw clearly in the dark, a low palette of blacks and brights and grays, and she was aware of tiny movements.

The men, by contrast, saw her indistinctly, and to some of them she seemed to hang above them like a brooding and expectant beast, poised to jump. They had guns but did not use them. When she came down the slope they pulled away, trapping her in a circle of light. None would approach her. And to her it seemed as if they were the beasts, not she, and they were cringing in silence when she moved, as if afraid she might notice them. Though some of them were shouting, and Zelea Codreanu was telling them what to do, Miranda heard nothing of all that. But she was surrounded by a ring of tiny squeaks and groans she heard over the roaring in her ears, the pumping of her heart. Their faces were inhuman, distorted not just by thuggishness and fear, but by a new kind of nature. In each of them she could see a spirit animal scratching and struggling to get out, as if caught in a transparent human bag. In some cases the membrane had already peeled away, revealing the stalklike eyes and active mandibles of insects and shellfish or the unformed faces of baby animals, as if seen through a splitting caul.

Only Codreanu had kept his human shape. Or it was as if the caul had ripped to show the same face underneath, made shiny and new and even more beautiful. Pale skin tinged golden in the torchlight, soft, long-lashed eyes, red lips that were open now to cry out exhortations and political rants. But it was as if the shell that had surrounded these words had also cracked apart, revealing something soft and quiet. The Roumanian words had cracked apart to reveal a core of French: "Longtemps j'attendais—now I have you."

Roumanian was the language of Zelea Codreanu. But the vampire spoke in French. Miranda looked up at the moon. With her new, quick eyes she saw a bird fluttering overhead, and with her new ears she heard a voice that might have been inside herself. "Don't be afraid." But she was not afraid.

She reached out her hand, which was indistinct to her. But she could see the claws. She could feel the movement of her joints and muscles. She could hear the pounding of her heart. She stepped into the grip of a young man and with a sweep of her hand she slit the membrane that covered him from top to bottom. The bag deflated and collapsed around an animal that was neither large nor fierce, a little dog that yipped and complained when she reached down to grab him underneath the belly and flip him into the air, into the water. A long pole with a sharpened end clattered to the stones.

All of them—bugs, beasts, and scuttling crabs—now spread away from her into the dark. They were the frightened ones, and it was right they should be frightened. She leaped after them, grabbing them and throwing them aside. Flung down, one of the torches made a fire in the small dry grass. Through its light she saw the vampire start away, running down the flat spine of the island toward its low south end. But in a bramble patch he tripped and fell, and she was on him.

She turned him over. He was weak under her hands. He also was afraid and she could feel it. The moon shone in his face. His fear was like a tremor in his flesh. It thrilled under her fingers while she waited to do—what? Her hands were stiff with power while she waited to do—what?

Zelea Codreanu lay on his back. He was a man in his early thirties with pale skin under which she now saw a blush of color. His blood was rising to the surface. He opened his lips and she could see his teeth, smell his breath. In an instant she remembered all the small things she had heard about him during the previous days, how he'd been born into a peasant family in Galati. How he'd been taken in by the Sisters of Diana and sent to the temple school where he'd excelled.

Not another one, Miranda thought. Not after the policeman in the garden of the Russian consulate—as she looked down she could see her hands again. There was a change, and the vampire understood it. His eyes opened, and with a surge of strength he turned her over and put his hands around her throat. "Ça-y-est maintenant," he whispered. "Let me."

She had hesitated too long. Now his red lips were near her own. One hand was on her throat, while with the other he was touching her on the neck and shoulders. But she was not frightened, though the vampire's thumb had pressed into her windpipe. She had resources, wells of power and disgust. But she couldn't breathe. Her hands pulled uselessly at the vampire's hands; his mouth was near her own. "Is this what you like?" he murmured, before he bit her on the lips, drawing blood.

They lay in the short grass above the beach. Miranda could hear the susurration of the river. And then something else. "Papa! Papa! Est-ce que c'est vraiment vous? Ah, comme je vous cherchais—how I was looking for you!"

A girl stood on the riverbank below where they lay in the dry grass. "Papa, what are you doing—do you want to make me jealous? Who is she, please?"

Miranda felt the vampire's grip loosen on her neck, slippery now with sweat. She saw him raise his head, and so she twisted underneath him, batted at his hands. At first she didn't think he recognized the girl. But then a flicker of something passed across his face. "Livia," he murmured.

"Papa, is this how you repay me? After I have given you so much?" The girl had climbed up the slope and stood above them now. Her saturated dress trailed behind her. Weeds hung from her wet hair. She carried a knife with a serrated blade. Around her throat shone a gaudy necklace, alternating yellow and gray stones.

Down by the dock the torch had lit a fire. Miranda saw the girl by the light of a smoky fire, which was spreading through the drought-starved reeds. Miranda had turned her head so that her cheek was against the stones and she could breathe. She studied the girl's old-fashioned hook-and-eye-laced boots.

Miranda pushed up and pushed away with all her strength, and she was free. She saw the gleam of the blade as the girl raised it up. The vampire also raised his hands to protect himself. The girl had grabbed him by his long hair. Then she was hacking at his face with her knife; Miranda rolled away over the stones and staggered up. Beyond the struggling figures, the fire had begun to spread up the east slope of the hill toward the dell and the salt cave. Ludu Rat-tooth was chained there on the salt throne.

It was Miranda's instinct to escape, to run away. Whoever she was, wherever she had come from, the girl in the high boots didn't need her help. The vampire was on his knees now as the girl cut him with the knife. Miranda backed away from them. And then she turned and staggered up the hill. But she stopped when she heard the voice, whether the brandywine bird or else something internal—"You must fetch him."

In her mind she caught a glimpse of Ludu Rat-tooth, locked and chained. The fire was burning in the dry underbrush. The Gypsy girl was her first duty and Miranda continued up, climbing where the grass was green. Then she stopped again. "Go back," said the voice. "Fetch him. This is your chance."

Twenty feet above the riverbank she turned around. Below her she could see the vampire's body sprawled out on the pebbles. Beyond it the girl had waded out into the water. She stood with the water around her thighs. She had her back to Miranda and was staring out over the calm dark river, lit now with reflections from the fire.

"Don't worry about her," said the voice.

That was bad advice. As Miranda stumbled down again, Livia Hirscher turned in the water and came to shore. The fire burned in patches over the low end of the island. The air was full of smoke. In her big wet dress she flounced ashore and met Miranda at her father's body. Jealous, she was snarling more like a wild beast than a human being. But then the brandywine bird flew around her head, pecking at her eyes. And she was flailing at it with the knife until her slashing strokes unbalanced her—her wet leather boots, the yards of wet cloth around her legs. She fell to her hands and knees with the bird still in her hair, while Miranda dragged the vampire by its wrist. She pulled it through the high grass. Now she knew what she was doing. Mary Magdalene had locked this creature in a prison for a thousand years.

But Mary Magdalene, doubtless, had been muscular and tall. It was hard work for Miranda to move the body a few yards. And she wouldn't have managed it if she had not felt the body change under her hand, diminish and dry out. The wrist clenched in her fingers grew thin as bone—she didn't look back. She climbed from the west side of the hill and found the path. There were the cedar posts, the baskets and bedrolls. Below her the fire struggled and spread, and the air was full of smoke. She threw the body down the slope into the dell, then staggered after it and dragged it to the entrance of the mine among the wooden crosses. The sky was murky red.

She pulled the vampire by his wrist into the salt chamber. There was the lighted lantern. There was Ludu Rat-tooth on the salt throne, conscious now, her eyes shining with fear. The chains, undisturbed, were around her arms. She struggled to pull them from the wall. Miranda slid the locks out of their rings. The girl was free.

"Miss, what is that?" she asked.

"Codreanu."

Openmouthed, terrified, the girl was no help. But Miranda pulled the dry black body onto the seat and locked him fast. Ludu Rat-tooth was making little squeaks and cries; tears burst out of her. Miranda worked grimly, her teeth clenched and set. She wrapped the chains around the shriveled corpse which was not dead, not altogether dead. She could feel a tremor underneath her fingers. "Go," she said, and the girl left her, staggering to the tunnel and then out the door.

"Go," said another voice. Miranda turned and recognized her aunt, whom she had seen in dreams and photographs and once in tara mortilor. Now Aegypta Schenck was coming toward her over the rough floor, out of a corner in the chamber where she'd hidden in darkness. She was dressed in rich, old-fashioned clothes, with a lamb's-wool hat and a stole made of fox fur. Miranda could see one of the wicked heads hanging down.

"Oh, my child," said the old woman, "oh my dear child," and proffered her gray cheek to kiss. From the depths of memory Miranda summoned up the scent of the perfumed powder her aunt wore, and she was hugging her around the neck. "There, my child—there, there. That's enough. You must leave now. Leave him to me."

Miranda hugged her and rubbed her face on the fox fur. Then she turned away out of the tunnel, out to where Ludu Rat-tooth was waiting in the smoky air. They even managed to rescue their food and their blankets, dragging them after them as they climbed down the west side of the hill away from the fire. Then they carried their bundles south along the low ridge of the island, past the deserted beach and to a circle of bare ground where they sat watching the flames lick the crest of the hill.

And as they watched, Miranda found herself gradually overcome with nausea and disgust. She was clutching a beaded purse—where had it come from? Had her aunt thrust it into her hands? It had more money in it, she could tell, and she unbuttoned the flap and let the coins spill on the ground. There was a letter: many fragile pages, which she unfolded. She held them up close to her face. Just barely in the uncertain light, she could see the tiny words. "My dear girl. You will go to Mogosoaia, where I have left my key. . . . If you are as I think a princess of Roumania . . ."

She couldn't stand it. What was this, a steeplechase? A scavenger hunt?

Once on her birthday Stanley had sent her and her friends racing all around Williamstown searching for little paper clues.

She almost ripped the letter into pieces without reading it. She almost left the gold coins where they lay, except she didn't. Instead she snatched them up angrily and thrust them into her pockets, along with her aunt's folded pages.

"Look, miss!"

Now Miranda was aware of a new noise, and she realized she had heard it intermittently. It was thunder, and on the black horizon she could see the lightning stabbing down. There was a wind that blew the smoke away from them, and then a few drops of rain.

13   *The Wrestling Match*

PETER WOKE UP WITH the words of the poem in his ears, as clear as if he'd heard them spoken:

> So the sun went down and the stars came out all over the summer sea.
> But never a moment ceased the fight of the one and the fifty-three.

He lay on his back in a dark room on a white slab of a table, and his hands and feet were bound. But he could move his head, which still ached where the guard had clubbed him from behind. Aristophanes Turkkan had bit his hand. Afterward they had taken him to a different prison, to a private cell.

And they must have drugged his food or something, because he couldn't remember coming here. How many days had gone by? Had the man really hit him so hard? Above him was a stone, vaulted ceiling. There were barred windows high up on the walls. Sunlight came from them. The air was stuffy and hot. But he was not in prison, Peter decided, because of the statues carved in niches in the left-hand wall. Four stern old men with flowing beards. One was obviously Moses. One was Ezekiel with his wheel. One was Elisha with a raven on his wrist, Peter guessed. His mother had loved myths and Bible stories. One statue was of Daniel, his hand touching the mane of a sleeping lion.

With difficulty Peter turned his head to the other side. He was surprised to see the room stretch out into the darkness, and four living men against the far wall. In contrast to the prophets close at hand, they had their backs to him. They were grouped around an ornate piece of furniture, a sideboard or a desk on which a gas lamp burned. And now Peter could hear they were conversing in low tones that competed with the roaring in his ears. He strained to understand, but could not because they were too far away, and because of the pain in his head, and because they spoke in Turkish.

Occasionally they glanced back toward him. If he had set himself to guess what they were saying, by their looks and glances he would have discovered something of the truth: "Biliyorsun bu küzey—you know in these northern places there is a great deal that modern science does not claim to understand. The magic of today is the science of tomorrow. We men of reason think we have the answer to all things, answers that have banished superstition from the borders of our own country. I must claim that I have seen in my examination a young man not yet twenty-five. But these matters are subjective and are not accessible to proof. You say he is Roumanian? I must confess to you all things are possible, because this is a barbarous race without an understanding of the one sole author of all natural law. And in places where there is no God— surely we have all heard stories of demons who live forever, vampires who live on human flesh. I myself had the good fortune to see the Chevalier de Graz on the wrestling ground when I was a young man. I do not think you would have been able to subdue him in your chambers and bring him here. . . ."

Of the four men, the one who spoke most closely resembled the prophet Elisha. He was small, stooped, slight. His narrow hips, narrow face and high-ridged nose were like the statue's.

"O bir kahroman degil—he is not an over-man," interrupted another. If he'd been wearing robes that touched the floor, if he'd been carrying the tablets of the law, or if the sculpture of Moses had been dressed in a janissary's uniform with gold epaulets, there might have been a strong resemblance. "Halil smacked him with his rifle butt. I never saw this man but I assure you . . ."

Elisha raised his hand. "Don't tell me anything, please. I don't desire to know what you have done. You ask for my advice and I have given it. These things are subject to a kind of proof—evidence of demonic possession or a fugue state. You understand that we are talking about Roumania where all things are possible. Twenty years with no memory except of these things he has told us, magic worlds in North America and so on. I must confess to curiosity, because as you say the likeness is extraordinary. And there is no mistake about the birthmark. To suggest a tattoo is foolish. . . ."

It was clear to Peter that Elisha and Moses did not like each other. He saw their faces in profile, one glowering, one subtle. But now the biggest of the four looked toward him, and he recognized Turkkan. "It's no tattoo, I'll tell you that. You forget I wrestled with the man—I myself! One fall, just as a favor before the main event—I saw that mark under my nose as he tried to twist my head off. I bit him then and I bit him now. When I see that mark, I bite—I am not proud of that. But can a man fight against a devil? Look, you see."

Peter was too far away to see what the cadi was holding, an old photograph of Frederick Schenck von Schenck bowing to the sultan after the Peace of Havsa. Staff officers surrounded them, including one young captain of dragoons.

"It is extraordinary," repeated Elisha.

To the four men who examined it, this photograph depicted the most humiliating event in Turkish history. All four now turned to look at Peter where he lay. "You see he is awake," said Aristophanes Turkkan. "Come, you see. Bring your medicine."

He spoke in English now. Red-faced and bald, he resembled neither Daniel nor the sleeping lion. Peter was not reassured by his apparent friendliness as he walked forward with his arms outstretched, his glasses twinkling. "Domnul Gross, how are you feeling? You see we have brought you to hospital after your injury. This is Adnan Mejid Pasha, and this is Dr. Baz—you see he was educated in Somalia! You are in good hands!"

Elisha was holding a small leather case and a white piece of cloth. The fourth man, whom Turkkan had not introduced, hung back. He was light-haired and subservient—the chauffeur, Peter decided. Ezekiel the chauffeur, with his wheel. Groggy and confused from the blow to his head, Peter looked back and forth between the four faces as Dr. Baz took his pulse, then peered into his eyes with a white light.

"Put a pillow under his head. That's a good chap," said the doctor.

Peter lay on a cold, hard, white, enamel surface. His wrists and ankles were bound with leather straps. "Where am I?" he asked.

Turkkan ignored the question. "You have made a claim that is extraordinary. You've been convicted—you remember this? You've been convicted of a ghastly crime. But even so, we'd be—what is the word? We would be remiss, I tell you. So we have asked my friend to give you an injection." He bent over the table. Peter was aware of his powerful shoulders and arms, his fat, short neck, and the smell of anise-flavored liquor that clung to him.

Dr. Baz now spoke. "You will be pleased to tell me your parents' full names. Tell me their birthdays and the years during which they were born."

"No," said Peter. "Take that light out of my eyes."

"Tell me the dates of your schooling and at what academy. Were you good friends with your father, do you think?"

"Please turn out the light."

Someone was chafing Peter's right wrist. On the other side he heard a hiss of contempt from Moses. "This is a waste of effort. A waste of money also. Why does he deserve this treatment?" Then more words in Turkish, and then a whole conversation that Peter didn't understand. He closed his eyes.

Occasionally he distinguished Aristophanes Turkkan, who had kept to English. "It would have been simple for him to invent these answers to your questions—no. You see it is because he cannot remember that I must believe him . . ."

Later, Turkkan again: "My friend—doctor, I am tired of these objections. You must use your specialty. You see I am here as an officer of the courts. It is not for nothing that we brought him to your gates!"

Then more grumbling from Moses, and Dr. Baz burst into English once again. "No, it is too much. How dare you call me these names? This is not animal magnetism or hypnotism or any quackery. These are modern scientific techniques, invented at University Hospital in Addis Ababa, and useful in your own department—no, you insult me, I insist . . ."

Peter felt the doctor's hand on his elbow and a wet, cold cloth on his inner arm. He knew what was going to happen next. "You will not be alarmed," said Dr. Baz close to his ear. "This will be finished in a few minutes and will have no terrible effects. It is a solution of sodium thiopental. You will experience some burning." Then to the others: "Ask whatever you want. In ten minutes you will see."

The needle hurt more than he expected. Peter opened his eyes to see the faces of the prophets hovering over him. The doctor wore a pair of cotton gloves. In his right hand was a glass-and-silver syringe. With his left hand he pressed a wad of gauze into Peter's forearm.

"Look for the dilation of the eyes," he said. "Ask what you want. Go on."

But they said nothing. They just stared at him, and in time he was conscious of a new sensation in his body. His hands and feet had been chafing uselessly in their leather bonds. Now they lay quiet. The pain in his head was gone, the roaring in his ears. A hot feeling of relaxation came over him.

"Ask him what you want!" repeated Dr. Baz. "The first minutes are best, before the self can reassert its own identity."

There was another pause, and then Turkkan: "What is your name?"

It took a lot of effort for Peter to respond. In time he opened his mouth and cleared his throat. Then after a few false starts he began to speak, and his own voice was flat and unfamiliar, as if he listened to a tape-recording of himself. In his mind he was reciting:

Ship after ship, the whole night long, their high-built galleons came,
Ship after ship, the whole night long, with her battle thunder and flame,
Ship after ship, the whole night long, drew back with her dead and her
    shame. . . .

But the words that actually came out of him were different words, spoken in a different language. The poem seemed to float upon their current—Spanish galleons on the sea. At moments a wave surged up, threatening Peter as he stood upon the deck of the *Revenge*.

And the pikes were all broken and bent, and the powder was all of it spent,
And the masts and the rigging were over the side . . .

And in time he heard a long expulsion of breath and then: "It is that man. It must be."

There was silence until he spoke again. He heard his voice go on and on, finishing the poem, flubbing the ending, then starting it over. He heard the contrast between his words and the English words. Then Dr. Baz spoke again. "I have no explanation. Ask him something else."

Peter was conscious of the heat in his body, and he couldn't move. But these men had no power over him. He spoke loudly, taking a new, perverse pleasure in the ugliness of his own voice. Then he heard an interruption. "This is all I want. It is enough to hang him. Ask him about the night of Nova Zagora in the rain."

It was Moses who had spoken, Mejid Pasha. Peter stared up without blinking and without fear. The man seemed to look down from a long distance. His uniform—black and red, with gold epaulets and gold buttons and colored ribbons across his chest—seemed small for him. Peter could see it was a little bit too small, especially around the neck where the stiff collar pressed into his skin. His beard was short and almost black, his forehead high and bald. His face was full of indignation and disgust, and his teeth were bad. As he spoke, and even from that faraway distance, Peter could smell his breath.

"Ask him about Nova Zagora. He won't tell you. I say he is a coward. All your drugs won't turn a liar to an honest man—I know this. I was corporal in an artillery regiment."

His face as he looked down seemed pale and cold as stone. Peter stared at him, then looked past him at the statue of Moses in the wall, holding the ten commandments above his head. "That day we drove them through the black trees in the rain. We stopped at darkness—this was two kilometers from the front. At day we pull the guns out of the mud along the road. One of the caissons is stuck to the axles and we could not pull it out. It was turned onto its side. We cut the horses loose, and the captain told me to go up to a small village on the hillside to find a team of oxen. So I come into the village, and this is the story I hear about the Chevalier de Graz. A Bulgar woman tells it before she died. All the men are gone to fighting, so de Graz comes with ten men over the wall in the black night. Some Jews come out with hunting bows, slings and stones, harquebus and blunder, what they have. They are boys. But this man gives the order and the Roumanians put the barns on fire. They shoot into the houses. It was raining—I remember this night. In the day I come into this place and find the woman lying in the mud. She tells me the barns are full of hay. Her own mother was shot in her kitchen, and she comes into the yard to beg for life. The rain was like buckets, she says, but the barns were burning because of the hay. She saw this Chevalier de Graz. His face was black with soot like a devil, she says. There were boys and women lying in the mud. But de Graz goes down and takes a calf across his back. He says he cannot tolerate to see animals suffer. They were in black uniforms without marks, and more than two kilometers from their places past the stream."

Peter didn't want to hear this story. And so now the poem in his mind took on a new purpose:

> For some were sunk and many were shattered, and so they could fight no
> more.
> God of battles, was there ever a battle like this in the world before?
> And he said, "Fight on, fight on," though his vessel was all but a wreck . . .

While he recited, he waited for someone to defend him. He waited for Aristophanes Turkkan to defend him, because Turkkan was a wrestler. Peter imagined he might understand these things, and he was happy when he saw the broad thick face above him, the glinting eyeglasses and waxed moustache. He smelled a new smell that was not the breath of Mejid Pasha, but the honest stink of sweat and booze. "It is true I heard that story about Pieter de Graz. Who has not heard this story? But I did not believe it—have you tried to lift a calf? What kind of imbecile would do this? Two kilometers, you say? It is true—you would have to a super-man. But with an empty skull!"

"This I heard. This woman does not lie to me."

"No lies, but it was dark. And you said the boys shot at them when they were coming over the wall."

"Fool—he has the truth injection, but not you. Why? You must ask him!"

The truth injection, as they called it, was having some side effects. Peter found tears on his face. The leather bonds around his wrists were slick with sweat. In his mind he recited the poem once more to its ending, which he flubbed again. His audience listened in shocked silence and then started to argue one more time. "Why must you defend him? Turkkan—are you a traitor to us? I am glad he must be punished like a criminal for Jacob Golcuk's sake. You don't believe what he has said? I think you are not sane or drunk. This punishment is too good in Trebizond. But to you he is a hero."

Turkkan's voice: "You do not understand. But I gave him my promise in those days. Not with my lips, but in my head. I saw him defeat our champion and exchange gifts like Glaucus and Diomed. To remember is to be a man. Giants walked among us. . . ."

LATER WHEN HE TRIED TO piece together his broken experience, these fragments were all that Peter could remember of this conversation. The whole day was lost to him except for these small pieces. Later he imagined he'd lost consciousness again, because unlike the captain of the *Revenge,* he was unable to fight to the end.

When he awoke, he was in darkness. But he was in a different place, a small room that was cooler and less stuffy, a comfortable room, he could tell without looking, and he was lying on a comfortable bed. He moved, tried to sit up, and found his wrists were shackled together with a two-foot length of chain, and his feet also.

The chain clinked when he moved. The links were small and smooth, and he could not get his fingers into them. With all his strength he tried to pull his hands apart. But his left hand followed his right, because it was still weaker.

A cool draft came from somewhere. The mattress lay on the floor and he sat cross-legged on it, which the chains permitted. His headache had returned, and when he stroked the back of his head, he found an egg-shaped bruise behind one ear. The inside of his arm was sore.

What had happened to him? Fragments of the day came back to him in no particular order. He supposed he was in some kind of holding cell, though it was incomparably nicer than anything he'd seen before in any Turkish prison. It didn't stink of urine or bat shit. And he was alone.

Perhaps this was a cell for condemned prisoners. What had Mejid Pasha said? He was to be transported to a penal colony in Trebizond, which was— Peter happened to know—in eastern Anatolia along the coast. None of that sounded very good, though maybe there'd be some way to escape. After all, he was the Chevalier de Graz, or he supposed he was. No cage could hold him, he supposed.

Besides, it was impossible to despair completely in this room, where the air was scented with some trace of perfume. This was Turkkan's doing—maybe Turkkan had prevailed after all. And even if he hadn't, Peter could imagine still convincing him that this was all nonsense—he was who he was, not some middle-aged war criminal. Never had Peter felt less like the Chevalier de Graz than he did at that moment.

In retrospect it had been a truly terrible idea even to mention de Graz's name in the land of his enemies. Or at least without learning more about him. But it was a mistake that could be rectified even now. Like the Aegyptians, these Turks were rational people. Roumanian conjuring, demonic possession—it was obvious they found these explanations only half-convincing.

Now he was accustomed to the darkness. He saw the dimensions of the room, saw the outline of the furniture. The doorway was in front of him, and he saw a light burning vaguely behind a gauze curtain that bellied out toward him. He could hear a sound of whispering from an adjoining room. Then stifled laughter, and a shadow slipped inside the door.

So he was in a private home. That much was obvious. Peter felt a spasm of relief; he sat cross-legged, watching the shadow. First it stood against the wall. Then it ventured a little toward him without making a sound. There must have been a carpet on the floor. The shadow made a sudden movement—Peter already had decided her sex even before he smelled the fragrance that accompanied her as she approached. It was rosewater and glycerine, which had also been his mother's favorite cologne.

God, it was a relief just to feel her with him in the room! In this country he had not seen many women. Usually they kept at home. In the markets you could see old women and servants, and sometimes young girls going to school. But for the time he'd been here, Peter had not spoken to a woman his own age. "Who are you?" he asked. "Please, where am I?"

Again there were stifled giggles and another shadow slipped into the room. He didn't move and they came closer, whispering to each other. Careful to keep distance, they stood on opposite sides of the bed while Peter filled his nose and lungs with their fragrances. The second girl was wearing a citrus smell. It was bitter and astringent, unlike the cloying rosewater.

"Please," said Peter. But then he heard a new sound of heavy footsteps and saw a new light. The curtain was pulled back. Aristophanes Turkkan stood in the doorway with a lamp in his hand, while at the same time the girls fled through the opposite door. As the lamplight chased them, Peter was aware of their long dresses and thick braids before they disappeared.

"Shoo!" Turkkan said. "Shoo away! Ah, my gazelles' horns," he said as he held up the lamp. "They are my daughters—see? They would tell if you're awake."

"I'm awake."

"And not feeling good or well, is it not so? Let me help you."

He came into the room, carrying his lamp. He was dressed in a long, embroidered, linen gown. On his feet were leather boots. "Come, my friend. You are in the house of Aristophanes Turkkan!"

He bent down to peer into Peter's face. "For one night only. But do not think any thoughts. I am an officer of the courts and there are soldiers here. Come," he said. "I have let you sleep as long as I can, but supper is ready. Let me help you."

The chain ran taut as Peter reached out his right hand. Turkkan guffawed. "You must not offer me that kind of food again. A tattoo! What an idiotic notion!"

He brought Peter to his feet. And when he swayed and almost fell, Turkkan put his big arm around him. "Come," he said. "Come here."

He led him out of the dark room and into a gallery of rose-colored stone or stucco, hung with painted miniatures along the inner wall. Two feet thick at least, the outer wall was pierced with unglazed windows that stretched from floor to ceiling but were only a few inches wide. After a few steps Turkkan's solicitude had changed into impatience; he clamped Peter by the neck and hurried him along so quickly that it was as if a jerky, silent film of courtyard life were being shown along the left-hand wall, framed by the slitted windows. The yard was full of soldiers lighting fires and stretching out their tents. Savory smoke blew into the gallery and into the red sky. It was the dinner hour.

The chain between Peter's ankles slapped along the tiles. He had to take mincing little steps. "Come," said Aristophanes Turkkan. "You see I do not lie to you—this house is full of soldiers. They will shoot you if I give the word. I myself will shoot you." He gave Peter's neck a friendly squeeze.

"Where am I?"

"You are in my house! My personal house—for one night you are my guest. I am not afraid of you. Tomorrow you are off to Trebizond with the other prisoners and your name will be Peter Gross. Tonight you will want nothing, I promise you!"

"But my name *is* Peter Gross," Peter murmured. Now that he thought about it, he had no idea how to undo the damage he had caused by taking a false name, or even if it made sense to try. Peter Gross, apparently, had been convincted of the murder underneath the bridge.

They had reached the end of the long gallery. Now they came through several small antechambers and into a larger room that was full of rich and delicious smells. There were windows above Peter's head along the walls, and from the vault hung a row of slow fans. Below them in the center of the floor, a low table was surrounded by pillows, and on it burned a dim electric light. The bulb was covered with a perforated shade so that the light made a pattern on the surface of the table. It shone unevenly on bottles and covered dishes. The carpet was soft under Peter's bare feet.

Besides, it was de Graz that Turkkan wanted to entertain, de Graz he had invited into his house. Peter Gross would have been in Trebizond by now. So already he was ahead; when he sat, pressed into a cushion by Turkkan's strong hand, the small-linked chain between his wrists coiled into his lap, and he looked down.

For the first time he noticed the clothes he was wearing, a pumpkin-colored pair of pajamas. He had not seen them in the Eski Seray, where even the condemned prisoners had been dressed in their own clothes. But he assumed the pajamas were some kind of prison uniform—his spirits, which had been restored by the girls' perfume and the pungent food, now wavered. The chain slipped and coiled in his lap. It dragged on the cushions as he crossed his legs.

But he couldn't stay miserable when he was so hungry. Who knew what the future kept for him? He'd given up predicting a long time ago. In the meantime savory smells came from the dishes, made of rose-colored porcelain. Aristophanes Turkkan was lifting the covers and sniffing at the steam, though Peter noticed there was only one plate, only one knife and fork. "Eat, my friend!" Turkkan said. "Eat! Here there is honey lamb, rice with dried grapes and almonds, yes, but first—hot towels!" These he uncovered from a large pot, and as he wiped his own red face and hands he recited a short prayer in a language Peter didn't recognize. Perhaps it was Hebrew.

"Let me serve you with my hands, for old sakes!"

Peter ate and drank. At first he took small bites. The food was spicy, and the more he ate, the more ravenous he became. He ate until his cheeks ached from chewing, and the cadi served him delightedly. The chain clinked as Peter moved his hands.

The old man sat back in the pillows. When Peter lifted up his long spoon to start on a dish of yoghurt and cinnamon, Turkkan spoke. "Tell me, my friend. Now you must tell me the truth. Not for that damned drug, but its own sake. Is this some fantasy of darkness, that you appear before me? Are you a devil, as they say? Or have you come again from the fountain of youth? Tell me what has washed away your memory, so you remember nothing of these things. Tell me how we must explain this at long last?"

How could he explain? Peter wiped his lips. Forget Turkkan—how could he explain this even to himself? De Graz lived inside of him. Sometimes Peter kept him quiet and contained. Sometimes he prowled free. Any time, Peter supposed, when instinct might take over, which was another reason not to trust yourself.

Peter's father sometimes quoted an old radio show: "What evil lurks in the heart of men?" Reassured now by the memory, Peter smiled. He put down his cup and washed his fingers in a glass bowl. He dried his hands on a linen towel. Then he found himself staring at a row of cabinets that lined one side of the room. Glass-fronted, they were full of bones.

"You laugh at me!" Turkkan cried, suddenly delighted, laughing, too. "Bah, it is ridiculous. Bah, we are men of action, you and I. These mysteries are not for us. Old graybeards talking."

Now his eyes followed Peter's eyes. "I see you looking at my collection.

Please, it is the interest of an old man. You also are interested in archeological remains?"

Peter didn't answer, and Turkkan leapt up. "Let me show you the pride of my collection! Of course they want to take it away and bury it. What ignorance—but I am an officer of the courts! Let them try!"

Now he had opened one of the glass cabinets and lit a lamp. Peter came to join him, and found himself looking at many rows of fossilized bones. Some were small, some large. All were carefully labeled in delicate handwriting, drawn in black ink upon the bones themselves.

"My daughters help me," Turkkan said proudly. "You see they have been educated in taxonomy abroad. Let me show you this new thing, of which it is a question of a battle in the courts."

They squatted down, and Peter found himself peering at a single, long, enormous tibia, stretching the width of two cabinets. "We have legends in this country," Turkkan continued. "Graybearded scholars come and look and say this is the leg of Goliath the Philistine. Others scratch their beards and say it is the leg of Hector of Troy. You see they have a scholarly difference of opinion! All these bones, it is the same. They are heroes or giants, and must be taken away and buried with honor—what a loss to science! When in fact they are not human bones at all. Always the past is like a mirror and we see ourselves. I ask you, is it possible Hector of Troy was seven meters tall?"

"'Giants walked among us,'" Peter quoted.

"Ha! I see you make a joke. But I wish you to imagine seven meters—what about his wife, the lady Andromache? Was she also seven meters, or else six and a half? I would like to have seen that! Besides, we have found much armor in the ruins of Troy. Many plates and dishes—no, it is ridiculous. These bones are not found in those places. They are deep, deep, deep inside the earth where they have turned to stone. But sometimes the earth surrenders them. I tell you if we could only find a skull. But it is frustrating! The skulls break and shatter, because the bones are thin."

Peter found himself distracted by a happy memory. Several times his parents had taken him to the Museum of Natural History in New York. "The skulls are hard to find," he said.

"Yes, of course. I see you are a sensible man! Is it not obvious? These are animal remains, but animals like we have never seen. The little elephant, the feeble mammoth—it is not like that. Come, my daughters have made sketches. This is of a find near Trebizond. Perhaps when you are digging in the mine, you will find something like this and send for me. Ha—another joke! No, my friend—I am sorry to have hurt you. I am an old fool."

The drawings were exquisite, huge beasts in red pencil and watercolor, their skeletons superimposed in hard black ink. They were dinosaurs, obviously, but none he recognized—no triceratops, no stegosaurus, no tyrannosaurus rex. He recognized none of the names that were so carefully printed, in Roman letters, under their enormous feet. But the drawings were so beautiful. "Your daughters, they are very skilled," he said.

But he was thinking about the bones in the natural history museum and about his parents. Without warning he had tears in his eyes. He reached up to wipe them away and the chains clinked. "No, my friend," continued Aristophanes Turkkan. "You must not hide these things. It is a man who lets his tears fall. Come with me!" And he led Peter to a side table where there were bottles and glasses laid out.

"I think we will not sleep tonight," said the old man as he lit a candle. Then he unstoppered a bottle and poured out a stream of green liquid into two long-stemmed glasses. "This is the green serpent that has coiled inside my heart. But if you are a man, you do not care. See how it glows!"

Settled in the delicate spheres under the candlelight, the liquor shone. "Warm it in your hands, you see. Wash your breath with it. It is absinthe from your country. Always from your country. Everything that is not as it appears, I think it is from your country. Everything that is a mystery. Men whose faces have not changed for twenty-five years. In this fight between barbarians and honest men, I think you have all the weapons, all the powers. It is why Mejid Pasha is afraid of you."

Peter had managed to interrupt his tears. But his voice still felt lumpy and uncertain. Finally he blurted out, "Is it true what he said? Did the Chevalier de Graz carry a cow across a battlefield, rescue a cow when there were people dying?"

"It was a calf, I think. No man alive could carry a cow such a distance, not even the Chevalier de Graz."

Turkkan had picked up one of the glasses. Warming it between his hands, he made the liquor turn in a small whirlpool before offering it to Peter—"I have been a judge for a long time in the courts of this city. Certainly there is a difference between the truth and a lie. But in the house of what is true, there are many chambers, and some are sealed from the others. Today you have taken their truth serum, and I apologize for that. That is something for criminals, which you are. But you are also a man and a champion, and so I offer you this other serum for the truth. Smell! It is from Targu Mures!"

Peter took the glass. The liquor in it was intolerably sweet.

"It is a taste to hide the wormwood," Turkkan admitted, smelling his own glass. "I beg you to examine the stone bones of these creatures and examine my daughters' sketches while I tell you another story which is also true because I saw these things myself with my own eyes. I am right to think you don't remember—this was before the Peace of Havsa, so we were still at war. But all alone a man crossed through the line, unarmed, without speaking our language, already famous to us because of the wrongs he had done to us at Nova Zagora and other places. I tell you we might have been justified in shooting him where he stood, or striking his head from his shoulders and sending it to Schenck von Schenck. I tell you arguments were made. This man acted as nothing, and then asked if it was true as he had heard, that every year there was a wrestling competition in Adrianopole, the yagli-gures festival on Sarayici island—oiled wrestling, we call it. It is the most important competition of our national sport. And this man stood there, cold as anything; I tell you he was not a giant but an ordinary man. Smaller than myself. He was no great reptile as you see in my daughters' drawing. And so we laughed to think that he would fight against Vassilye the Greek and Mehmet the Conqueror, who had won the open competition for three successive years—the greatest champion of the age, we thought. And so the colonel said, why kill this man? Why take him prisoner? Mehmet the Conqueror will kill him with more glory to us, and we would put his bones into a bag and send them back to Frederick Schenck von Schenck, whose soldiers were pressing us so fiercely—if we'd only known how weak they were, and how they'd brought every starving boy onto the line to press us, while we held many back because of the caution and stupidity of our generals, who were not used to fighting a madman like von Schenck when he was keeping nothing in reserve—it doesn't matter. This boy was not yet twenty and he stood there with his hands behind his back, a look of stupid pride on his face as we all thought."

Still Turkkan was smelling the absinthe in his glass and had drunk none of it. He lifted it up, inspected the green glow.

"They took him for questions and he said nothing. You cannot imagine the impudence! So I was sent for, because I was a famous wrestler in the camp—I had received the silver cup from General Fernandes-Cohn. The general told me to make a fall with him, and so I did, in the stadium of the Janissary Corps.

I tell you I was the stronger man, but it was like struggling with water, or like Menelaus and Proteus in the story. I called him the Proteus man. Never could I hold him or catch a grip until I found myself straight on my back. I saw the mark before my face and I bit him—so, I am not proud of that. And I will try to make it up! Tonight I will try, my friend.

"So you must understand the arrogance of this man as he stood under the torches on Sarayici Island. A crowd of many thousands, and they wanted Mehmet to tear him to little pieces. It was the only reason we allowed it, to see the enemy beaten like this. In the army our spirit was low, though we had the stronger position—every day the stronger position as we retreated from von Schenck. We knew this man was a staff officer, aide-de-camp—we knew his reputation. This story of Nova Zagora, it was one of many! So the sultan promised Mehmet the Conqueror a diamond ring from his own finger."

"I don't remember," Peter said. He drank the absinthe in little sips. And sometimes he looked down and touched the sketches of unknown dinosaurs.

Now again he felt burdened and suffocated by the weight of this new story, though he longed to hear it: "So they stripped down naked in the pitch, and the boys came out to grease their bodies with the olive oil. I tell you, the Chevalier de Graz did not stand up to the shoulder of our champion. I alone thought he had a chance because of my experience—I kept my opinion to myself! I put some money on his head, though, in a bet, because I felt shamed by my loss, and shamed to see this one man standing against death in the city of his enemies, and a crowd of many thousands as I said. I put my money as a token for his courage, and I'm glad I did! In those days I was only a poor soldier. My father would not live in a house like this and send his son to school as I have sent my daughters. So my friend, I owe you many good things. I ask you, why did you kill this thief and criminal, Jacob Golcuk? If not for that, I would put you on a train to Bucharest with my own hands."

It was true, the intolerable green licorice taste hid another bitter flavor, which now touched Peter on the tongue. "So I beat the champion," he said.

"Three falls! Three falls! The first, we thought it was an accident, though I made double my bet. It was so quickly, we thought Mehmet had slipped. But I knew he had not gotten his grip, this man who could squeeze a brick to powder in his hands as I have seen him do. De Graz slipped through his fingers and then turned him so he fell.

"The next pass, it was the longest, and we saw the strength on both sides. Mehmet was careful now. I think he saw the diamond ring on one side of his mind, and anger and contempt of all the Turks upon the other—this for a man who had never lost a match. Who had never taken a fall, but now had taken one. In the crowd we thought he slipped, but he knew better. I thought I saw it in his eyes as they grappled and broke apart. Still he was always off-balance or stretched too far, and he was never in a place where he could use his strength. I tell you it was like fighting water or a nest of snakes, because he turned so quickly. But then his foot was behind the giant's knee, and the giant fell. Even though he rolled right up to continue fighting, there was no doubt of it. There was no accident this time. There was a terrible moaning from the crowd, and the princes of the court stood to go."

Peter's glass was empty and he put it down. Still Turkkan had not taken the first sip of his liquor. Still he frowned, and examined it in the light.

"I was in the seventh row. Right then as I stood there, I knew the war was lost. Not just the pehlivan competition, but the war with the barbarians, which we had fought for so long. In my great-grandfather's time our soldiers had reached the gates of Bucharest. Yet here we were, beaten by a boy as it occurred to us. I tell you, that fight was worth a brigade of soldiers to the enemy, and von Schenck knew it. Four weeks later he broke through at Havsa and the sultan gave him peace. And he was happy to take it, because he had no army left, as we found out when it was too late. I tell you he was a devil, this man with his tricks and stratagems. And now his daughter has come to life in Braila! I tell you they will never catch her. Ceausescu the white tyger is finished now, I tell you."

These words broke unexpectedly into Peter's thoughts. But he didn't want to talk about Miranda with Aristophanes Turkkan. "And the third fall?" he asked.

"Was over in a minute! Less than that! I was in the seventh row, and I could see Mehmet's face. This was a man who had never lost! When the judge gave the signal, he threw himself immediately on de Graz, hoping to take him by surprise. Once more he hoped to crush him with his strength, but the boy turned under his arm. He stepped behind him and struck him in the back between the shoulder blades. It was the first time he had struck him."

Now Turkkan drank his whole glass in one gulp. "I know!" he said, after he had wiped his mouth. "I tell you these things and they mean nothing. It is a story that has made you melancholy, I see. But it was something I wanted to set against the story of the calf, for we have all done terrible things. Because we are men upon this earth. Now tell me, why did you kill Jacob Golcuk? How could you take a fall from such a one? This is our last night and you must tell me. To-morrow there will be a penal convoy to the east."

"I didn't kill him."

The old man stared at him and shook his head. "Alas, my friend, I don't be-lieve you. But if it gives you pleasure to say nothing, I will understand. We have one night only, and it belongs to you. Where will we go, what will we see? If you like, my girls will come talk to us on the subject of their researches. I can see you are interested in these great lizards."

As he spoke, one of the girls came toward them across the open floor, bear-ing a sprig of paper in her hand. And despite what he'd said, her father seemed embarrassed she was in the room. "Please," he said, "you must see that we are busy!"

It was the first bad-tempered remark Peter had heard from him. But she came forward unabashed, the sprig of paper in her hands, until she stood with them—a tall young woman with two circles of fat braids. She was the one who smelled of citrus. Her face was freckled and her features were strong, and she stared at Peter out of her intelligent, small eyes. She smiled as she was speaking, and her tone seemed to suggest a trace of mockery both for her father and for him, although her words were straight enough. "Please sir, a man came to the door with a message for our guest. When the steward questioned him, he went away."

She spoke in English, and her father answered. "And what business is that of yours?"

"I thought it was important, so I came. I wanted to greet our guest and make him comfortable in our house. My name is Mariamne Turkkan, and you are welcome, sir. My sister is too shy."

In her left hand she had the sprig of paper, and she held out the other one to shake. Her grip was strong and hearty. She paid no attention to the clink of Peter's chain. "I see you are looking at my drawings of the thunder lizards. Do you like them?"

"It is enough!" said her father. "You see he does not suffer for adventures. Now I must ask you for the message as a matter of law. You must put it in my hand."

"But Papa—that is rude. It is for Domnul Gross." Still she was smiling, as if at a joke Peter didn't understand.

"Not so rude as this man is," grumbled her father. "You forget he is a pris-oner of the courts. Now you remind me of my work. Give it here!"

"Papa, I'm not sure what you're saying. The steward will tell you—"

"Give it here."

"Well then, of course we are all curious. I am sure Domnul Gross . . ." and she gave Peter her frankest smile.

The sprig unrolled in Turkkan's big palm. Three words were written on it in Andromeda's slashing script. *World Wrestling Tonite.*

"There, you see?" laughed Mariamne Turkkan. "Papa, I'm not sure what you suspect."

"I do not suspect, except daughters of mine will behave like gentle ladies in my house. Is that too much?" And he went on in Turkish while Peter watched his face. He didn't seem especially angry, nor did his daughter seem embarrassed.

"Do you like the drawings?" she asked.

"You are very skilled," said Peter

"Enough!" bellowed her father. "Get away from here!" As the girl retreated, still smiling, he crushed the paper in his hand and threw it to the floor. "Where were we? You must forgive her. She forgets you are a prisoner under sentence."

But the next moment he forgot it, too. "My gazelles' horns," he sighed. He poured himself another glass of absinthe and held it up into the light.

He had left the crumpled message lying in a corner of the floor. Peter looked at it, and looked again around the room at the upper windows, now dark, the slow fans, the litter of food on the small table. The girl's appearance and Andromeda's note had combined to lighten his mood.

Turkkan drank his liquor. He put down his glass, and with a napkin he wiped his moustache and his bald, sweating forehead. He took off his glasses to polish them. His eyes seemed suddenly mournful, until he replaced them and turned into the light.

He talked for a few moments about his daughters, about how difficult it had been to raise them since his poor wife's death. This led him to a brooding silence as he stared at the closed door at the far end of the room.

"Enough!" he said at last. "We must find some more amusement for this night. We have many hours before you leave us. What must you do? Mariamne is a chess player, and her younger sister can play and sing."

He seemed to have forgotten he had just chased Mariamne from the room. Peter dreaded the idea of sitting up with him, drinking absinthe. Besides, there was Andromeda's note. "Is there a wrestling competition?" he asked.

"Ha! It is impossible." Turkkan shook his head with something like amusement on his face. When Peter persisted, he cut him off: "You forget your situation."

But later, when they had sat in armchairs and Turkkan had smoked his pipe, then abruptly he changed his mind. A servant had come with more cups of coffee, and Turkkan told him to prepare the car. "Why not?" he said, his spectacles glinting fiercely. "Am I not a man? Is this not your final night? Is this not the sport of emperors?"

He stood up, put down his demitasse, and stripped off his embroidered gown. Underneath he was dressed in his khaki uniform. Around his waist was a leather belt, from which hung a long holster. He unbuckled the flap and showed the handle of a gun. "I will be with you every moment. I will not stop to shoot you dead."

"I understand."

"You think you will try something? Maybe you will meet your accomplices—go ahead! There will be soldiers there. At every competition there are many officers of the janissary police. De Graz, we are not afraid of you!"

Now quickly he led the way, while Peter took mincing steps because of the chain between his ankles. When they came out of the room, Turkkan held the door for him. "My friend! This will be a pleasure! This will be a privilege to see some matches in your company, even though this is the ordinary Friday competition and there will be no champions. It will be something for me to tell my daughters' sons. I mean when they are married and have sons, and are not such a worry to their father."

"They are lovely—"

Turkkan glared at him. "My friend, you do not laugh at me! What is beauty in this world, when compared to the love in a good woman's heart?"

Touched in spite of himself and his own troubles, Peter now preceded Turkkan down the long hall. Once he felt a sudden jab in his ribs, and turned back to find the old man had poked him with the muzzle of his revolver— "Shoot you dead!" he whispered. "I shall not stop to shoot you dead!"

A steward met them at the bottom of the hall, carrying his master's tarbush and fly whisk. The tarbush was a red pillbox hat with a black tassel, and Turkkan slid it onto his bald head while he was talking to the servants who now clustered around. He had replaced the revolver in his holster. The fly whisk, made of white horse hair at the end of a carved, ebony stick, he put under his arm. "Is the Pharaoh ready?" he asked.

THAT SAME NIGHT IN ROUMANIA, far from the civilizing influences of Adrianople, Bucharest, or even of Brasov, General Ion Antonescu sat in his hut in the Carpathian mountains. This was north of the village of Nucsoara in the Doamnei valley, a high, lonely, uninhabited place, where the partisans of the former empress had their camp. Valeria Dragonesti lay sick from a wasting fever. Doctors had come.

Long accustomed to the luxuries of the Winter Keep, she now lay on a rude mattress of pine needles in the hut's inner room. Outside her door the general sat before the fire reading a letter. Light came from the oil lamp on the surface of his writing desk, a rough-cut plank between two stumps. It shone on the woodpile and the dirt floor, the hearth and chimney. Antonescu sat on the only finished piece of furniture, an upholstered armchair taken from the wreck of the empress's hunting lodge. The fabric was now ripped and stained.

That spring, after five years of fighting, the fortunes of Antonescu's partisans were in decline. The previous summer, after the success of several bold raids, the German military governor of Transylvania had organized a response. He had pushed Antonescu back into the most inhospitable regions of the mountains, and had allowed him to suffer there over the cold winter.

Communications were difficult, which gave the letter he now read a double importance. He pored over the fine stationery, the elaborate, cursive, feminine script:

> . . . I have information I must share with you regarding the importation of proscribed armaments under the protocols of the African States. As you know, those protocols have forbidden the sale of any kind of automatic weaponry and advanced rockets, for fear of unbalancing the European powers. But I have reason to believe that the usurper has made an expensive purchase, leaving Constantinople on the train to Bucharest, hidden in a shipment of caviar and fruit preserves that will necessitate the ice-cooled car. The name of the train is the Hephaestion. It will cross the border at Dobric at two o'clock at night. . . .

And here the letter named the date.

The general had received this letter many days before. With characteristic energy he'd made his plans. If it had not been for the empress's illness, he personally would have supervised the derailment, whatever the risk—because of his huge size, disguises were no good for him. But he would have journeyed by night from safe-house to safe-house. The cause needed a victory, and he needed to find one, if only to come back and whisper news at Valeria's bedside, words of encouragement and hope.

General Antonescu sat in his armchair with his long legs sprawled out, reading and rereading the precious letter. There was nothing left to be done. It was not his fate to be there when the train crossed the Danube at Silistra and made its lonely progress through the Lalomitei marsh.

From the inner room he heard the empress cry out. There was nothing he could do about that. She was in the care of her devoted nurse who soothed her forehead and pushed back her hair, which in the past year had turned a lustrous shade of white. There was nothing he could do except upset her with his awkward movements, bump his head among the rafters. But he could not sit and listen to her cry, and so he pushed himself upright. Ducking his head, he stamped out of the door and stood outside, breathing in the cold air. The last light of the evening vanished from the rock face of the mountain, visible above him through the tall firs.

And though he stretched his arms and hands, though he stamped among the rocks in his high boots, though he opened the neck of his old uniform, still he could not shake the feeling of confinement.

NOR WERE THE CHAINS OF need, frustration, and anxiety that hampered him less strong than the chains around Peter's wrists after they'd been checked and rechecked by the soldiers. In a luxurious neighborhood outside the city of Adrianopole, he got into the rear seat of the cadi's Pharaoh motorcar, a long, open, stylish, internal-combustion vehicle. The air was wet and hot. A soldier sat in the front seat next to Ezekiel the chauffeur, and Turkkan squeezed in beside Peter in the back. Outside the wall of the cadi's house a narrow lane passed through a grove of fruit trees, some of which were still in flower.

The chauffeur turned the car onto the road. Cautiously peering ahead through the small windscreen, he opened up the *pop-pop* of the engine to a grumbling roar. Then he was off down the small hill through the deserted roads, until after fifteen minutes he came in through the old brick gates into the crowds. Still tinged with the colors of the sunset, the sky above the city was a soft, heavy purple, shredded and pricked by the carbide lanterns of the shops.

Now the chauffeur pressed his horn and flashed his headlights. They caught intermittently at the legs of people in the streets, who turned aside to let the Pharaoh pass. All roads led to the Hurriyet Meydani, the old town square beyond the synagogue. There a pitch had been laid out for wrestling. There the car came to a shuddering stop, and its clouds of greasy smoke drifted away.

At the opposite side of the square, Peter could see grandstands and a temporary barricade. The pitch was laid out under a four-cornered skeleton of wooden poles that supported the lights. Around it moved a crowd of spectators, vendors, and pickpockets, waiting for the next match.

Soldiers and black-uniformed janissaries made a passage for the cadi. With his hand over his holster he led Peter up the stairs into the grandstand. It was mostly deserted, as was the one across the way, for reasons that were soon apparent. Men bet money on these matches and the odds would change even when the fight was on. It was a complicated process and required an open area for negotiation—the bettors' circle around the pitch itself.

Even when the match had started, it seemed to Peter no one paid attention. Instead they hunched over their calculations, calling out numbers, paying out money, arguing among themselves. Peter sat between Turkkan and the soldier in the front row of the grandstand directly over the railing. A hundred feet away over the heads of the crowd, two enormous naked men, their skin greased and slippery, grappled and fell back.

The umpire blew his whistle. "Who are they?" Peter asked.

Turkkan shrugged. "It's not important. They are condemned prisoners. If one of them will win eleven matches, he'll be free. It has never happened."

He glanced back at Peter and smiled. "You must not think about this. This is not for you. This is by special permission only. In the morning you are gone away. No, I am sorry to remind you! Tonight we are friends—watch! Watch! Would you like some lemon sherbet? It is very good."

Turkkan bought some sherbet on a stick, as well as some sugar-cane juice. "This will chase away the green serpent," he said. "These are the simple pleasures—look at that black man. But he will take a fall!"

After a moment Peter found himself watching the fight, and then the next one, and the next. He could not take his eyes away. The men fought on a bed of black sand that stuck to them. Some of the wrestlers were subtle and quick, others relied on force. When they grappled there were many tiny tricks of balance, and Peter found that he could soon predict the outcome just by looking at the wrestlers' hands, the placement of their feet.

He leaned forward with his elbows on his knees. "Ho, you find it interesting, our little display!" Turkkan said. "I'm sorry you will not be here for the yagli-gures—let me give you some pistachios. And let me ask you, do you see that old man across the way? In the place of honor in the front. That toothless old man with the red beard—do you recognize him? No? I'll tell you that is Mehmet the Conqueror who is always coming to this place. Men shake his hand, boys ask for his blessing—what about you? In this city he is a great man."

Peter followed the pointing finger. There in the first row of the opposite grandstand on the far side of the pitch, the man sat. His red hair was streaked with gray. To call him old and toothless was not fair. He was smiling and talking to his companion, who shook his head.

Embarrassed in a way he didn't understand, Peter raised his eyes. A few rows up in the grandstand there was almost no one. But Andromeda was there as he had hoped, carefully dressed as a young officer, and she also was nodding and smiling to her companion, a squat, fox-faced little man in a leather cap and an old leather coat, decorated with patches of fur.

"By God, who is that?" muttered Turkkan beside him. He pointed with his fly whisk and then spoke rapidly to the soldier on Peter's other side, who stood up to get a better look. Peter was still watching his friend, who now appeared to see him for the first time; she smiled and blew a kiss.

"By God, who is that?" shouted Turkkan. He stood up in his seat as the soldier hurried down the steps. Now janissaries were pushing through the crowd. Peter saw Andromeda slide underneath the seat of the grandstand. She must have dropped through the scaffold underneath, but it was no use. The guards caught her at the barricade. They led her back into the bettors' circle until she stood under the cadi with an insolent smile on her face.

"Not that one!" shouted Turkkan. "You idiots—where is the other one? Find him for me." But in the confusion of the crowd, the fox-faced man had disappeared.

"This is the one," said a policeman. "This is the pickpocket of the Ali Pasa Carsisi. I am sure."

But Turkkan interrupted him: "It is not the man I want. By God, don't you think I know the difference between a dead man and a live one? Have I not seen him in my court since he was ten years old? Imbeciles—that was Jacob Golcuk!"

All this time he had been speaking Turkish and Peter had not understood him. But he understood that name and now he realized he had recognized the man in the leather coat. Turkkan stood up in his seat, waving his fly whisk—"This is a catastrophe! How dare you answer me? Release this man!"

The policemen stood away from Andromeda, but Turkkan was not satisfied. "No, you fools—this one! This one here! Strike off his chains!"

"Sir?"

"I will answer for it. This is on my authority. Is this a nation of laws?"

Red-faced, spectacles glittering, tarbush slipping from his forehead, Aristophanes Turkkan shouted and gesticulated to the crowd. The wrestlers, who for several minutes had been pushing at each other halfheartedly, now stopped altogether, though the umpire had not blown his whistle. Covered with black sand—for each had taken a fall—they stood uncertainly under the lights. Janissary policemen gathered near the barricade, but not one moved to do as Turkkan had suggested, not even the soldier who'd come with them in the car. They seemed anxious for another authority, and then they found it. Adnan Mejid Pasha was striding through the crowd.

There was a language of gestures, and Peter understood it. But then he looked into the faces of the people where he saw a range of passions. The wrestlers stared up at him with piglike eyes. Across the way, Mehmet the Conqueror had struggled to his feet.

Andromeda stood close to Peter on the other side of the railing. When he looked at her, she winked. Alone in that gathering, she did not seem excited or upset.

Adnan Mejid Pasha had climbed into the grandstand. Now he pushed forward to where they were, in the middle of the first row. It was obvious to Peter what he was saying, though it was in Turkish: "What are you doing? Are you drunk? How can you bring this prisoner here?"

"He is no prisoner! My friend is a free man. The Chevalier de Graz is free to go!"

Peter's name caused a ripple of sensation as it was flung into the crowd.

"What is this madness? Turkkan—I command you. Lower your voice at least."

"I will not lower my voice. I will proclaim this. I have seen Jacob Golcuk—you have all seen him. I am the judge in this case and I declare that I am satisfied."

"Where did you see him? What does this mean?"

"He ran away. It doesn't matter—I was not mistaken. Ask this man." And Turkkan pointed to Andromeda below the rail.

As interesting as this was to try to interpret, Peter only gave it half of his attention. For he was watching as Mehmet the Conqueror pushed slowly through the crowd, his right hand on the barricade around the wrestling pit.

"It is true," remarked Andromeda, smiling and cool. "That man was Jacob Golcuk."

Mejid Pasha leaned down to look at her. "And you are . . . ? Bah, I don't care—this is insanity. What motive could he have?"

Mehmet the Conqueror, as he approached, seemed to have trouble walking. His big hand was on the barricade and he limped with every step, favoring his left leg. Though tall, he was bent over and his chest was sunken in. His hair was red and gray, as was his beard.

"So we must catch him to find out," retorted Aristophanes Turkkan. "In these past months I have signed several warrants for his arrest. There are reasons he would want to seem as dead."

"Then why give his name to this stranger? Why would he come here?"

Andromeda said: "He gave me a false name but I recognized him. He's not the only man who cannot stay away from these matches. I believe he makes his money here."

"You shut up! You have no standing in this place. Am I right to think you are a subject of Roumania?"

"He's a pickpocket," added one of the policemen.

Peter was looking at Mehmet the Conqueror. Now he had left the barricade and was crossing the bettors' circle to the grandstand. He was dressed in evening clothes, and his lapel was adorned with a commemorative ribbon and a crescent moon. Now Peter could see a cane in his left hand, and he leaned on it as he limped slowly through the crowd, a smile on his face. "It is the Chevalier de Graz," he said. "By God, it is the Chevalier de Graz."

Tears stood in his eyes. He made one final push and flung himself onto the railing in front of Peter. Then he brought up his cramped, massive hands and seized Peter by both forearms above his manacles. The gold-headed cane clattered to the ground.

Peter looked into his bleared, rheumy eyes. The old man's hands were still powerful, and they pulled him forward so that Mehmet the Conqueror could kiss him on the cheeks. "Why is this man chained like a criminal?" he asked in English. His teeth were yellow as old ivory, and his breath was flavored with mint or fennel.

The crowd had gathered close now. They pressed against the railing where Peter sat. Even the naked wrestlers had come out of the pit. Mejid Pasha spoke to one of the policemen. "You must take him into custody to the Saraclar station house. Tomorrow he is off to Trebizond."

The crowd pressed against the railing. "No," said Mehmet the Conqueror. "I will see him fight again." Again he pulled Peter down to whisper in his ear in English. "All my life I never took but three falls."

Now there was a lot of shouting. Turkkan had his hand upon his gun and made a broad pantomime of drawing it. The janissary police, who'd seemed so numerous before, now were scarce in their black uniforms. But Mejid Pasha had not given up. "I tell you he's a criminal. He is the butcher of Nova Zagora—does anyone remember? Am I to let him go on the word of a drunken fool and a Roumanian thief? Captain—"

Now a blacksmith was coming to the rail with a big hammer and a chisel and an enormous pair of shears—a bolt-cutter with handles several feet long. The policeman and Mejid Pasha stood together in earnest conversation—the policeman was unarmed, Peter saw. And now suddenly Mejid Pasha pressed his way out of the grandstand, and the police retreated to the edges of the crowd. "He'll come back with a company of soldiers," said Andromeda. Then to Aristophanes Turkkan: "Sir, there is a night train to Bucharest, I beg you—"

The blacksmith had the bar of Peter's lock in the small beak of his bolt-cutter. But he could get no purchase on the hardened steel. Then Mehmet the Conqueror pushed him aside and took the ends of the bolt-cutter in his massive, cramped, arthritic hands. Four hard snaps and Peter was free. Once the manacles were off, he could feel how much the chains had hurt him. His wrists and ankles were chafed raw.

Turkkan reached to shake his hands. "My friend, I am glad for you. You see in their own way these people can appreciate our art."

Again Peter found himself staring into the face of Mehmet the Conqueror. And he felt something inside of him as he looked at the old warrior. It was not sentimentality. Instead it was a wave of ferociousness that filled his mouth with spit. "I want to fight," he said, words which astonished him. "You'll let me fight."

There was a sudden silence as all the chattering around them ceased. Then Andromeda raised her voice. She spoke to Turkkan, "Sir, there's no time. That man will return in half an hour."

"Bah! What are you talking about? We are here as watchers only."

"I want to fight," Peter said. The words sounded less strange at the third repetition.

The cadi shook his head. "But it must be impossible. You are my guest and you have seen these people. There are no champions here."

"I know the rules," Peter said, surprising himself. "Isn't there a spectator's challenge?"

"Yes," confirmed Mehmet the Conqueror. Several people in the crowd nodded their heads. Then no one said anything until Andromeda interrupted the silence once again:

"Sir, you must know that man will come with soldiers. If you could lend us some money, there's a train to Bucharest—"

"He can do nothing! Mejid Pasha! I am the judge in this case."

Now suddenly Turkkan had changed his mind. "Bah, if it will give you pleasure! A friendly match, a single fall, if you are sure. Afterward you come back to my house to celebrate. All Roumania will be my guest."

The crowd, who had been so eager to free him and protect him, now was eager to see him in the pit. Peter stood at the rail, squeezing his wrists, looking over the expectant faces. Of course. They had been raised on stories of his skill. He would not disappoint them and dishonor himself.

Andromeda grabbed hold of his arm. He leaned down to listen, and she whispered in his ear. "What is your problem? What do you think happens when you lose?"

He shook off her hand. He looked up to see a man step into the pit. He was dressed in a towel-cloth robe, which he now dropped. Naked, he put his hands on the barricade—"I am Roderick of Burgos. Champion I may not be, but I have heard of Nova Zagora. Even in the Spanish Empire we've heard these stories. Now I stand here for the honor of my adopted country, against a man who has stepped out of a children's fairy tale and a pagan sorcery that has kept him young and strong. I, too, am strong. So now I spit. . . ."

Peter understood none of this. But he understood the language of the Spaniard's body. He recognized the formal, measured, flowery phrases that indicated an official challenge. The recognition came from far inside. The crowd had opened up in front of him, from the railing of the grandstand to the barricade around the pit. Without thinking, Peter spat into the dirt.

Andromeda reached to take hold of his arm again. She pulled him down, though he resisted. He could see the golden hair that glistened on her cheeks. She whispered in his ear. "You've got to know you're not the Chevalier de Graz."

"Shut your mouth," he said, and his voice was light, harsh, ugly.

"All right. I'll put my money on the other guy."

She let go when he swatted at her, pushed her away. "One thousand piastres on my friend!" shouted Aristophanes Turkkan. The crowd was shouting and cheering as Peter ducked under the railing and stepped down. The bettors in the circle now were haggling and calling. Folded banknotes stood out from between their knuckles as they gesticulated and made their calculations.

For a while Peter stood there in the gap. The lights seemed harsh and glaring now. The crowd was massed along an open corridor between the grandstand and the pit:

Thousands of their sailors looked down from their decks and laughed,
Thousands of the soldiers made mock at the mad little craft,
Running on and on, 'til delayed,
By the mountainlike San Philip, of fifteen hundred tons. . . .

From the grandstand, Roderick of Burgos had not looked so big. Peter judged he was about thirty years old. He was clean-shaven and his hair was black and curly. Scars and welts stood out on his shoulders and biceps. But his legs were small, Peter noticed, and he had a purple bruise over his right knee.

As if by reflex as he stepped forward, Peter found himself measuring and judging each characteristic and detail of the man in front of him, from his high-arched, hammer-toed, broken-nailed feet, to his heavy, scarred eye ridges and forthright stare. His nose had been broken at least once, and he was missing a tooth. His knuckles, also, were thick and bruised. He'd had a couple of falls in his career, Peter thought.

There was a feeling in his stomach that was not fear but a species of relief. Since his arrest and long before—perhaps since that terrible night with Raevsky on the bridge, perhaps since the morning he had woken in the snow with his new hand, or perhaps since his first school days at home—in various parts of his mind he'd been afraid. To function he had had to live with fear. To close out fear had been to close out sections of himself. But now the barriers were down. Air moved through him end to end. As he stepped between the two masses of spectators, he felt the world under his feet, the paths that led to him and away. Behind him stretched the Aegyptian desert, and in front of him the earth curved north into Roumania, and there were the mountains, valleys, great rivers, and forests, and there was work to be done and wrongs to be set right. And there was a dream that was languishing in danger, and a woman he had sworn to protect. And his way to her was at that moment blocked by a rickety barricade. And behind it stood a broken-down Spanish fighter named Roderick of Burgos whom he'd beat with one hand because his left hand was weak—that was his shame, his secret to hide. He felt no anger or urgency. He saw himself duck under the rail. Roderick of Burgos had retreated to the center of the pit.

The crowd made a noise like the sea. Peter stood testing the sand under his feet. Then he stripped off the pumpkin-colored shirt, the pumpkin-colored trousers. The boy came with the oil but he waved him away. He would fight in the Roumanian fashion, ungreased, though he might give up a small advantage. He disdained any stretching or preparation. He stood with his legs splayed, his eyes closed, listening to the directions of the umpire—they would fight a single fall, apparently.

The ending of the poem now occurred to him, as clear as if he saw it on the page:

And the water began to heave and the weather began to moan,
And or ever that evening ended a great gale blew,
And a wave like the wave that is raised by an earthquake grew,
Till it smote on their hulls and their sails and their masts and their flags,
And the whole sea plunged and fell on the shot-shatter'd navy of
    Spain . . .

At the same time other images occurred to him as he stood with his eyes closed. They were like a series of photographs or flash cards, changing as he looked at them: faces, stone buildings, landscapes, horses, dogs, none of which had been part of his life in Berkshire County. They came in such profusion he could not make sense of them. They did not combine into a net of stories. They suggested nothing to be put in language. But each one brought with it an emotion, which he experienced as waves of hot and cold, dark and light.

Then he felt a blow upon his chest and he almost fell. Roderick of Burgos was there. Peter opened his eyes and saw the great heavy hand come swatting at him again. But it seemed to travel slowly as if pushing through an obstruction—Peter himself at that moment was not capable of moving quickly. But he could move faster than the ponderous hand that seemed to make a noise as it pressed through the air. Around him was the roaring of the crowd.

Laboriously and sluggishly, he ducked and turned away. Another hand now came to seize him by the shoulder. It moved with absurd slowness and he turned away from it. Burgos's leg was at the level of a stool, but he stumbled over it and almost tripped. Then he pushed his foot under the man's heel and lifted up, expecting him to jump away. There was all the time in the world. But he was as awkward as he looked. He lost his balance. Peter seized him by his waist, and twisted him, and flung him down.

The Spaniard fell onto his back. Then there was time for him to roll away and get back up before Peter, after long deliberation, knelt down on his chest. He pressed the man's head into the sand. Holding his left hand hidden behind his back, he grabbed hold of the man's chin in his right hand and pressed his head back, and then released him, and then pressed him back, and then released him. And every time the back of the man's head struck the dark surface of the sand, it was as if a new part of the story was shaken clear in Peter's mind; the man grabbed and flailed and tried to twist under Peter's weight. "De Graz!" shouted the crowd. "De Graz!" And de Graz paid no attention either to the crowd or to the struggles of the man, but instead he was listening to the stories in his head as they arranged themselves and joined themselves together. Slippery as expert wrestlers, they moved away as he approached them, but they were there, and he knew them after all, and Roderick of Burgos was beaten, and with him Peter Gross had also taken a fall, after fighting long and stubbornly and valiantly to keep upright:

. . . and the little *Revenge* herself went down 'mid the island crags,
To be lost evermore in the Main.

ANDROMEDA HAD CLIMBED INTO THE grandstand to sit in Peter's seat. She'd not waited for an invitation from Turkkan. Now she hunched her shoulders and slid down, and leaned back on the empty bench behind her. Her pale eyes were closed to slits, and her long boots were thrust under the railing.

She was the first to sense the change in the man in front of her, even before Peter himself. When he released the Spaniard and let him up, he stood splay-footed in the sand while the people cheered. Naked, legs spread, he stared at her with eyes as unself-conscious as an animal's. He didn't blink. In the language of his body there was no shame or awkward diffidence, nothing that suggested her old friend Peter Gross, who had stepped into the pit a few minutes before. Instead in his tense body and proud face the part of her that was Prochenko recognized a comrade and well-worn adversary.

No, it was not right to call him proud. That was the mark her envy put on him. He was too innocent to be conceited, too unaware of the world's attention. He was a man of action and desire and one other thing, a glimmer of irrationality that was apparent in everything he did.

Andromeda slouched in her seat. Though it was a hot, humid night, she felt gooseflesh on her skin. There was, however, work to be done, and so she turned to Aristophanes Turkkan, who was chuckling and clapping. "Hum? Did you ever see such a thing? Less than one second! And he was not in the best condition, I can tell you. Stuffed with food and drink. And for three days he has had the chains on his hands."

"Do you think there are some clothes he could borrow?"

"Hum? Yes—I should think he'd have some clothes. I will give him my own coat. Tonight he is a guest in my house."

With her long fingernails Andromeda scratched her forearm underneath her French shirt-cuff. "Sir, I think we will refuse your offer. Mejid Pasha will be here. I think this man should cross the border."

"Mejid Pasha—bah! I am the presiding judge."

All this time Pieter de Graz had been staring at her. But now he turned and rubbed his face in the towel that the boy held out for him. Andromeda found herself admiring his muscled back and buttocks—she was worried for her friend. She knew that she and Sasha Prochenko were similarly made. Both had a layer of bravado and a layer of embarrassment around their hearts, as her father in Berkeley had once poetically described her. But Peter and de Graz were miles apart.

"Even so," she said.

The crowd began to move around the betting circle once again. The bookmakers were collecting money and paying it out. Men came out to rake the sand for the next match. Aristophanes Turkkan got to his feet, yawned, stretched, scratched his chin. Then he pushed his way off the grandstand and stamped down the steps. Andromeda got up, too.

She found him urinating beside the scaffold in the back. She waited until he was finished. "Please."

Buttoning himself, he turned to face her. They were in the shadow of the stand, away from the lights and the pressure of the crowd. They could hear the muted sounds of the barkers. "I don't want to speak to you," said Aristophanes Turkkan. "The Chevalier de Graz will be my guest. But you—with you Roumanians there is always trouble. So you must go away and then we will have peace again. I give you this, and you must not be asking for another gift. Hah!—and one thing more. I will not ask for witnesses from the bazaar."

"Sir, Mejid Pasha must not find us. The chevalier and I must leave this place. You can't let Mejid Pasha overturn your wise decision."

The old man's attention was now divided by an announcement from the umpire in the pit. But he turned back to look at her. "Why are you always mentioning this man? You must not insult me. This is justice and not victory. I am having some demands upon my time."

His expression of disdain was eloquent. And something else: Quite suddenly he was drunk. He swayed on his feet as he stared down at her. Andromeda imagined he was disgusted by Prochenko's effeminacy. She stepped closer so he could smell the perfume on her skin and see the gold hair on her neck. "Sir, I'm grateful. I'm appealing to your love of justice. What's the good of giving him his freedom if tomorrow he is locked away? My government will thank you. When he gets home you will receive an invitation from the Countess de Graz."

Aristophanes Turkkan reached out his big hand. He brushed the shoulder of her silk shirt. Then he seized hold of her earlobe as if to find his balance. He pulled her to him by the ear, and she could smell the liquor on his breath. And something else when he had belched, some hint of vomit. His hand was powerful. She did not resist him. "Do I care for the thanks of my enemies? I tell you I would never enter such a country of devils!" He shook her once and let his hand drop to her arm.

You old goat, Andromeda thought, as he caressed the ball of her shoulder.

He was a tall, big-chested man. He drew her close and whispered into her ear. "What do you want?"

"Sir, the loan of your car. In four hours we could cross into Roumania."

"You are quite insane." But he was still squeezing her shoulder.

Now there were some more muffled announcements as a new match started. The Chevalier de Graz was walking among the scaffolding, looking for them. They saw him moving among the long corridors of supporting struts. Aristophanes Turkkan murmured in her ear. "Am I right in thinking you would take this motorcar and disappear in the dark night? That there is nothing real or sane about all this? I think we have been flying among ghosts and shadows, and so now we must come back to the ground. Does he look like a man of forty-five and more?"

De Graz had not reassumed his jailbird overalls. Instead he'd found some new clothes from somewhere—perhaps from the umpires or his fellow wrestlers. He was dressed in pale tight trousers that left his shins bare, and he wasn't wearing any shoes. His shirt was loose around his neck. Now he turned and saw them. He came striding down the tallest corridor under the scaffold, spattered and striped by the light that filtered through the planks. He stepped through the empty bottles and detritus until he stood beside them. Turkkan let go of Andromeda's shoulder.

She said, "You'd come with us. I am asking you to take us to the border."

Then came de Graz's light, irritating, well-remembered voice, joining in as if he'd overheard. "You must have no concerns about the safety of your property. I give my word of honor in return for your generosity."

This kind of idiotic nonsense had always been typical of de Graz. But because he spoke without a trace of irony or self-consciousness, it had an authenticity that was effective sometimes, though not at that moment. Turkkan stared at him.

"My friend, you will not come to be my guest, me and my daughters?"

"Sir, I long for my own country."

"Bah!" Turkkan was immediately angry. He made a theatrical gesture with his arm, which had the effect of throwing him off balance. Staggering forward, he smacked his forehead on a protruding wooden strut under the grandstand. "Cowards!" he shouted. "Assassins—great Jehovah!" and fell heavily on his back.

Andromeda and de Graz knelt down. The old man wasn't hurt. He was just stunned and drunk. He groaned as Andromeda slipped her hand between the buttons of his coat, searching for his pocketbook among the folds of his damp undershirt. But de Graz caught her wrist in his right hand. He squeezed until her muscles failed. At the same time he was staring at her, smiling. His eyes had always been a little dilated, she now remembered. And as always he'd forgotten the task at hand. It was going to be up to her to drag his stubborn carcass to Roumania.

"Laissez-le," he whispered.

"What about the gun?"

"Laissez-le."

But someone had already heard the old man's cries. Around the corner of the grandstand came the chauffeur and the soldier and two other men. Andromeda recognized one of them, a tall, emaciated man. He'd taken charge of her last bet—fifty piastres on Roderick de Burgos.

"Crud," she murmured, a word her mother had been fond of in the house on Syndicate Road. The soldier had a gun in his hands, a strange, short, modern-looking rifle with a barrel of black steel.

"Double-crud," she murmured. She stood up, forced herself to smile. She spoke in Turkish, "Oh, I'm glad you've come. The cadi has hurt himself."

But the soldier wasn't having any of that. The men behind him were jabbering and swearing, but he said nothing. Andromeda showed her empty hands, then clasped them together. "Bey efendiler—gentlemen, where is the hospital? Look what has happened! He was drinking, I suppose."

The idea was to get all of them inside a car. If de Graz would just get up and show himself also to be harmless, then . . . But it was not to be wished. He was still squatting over the body of Aristophanes Turkkan. She had scarcely finished speaking when he lifted the old man's revolver and fired.

No doubt if he had gotten a clear shot, he would have pierced the soldier through the brain. He was quite a marksman. But two things happened as he pulled the trigger. First, the old man started to bellow and seized him by the wrist. Second, the gun misfired when the hammer came down, and there was a flash of light. De Graz cuffed Turkkan with the ruined gun, then threw himself at the soldier as he now stood uncertain. In just a few seconds he had seized the rifle by its barrel and twisted it away, and slapped the soldier down with it as well as one of the other men—not the bookmaker, Andromeda saw, which was a pity. Tall, with a long neck and big Adam's apple, he backed up beside the grandstand while de Graz took a few steps toward him.

"Don't be such an asshole," Andromeda suggested uselessly. She ducked under the grandstand and started running down the corridor of scaffolding. De Graz came after her, and it wasn't until they had come out the other side into the crowd at the entrance to the pit that they realized the bookmaker had followed them. De Graz had dropped the gun.

One part of the crowd was now discovering the three unconscious men and raising the alarm. But this part on the other side of the main grandstand had not yet heard anything about it. The distance was not long, however, and Andromeda strode quickly toward the gate. Beyond the barricade she could see black-coated janissaries—the next obstacle. But the way was now blocked by people in the crowd who came forward to meet de Graz and shake his hands. Roderick de Burgos was there, all smiles. And leaning on his arm was Mehmet the Conqueror.

"Friends!" he cried. And de Graz was such a preening fool, he actually stopped. "Thank you for the lending of your trousers," he said in English.

Another smaller wrestler now came forward to grasp his hand. And soon he was surrounded by a gang of men. Some were greased and oiled, naked from the waist up.

"Please," said Andromeda, "will you help us?" She gestured toward the uniformed policemen. There also, where the crowd was less, stood the sleek and shiny motorcar of Aristophanes Turkkan. Its long bonnet was silver, and its wheel guards were gold. There were several others cars beside it.

But no one was paying any attention to her. They thronged around the Chevalier de Graz, slapping him on the back. And when they pushed all together through the gate, it was less out of a plan to hinder the police than out of the natural carelessness of crowds. Perhaps a hundred people swelled through the barricade.

But no doubt Mejid Pasha was a cautious man, Andromeda thought, unwilling to risk a riot. He would stop them at the city gates, or on the road, or at the Roumanian frontier. Doubtless he'd sent messages by telegraph.

With the others she came to Turkkan's car. The chauffeur was standing beside the running board. Andromeda walked ahead of the crowd toward him. "Lütfen—please, your master sends his greetings. He asks if you can make two trips. First the Chevalier de Graz and me, along with one other. Next you will return for him."

"Benim emirlerim Eristofanis Bey'dan aliyorum—I take my orders from Mr. Turkkan."

He was no dope, Andromeda thought wistfully. And Mehmet the Conqueror now looked around. "Eee—so where is Turkkan? I thought he was going for a piss."

Shouts came from behind them. With obvious reluctance, the chauffeur left the car and walked back toward the wrestling pitch. The wrestlers moved to the next car in the line, a larger and shabbier vehicle that belonged to Mehmet the Conqueror. Andromeda thanked some dual version of God for this piece of luck, and because the passenger compartment was closed. What to do? The janissaries were sure to stop the first car on the road.

The bookmaker was still with them, the tall man with the Adam's apple who had followed them. "Vreau sa te ajut—Please, I want to help," he murmured in her ear, reaching for her elbow as she pulled angrily away. It took her a moment to realize he was speaking in Roumanian. He made a quick, possessive gesture down the line of automobiles. "Acesta e al meu—This one's mine."

"You go on ahead to the cadi's house," she said to Mehmet the Conqueror. "We'll wait for him and follow."

The old wrestler shrugged, then sat down heavily in the front seat of his motorcar. Roderick de Burgos worked the crank and slid behind the wheel as the engine came to life. Three other men squeezed into the back compartment; through its small rear windows, the space seemed full of anonymous biceps and torsos, which was the effect Andromeda wanted. She hoped the police would let it run at least out of sight of the fairground before they forced it off the road.

The car honked its horn and turned in a wide circle. Peter and Andromeda, still hidden in a crowd, came to the next conveyance in the line. This was even better, a windowless, closed van. Andromeda looked for the bookmaker. His dark hair was clipped close, and he wore wire-rimmed spectacles on his beak of a nose.

"Daca vrei banii—If you want the money I owe you," she murmured, "you'll get us out of here." They didn't have more than a minute or so. She didn't look back to the cadi's motorcar. Every moment she expected to hear his strident voice.

The van's rear compartment opened from the back with double doors. Peter, uncomprehending, got in while the bookmaker started the machine. It made a weak, nasty noise, then caught and held.

The way to Turkkan's house led down Talat Pasa Caddesi to the gate, east along the main road of the town. Andromeda pointed south over the cobblestones into the warren of small lanes behind the Ucserefeli synagogue. "Is it true he is the Chevalier de Graz?" the bookmaker asked. "My father was with him at Nova Zagora. These Turkish infidels, they never understand."

Confused now, the crowd had changed directions and was pulling back from them. Andromeda didn't turn around. "You are a patriot. Take this as payment, and when you get to the bottom of the Eski Carsisi, then you must stop for one moment. Then go on to the Dobric road as quickly as you can. Then you drive straight north toward the border, far as you can manage. If they stop you, you've done nothing wrong."

She pressed into his palm the ring she'd bought in Alexandria, her last stake on this gamble. Then she got into the back of the van and held the doors closed as it bumped away toward the domed mass of the temple.

Soon they were beyond the range of lanterns and torchlight. After only a few minutes the van stopped. Andromeda pulled Peter out, then rapped on the doors. The van turned at the corner.

She pulled de Graz along the wall beside the garbage ditch. The lanes here were deserted, and it was filthy dark. This was a commercial district. In time they could see the lights of the railway yard. The old city wall had been torn down along this side. The station was a few miles out of town.

They walked across the wide deserted yard among the boxcars on their sidings and the piles of lumber under canvas. They looked for the night watchman but saw no one. They crossed an embankment of crushed stone. The land was arid on the other side of the river. There were few trees, and they could see the moon. The air had lost the perfume of the town, and as Andromeda walked along the track, she was aware for the first time of a gunpowder smell from de Graz's hands, burned from the misfire.

"We've got to move," she said. The stones and splintered ties were hard under her boots. De Graz was barefoot, but he didn't complain.

She spoke in English, and he answered in French: "C'est loin?"

"Not far."

They walked on south. In time they saw the station on ahead, the four long platforms and the high gas lampposts, under whose light they could see black-coated janissaries and dogs.

But the train was there too, halted for the late dinner hour, taking on coal for the trip north. The long black steam engine led a row of silver passenger cars. Beside them men and women smoked and talked, while the guards walked back and forth.

"Mejid Pasha," whispered Andromeda.

"Vous êtes fou."

Folle, Andromeda corrected in her own mind. But she said nothing. It didn't matter. They stood in the cinders of the track, in the darkness under the half moon.

The engine was the second in the line. In front of it there stood a gray, closed, metal car without windows or markings. Sometimes, Andromeda knew, the trains from Constantinople would push empty freight cars in front of them in case Bulgar bandits had mined the track near the frontier. But this was different.

The track went round a curve north of the station. On the outside of the curve it ran along a raised embankment. De Graz and Andromeda now descended part of this steep small hill, so they could approach the station out of sight. The gray car protruded beyond the station platform, outside the circle of gaslight into the dark.

Now on their hands and knees, pulling themselves along the dry bushes, they came along the outside of the curve. Gouts of steam rose to the sky, and they were spattered in the hot spray. Presently they heard the long hiss. The platform was hidden by the arc of the train as they approached the mysterious gray car. Now in this one place they could stand upright, hidden even from the headlights of the engine, which shined through the struts of the car. They could see the driver's compartment, still empty. And it was impossible to imagine they could climb upon the car itself, under the driver's nose. And it was impossible to think they could find their way among the brightly-lit passenger cars. Surely the dogs would smell her, Andromeda thought, would smell her scent.

She put her hand to the smooth gray metal. Above her was a curved, pad-locked door. Squatting down, she looked into the carriage's underside. Once she'd seen a movie about people escaping from the Nazis—yes, it was just possible. Between the track and the recessed bottom of the car there was a distance of about three feet. Above the system of axles and struts there were steel spreaders at intervals, and between them a woven metal grille. These spreaders were not structural to the car, but they supported five oblong blocks of cork. Lying on her back, Andromeda dug her fingers into them. They were saturated with cold water.

"Help me," she whispered. But de Graz did nothing. He squatted on his heels on the railroad tie, peering into the greasy dirty belly of the carriage as she worked at the cork blocks.

"Get underneath here," she whispered, afraid that the engine driver would soon take his seat. The headlamps of the train shed a harsh, indirect light, which shone on both sides of the track. The cork blocks were made to be re-moved; you could slide them inch by inch off the edge of the grille until they fell—greasy, sodden, heavy—to the cinders.

"Slide them down," she whispered. But de Graz did nothing, and so she pushed them off herself. Instead of rolling down the embankment, they lay in the debris that lined the outside of the curving track. Now there was a space between the spreaders and the cold roof, and the grille would hold them. Above, a steel grating was set into the bottom of the car. Water leaked from it.

She and de Graz climbed into that space and lay on their stomachs end to end, peering down at the track two feet below them. They lay there a long time. Once they saw a man's boots as he walked around the car. Andromeda thought he'd have to notice the discarded blocks. But there was enough anony-mous junk along the track to hide them.

Toward midnight, with much screeching and hooting, the train started to move. Then, and in the next hours, Andromeda realized that the movie she had seen had not in any way tried to reproduce the experience of riding on the underside of a railway train. Thrown up from the track, chunks of cinder pelted them. And they were soaked with the cold water from the grate. Nor was it quiet under there. Nor was her position a comfortable one. She listened to the pounding shudder of the track for several hours, the screech of the bare wheels as they went around a turn. The ties were like a ladder below her, and she was clattering up the ladder to Roumania, Roumania, Roumania.

Finally they slowed and stopped. Andromeda expected they had reached a station, but there were no lights and no sign of a platform. Even the headlamps of the train for a moment were extinguished. Andromeda was in the throbbing, quiet darkness. "This really sucks," she whispered.

But when she turned her head she saw de Graz was gone. Above where he had been, the drainage grate into the car had been removed. Maybe this whole way he'd been working on it, and now she saw he'd managed to pry it from its bracket. It lay on the metal grille, a rectangle maybe eighteen inches square—enough to climb through.

She slid backward and then poked herself up through the hole just as the train started to move again. It lurched forward as she pulled herself up into a cold black space. "Are you there?' she whispered.

"Oui."

She sat down on the wet metal floor. Now the headlamps were lit again, and the only light came from the square hole. After a moment her eyes adjusted, and she saw de Graz standing near her, holding onto a bracket as the train went around a curve, examining a kerosene lantern that was set into the wall.

"I've got a match," she said.

There was a box of phaetons in her pocket, which she gave to him. And when he lit a match, she reached back to cool her hand against one of several refrigerator-sized blocks of ice, tied together in the center of the car.

The metal floor was wet, but she didn't stand up. She sat next to the square hole and watched the track go by. There was a small open space around the blocks of ice, illuminated by the kerosene lantern. But most of their car was taken up with freight: boxes of fruit, wooden crates of jars and bottles.

The light shuddered to the rhythm of the train. It fell on Pieter de Graz in his wrestler's clothes. She found himself staring up at him and he stared back. There was nothing else to do.

She cleared her throat. "Hey, you looked really cute out there without your pants."

She was talking about him in the wrestler's pitch, grappling naked with the Spanish fighter. She said it to goad him, but was not prepared for the ferocious look he gave her. His face, contorted with disgust, bore no resemblance to the face he'd had that evening when she'd first seen him at the pitch. Every feature was the same, but she saw no trace of Peter Gross.

"So are you still in there at all?" she asked, but he said nothing.

She persevered. "Do you still remember how Cardillo kicked you out of music class? I thought that was so cool. You just sat there with your eyes closed, humming that song, and you wouldn't look at him. Or what about the next time when you had that fight with Kevin Markasev?"

"Je me souviens—I remember."

"And Nova Zagora?"

"Je me souviens."

And that seemed to be it in terms of conversation. He swayed above her with his hand on the bracket, hour after hour. She leaned her back against a crate of pickled mangoes, stretched her legs out. In her pocket she found a packet of cigarettes, but every single one of them was spindled and damp. Hoping they would dry out, she held two of the best ones in her cupped palm. She put her head back, and even though it was cold in that cramped space, she found herself nodding to sleep. Once she looked up to see de Graz eating fish eggs out of a bottle. His lips were smeared with black.

"Vous avez faim?" he asked. But she wasn't hungry. She felt sick to her stomach in a way she recognized.

111

The Secret World

14   *The House on Spatarul*

IN BUCHAREST ON THAT same night, Nicola Ceausescu had left the People's Palace by a servant's door. She knew of the Hephaestion's departure from Constantinople, though there were yet many hours before it crossed the border. She'd arranged for Jean-Baptiste to meet it at the Gara de Nord, and to supervise in secret the unloading of her crates.

What was in them, she scarcely knew. Something deadly and important that had changed the politics of northern Africa. Some chemical or virus that had been developed by important scientists, and not a conjurer among them. Yet their descriptions of its properties suggested conjuring, as well as a slow, long-lived poison that could contaminate an entire city—that was the weapon she would use against the potato-eaters in Berlin! That was the weapon she would use against the Elector of Ratisbon, whose skill as an alchemist had blocked every attack out of the hidden world.

In any case she had not yet found time for much research! Jean-Baptiste had seen to the details. Everything would be all right. The Abyssinian technician would show her what to do. Jean-Baptiste would find a hotel for him; Radu Luckacz was away from town, she'd made sure of that! And even though she knew it was important to maintain appearances, still she had canceled her evening performance, a reading of Euripides she had prepared for a small audience at the National Theatre.

Over the past year she'd considered returning to the stage after an absence of two decades. This was her first attempt in that direction—it was not even a proper performance! Anxious beyond reason, after supper she resolved to walk the cobblestoned streets by herself, in her guardsman's uniform and cape. She was hoping to relax herself, calm her nerves, find comfort from an indirect communication with her people, and visit Kevin Markasev in the Strada Spatarul.

This was the boy who had wandered onto her doorstep in Cluj, the boy she'd sent to fetch Miranda Popescu out of Massachusetts. This was the boy who'd been arrested for the murder of a German officer in the first days of the occupation—close to the wall that runs the length of the Calea Academei, she reached out her left hand and scraped it along the bricks. As always when she found the halfway point between the palace and the comfortable house she had provided for him, a surge of guilt came over her and made her weak, made her grasp at the coarse wall for support. Surely she was an evil woman who would get what she deserved. But no—wasn't she a loving mother to her people, at least as far as the potato-eaters had allowed? Hadn't she rescued her country from Zelea Codreanu the vampire? Even his corpse had not been found.

Waves of hot and cold came over her as she dug her knuckles into the wall. She would make the Germans pay for stealing her son.

But even as she surrendered to them, she realized these feelings were an indulgence, and they grew and thrived on idleness. Since the beginning of the eastern campaign the German government had dropped all pretenses. Official documents were now prepared for her signature by the Committee for Roumanian Affairs. The baroness had no responsibilities except to agonize and fret, and to reproach herself for the sake of Kevin Markasev.

But surely she was blameless there too, because she'd saved his life! If not for her, doubtless he would have been executed or imprisoned for the murder of Sergeant-Colonel Boris Blum outside the Palace Hotel. And if she still held him in a prison of her own, surely it was only to protect him.

Alchemists and conjurers require hostages to keep them strong, the baroness knew or thought she knew. Imprisoning another soul was like keeping money in a bank account. Scientists had proved this. Her husband had proved it, drawing on the ancient knowledge of Hermes Trismegistus. She had studied the passage in her husband's notebook, and it was true. The Elector of Ratisbon kept her son and Clara Brancoveanu prisoners in his house. And she had Kevin Markasev.

That night as she approached the house on Spatarul, the baroness went over the justifications in her mind, which was her constant habit. It is an artist's challenge to pick out of the chaos of life the random, subtle pattern of fate. She approached this task as she did everything, with creative skill. But because part of her greatness of an artist came out of her unrelenting honesty and pitiless self-examination, she returned again and again to the same facts and was not satisfied.

She was dressed in a guardsman's uniform. Her boots made a clapping noise on the new stones. As she turned among the comfortable houses of the Strada Doamnei, she kept away from the streetlights. There were carriages in the road, men and women returning home from the theaters and restaurants of the old town. Instinctively the baroness took her hand out of her pocket where she had been fingering her tourmaline, Kepler's Eye. It was the source of her people's love, but she didn't want to feel their adoration at that moment. She wanted to pass unperceived.

That night she was depressed and restless because no matter how she tried to manipulate and invent, Radu Luckacz had too grandiose a part in the third act of her play.

This was the project she'd been working on, toward which the reading from Euripides was just a feint. The title of it was *The Tourmaline*. Except for the music and the songs she had not yet written a line, but on long walks at nighttime she brooded over every scene—there was no problem with the first two acts. In her mind they were complete. The curtain would open on a village in the mountains, a young girl born in poverty. One day, standing in the cold stable with a bucket of milk, a waking dream occurs to her, a vision of herself. And because she drops the bucket, she is afraid of being beaten. She runs away to Bucharest and lives there in deserted buildings and railway sidings. She does a thousand disgusting things to stay alive. But because some talents are so great they cannot be broken, and because some characters are refined by suffering, by the time she is a woman she is famous in the theaters of the capital and abroad. She chooses to marry the deputy prime minister of Roumania, a hero who has saved his country from the Germans and the treachery of a half-German general. She retires from the stage. The gods and goddesses give her a child.

The second act is darker, minor-keyed. The evidence against von Schenck was forged, as it turns out, invented by her husband, a jealous old man now driven mad by guilt. Desperate to find purity, he beggars himself with alchemical research and writes new laws against political and racial corruption. The victim of one of these is his own son. Wrongly convinced the boy is illegitimate, he has him diagnosed and interned. Bankrupt, broken by remorse, he commits suicide and leaves his wife alone.

Oh, this was work she could be proud of, she thought—an oratorio or else an opera, though perhaps there would be intervals of dancing. By the end of the second act her fortunes will have come full circle. Chased from her home, she lives in the streets again, pursued by unjust enemies—the Empress of Roumania, a German elector, and von Schenck's daughter. All she has to protect herself is her own wit and courage and a miraculous jewel. As the curtain falls, and the police swarm to arrest her on a trumped-up charge, and as German troops march through the streets of her beloved city, she discovers one more thing: her destiny, at last!

In front of her a group of officers came down the flagstone walk, laughing and chatting and smoking cigars. Afraid of being greeted or accosted, the baroness crossed the street and waited in the mouth of an alley between two houses.

The flaw in the plot, she knew, was in the final act, and it wasn't just because the actual events were not complete. But the trajectory and shape had already gone wrong, though there remained two obvious contingencies. First, it was possible this drama was a tragedy, and that she herself was the tragic heroine, undone at the moment of triumph by her mistakes and sins. Oh, and if this were so, what a slaughter she would leave upon the stage!

But it was also possible that that she would find a way to reassert herself, that she would chase the potato-eaters from her country and rule wisely and compassionately over Great Roumania. That she would become the white tyger not just in name. And even if she died in accomplishing this, the curtain would still fall on a crescendo of hope and love and the thanks of her joyful people.

So in either case it was right for the first half of the act to be muted and doubtful. All that would change with the arrival of the Hephaestion at the Gara de Nord. All that would change when she had the weapon in her hand, the thunderbolt that she had purchased from the Abyssinians—a mineral so poisonous that it had to be transported in lead-lined cylinders, as Jean-Baptiste had explained.

This was her experiment, a new weapon for a new age. And she needed a new weapon. The Elector of Ratisbon had thwarted all the conjuring she had attempted at long range over the German border. Still he was protecting his own country, as she would protect hers with this new slow-moving poison, as effective as a curse.

Radu Luckacz didn't know anything about it. There was a lot she'd hidden from him. She didn't trust him not because he was unfaithful, but because he had usurped her place at the center of the drama, at least in the final act. At least so far. And her cruelty to Kevin Markasev, a boy who loved her, also was a difficulty, though it could be explained.

Here was the plot of the last act, as far as she had sketched it out: Domnul Luckacz was a police detective in District Station Number Three off the Elysian Fields, on that night in early spring when she had been arrested. This was when German soldiers were first loose in the city. She had been apprehended by a Hanovarian officer and then turned over to the Roumanian police. As it happened (and this was the coincidence necessary to all dramatic plots, to intimate the hidden role of fate), Kevin Markasev was being questioned at the same station after the death of Sergeant-Colonel Blum, who had been shot outside the revolving doors of his hotel.

Alone in her prison cell, Nicola Ceausescu feels the thrilling presence of two men who adore her. She hears the boy's voice in the next room. The tourmaline vibrates in her hand. And it was true—when Radu Luckacz saw her that night, she begged for the boy's life. How could she not? She was to blame for his predicament. It was she who had hypnotized him, given him the gun to use against the Elector of Ratisbon, also a guest at the Athenée Palace Hotel. And it was not her fault that the idiot boy had ended up shooting the wrong man!

But after that (honesty forced her to admit), Luckacz had managed everything. It was he who had contrived her freedom in the chaos of events. It was he who had produced the body that was buried in the grave meant for Markasev. And it was he who had suggested that she speak at his funeral. On that cold day she had stood with the tourmaline next to her skin, and the entire crowd had felt its power. She had wept over the tomb of Markasev and praised his heroism, his youth, his virgin innocence, his courage, because he had been the only one to strike a blow for Great Roumania when German troops first marched along the Calea Victoriei. He had seen a poor fallen girl in the piata, abused and then abandoned by a German officer—was it any wonder that his heart broke in his chest? Was it any wonder that he seized his gun? Etc., etc.— long had he been tortured by Roumanian collaborators in District Police Station Number Three. But he had gone to his death without revealing a single name.

And—she must be honest—it was Radu Luckacz who had engineered the rest, the songs, the flags, the banners, the cult of Kevin Markasev. Her role had been symbolic: the white tyger, sent to comfort her poor country, and what Radu Luckacz had arranged she did not want to know. He also hated the Germans. But perhaps it was his hatred that allowed him to be so cold. Certainly he'd had conversations with the German authorities and with General Stoessel—von Stoessel now. When the Empress Valeria had fled the city, Luckacz had presented a symbolic alternative to the German high command, while the Roumanian political opposition—the socialists and democrats—were arrested and gathered up.

No, it was obvious she'd been complicit in a crime. She'd allowed her face to be a mask upon the face of German tyranny, which was why she was permitted to mouth her anti-German slogans—it was proof of how little the potato-eaters cared. It was proof of how secure they felt. All that would change with the arrival of the Hephaestion. Even now it was steaming nearer with its cargo of dreams, of freedom from foreign occupation and the schemes of Radu Luckacz, who (it must be said) had done everything he'd done because he loved her.

Now she stood upon the steps of a small house on the Strada Spatarul. This night, she believed, was the crisis of the act, when she would either descend into tragedy or ascend into greatness. Was it any wonder that her hands were trembling and her stomach was full of knots? Onstage, what was the song she would be singing at this moment? Yes, she had promised herself that she would sing—she herself, and not some younger actress. She grasped at the curving, wrought-iron rail, knocked at the door.

Or else the performance would be called *The White Tyger*. At moments she imagined she would need no script or score or rehearsal or choreographer, but would dance and sing the story to her people on the massive stage of Dinamo Stadium or else the smaller, intimate National Theatre, or else even the old Ambassadors, the scene of all her early triumphs. It alone had not yet been refurbished with German money. Curse them all! She heard the heavy locks drawn back. The high, black, double doors split inward.

A white-clothed orderly pulled wide the door and bowed to let her pass. She walked through the hall and then immediately up the stairs. At the top there was an antechamber where she waited, where she changed her clothes. Markasev didn't like to see her dressed as a man.

There was a cabinet, a clothes closet. The room was stuffy and overlit, the walls pale yellow with recessed gilt trim. The gauze curtains were restrained with golden tassels. It was a woman's room. The baroness stripped off her uniform and hung it up, stripped off her shirt, trousers, boots—she was not too old for this sort of thing. She was scarcely thirty-nine. Her chestnut hair still gleamed like a helmet without a trace of rust or discoloration. Her complexion and her skin were still the same. As for her face, she'd never cared for her small features, though people made a fuss.

Only her hands were not beautiful, the fingers heavy-knuckled, the nails bitten down and stained with nicotine. She held them out, dissatisfied, then inspected her small teeth in a gilt-framed looking glass above the cabinet. At moments when she turned her head, she could see in the reflecting glass the image of her spirit animal, a slit-eyed and ferocious alley cat, even after all this stroking and cosseting. A calico or a marmalade—no, she was a tyger, the white tyger of Roumania, she reminded herself, as she had to every day. Once, years before, she had seen the image in the glass. Once she had seen her spirit image in the adamantine glass. But not since then, no matter how she'd tried.

From the cabinet she took a new frock, also of the pale yellow that best suited her complexion and her violet eyes. As always it was a simple dress that fit her closely, ending at mid-thigh. Under it she drew on ash-colored stockings. She wore no jewelry except her husband's gold signet ring—too large for her, and with the pig's-head seal reversed. Why she kept it, why she worried it constantly, was a mystery even to her.

The guardsman's uniform she had thrown over a chair. From the pants' pocket she now drew the tourmaline, Kepler's Eye, glowing green and purple in its depths. Taken from the sorcerer's brain, it was a natural crystal, flawless and uncut, she thought, although sometimes when she rubbed it she imagined she could see a trace of subtle faceting in the rondelle style—the surface was not rough, not smooth. Sometimes the shape reminded her of something, some kind of crouching, sleeping animal, perhaps.

She wore no cologne, but she took the jewel and rubbed it over her arms, her shoulders, and her neck. She rubbed it underneath her armpits. Then she laid it on the cabinet, shook out her hair, made a grimace in the looking glass, and she was ready.

None of this would have been necessary if she'd not made a terrible mistake. But Radu Luckacz and Jean-Baptiste had arranged a series of posed photographs during those chaotic days. If they had hired a model, if they had taken their exposures of the substituted corpse, all would have been different. Soon there were posters and flags with Kevin Markasev's real face, medals cast in his honor and a mural at the corner of Dobrescu Street and the Piata Revolutiei. After that it was imperative to keep him locked away for his own safety! But because of her generosity she took time out of her schedule to visit him. No, that wasn't it.

She turned the key in the lock of the inner door. With her hand on the knob she paused, trying to understand once more the problem of her cruelty. At moments such as these she felt the most alive, as if she could give and yet withhold herself. And as she turned the knob she felt the flicker of a self-justifying rage. Her own son was now a prisoner in Ratisbon, far from his mother's arms. If she treated this boy badly, if she never let him out, surely that was no worse than what she suffered. Under the circumstances she did what she could. No doubt she'd have given him his own room in the People's Palace if she'd been able to. What could she do—give him a mask to wear? Cover his face with makeup from the theater? It was impossible. But surely she'd have loved to walk with him arm in arm through the streets of Bucharest, in the students' quarter as they had in the old days. Oh, she was robbing herself! Besides, wasn't she right to use him in whatever way she wanted, because she had saved his life?

No, she must be honest with herself. Her strength as an artist and performer, it had always come from her sincerity—she was the one who had hypnotized him, who had manipulated him into attacking the German officer. Since the time he had appeared at her summer house in Cluj, he had always done everything she wanted. She had even sent him on a journey to Aegypta Schenck's imaginary world, the town in Massachusetts where she'd hidden her niece. And Markasev had found the girl and brought her back. And if that fool Raevsky had been half as competent as this abandoned boy, by now she'd have the golden bracelet of Miranda Brancoveanu on her wrist. She'd have no need for any stupid tourmalines or any parlor tricks. She'd have no need for love or being loved.

She threw the door open. The orderlies had arranged Kevin Markasev for her visit. They had tied him to an armchair in the center of the room. He was gagged with a silk cloth, tied with silk ribbons that were nevertheless arranged so loosely, he could have freed himself at any time. The gaslight shone on his long face, his single eyebrow, his clipped hair, and the strange marks on his temples. When she saw him her anger disappeared, replaced by a kind of tenderness.

For here before her was the hero of the revolution, the angel of Bucharest, Kevin Markasev the pure, as he was known in songs she herself had inspired and performed.

"My dear," she said. "What have they done to you?" She came toward him with her hands held out, tears on her cheeks. With her own handkerchief she rubbed the sweat from his forehead—"Let me help you!" She pulled the gag from his mouth.

He said nothing, but he rarely spoke at first. In front of him there was a table and several porcelain dishes. There was a pitcher of ice water and she poured a glass for him and held it to his lips. He did not drink.

"Here, let me serve you," she said. And with her own hands she picked up some of the sweets and pastries from the plates—gazelles' horns from the Turkish Empire. Slices of candied ginger. She held them up, but his lips were tight, his brow furrowed and disapproving. It didn't matter. It was often like this at first. She held up one of the pieces of fruit. "Later we'll have coffee," she said. "Or would you like a cigarette?"

Unwillingly, mournfully, he opened his lips, and she brought up a ripe red plum. "This is for you," she said. But when her hand was close, he leaned forward suddenly and took her index finger between his teeth. He had a good grip on it, and he bit down hard, as hard as he could until his teeth turned on the bone. She howled and struck him with her open palm, while he looked up at her and smiled, her blood on his lips. When she was able to rip her hand away, she had a cut below the knuckle.

Tears in her eyes, she wrapped her finger in a napkin while Markasev sat back. The blood seeped through the cloth. He had hurt her! How unfair of him! Surely he must realize she was not like other women. If he loved her, he'd indulge her for the sake of all the beauty she had brought into the world. She herself had never hurt him willingly. She had meant no harm.

Still he was smiling at her, though his cheeks still bore the flushed imprint of her hand. His teeth were stained with blood. And now he started to speak in a low tone that was quite unlike him. "Don't touch me. You disgust me."

How handsome he had grown during these years!

"You must not touch me," he said, "not again. Now they visit me, not you, but others. Gently in the night and they don't leave. I think I spent all day on my knees. I don't eat—don't offer me this food. Don't tempt me with this, because you are an evil woman as they say."

"Who says so?"

"They are all around us. Now you've left me weeks and years, and I've come to sit quiet as a stone. And then they come around you little by little."

"Who?"

Now she looked at him and saw his face was gaunt, his cheeks thin. Still, how handsome were his burning eyes!

"Oh, they are goddesses. Aphrodite is there, and Cleopatra, and Queen Mary Magdalene. Sometimes birds come to my window."

The Baroness Ceausescu was relieved. Sometimes the orderlies had given him devotional literature, which he read with difficulty because of his lack of education. Perhaps that made him even more susceptible. The previous year he had imagined her as the moon lady, come to visit her Endymion.

No, this was different. Always before he had confused her with the goddesses and made her one of them. But now they warned him against her. The blood seeped through the napkin. "Please let me help you," she said. "My dear . . ."

"I hate you."

He had said it. And not in violence or anger, but with cold simplicity. She had no doubt he spoke the truth, and how could it be otherwise? She deserved more than his hate for what she'd done.

Now he closed his eyes. And when she spoke it was as if he didn't hear.

She stood for a few minutes feeling her anger grow. But she would forgive him and be as gentle as a goddess, because of the harm she'd caused. So when he continued to ignore her, she turned back into the anteroom where she saw Kepler's Eye glinting on the cabinet top. He hated her? He'd never said that before.

One of life's pleasures, the baroness knew, is to be cruel in little ways to those who love us. And who loves us more than our own selves? There can be no joy in punishing our enemies. The tourmaline shone on the lacquered top, one of the most valuable gems in Europe, glowing as if it were a source of light.

He hated her? How was it possible? The whole world loved her for the jewel's sake. Johannes Kepler had had thousands of lovers. A hundred thousand others had followed his funeral procession, though he was an evil man. And besides, how could anyone explain the events of the third act of her drama, except through supernatural intervention? Surely there was something miraculous about the way she'd acquired the gem. She had taken it from the body of

Spitz the jeweler, who had bought it from a debutante named Corelli, who had stolen it from her father's vault because she'd wanted to escape to Paris and become as great an artist as Nicola Ceausescu! No, it was not through her own gifts that she had risen this far!

All this time she had been pulling on her clothes again, hurriedly, distractedly, her trousers over the gray stockings, over the dancing shoes she'd worn. She stripped off the frock, put the jacket on over her undershirt. All the time the eye stared at her grimly until she couldn't stand it; she seized it up.

Then she was through the door again, the stone in her hand. Yes, she could be a goddess, she could be a maenad or Queen Agave, whom she had played to such acclaim on the stage of the Ambassadors. She pushed the stone against Markasev's mouth, cutting his lips until he cried out, and she was trembling, weeping. There was blood on her hand as she ran through the door and down the stairs. When the nurse came toward her, she said, "I can't bear it. This is the end—you can release him. Let him go wherever he wants. Give him this."

She emptied her pockets on the side table. There were several hundred marks in coins and bills. "Give him all the money in the house. You promise me?"

"Yes, ma'am."

The nurse was a respectable old woman and she spread her nostrils, wrinkled her nose as if she'd smelled an ugly smell. She suspected the worst—they all did. But there was nothing dirty about this after all. The baroness had never touched the boy—not in that way, or allowed him to touch her. Only she'd rehearsed for him, trying out songs and speeches she would then plan for the stage. Most of all she had indulged his love for her, which had been sweet until tonight. There is nothing sweeter than the love of someone you've misused.

"Do this and you'll be rewarded. Do not play a game with me."

"No, ma'am."

And the baroness staggered out into the street. It was past midnight. She thought about finding a cab. When she reached the corner, she listened for the *clop-clop* of a horse's hooves. But she had no money. She would walk, though she had left her boots in the Strada Spatarul.

She buttoned her jacket, then thrust the jewel into the inside pocket. "That is all," she muttered to herself again, except it wasn't. She took a different way, and in Lipscani Street, by the Old Absinthe House, amid some stragglers outside the glass doors, she felt a hand on her sleeve.

"Please, sir."

It was an area for prostitutes and prostitution. The baroness found herself looking into a face she recognized but could not place. She pulled away, stepped back. A horse-faced young woman in her mid-twenties, in a brown, out-of-fashion dress. Where had she seen her before? She had a nice shape.

"Please, sir, would you like . . . ?" But then the girl looked down at the baroness's feet, at her dancing shoes and stockings. "Excuse me. So you're not the type." She smiled.

The lantern on the wall above the restaurant cast a semicircle of light into the road. The baroness stepped out of it. "Mademoiselle Corelli!" she hissed.

Again in this coincidence—the hand of fate. The girl peered at her, uncertain. Then she staggered forward and grabbed hold of her arm again. "Oh, ma'am," she said.

Here was another person the baroness had destroyed. She had robbed her of her money and her jewel. No doubt the father had thrown her from the house, put her on the ladder where she now found herself close to the bottom. The baroness tried to twist away, but the girl was stronger. She was hurting the baroness's hand, especially the finger that still throbbed. What would happen if she called the police?

"Thank you," said Mademoiselle Corelli. "I saw there were tickets at the National. I waited for hours, but the performance . . . I will never forget you when I saw you that first time. You were like a goddess on that stage."

The baroness pulled backward until she stood against the wall. The girl continued, "Thank you for everything you've done. You have been a model for my life, for all of us. Let me kiss your hands."

She had the finger in her grip, and it had started to bleed and throb. The baroness shook her head. She couldn't stand the silence. "What are you doing here?"

Mademoiselle Corelli shrugged as if to say, "It's what you see."

But the baroness couldn't tolerate the silence. Yes, she was a model for all prostitutes, and suddenly she was afraid. "Come to my house," she said. "Come to the servant's gate. Come tomorrow and I'll talk to my steward. But you must not ask for me. You must not talk about these things. I can arrange payment for the jewel you lost."

"Ma'am, don't concern yourself. That was a fake after all."

In the narrow street, the baroness looked up at the sky. There was a mist above the city, come from nowhere over the half moon.

At first she didn't understand what had been said. She stood dumbly in the road, trying to disengage her hand.

"That's right," said the girl. "I found out from my father. I didn't know, but he would never have let me wear that tourmaline to that reception, not the real Kepler's Eye, not after the Germans had tried to steal it so many times."

"But I don't understand. Monsieur Spitz examined it—"

The girl laughed. "I didn't say it wasn't a real stone. Since that night I've learned something about men. Sometimes men are not the experts that they claim."

"My God."

"Yes, and you know I had a narrow escape that night. The Germans killed that Domnul Spitz for it, that's what I heard. So now the joke's on them. The potato-eaters, as you call them. My father wasn't going to say anything about it. He put in for the insurance and then hid the real stone in a secret place. Did you ever cash the cheque?"

"I owe you that money. Come to my steward as I told you. Now you must let me go. You must not say you saw me."

She pulled away. She turned her back, didn't look around, and the rest of the way down the street and up the Calea Victoriei, she walked without a thought in her head. But at Maximillian's Fountain she paused.

The jewel was a fake. Of course it was. If it had been real, Markasav would not have said what he'd just said.

All these years she'd been a dupe, a fool, craving warmth from a cold stone. Impulsively, theatrically, against her better judgment, she threw the tourmaline into the shallow bowl under the spray.

The street was not deserted even at that hour. It was only a few minutes later that she returned, panicked, to retrieve it—what if the girl had lied, or else her father? What if Markasev had lied—surely he loved her still? And there the stone was, still waiting for her, glaring balefully from the water.

She stared back at it a moment, then abandoned it again. The third time she went back, and it was gone.

15 *In Mogosoaia*

THAT NIGHT MIRANDA SAT among bales of the previous winter's straw, in a thatched stable on the old Brancoveanu land in Mogosoaia, fourteen kilometers northwest of Bucharest. Confiscated after the arrest of Frederick Schenck von Schenck, the fields were rented out to farmers, though the palace of Constantin Brancoveanu stood empty across the lake, boarded up.

Besides Miranda and Ludu Rat-tooth, the stable was full of men. These were friends of her father, veterans of the Turkish wars. Since Zelea Codreanu's death, since she'd left the marshes, almost every night had been like this—men gathering in out-of-the-way places, at Robeasca and Sarata Monteoru and Urziceni, all across the Wallachian plain. Coming so soon after the events at Braila, news of Codreanu's death had spread throughout the country.

From Insula Calia, Miranda and Ludu had returned to the marshland around Caracalui, and there they'd met the first of the old men, Captain Dysart of the Emigré Battalion, which had fought with such maniacal fury against the Turks. Even the Gypsies treated him with awe, a small bow-legged man, blind in one eye, dressed almost in rags, with white hair down to his shoulders and a white moustache. Miranda was drawn to him because he spoke to her in English, avoiding Roumanian when he could. "Here you are, by God. The last time I saw you, you were in your little dress. But you look like your father!"

It was hard not to be touched by the tears on the man's face, scarred with burn marks or acne. "Mademoiselle—miss, at long last it will be all right!"

He had a way of speaking that made it hard to take him seriously. "Dear miss, just to see you is to feel a new hope in my old breast. But touch my arm—touch it! You see there is still strength in these biceps. . . ." Then he'd wink at her as if she'd caught him in a joke. For in many ways he was a thoughtful and intelligent man, as Miranda found during that first day, waiting for darkness in Doamna Lyubitshka's cottage in the reeds. He didn't drink, didn't smoke, didn't curse. And he was clever about politics, not just in Roumania but Germany as well. He explained to her about the Committee for Roumanian Affairs, and the war party and peace party in the Reichstag.

He showed her the placard Radu Luckacz had hung in all the towns, a woodblock print of her on horseback, a long revolver in her hand. Though it offered a reward for information, it could have served as a recruiting poster—at dusk Dysart brought her up into the village, where he introduced her to the first gathering of toothless, old, and middle-aged veterans. Some of them proposed to help her. "Come with me to Bucharest—to Mogosoaia," she'd said, because that's where she was going. And they had nodded and smiled. Mogosoaia, where the grave of Aegypta Schenck von Schenck had already become a shrine.

Many of their sons, many of the young men in the delta were on their way north, conscripted by the Germans for their war in Russia. And many of the rest had land to work, lines and traps to check, families to raise. The ones that came with her were like Dysart, without wives or homes. Six men followed her that first night, and landed with her on the west bank of the Danube near the town of Gropeni. As they unloaded horses and supplies, all bought with her money, she saw they were a mixed bunch. Ludu Rat-tooth didn't admire them.

It didn't matter. The important thing was to move forward step by step. The important thing was to have a plan, and Dysart was helping her with that. As the stars were paling and they rode up a ravine onto the plain, Miranda let herself imagine all Roumania was with her, that all she had to do was stand up and speak for everyone to hear. What had her aunt said? To be a voice.

So every night she sat and listened, and people came to her. They touched her hands, admired her bracelet, and talked to her about the good old days before the generals conspired against her father, before they put Valeria Dragonesti in the Winter Keep, before the Germans had come to Great Roumania. As she listened, Miranda started to imagine what these changes had meant to ordinary people, at least the ones who spoke to her, at least in this locality. Up to this point it had been hard enough to piece together all that had happened, and understand it as a story about her own family, a personal story about her mother, father, aunt, and now herself. But now as old men and women talked to her beside the campfires, she heard a story that was always fundamentally about money and injustice—the corruption of the courts. How a class of local tyrants had grown up under the empress. And when the time came they had shifted their allegiance to the German authorities. The vampire had been one of many.

Miranda didn't want to think about Zelea Codreanu. She didn't want to think about the events of that night, though of course her victory over the vampire was the cause of her present reputation. But with a stubbornness that had become her method, she had consigned the events that had occurred on Insula Calia to a special mental category: that which could not be explained. And if she was to move forward step by step, she had to wake up fresh from those nights as if from a disordered dream, as she had woken in America and in her father's garden.

When she had been a high-school student in Massachusetts, every morning she had eagerly gone over her dreams. And now just as eagerly she strove to put them behind her, keeping only the few things that she could not forget: "I thought you'd be a voice . . . for Great Roumania."

On the first morning and the second morning she had wondered what that voice would say. But as the people came and talked to her, she knew. None of this was about her. Many voices could combine into one voice.

On the third day in the morning they were surprised by ten policemen after breakfast in the town of Ghergeasa. By that time she had almost forty men and the entire town had come to see her. But fewer than twenty continued with her after the fight, and not because of casualties—no one had been hurt. As before, she hadn't understood much of what happened until later. Guns were fired. Dysart had his hand on her bridle until she slapped it off. The policemen had ridden away north.

But that evening and the next, around a fire outside a barn or in a copse of trees, she sat and listened to the stories about hunger, and hardship, and the usurper, and German tyranny. And sometimes stories about her father, because each of the old soldiers had his personal encounter to describe. In the gaps between them, she could catch glimpses of the man himself.

The general had not cared for distinctions between officers and ordinary soldiers. A gap-toothed man named Sorin told her, "Once we were on the Strymon River north of Thessalonike. The Turks were on the other side of a high stream. We didn't have anything but beans and hard green peaches in the trees. The word came that there was a run of some small fish, I never knew the name. We crept out of our holes when it was still dark. The general came too, and I've never seen anything like it. The fish—they jumped out of their holes in the earth. The stream had come out of its banks and flooded a small hill like a waterfall over the rocks and the tall grass. And you could find the fish jumping and sliding down. There was eels, too. We took our boots off and caught them in our hats, and the general was laughing like a boy. It was like a holiday or being out from school. We built a fire in the clearing and roasted those fish on sticks. I sat next to the general and he was telling jokes. But then we had bad luck because the Turks crossed downstream and cut us off—it was that devil, Kemal Bey."

"What did he look like?" asked Miranda. "I mean my father."

"Oh, he was no hero in his face, that much I can tell you. Not so tall and strong. A high nose like yours. Ears even bigger. Not much of a chin. You never saw him?"

"No."

"Not a picture?"

"No." Miranda wondered for the first time why this was so, why there hadn't been, for example, a portrait in the castle on the beach.

"So, I can tell you about that," said an older man, as though she'd asked. "The general had superstitions. The photographs were blurred because he'd always move. He said it was bad luck to stop in time. You know there were always things like that, never a fight on a Thursday. Never when Mars and Jupiter were in conjunction. I forget all of it. He used to get letters from his sister."

It had been drizzling and raining since they left the river. Nevertheless this was a beautiful country, the flat plain of the Danube, the tara Romaneasa with the city of Bucharest in the middle. There were orchards, wheat fields, and pastureland with many cows and sheep. The small, thatched, wood-and-stucco villages were built around a graveyard and a temple of Demeter with a bell tower and a tiled dome. The straight muddy roads were lined with poplars.

Miranda rode the big black gelding, and Ludu followed close behind. Miranda could tell she found the landscape ugly and depressing. Every mile they came inland she seemed more distracted and sad. Before, she had been full of her opinions and judgments. Now she was mournful, silent, perhaps because she realized finally and forever that her home was gone, her family dispersed or dead.

But if that was true, why did she want to talk about them and nothing else? Only the mention of her house—burned now, probably—her father, her brothers, could bring even the smallest, sourest smile to her. And she still didn't have anything good to say. As Miranda learned more about her own father, she learned about Ludu's too, stories that made a kind of counterpoint. "Sometimes he'd drink all night and there would be no stopping. He'd send Gheorghe out with all the money in the house. When that was gone he'd pull himself around looking for things to sell—all the silver work he'd made during the winter. He never took any of our clothes, I'll say that for him. This was for days, and we'd run off to sleep outside or with the neighbors—we'd leave him alone. Then he was tired out, and we'd go back and find him sleeping in his chair or sprawled out in the dirt if he had fallen and could not get up. He was helpless without us and he knew it. Then months would go by and he'd never touch a dram. I'm worried about him now, I'll tell you that."

This came out of her at Mogosoaia, where they had arrived during the day. Miranda didn't know what would be kinder, to force the girl into the facts or let her continue in delusion. What was the use? And maybe she knew better after all. Miranda's own memory of that night, when the vampire had squatted over Dinu Fishbelly, now seemed like a dream. So maybe somehow the old Gypsy had survived.

Now past midnight, they sat in the stable while the men were talking. And when Ludu fell asleep in the straw, Miranda got up to go outside and watch the mist come over the sky, hiding the stars. The stable was on the edge of a wood, tall beeches and oaks. She looked north over the knee-high grass toward the unlit bulky building across the lake. Nothing here looked like home.

She stood a few minutes in the doorway listening to the men, watching the carbide lantern shining on their faces. Where was Dysart? He must have slipped away when she wasn't paying attention.

She saw Ludu start awake and look around. She'd woken up as soon as Miranda was gone. As they'd come farther from the coast, she was less and less able to stay alone, to leave Miranda by herself even for a moment. Sometimes that was comforting among these older men, and sometimes it was frustrating, as now. Miranda stepped away under the trees, and in a moment she saw the girl come out the door and look around. Then she came to stand beside Miranda in the darkness, and together they listened to the buzz of voices inside.

From near Ploiesti, Dysart had ridden ahead to find support in Bucharest among important people he had known from years ago. This revolution, or whatever it was, could not be achieved with these old soldiers from the marshes and the villages. Dysart had brought richer, better-connected people from the city to meet her, and they were harder to impress. One, Count Sfetcu, who worked in the treasury office, spoke for many when he said: "That she is the daughter of my old comrade Schenck von Schenck, I can see for myself. That she is a bold young woman and a patriot, no one can doubt. That she is responsible for the rain in the Dobruja, that she is the savior of Roumania—these are children's stories. We already have one white tyger, and she is an agent of Germany. Why should we want another?"

Sfetcu was a goat-faced man who talked about her as if she wasn't there. But he had a point. The problem, Miranda understood, was not with Nicola Ceausescu, or Radu Luckacz the police chief, or the Roumanian home guard, but with the German army. That was what mattered. And if no German soldiers had come to stop them yet, it was because so many had moved north to Lithuania, or east across the border into the Ukraine. Miranda had a little bit of time, but not a lot. The German governor of Transylvania had troops at his disposal in the oil fields.

But de Witte's letter had given her some breathing space. That was the advantage she'd taken from the mistake she'd made. Now she listened to the forest sounds, the peepers and cicadas, even though it was a damp night. Ludu said nothing, an anxious look on her chapped, spotted face. Though the moon was hidden, there was still light enough to see. Above her rags of mist glowed faintly against the black sky. Worried and frustrated, Miranda turned away, took a few steps under the trees. Where had Dysart gone?

No doubt he had walked out in disgust, because when people started to talk about political or military strategy, it always seemed a little unreal. Not long ago Miranda had been a high school student. She was not the one to be manipulating armies. The fiasco in Lithuania had taught her that.

So if she stayed with the guns and horses, always she'd depend on other people, on Dysart or Sfetcu or the rest of them. Doubtless her aunt had understood, and it was why she was always leading Miranda to places like this one, where another way might be found. But if that was true and she had grasped the truth, why was she so resistant? Here she was in Mogosoaia after all, as she had gone to Insula Calia. It's not as if she'd had a better idea. But why was it so hard for her to take what was offered? This was the Brancoveanu land, the forest where her aunt was buried.

As she came out into the open air, her mind was still occluded by the stable talk, the close, inside atmosphere. All this talking could not change the obvious. The Germans had no energy to spend on her because of the war in Lithuania—that was her strength. Her weakness was she didn't know this place or these people, didn't know whom to trust.

In the first days after Insula Calia, she'd wondered if her sole presence was enough to bring a change in a rotten and unpopular government, like the velvet revolution in Czechoslovakia. And unlike what had happened in Romania, starting with the riots in Timisoara and the murder of Nicolae Ceausescu and his wife—it was all so complicated. That was the version of history she'd learned when she was growing up, that Stanley had made sure she learned, forced her to learn over her objections. It was her history, he'd said. No doubt it had been included in her aunt's book as a cautionary tale and not a model to be followed, although who could tell for sure? This much was clear—for Dysart and the others she was just a flag to hold, an emblem of her dead father and their own dead selves.

She was tired of them and frightened of herself. All the way across Wallachia she had been pursued by nightmares and regrets. At moments when she closed her eyes she could see the neat, singed hole in de Witte's shoulder. And if at times she couldn't see the dead policeman, she could feel the gun's recoil as she had shot him. She could feel the bruise in her palm. It was not enough to say she'd had no choice, at Queen Mary's hermitage or in Braila, or Insula Calia either—no, she had traveled along a road, and the start of it had been when she'd fired on the vampire over the body of Dinu Fishbelly.

Maybe she had been seduced by the unreality of that moment. Then came the singed hole, and then the chaos in the garden of the Russian consulate in Braila—a man was killed, she'd later read. She'd killed a man—was it possible? She couldn't imagine it, and if there were moments, like now, when she felt sick with remorse, there were also moments as if none of it had happened, not the vampire, not de Witte, not the policeman. And none of that craziness in the salt cave, which seemed now like a fantasy.

She didn't want to feel again the place inside of her where violence seemed natural. She was her father's daughter, as her aunt had said. Surely there was another way to control these events if she could learn it. Maybe it was like learning to ride Ajax, her black horse.

Miranda stepped away into the wet grass.

"What are you doing?" Ludu whispered. "Come back."

How Miranda missed Andromeda, and Peter, and Captain Raevsky, too! She'd asked Dysart about him, who'd shrugged. "He was Ceausescu's man and then the widow's. Who can blame him?" He'd kissed his bunched fingers. "She's a beauty."

Now there was a mist over the moon and the whole sky seemed to glow. Miranda walked through the wet grass at the edge of the wood. She was wearing riding boots, trousers, and a white shirt. Around her neck was the locket with her mother's portrait. Around her left wrist was the bracelet of Miranda Brancoveanu. Thrust into a pocket under her shirt was her father's gun. She had lied when she had told her aunt that she'd thrown it away. It's what she'd meant to do, as part of her had meant to throw away her aunt's new letter and her aunt's money.

That would have been a mistake. And the letter had told her she must go to Mogosoaia; here she was. And though the letter had begun with orders and directions, it had not gone on like that.

Now the night was beautiful and soft and there was moisture in her hair. From time to time the mist would blow away, revealing blue-cast stars. "What's that one?" asked Miranda.

Ludu gave a furtive glance back toward the stable. When she spoke, she whispered, "Oh, miss, that is the part of Mircea's arrow when he killed the black bull. Over there. It's hidden in the trees."

"And this one?"

"That is Jupiter. The god himself. See how he glares at us! King Jesus . . ."

Miranda liked to listen to her talk. And she liked the idea of comfortable old Jupiter among the unfamiliar constellations. On a night like this sometimes Stanley would point the planets out. "Tell me," she asked, or tried to ask. "Is the planet Jupiter . . . ?"

But she found her Roumanian, fluent in most subjects, contained no word for planet. The French word had been taught her by Mr. Donati, but it meant nothing to Ludu. So she tried to describe what she meant, but got only confusion. "No, miss, it is the god himself."

But the girl laughed. As they left the proximity of the stable, she seemed happier and more cheerful, and by this time they had reached the corner of the field. A cart track led under the canopy of the wood. "This is the way to Mother Egypt's tomb," she said. "That old man told me. That Sfetcu."

"Let's go see."

"But the captain," protested the girl, meaning Dysart.

"So? We'll probably meet him on the way."

Miranda stepped into the center of the track and turned into the wood. She didn't pause or look back, and presently she was aware of Ludu Rat-tooth following her. The darkness was intense under the trees. But the ruts were easy and the path was clear.

In time they came to a burned-out cottage. There was a clearing and more light. Miranda stood looking at the collapsed and blackened beams, covered now with vines. "Tell me," she said. "Have you ever seen a white tyger?"

"Miss, no one has seen one. They are very rare."

"But they exist?"

"Yes. They live in the mountains in the snow. People hunt them for their skin, but they don't find them. They are very ferocious, very shy. Once my father's father met a man in Pietrosul who had a skin he was selling in the market. No one could buy it, he was asking so much."

"How big was it?"

"Oh, they are small!"

"Like this?" Miranda asked, moving her hands three feet apart.

"Half that. Like this."

"And striped?"

"Very faint. Silver stripes."

Miranda laughed, and they started walking again along the track into a wood that turned gradually to pines. The land was rising and there were ridges of white rock.

A cool wind came out of the trees. Above them now the mist had blown away. "Tell me," Miranda said. "I heard this story—how can I say? That people have an animal. Sometimes you can see the animal come out—"

"When they are dead." Ludu completed the sentence, then put her hand on Miranda's sleeve. "You shouldn't talk about this."

"Why not?"

"It is against the law! Not everyone can see these animals. Witches and conjurers . . ."

Miranda considered this. "I don't understand. You remember Insula Calia. What about all that? What would the law say about that?"

Ludu held onto her arm until she shook her off. Then the girl came close, and Miranda could smell the onion on her breath, see the corner of her rat tooth. "But there's a difference!" she cried. "King Jesus and Queen Mary Magdalene—they can light the fire in the dark. The rest is the devil's work."

Miranda smiled. "Where I grew up there was no magic. People were pretending everywhere you looked. Here it's the opposite."

She couldn't tell if Ludu was offended. She didn't care. So the white tyger was a little guy, wombat-sized, bunny-sized! She felt inexpressibly relieved. No, but ferocious. More like a ferret or a stoat.

Ahead she saw the glimmer of a light. A new ridge of moonlit rock appeared on her left hand, a pitted, undercut surface that soon rose above their heads. Small, spindly conifers grew from the crest of it, visible now the high trees had given out. There were knee-high gorse bushes, and the path through the middle of it led parallel to the cliff. Then the undergrowth subsided as they came around a buttress in the rock, and they saw the lantern and the house and the cave mouth and the tomb.

The lantern was set into a niche in the rock. It shone upon the pale grass. Mother Egypt's house was built into the cliff nearby, a bark-faced building with a long, low pediment and an overhanging roof. The door was open and a light burned there, too.

This was the house Miranda's aunt had lived in when she was the warden of the shrine. "Mary's fountain," whispered Ludu Rat-tooth. "When Julius Caesar fought against the Dacians, he tracked her to this place. She took off her armor and was washing in the water. He wanted to have her like a dog. But when he saw her, he was too ashamed."

"Yuck. That's quite a story."

Ludu was full of tidbits. "Some Gypsies say he dragged her to the cave, and that was the beginning of the Brancoveanus." She shrugged. "I like it best the other way."

"Me, too." Miranda was more interested in the tomb in the middle of the clearing, in front of the cave mouth. She would have gone to it, only Ludu grabbed her by the wrist. Someone had appeared in the entrance of the house, a tiny huddled figure. The candle she carried illuminated a small round face. Miranda only glimpsed it for a moment before the light flickered and the woman cupped her hand around it. But that moment was enough for her to see a face almost too strange and simian to be ugly. Painted yellow in the candle light, for a moment it seemed almost featureless.

Ludu Rat-tooth still had hold of Miranda's wrist. "Ah," she said. "Oh God, miss." She pulled hard on Miranda's hand, until Miranda twisted toward her thumb and freed herself. She held her arm up, took a step forward.

"Come back," whispered the girl.

But the woman with the candle had walked out into the clearing. And now Miranda could see more lights among the trees and four more figures shuffled out of the woods near the cliff face.

"Baron Ceausescu made them wear masks," breathed Ludu in her ear.

As the lights came together around the tomb, Miranda could see better what it was, a raised mound covered with talismans and knickknacks. The woman from the house was stooping to light candles among them and little oil lamps. By the accumulating glow, Miranda could see photographs, books, and scraps of paper, strands of beads, bouquets, and bundles of dried herbs.

Though she and the girl were hidden in the darkness, the woman now turned to them. Holding her flickering candle, she called out. "Come! Come forward."

Ludu tried to catch hold of her again, but Miranda stepped away. The girl's terror fed her sense of calm, but that wasn't the only thing. She could smell a perfume of hot oil out of the lamps, and she could see candles glimmering in the woods and in the grotto's mouth. They almost looked like lightning bugs, and in a moment she was reminded of summer evenings in Berkshire County, standing in the backyard with her father or on Christmas Hill behind the art museum.

"Come," said the little woman, beckoning.

She brought Miranda to the house where there was a larger lantern hanging inside the door. And there Miranda got a better look at her, a tiny woman with long arms and a hunched back—she would have seemed deformed except for the others around the tomb. She wore a kerchief on her head, and a homespun dress that covered her completely. But from the hair that grew on her neck and hands, Miranda guessed her entire body was hairy. Only her face was not, and perhaps she had shaved her cheeks, because they seemed scratched and raw. She had a yellow complexion, and her mouth and jaw bulged out. There were ridges of bone around her eyes. Her nose was flat and very small.

Miranda was happy to see her and didn't understand why. Though maybe it was because the woman seemed so glad herself—her lipless mouth smiled widely, revealing big teeth. "The white tyger," she murmured, and Miranda could hear the others whispering the same phrase in the dark. "The white tyger, the white tyger."

Miranda tended to distrust that kind of talk. But there was something charming about it on that quiet night with the warmth of summer in the air. "Ludu," she said over her shoulder. "Come. It's all right." But the girl stayed in the shadows.

Miranda put her hands out and allowed the monkey-faced woman to clasp hold of her thumbs and draw her to the threshold of the house. It was comfortable inside, Miranda saw.

The woman's voice was small and soft. "This was where your aunt lived in the last months of her life. She died in this room."

"Lovely," Miranda whispered.

But the woman didn't hear the sarcasm in her voice, and Miranda hadn't wanted her to hear. There was something in the soft warm air that was making her a little giddy. "Mother Egypt was always kind to us, so you'll be kind. She told us to wait and so we waited. When you wash in this water, all Roumania will be clean."

Even allowing for the magic and enchantment of the night, this was too much. Miranda guessed it was only a matter of time before her nemesis and namesake would be mentioned—"You'll be kind to us," the little woman repeated. "Miranda Brancoveanu gave us this forest as our own. She came here when she marched on Bucharest. That night the world was changing."

"Well, what do you know?" Miranda murmured. She was in a mood where none of these serious things seemed serious. She stepped into the room, which was nevertheless extremely dirty. There were dirty sheets over all the furniture. But there was something familiar about the room, and she was trying to figure out what it was when the woman started to talk again.

"There is a poem about the statue Mother Egypt brought from Prague. This was when you were a child. She told us to touch nothing."

"What statue?"

"In the cave."

Miranda had been walking through the room while the woman spoke. She realized she'd been here before, but when? What had her aunt said? The last memory she'd been permitted to retain when she'd been sent to Massachusetts was Mogosoaia station. It was the place where her aunt had pressed the book into her hand.

Miranda stood in the doorway of the inner room. To her left was a cabinet against the wall, an armoire with the doors pulled open, and she imagined she might find the lamb's wool cap and fox-fur stole that she'd last seen in the salt cave. Against the far wall was her aunt's big bed, and on the wall a rough-hewn crucifix, which she found herself examining as she listened to the poem. It took her a few words to realize that the woman had switched languages from Roumanian to heavily accented English:

Her eyes are shut,
Her breast is cold,
Her limbs are made,
Of solid gold.
Salamagundi.

There is a lock,
There is a key.
Now you recite this
Back to me.
Salamagundi.

Miranda was pleased by the badness of the poem, which suggested another facet to her aunt's character. She laughed—"Tell me again." Because there was something else. The second time around, she realized she had a picture of someone in her mind as she was listening. A woman stood naked, eyes shut, bending over from the waist, her left hand stretched behind her and to the side as if warding something away.

No, not a woman—a statue of a woman. Was it possible she had seen a statue like that, perhaps at the Scythian gold exhibition in the Smithsonian, where there had been a pair of tiger earrings like her tyger beads? No, but she'd imagined it before. She'd pictured it in her mind as she was doing now, and she was standing on the streets of New York City looking at a sign on a house in Greenwich Village, asking her father the meaning of a word that was printed there.

The woman continued in her droning singsong:

If you solve
The mystery
Of these chopped meats,
This cup of tea,
Then bring the answer
Back to me.
Salamagundi!

Once Miranda had asked her father what the word meant, and he'd told her out of his store of useless knowledge. It was a salad of chopped meat and olives, oil and anchovies, and he'd repeated the word, and she'd imagined in her mind's eye the statue of Aphrodite in the cave, her hand stretched back, her fingers spread. Just for a moment, and it had gone away, but she remembered now. "It's the kind of thing people eat in Dickens novels," Stanley had said.

Salamagundi. What was the phrase in her aunt's letter—she would find a key? A key to what? But now it was as if the word really was a long, strange key for a little lock, and all she had to do was hear it for her mind's eye to flutter open a bit more, and she remembered her aunt bringing her into this room— she didn't live here then. She lived in another cottage, but she'd brought Miranda here, and everything was different.

There was no armoire and no bed. But one thing—yes, the crucifix. Two rough pieces of wood with the bark still on them; Miranda stepped across the room and pulled it from the wall. She pressed her thumb into the little groove her aunt had shown her, and twisted her thumbnail the way her aunt had shown her, and slipped out the whittled plug the way her aunt had shown her, and shook the key out into her hand—a long, flat strip of gold with complicated ridges on the upper side.

Her aunt had planted the long word as a mnemonic key, and it had given her the actual key. Fingers trembling, she held up the golden strip. Paying no more attention to the little woman or her awful poem, she rushed through the house again and out into the air. Nor did she look for Ludu, but turned immediately to the cliff face. She stepped into the mouth of the cave, where she smelled a hot sulphurous smell.

The tunnel was lit with two flickering oil lamps set in niches in the rock. Ahead there was a brighter light that shone upon the troubled surface of the pool. And on a rock beside the water on the far side of the cave stood Venus Aphrodite. Even in this world it was ridiculous to think the statue represented Mary Magdalene—though a breastplate, a shield, and a helmet all were gathered at her feet. Mary Magdalene had never been so embarrassingly naked in her life. The goddess stretched out her golden arm. She looked terrified and her eyes were shut.

At first Miranda thought she'd have to step into the pool to reach her, but she didn't want to touch the water. The pool was in a raised rock basin and the statue was on the far side. And there was a way of climbing into the niche that held her. Miranda climbed up the rough steps. And she could see the keyhole in the helmet's empty eye, and she slipped the gold rod into it.

"Ludu!" she cried. "Ludu!" But she was alone. None of the strange women had followed her.

The rod slid into the grooves of the lock, but nothing happened. Hot and out of breath, Miranda lay on the rough steps. Looking around, she could see she was in a circular chamber cut from the living rock. And though the brimming water was different, and the smell was different, and the grain and color of the stone was different, still she recalled with a kind of loathing the salt cave at Insula Calia. She recalled especially the greasy, knotted feeling in her stomach and the taste of salt in her throat.

There was a whirring sound and the statue started to move. There was a music box hidden in the base. It played a plinky little tune.

The notes reverberated in the vault and on the surface of the pool. Miranda put her head down on the stones, trying to listen, trying to remember—a Gypsy melody, she thought. She wished Ludu were here.

Now she could see the clockwork joints, so cunningly made that they'd seemed solid. Aphrodite was moving now, making a little, jerky dance in rhythm to the music. Her golden eyelids fluttered open, revealing eyes that had been crafted to look human, with a white circle around a gold iris, especially as the cave filled with a new roaring and a new wind, and the lamps glimmered out. Then there was darkness except for the dancing golden statue, which seemed to shine. Light flickered around her like the beads of light around a disco ball, an impression furthered by the music, louder now in the sudden dark. Miranda had her cheek pressed into the rough stone, and when she raised her head she saw the cave had changed.

Light seemed to come not from the statue but from the pool, as if a cold blue lamp were burning underneath the water. And the dimensions of the place were different. Before, chunks of many-colored, pitted rock had swelled and jutted from the roof and walls, but now all that was smoothed away. The texture of the stone had changed. Looking up, Miranda could see now that the entire ceiling above her was covered with painted figures. And they bore no similarity to the crude, daubed images that had decorated the cave along the Hoosick River in the snow. Those were new and these were ancient, cave paintings as beautiful and rich as those in Lascaux or Altamira, which she'd seen reproduced in *National Geographic* articles and in textbooks. There were the same burnt colors. There was the same use of contours in the rock to define flesh and muscle. There was the same riot of superimposed images, suggesting they'd been applied at different times over the course of centuries, perhaps millennia. There were no human figures but only animals: horses, bison, cattle, elephants, and rhinoceroses, all pressing against each other in a crowd, except for one place in the vault of the roof where an animal sat on its haunches, a white tyger, without a doubt. And while everything else was chaos and stumbling movement, the tyger itself was quiet, surrounded by a circle of blank space on which a circle of animals pressed in vain. It sat staring down in the center of the vault, its white coat striped with silver, its tail curled around its feet. Its mouth was closed, its massive paws relaxed. There were no teeth or claws. What had Ludu said—bunny-sized! It was the biggest animal there.

The music was gone now but the statue still moved, still scattered beads of light that spread over the vault. Below, the surface of the pool glowed. No heat came from it, no sulphur smell, and the surface of the water was smooth and still. But Miranda could see movement in its depth.

This was the true, transforming water of Aphrodite. Like Insula Calia, this place was a point of contact between two worlds. If Miranda washed in this water, she would step out of the grotto's mouth and find the world had changed.

This had been her aunt's plan all along. Nicola Ceausescu was a conjurer, the Elector of Ratisbon was a conjurer. If she was going to struggle with them to make something better out of the world, then guns and horses would not be her weapons—not her father's pistol and not broken-down old soldiers like Captain Dysart. Nor could she win by taking on the German army. But she would fight with her own weapons in the hidden world.

And it was true—she did have weapons there. Insula Calia had proved that—not just her aunt's weapons, but her own. It was she who had destroyed the vampire, a chain of events that she remembered now.

After her book had been destroyed and she had come into this world, and after she'd been dragged through time into Roumania, and even after Insula Calia she had tried to convince herself that all those magical, unexplainable events were aberrations. It was how she'd managed to stumble forward—first things first. Step by step. The big picture was for morons, as her adoptive father had once said.

It was a strategy that had kept her safe and brought her to this place. Every morning she had tried to wake up fresh as if from a dream. The morning after she had seen her aunt in Insula Calia, she had tried to look forward and not back.

Now she imagined she had come to the end of that kind of journey. She was looking at the big picture now, that was for sure, moron or not. If sometimes on the way she had resisted and refused, it was because it was too threatening to find another reason for the world, another principle of experience that was not the same as Stanley's careful strategy. In this cave, as in the salt cave, was the access to that principle.

Stiff and unsteady, she climbed from her perch next to the statue. She found she was peering over the edge of the stone basin into water that seemed impossibly deep.

Fascinated, frightened, she reached out her hand. Every action now was irreversible. Behind her were the tunnel and the grotto's mouth leading out into the comfortable darkness.

And because it is hard not to look back, she paused now to reconsider. Were these her own weapons after all, and her own choices? Certainly during the moments she had already spent in this new world, when she remembered them later, she had not felt her choices were her own. At Insula Calia, fighting with the vampire and his men, she had not felt she could stop or go the other way. But it was as if some animal nature was driving her forward, something she couldn't quite control.

And maybe instead of learning to control it, she had confused this sensation with another—one that made more sense to resent. For at these uncontrolled moments, in another way she had felt just like this clockwork mannequin, moving to a tune she had not written and scarcely recognized, a tune her aunt had sung over her cradle, or else paid a servant to sing, maybe, years before.

Now she examined her own feelings. For a long time it had been second nature to resist. But she'd always come to the brink eventually, and here she was.

Oh, but this seemed different and irrevocable. She could drown in this pool and never find herself again. Maybe it was all right to take a step away and reassure herself. There was no urgency tonight. And maybe this was not even the right moment. She knew the cave was here. She knew how the key worked. That was the important thing. These decisions could never be made lightly.

And so she turned away, stepped back toward the cave's mouth, where there were people waiting under torchlight—familiar faces, though the small, misshapen women were all gone. But Captain Dysart was there, beckoning her into the night.

As always there was something ridiculous about him, his white hair and white moustache, though just in the time she'd known him he'd exchanged his ragged shirt for fashionable, expensive clothes. Her money had helped him with that—the light shone on his patent-leather boots. She didn't look him in the face, didn't look into his single eye, because she knew he was angry. "What, you must not go away like this. We have been searching and searching. You must understand it is so dangerous—"

He drew her out into the clearing by the grave. Miranda interrupted him. "Where are the women that were here? Where is Ludu Rat-tooth? Did you see her on the way?"

"Pah, that Gypsy! No, there is someone else I think that you must meet."

Maybe a dozen men were in the clearing. They were dressed in policemen's uniforms. The torches shone on silver buttons and high helmets. Their leader stood with his hands behind his back. He was a small man in black street clothes. He didn't smile or acknowledge her. His gray hair was combed back from his forehead, and his moustache was luxuriant and black.

Confused, Miranda looked for Ludu Rat-tooth. Who were these men? She could feel the expression on her face begin to change. And when they saw her new expression they came forward, pretense abandoned.

She forced herself to smile. Smiling, she ducked away from Ernest Dysart. Arm outstretched, fingers splayed, she ran back into the tunnel with the men behind her, knowing if the golden mannequin had come to the end of her dance, then she was trapped. If the cave had changed back, she was trapped.

But there above her was the enormous painted tyger in the center of the vault, and there was the statue turning on its base—arm outstretched, fingers splayed—and there was the basin of blue water that Venus Aphrodite had touched, and Mary Magdalene had touched, and Miranda Brancoveanu had touched during the siege of Bucharest the night before she led her raid on Vulcan's barbican. Good enough for them, good enough for her—Miranda put her hands into the pool and slopped the water on her arms and neck and face, and for good measure drank some.

The water in the pool was bitter, acrid, sulphurous, disgusting. And it had no immediate effect. She could hear the racket the police made in the tunnel, the echo of their voices. So maybe she was mistaken after all. "Help," she thought, "Help me," she thought, and this time she meant it.

16   *A Derailment*

AT FIRST LIGHT THE Hephaestion came steaming to the town of Chiselet on the edge of the marsh, sixty kilometers southeast of Bucharest. Andromeda woke in the baggage car at the front of the train. She had in her belly a dissatisfied feeling, a queasiness that had nothing to do with the cramped, damp space, the smell of tar and oil and hot metal from the square hole in the floor. For several minutes she lay curled up on her clothes. Nor did she lift her heavy head from off her paws.

But with new eyes and the gray light from the hole, she could see details of the compartment hidden from her the night before. With her new ears she heard the same noises in a different way, softer, muted, and yet more complete. She lay listening to the scrape of the metal wheels, the shuddering rhythm of the ties, and yet she wasn't bothered and deafened by them as before. It was as if her hearing was less sensitive but more acute, and in the space between the larger noises she could now perceive a range of others, the drip of the melting ice, the scurrying of some rodent, and Pieter de Graz's breath as he swayed above her, his hand in the leather strap.

She stretched and yawned. And as soon as her mouth was open she could smell a number of new smells, wax, fish eggs, and fruit preserves, sawdust, grease, and gunpowder, urine, sweat, and straw.

There was a smell she couldn't identify, and she raised her head. She lay curled up in a corner between two vibrating blocks of merchandise, strapped down and covered with tarpaulins. Beside her head wooden crate was packed with cylindrical containers. Their rounded edges, their smooth, mirrored, metal skin seemed out of place. Carefully stenciled along its side were letters she couldn't read.

Above her de Graz said something, and she tried to understand his tone of voice.

It had been a long time since she'd been able to interpret the words of men. When she first woke on Christmas Hill when everything was new, then she'd understood. Especially she'd caught everything Miranda had said, perhaps because she knew her well. But steadily there'd been more guesswork and interpretation as her body changed and thickened, her hair grew coarse and dark along the spine, along the ears.

But even now she thought she didn't miss much of importance. Pieter de Graz grunted above her. Already she missed Peter Gross, whose body had always given out a light and pleasing odor, even when he hadn't washed for weeks. This new smell was rank and coarse. There was something apelike in the way he smelled, something apelike in the way he hung above her from the strap.

Andromeda yawned, stuck out her tongue. Then she settled her head between her forelegs.

She didn't have long to wait. She listened to the shudder of the train. They were moving fast, the straight track a blur beneath them. She heard the whistle, a high, screaming sound, and then the scrape of metal as the brake came on. The wheels locked and the train slid forward. Andromeda started up, her claws uncertain on the metal floor.

De Graz already had his head out of the hole, and then half of his body. When he came up there was a different tone to the language of his grunting. Andromeda could see the ladder of the track that had led them to Roumania; at every instant the rungs were more distinct. The rhythm of the ties was slower, though the screaming of the brake hadn't changed.

Pieter was hanging from the metal cage beneath the hole. Above him Andromeda watched the rungs of the ladder, thicker and darker all the time. She could see the stretches of cinder between them. She'd heard in Adrianopole that bandits sometimes stopped these trains. That's why the engineers put the baggage car in front, she now remembered ("What an idiot!"), in case the train went over a mine.

De Graz was crouching in the metal slot, and she imagined for the first time he was waiting to drop down onto the track. If so, he would be ripped apart. And what about her? What was she supposed to do? What a jerk he was—the whistle was still screaming and the car lurched from side to side. But it was slower now, much slower, as she could tell from the rhythm and the solid ties.

De Graz climbed out of the hole again, picked up a hammer from behind one of the bins. There were some ventilation windows on the side of the car, fastened on the inside. He undid the steel clasps, pressed the windows open, a half dozen long, rectangular holes on top of each other, set into a louvered wooden frame. This he attacked with the hammer and a crazy fury that she recognized. He threw the entire weight and strength of his body into each blow. Andromeda could see the trees rushing past outside, more and more now as the frame gave way. De Graz pounded out a ragged hole maybe two feet square, and now he was scrambling through it with the hammer in his hand— what was she supposed to do? But no, she heard him clambering on the outside of the car, and then the blows of his hammer on the padlocked door, one, two, three, four, five, and then a crash, and the door slid open.

De Graz was nowhere to be seen. The train was still going about five miles an hour. She crawled to the open doorway and looked out. There was a path beside the track, and then a steep embankment, and then trees. But my God, to jump seemed crazy; she leaped forward, hit the ground, collapsed and crumpled with a pain in her foreleg. She kept her head pressed down beside the rail. She remembered a fall from her mountain bike outside her mother's house on Syndicate Road.

She pressed herself into the dirt and listened to the cars trundle past, first the screaming engine and then the rest. One, two, three, four, five. And then the gray sky above her and some steaming rain and pebbles, and she raised her head to see the back of the train receding down the track. It seemed to go very slowly now, and other passengers were jumping from the rear platform onto the path, or rolling down the embankment on either side, still in their nightclothes.

Then there was an explosion that Andromeda couldn't see except as a flash of light. But she heard the roar, felt the concussion. Ears down, teeth bared, she watched the train come off the rails. Slowly, at just a few miles an hour, the front car hit an obstacle and couldn't proceed. But the back cars were still moving. One by one they collapsed onto each other and continued down the embankment on the right-hand side, away from her in a relentless grind of metal.

But the baggage car had blown up and had fallen to the left. As she watched, the steel skin of the compartment was ruptured and fire burst out of it, an immediate conflagration as the car broke apart. In front of it the track was broken over a trestle bridge, and there was a pile of stacked timbers. The whistle blew once and was silent.

Andromeda kept her head down. After a few minutes there was a silence that washed over everything, washed over Andromeda as she lay in the dirt.

In time she was aware of some new sounds, birds and squirrels chattering and buzzing in the trees. And then people whimpering and calling out like weak young pups, over on the other side of the embankment. The train lay sprawled and wheezing there. No one was with her on the track itself, and no one had the vantage point to see, as she did when she pulled herself upright and hobbled forward, the different views on either side of the embankment. On Andromeda's left, men were coming out of the woods to stand around the broken baggage car, which was on fire. But after the first few explosions, everything was quiet there. The sun was coming out now from behind some clouds.

The engineer must have disconnected the car before it went over the mine. On the right-hand side of the embankment, the passengers gathered in dispirited little groups, men with their hands in the pockets of their dressing gowns. Andromeda caught the odor of a cigarette. Two cars stood almost upright down the slope, and two lay on their sides.

Andromeda saw Pieter de Graz pulling himself out of one of the fallen cars, walking upright underneath the line of windows, carrying a child in his arms. He jumped down and laid her on the ripped-up grass, bent over her as others stood around. Then he pulled himself onto the train again and disappeared into a window. A few minutes later he poked up again, dragging up a woman who was bleeding from both legs. He laid her on the side of the car, where she cried out. Men came to help her as de Graz lifted her down. He was the only moving part in that broken machine. Again he disappeared into the overturned train.

On the other side of the embankment, bandits were in the baggage car. And in the distance beyond the trestle bridge, some people were hurrying through the fields along a dirt track. There was a town not far away. The church had a double onion dome.

None of these three groups of people, separate and converging in a small space, was likely to have any use for Andromeda. A woman in her bathrobe shouted and pointed. A bandit raised his rifle. Favoring her left side, Andromeda jumped down the embankment into the long grass. Her paw wasn't broken, she decided. But her feet and legs were bruised and she was bleeding from a gash along her ribs.

The wood was full of briars and dead trees. Andromeda lay down several times and licked her feet. As she left the railway line, the ground got soft and wet. Soon she was wading through water between hummocks of dried grass. Crows flapped from tree to tree.

During the night the train had crossed into Roumania. Curled up on the floor of the car, Andromeda had thought about the morning with anticipation and nostalgia. Prochenko was not sentimental about the beauty of his native land. It was Andromeda who longed to see the majestic rivers, the mountains, and the forests.

In Prochenko she'd felt as if she were discovering old parts of herself, re-learning skills she'd always had. Her double memory had fused into a single impression of the past—high school and military school, California and New England, Roumania and Ukraine. Prochenko's family was from Rymarivka across the border. His father was gone, his family was busted up, his mother drank too much.

But in her dog's shape, each part of her humanity seemed muffled and un-real. It was natural for her to leave de Graz and wander out into the swamp. She felt no loyalty to him. She felt no dogged loyalty to Miranda, even though she'd laid on the cold floor of the baggage car the previous night, listening to the throbbing engine and the shudder of the rails: find her, find her, you must find her.

But now she limped away. Her heart was full of feelings that had nothing to do with her hurt paws, or the swamp, or her arrival in Roumania. Nor did she care that she'd escaped death. None of that held any interest. She squatted to piss and then went on through the dead trees, her nose crowded with signs and smells that made a map in front of her. She followed the tiny paths, and came first to some wood lice in a rotten stump, which she scratched apart. Then there was the smell of otters but she didn't see them.

Bees flew among the wildflowers. The sun came out again. She lay down on her stomach and licked at the pads of her feet. She must have hurt herself worse than she thought, because she was conscious of a smell of blood that in-terfered with other smells.

She spent the morning hunting for rodents and frogs. Then she lay licking her paws and the wound in her side. The ground was wet under her. When she heard men in the woods, she ran from them back toward the train track. Over the smell of her blood she caught a peculiar scent of someone else's, mixed with gunpowder and grease and sweat—a trampled path through the undergrowth. Someone had pulled himself away from the wrecked train, maybe to escape the bandits. Someone had pulled himself into the small trees. There was a smell of feces now. There was a sound of shouting and pounding from the track.

On three legs, forefoot poised, Andromeda looked that way, then bent her nose into the trampled grass. The man had slid along here like a slug. When she found him, she did not recognize him—a black man in expensive clothes. He had dragged himself into a thicket of high briars and could go no farther. He sat holding his stomach, and when he saw her he started to cry and grunt and argue—not loudly, because he hadn't the strength. He held onto his stomach, and she squatted in front of him under the thicket, waiting and watching, her head cocked to one side—he had nothing to fear from her. She wished him no harm. She herself was hurt and tired, yet still joyful, tongue lolling from her mouth. Maybe in an ideal world there could have been some communication of hurt spirits. But in that thicket, half a mile from that railway track, Andromeda listened to him groaning, watched his lips twist and falter, his chin tremble. He spoke words but she couldn't understand them. Inside all the other stinks there was the stink of fear, which was unnecessary. She was waiting for his clothes.

She saw a silver cylinder lying in the mud. Andromeda touched the metal with her nose, but there was no smell. At least there was no smell that could compete with death.

In time, toward evening, clutching his stomach, the African slumped onto his side. He didn't live to see the transformation. Andromeda got up and came to him and put her burning muzzle by his face. On the dirty leaves under his mouth she saw a tiny salamander, newborn, struggling to lift its head, warmed and invigorated by the man's last breath. It was blue and red and yellow, lapidary in its nest of powdered leaves, and it had no scent at all.

Where that jewellike creature lived, she felt rather than thought, all creatures might lie down in harmony. And even the most elusive and beautiful, with her white-striped fur as delicate as gossamer or thistledown, and her white teeth as sharp as knives, might climb down from the trees and walk upon the ground.

17 *Truth-telling*

SEVERAL DAYS LATER, IN the evening, Radu Luckacz, surrounded by policemen, stood on the steps of District Police Station Number Three, trying to understand the crowd. More than a thousand people had waited in the rain, newspapers and umbrellas above their heads, to watch the public exhibition of Count Sfetcu and the other conspirators. A scaffold had been erected in the center of the square, and the prisoners had been paraded briefly and then driven away. But in spite of the weather, the crowd did not disperse. What did that mean? Nor did the people sing, or chant revolutionary slogans, or raise their fists. But they stood glumly in their wet clothes.

Radu Luckacz knocked his fists together behind his back. The problem was, he thought, that he had made no public statement, issued no proclamation, commissioned no editorial to tell the crowd what it should feel. It was because of his own ambivalence. On the stone steps below the mural of the martyrdom of Kevin Markasev, he stood as glumly as the rest. This event was regrettable and sad, he knew. That it was necessary, he wished he could be sure, though he had signed the order of arrest.

At that moment he felt on his shoulders a burden of failure. And later in his car, as he was driven through the wet, dark streets to his evening meeting with the baroness, he reflected on the sadness of the day. How hard it was, he thought, to keep one's own hands clean! At supper in his modest house, the police at watch outside, Radu Luckacz sometimes felt an overwhelming desperation as he sat in silence with his wife and teenage daughter. How could he explain to them what he had done that day? How could he explain it to himself? Yet wasn't it a worthy goal after all, to maintain a functioning Roumanian state, a functioning parliament and post office and police force, even under foreign occupation? Wasn't it a worthy goal for a freethinker and a liberal to oppose the minions (as he might have described them in his unwritten editorial) of monarchy and superstition? Even if he was forced to make a bargain with a snake like Ernest Dysart, wasn't it still worth it after all?

And the baroness must be protected. In his mind she personified the spirit of Great Roumania. Her beauty, her artistic genius, her generous heart—the government could not exist without them. Now that she'd embarked upon the first of a new series of public performances, her people stood outside the theater in long lines. The house was limited, the audience kept small. Afterward, well-dressed men and women sobbed and whispered in the coffeehouses and the streets, conscious they had burned their hands upon some spark. Or else caught a glimpse of the white tyger, though Radu Luckacz despised the manipulation of these empty and outdated myths. Deeds were better, like the new pediatric hospital the baroness had opened and endowed with money from the German government.

His car turned up the Calea Victoriei. At the end of the street between the ornate stone façades, under the lights he could see a shoulder of the People's Palace, a monument to the excesses of the old regime. The baroness lived in part of the south wing, while the rest had been turned into a museum. In the wet dusk Radu Luckacz saw lights shining on the second floor. As usual there were some people gathered at the fountain in the square, hoping to see the baroness's shadow cross the blind.

He hung up his own hat and coat in the vestibule, and then walked up the stairs. On the landing, a horse-faced woman waited to let him pass. Dressed for the opera, perhaps, she looked familiar, but she bowed and hid her face and he continued on. He could hear the sound of the pianoforte in the small drawing room. It played a few notes, then stopped, then went on again.

He knocked. Jean-Baptiste was there, dressed in his old-fashioned, threadbare livery. He shrugged his high, narrow shoulders, put his finger to his lips, guided Luckacz in. A number of upholstered chairs were arranged in front of the piano, but they were empty. The baroness herself sat at the keyboard. A candelabrum stood atop the instrument, though the rest of the room was dark.

As always when he saw the woman, lit as if with inner radiance, he felt a mixture of unpleasant feelings that he had learned to call love. There was vertigo and nausea first of all. Then there was the desire to stumble forward, to grab hold of her and clutch her and rub his face against her bosom, though she was Baron Ceausescu's widow and he was a married man. But what wouldn't he give to go down on his knees and kiss the front of her dress? A cry came out of him, sublimated to a cough, and she started up. Then she stood away from the instrument and came toward him, smiling, holding out her hands. "My friend, I was expecting you!"

Jean-Baptiste had left the room. Luckacz struggled forward, his desire to clutch her now transformed, as always, into harsh, officious speech, buzzing and rasping in his ears. He scarcely knew what he was saying. But she interrupted him, held up her bitten fingers. "Thank God you've come! I've been so frightened. Please forgive a woman's weakness, but I've made myself afraid."

"Ma'am . . ."

"Oh, I've been foolish! And the night is so dark! Look what I have done." And she led him to a sideboard under the candlelight where there were some plans laid out—a circular small building and a naked woman. He could make no sense of it.

"It's my tomb," she said. "My mausoleum. I've had the artist draw it up."

He didn't understand, said nothing, and in a moment she continued, "The statue is inside. Lying on the lid of the sarcophagus. But there's no place where you can get a look—just perhaps a shoulder or an arm. The walls of the building hug so close. You can just see part of my body if you crane your neck—what do you think? It's my own idea. The plan itself is like a birdcage. Oh, but my soul has been a prisoner!"

He stood staring at the drawing, which he now saw was beautifully rendered in pen and ink. But he couldn't make out much of the detail, it was so small.

"Ma'am," he said, then swallowed. "Did you pose for this?"

She laughed, touched his arm. "My friend—what do you take me for?" Then she grew plaintive. "I've been at my wit's end. Tell me some good news! Oh, I can see it in your face. You've come from the execution."

He winced. "They haven't yet stood trial."

"And do you blame me for my morbid thoughts? Did they curse me? Did they curse my name?"

"No," he said, which was the truth. She was distressed, and he yearned to comfort her. But it was hard for him to look her in the face, to tolerate her clear eyes and perfect skin, the bitter smell that clung to her. So he stood looking at the drawing of the naked woman until she turned away from him back to the piano, and he felt he had to speak again, grind forward in his nasty, nasal, Hungarian-accented voice. "Madam, I am pleased to have good news for you. This is from several sources, including someone who has come recently to join us. It is news from Antonescu, who can't keep his men from running away. The so-called empress is on her deathbed. Valeria Dragonesti. She will not last the week."

He couldn't look the baroness in the face. She dropped the cover on the piano keys, which made the strings vibrate a little. "What about the train?" she asked. "The Hephaestion? That was Antonescu's work."

"But they achieved no benefit. Obviously there were armaments inside the baggage car. Whether they were meant for him or else for some other faction has yet to be determined. But they were detonated by the force of the explosion. The train was wrecked, but there were only several injuries, because of the heroism of—"

She interrupted him. "That's your news? A queen of Great Roumania is dying? My friend, I had hoped for better news than that. What about Miranda Popescu? Have you found her?"

"No. There must have been another exit to the cave, though we have searched—"

"And how many of my citizens have gone to join her in Mogosoaia? Tell me!"

"Ma'am, there are always malcontents."

"Tell me!"

"I don't know the number. It is troublesome. That's why I say the German ambassador—"

"Always it is you and your German ambassador! What does that say about my people's love if I must call in the potato-eaters to protect me? I must call in the soldiers of our enemy—"

"Ma'am, they are not . . ."

He couldn't finish, couldn't hear himself say the words. But she understood him. "What do you say? Weren't they the enemy when they burned Buda-Pest and drove your father from his house? When they marched into Transylvania? Haven't they stolen my son and kept him away from me?"

She'd come close to him, put out her hand to touch his sleeve. He was staring at the pen-and-ink drawing, the small breasts and narrow thighs. "It's so cold in here," she complained, turning away. "I'll have Jean-Baptiste lay a fire."

"What I say, ma'am, is there is a worse enemy than they."

"Tell me about that."

"Ma'am, I've already—"

"Tell me!"

He ran his forefinger along the drawing of the woman, then put his whole hand over it and raised his chin. He turned to face her as she leaned over the sheet music, rubbing her arms—the music was handwritten. He could see that now. The light shone on her chestnut hair, tangled and unbrushed. He observed for the first time what she was wearing, a high-necked blouse, stiff and starched over a black wool skirt. She fumbled with a jeweled cigarette box, the property of the former empress. She drew out a sobranie cigarette and held it under her nose. "I must give these up," she said. "They're hurting me."

"What does your doctor say?"

She shivered. "I will not let him touch me. What does it matter?" She flicked her jeweled lighter, lit the cigarette and sucked on it. "Tell me about this enemy who comes to fight me from another world."

"Ma'am, I've already—"

"Tell me again!"

She turned to face him, blowing smoke in a long stream, and he could see her violet eyes. As always when she looked at him, he took a refuge in lame-footed pedantry. "I believe the Germans can help us because of what they have achieved in their own country. This is in spite of their arrogance and the misery they have brought to weaker nations. Perhaps because of it—they are entirely modern in their own affairs. If there still remains some religious activity, it takes the form of nationalistic celebrations—public prayers to Odin, harvest festivals, occasions of that nature. It hurts me to say it, because of the harm they have done you and the contempt with which they treat you, but we can learn something. . . ."

He let his voice trail away. Blue smoke coiled above her in the darkness above the candle flame. He could see now there were dark shadows under her eyes. Had she been weeping? She stood hugging herself, and perhaps it was just an irritation from the smoke, but her eyes were full of tears.

"Tell me about Miranda Popescu," she whispered.

"Well, as you know, we'd been alerted by the mercenary, Dysart. We surrounded the place with twenty men. Twenty-one, myself included. You know the place. It was the Aphrodite fountain where Aegypta Schenck was killed. A painful circumstance, although because of it I was able to introduce myself and offer you my services—I tell you only what I saw. The place was kept by that degenerate race of aboriginals that so disgusted your late husband, though I am a liberal in this matter, I assure you. We must build our nation out of whatever lumber . . ."

A tear dropped down the baroness's cheek. "Miranda Popescu," she whispered.

What would he have given to have taken out his handkerchief and wiped that tear away?

"Ma'am, I'm coming to that. Believe me when I say I have no explanation. She came out of the mouth of the cave, and I saw her. There was light from the doorway and the cave itself, lanterns on her aunt's tomb. I saw her clearly. She is as I told you. It doesn't help to tell these things again—"

"It helps me."

"Very well. Only it reminds me of my failure. She is medium height and dark. She was dressed in riding clothes. When she saw me, she slipped from Dysart and ran back into the cave. My men were after her, except at that moment—how can I explain it? This was an illusion that came out of the ground. It rose out of the tomb, some miserable piece of prestidigitation, I can assure you. Something a magician might perform upon the stage. Smoke, colored lights, perhaps, and I am ashamed to say my men would not go forward past the entrance of the cave. There was darkness and some kind of electricity or thunder in the air. I am ashamed to say I cannot explain. For this reason if for no other, I wish I had a consultation with the German scientists, or else the extracts from the meetings of the scientific conference in Basel—"

"Please," whispered the Baroness Ceausescu.

"As you know, I went in by myself. And she had disappeared. There was no crevice in the rock where she could hide. Of course when daylight came we searched the complete locality."

"Of course."

LUCKACZ HAD STOPPED SPEAKING, AND for a moment all was quiet in the little room. Nicola Ceauseseu ground out her cigarette in the gilt ashtray. But her hands couldn't be still. She picked a fleck of tobacco from her tooth and then gnawed briefly on a hangnail while she watched him. She rubbed her hands together, put them behind her back while she stood watching his starved, diminished face, his long gray hair combed back, his glossy black moustache. Next to the German ambassador he was the most powerful man in Bucharest, she had to remind herself. Now that he'd allied himself with German interests. . . . Then why was it that every day he looked more crowlike and unkempt in his rusty suit of gabardine?

"What would you suggest?" she asked.

"Ma'am, since the day you moved into this building, there have been no German soldiers here in Bucharest or tara Romaneasa out of respect for you. Now I think that is unwise. Mogosoaia is two stops on the train."

How was it possible, the baroness thought, that in so short a time she could have lost her people's love? Everything had changed since Miranda Popescu had come, since Kevin Markasev had left the house on Spatarul, and most particularly since she had thrown away the tourmaline. But no, it was a fake! It was quite obviously a fake, unless (and this would be a bitter injustice) Mademoiselle Corelli had lied to her. How horrifying it would be, she thought now, as she'd lain awake thinking the previous night, to have thrown away the real stone, thinking it was false. How much worse than her reliance on a false stone, thinking it was real!

But no, the girl was too stupid for such a trick, and what would be the point? She had come during the day, and the baroness had fed her and given her money, spoken to her kindly in this room, though with an anxious heart. And the girl had told her about the safe where her father kept his jewels and curiosities, the secret place she'd mentioned in the street. Unless the girl was a spy, a creature of some foreign power, or else Radu Luckacz's creature, or else the Elector of Ratisbon's . . .

Tears in her eyes, the baroness imagined what would happen if Luckacz turned against her, because without the stone she had no hold on him. He easily might slip away once she had lost the secret of his affections. Tears in her eyes, she examined the roots of his black moustache. Without the stone there was nothing to keep him here, certainly not the charms of a defenseless, guilty woman in her thirty-ninth year.

"I won't allow it."

"Ma'am—"

"I won't allow it. You must not suggest it to me. Go—you have upset me now. Do you really think I would consent to this? That I need foreign soldiers to protect me in my own city? Or is this just a plan to make me more unpopular? I notice you have tried to keep me shut up here. I notice the piata and the park are full of your men. I won't have it—let my doors be open! I have no secrets—I'm an artist."

"Yes, ma'am."

Artist she might have been, famous throughout Europe at one time. But this was not her most effective speech, the baroness decided. She needed Luckacz to come toward her, sighing, wringing his hands or holding his hands out. She needed to feel some heat from him because the room was cold. Instead he scratched his ear, scratched his jaw, and looked down at the drawing of the mausoleum that she'd planned for Belu Cemetery. "Go," she said. "You must not keep me like a prisoner. You have hurt me and disappointed me and kept me from my work tonight—my life's work, though whether it's a comedy or tragedy is not so plain."

Why was he so stubborn? Why did he cock his head and peer at her, curious as a crow? This much was clear—she'd lost his love for her, and she'd lost Kevin Markasev's love, and she had lost her people's love.

And now Antonescu had robbed her of the weapon she had bought from the Abyssinian colonels. Broken the treasury to buy them, or at least she'd emptied the discretionary account the Germans permitted her, except for the money Jean-Baptiste had secreted away. That weapon had figured in the third act of her play, when she'd decided to become the white tyger in more than name alone. She'd decided to throw out the potato-eaters and redeem her country; now that option was closed to her. Or was this just another obstacle to overcome?

She picked up the sheet music from the piano stand. She made a show of studying it as Luckacz bowed, let himself out. There was another reason why she'd chased him away, why she'd wanted him gone. She looked at the square clock on the sideboard. It was almost eight o'clock.

She had prepared something for this night, a conjuring. If she'd managed to receive the weapon, it would not have been necessary. But without the weapon, she felt she must know something, or else what? She'd go mad—no, that was not true. That was the kind of sentimentality she'd always tried to avoid in her work. But she had lain awake the previous night, and she had thought of it like this: There were things she wanted to know, and felt she must know if her life was going to achieve the shape of a great piece of art.

If she was to overcome the obstacle of the derailment, she must find out the truth about Johannes Kepler's Eye. Had she been blessed by the great sorcerer or stumbled forward on her own? Who could tell her now but her own husband, the red pig of Cluj, dead for thirteen years? He was the one who'd given her the secret, spelled it out on the ouijah board in her house on Saltpetre Street. That had been a long time before, and already his soul was in the circle of brass. It would require a great conjuring to reach him now.

That afternoon she'd given a matinée, but cancelled her evening's performance. At nineteen minutes after eight, the God Saturn, caught in his dark, frozen round, would pass over the point of Cleopatra's spire near her temple in the old court. Things were possible at that moment. A word in the proper place might brush against his cloak, might catch there like a burr, might travel far. It was a chance, but it wouldn't do to prepare for it. No rehearsal was the best rehearsal, as she'd learned from her years on the stage. So she studied her sheet music a little bit more, calming herself, waiting for the chimes of the small clock—they didn't come. She looked again. The gold hands hadn't moved, still marked three minutes to the hour. The clock had stopped.

Then all her calmness left her in a moment and she fled the room, calling for Jean-Baptiste, hurrying up the stairs. The clock on the first landing told her it was twenty minutes past. But when she was running down the hall toward her personal apartment, she saw an ormolu timepiece on a small table—ten minutes after eight. It wasn't until she'd crossed the threshold of her bedchamber, pushed aside the rice-paper screen that hid her secret alcove, that she saw she still had time. Her absolute chronometer stood on a lacquer table, a gift to the former empress from the Maharajah of Singapore. The spheres were turning. She had ninety seconds left.

"What do you want?" called Jean-Baptiste, rude as always, from the hall outside her room.

"I have a headache. I must not be disturbed."

"I don't believe you. Who'd come see you anyway on such a night?"

"Go!"

While she spoke she'd been commencing an internal prayer, the kind that an experienced practitioner can set revolving among the lobes of the mind, a perpetual machine, and sometimes it took hours for it to slow and stop. It was a prayer to the goddess. At the same time she was fussing with Cleopatra's altar, a small brass statue she'd erected on an inlaid bench.

The statue was a clockwork one, and she wound it and got it moving with four seconds to spare. Now she was chanting out loud, a different prayer in contradiction to the first. For though the silent words were full of self-abasement ("Have mercy on me, forgive me, I am mud under your shoes. . . ."), the spoken words sounded presumptuous and proud: "I am the best-loved of your servants. Here I command you to help me to this terrible . . ." For it was only in the frictionless space between the prayers that the goddess's arrow might fly. The brass statue, which now was turning on its base, showed Cleopatra in the shape of the great huntress of the Nile on the day when she had overcome the crocodile. Dressed in padded armor, her beautiful head encased in a padded helm, she drew her bow and tilted backward as the crocodile swam through the arc of the heavens. It would become the brightest constellation of the summer months. It was not figured in the statue, though the goddess stood on a trampled nest of eggs.

But on the tiny brass arrow that would shoot a meter or so toward the ceiling, the baroness had affixed a tiny scroll. She had curled it and tied it around the shaft. It was not true she'd not prepared. On the scroll she had inscribed these words in minute letters: "My dear husband, please, we must adapt to the new times. . . ." It was the message that the goddess had dispatched to Julius Caesar after his death, begging him not to punish her for taking Marcus Antony for her second husband. But he did punish her.

That day the baroness had sent her steward, Jean-Baptiste, to Cleopatra's spire in the city. And in the secret, top compartment she had asked him to deposit a small bucket. On the handle of the bucket was the burr that she'd prepared, a sphere of wire hooks. In the bucket was the small silk nightgown she had worn throughout the previous week until it smelled of her. And pinned to a rosette of folded fabric in the center of the bodice, there was a piece of paper torn from the corner of an envelope, and one word in purple ink.

Jean Baptiste had unhatched the section of the roof over the compartment. That evening, at 8:19 and twenty seconds precisely, watchers in the square below might have observed a small, unsteady beacon rise into the sky. But in that spitting rain there were no watchers. In any case the beacon was soon lost among the clouds. Even the baroness, peering south through her bedroom window, saw nothing. Alternately gnawing on her cuticles and smoking her sobranies, she settled on her iron bedstead and commenced to wait.

Past eleven she undressed and went to bed. But she left a single lantern burning on her nightstand. When she awoke, disoriented, in the middle of the night, she lay quiet for a moment, watching the shadows turn and dance over the ceiling. At first she thought they came from outside her window. Lights from the traffic in the Piața Victoriei, although she couldn't hear anything. No, the lights from the carriages and trams had never reached into her room.

But perhaps there was some new brightness in the square. She remembered the bonfire lit by students on the night the Empress Valeria had left the city, while train after train of German soldiers unloaded in the Gara de Nord. Was it possible that she had seen the shadows dance across her ceiling from the light of that big fire? No, the window was dark, and when she raised herself onto her elbow, she could see the source of movement. The brass statue of the goddess was turning on its base, tilting backward as if shooting at the ceiling, though the quiver was empty and no shaft flew.

Now the baroness could hear the trigger in the statue's outstretched arm snap uselessly, over and over. She sat up in bed. "Are you there?" she called out.

She had left the window open a small crack, and now she felt the narrow wind that had managed to squeeze through. It troubled the flame of her lantern. "Are you there?" she cried out, already a little bit impatient at these histrionics, even more so when she smelled the barnyard odor that had always clung to the red pig, the smell of mud and food, excrement and death, that now was unmistakable.

What form would he take after so long? Surely he was trying to frighten her. It was intolerable—she slipped out of bed and ran to the window, closed the casement, turned the latch. The windowsill was wet. Below her the piața was deserted in the rain.

So she was not prepared to see him as she most remembered him, dressed in his velvet smoking jacket and his old-fashioned trousers and stockings, curled up in a corner of the big leather armchair she had brought from his laboratory in Saltpetre Street. His linen was white, and he had shaved. His eyebrows were thick as always, and his forehead shone. His long, sensitive fingers played always and forever with the medal pinned to his lapel, the eight-pointed Star of Roumania that Valeria IX (who now lay dying) had given him for his testimony against Prince Frederick. His face was covered with fine wrinkles, and his large ears were as delicate as bats' wings. But his eyes were as always, generous, calculating, kind.

"My dear," he murmured, "it has been so long."

"You startled me."

"Did I? I beg your pardon, but you should not be surprised."

On the rough matting, her bare feet were cold.

"And not because you sent for me," he said. "These tricks"—he gestured toward the statue, quiet now—"would not have hurt the slumber of a mouse. I must insist you should be studying my work more closely. Though I've often come to help you, too, if you must know. That business with Monsieur Spitz and Livia Hirscher!"

Always she had found his condescension irritating. But she was surprised to discover she was glad to see him. With the lantern light behind his head, he seemed to glow around the thin, flushed ridges of his ears.

There was a time when she'd respected him, even perhaps loved him a little bit. He'd been the deputy prime minister, after all. And some of those feelings still persisted after her marriage. Now suddenly she remembered the first time she had run her hands under his shirt, touching the puckered scars where he'd been wounded in the Turkish wars. He'd been a hero and Prince Frederick's friend, until he turned on him.

"What brought you, then?"

"My dear, I never go where I'm not wanted. I'd see you every night if you would let me. Sometimes I have spied—I'm glad to see you're still wearing my ring."

She drew it off, clenched it in her hand, surprised by her own pettiness. In some ways he had been an impressive man. In other ways he had been disgusting. "Let me tell you why you're here," she said. "I'm glad you remember Monsieur Spitz."

He smiled, showing his false teeth. Sometimes they had given him pain. It irritated her to have to remember, but then suddenly he closed his mouth. When she said nothing more, he spoke. "My dear, I was proud of you. That night you took the first two steps. Now you have much more than I gave you. I regret that."

How odd this seemed after so long! It was almost as if he'd never died. He seemed so lifelike, sitting in his chair. "Tell me about Kepler's Eye," she said.

He yawned, covered his mouth with his long hand. "You know everything you need to know."

"Johannes Kepler had a thousand lovers. Once I thought I had a million. But the girl tells me the jewel is false."

Now in death she found him easy to read. Easier than when he'd been alive. There was a sadness in his pink and wrinkled face, and also some impatience. "I am not a jeweler. It was good enough to fool Claude Spitz. That should be enough for you, I think."

But it wasn't enough for her. Honesty had always been her power and her strength. "Please, I must know."

Again a small, impatient look. "Here you are living in the Winter Keep. Surely you have won the game. Why trouble yourself now about the rules?"

But she must trouble herself. This was the night of Saturn's festival, a night for uncomfortable truth. In the countryside, among the common people, no one would tell lies on such a night. "What about the white tyger?" she asked. "I saw it in the pyramid one time and never again, although I looked and looked."

"I see you are an idealist," he said after a moment. "This is true: I wanted to help you. Perhaps you remember how unhappy you were."

She remembered.

"I tried to give you things," he said. "The stone, the boy."

What boy? But she knew.

"I was happy to see you," the ghost continued. "Was I wrong to let you see yourself as others see you? Love yourself as others . . . I thought you were the most beautiful woman I had ever seen. I still think so."

In a moment he went on. "It was confidence you lacked. Faith in your own power. Was it so terrible to lie to you?"

The baroness felt tears come to her eyes. "What about the boy?"

Sadness and impatience—"Dear, it does no good . . ."

"I want to know."

Uncomfortable truths are told on the night Saturn crosses over the city. Perhaps a sense of that tradition lingered in the ghost. He smiled and sighed. "He was my gift. A prisoner for you to make you strong. To help you in your conjuring."

When she said nothing, he went on. "Let me tell you. When our son Felix was born, I resented the time you spent. I was angry at night because your door was closed to me. So I took him away, and I regretted it. Later in the power that comes from death, I wanted to replace the son I took. I wanted to give you someone to love you every day. Someone to do everything you needed. It was my way also to be close to you and see you through his eyes. Please don't look so horrified! I think my two gifts made you what you are."

He was talking about the false stone and the false son, Kepler's Eye and Kevin Markasev. After a moment he went on again. "Did you think it strange he had no past, or that his past was whatever you suggested? Or he did everything you asked? I put him in your hands in Cluj. He was like a puppet that I made and gave to you, though I kept hold of the strings. Dear, you look so angry. Don't tell me you never guessed. What is a child, except something you create through miracles?"

The baroness turned away to hide her face. She glanced out of the window. If she'd been able to concentrate, she might have seen a moving shadow between two government buildings on the other side of the piata. But she couldn't see farther than the windowpane. The reflection cast her back into the room.

"How do you think a man can make a child?" the baron continued. "No, that is true alchemy. After Felix was sent away, I had no opportunity. I mean in the normal way. I had some of your blood, some of your hair. Some part of myself and a connection to me. Then I put him with a farmer in the country. But I almost lost him several times. Always I could see you though his eyes. Do you want to know where he is standing now? Right now?"

She closed her eyes. "Why did you?" she asked.

"My dear," murmured the ghost. "You must know the reason."

It was because he loved her. She knew from the peculiar simper in his voice that he was primed to talk about how much he loved her. Every day the subject had dripped out of him the last months of his life. Death had not, apparently, exhausted it.

But she couldn't feel anything but anger, a sudden rage. It burned away all caution. High up in her palace room, she made one of the unbalanced, daring leaps that were the secret of her creative art. "A miracle? It didn't feel that way. You must know Felix was not your son."

This was a lie. Now she opened her eyes, saw her reflection. Was it possible for a ghost to feel pain? She thought if he could love, then maybe he could feel some jealousy. Oh, he had robbed her, and she would rob him, too. "Do you remember there was a Danish ballet company at the Dinamo that spring? Do you remember the lead dancer, Koenigslander? We had fun, I tell you!"

This was a double lie on a night of truth. Never with anyone had she found pleasure of that kind. Miserably she stared at the glass pane.

If she'd been able to look past the reflection in the window, she might have seen a moving figure under the streetlight. It was Kevin Markasev in the rain, looking up at her window. She couldn't see him, even though she was thinking about him at that moment. How could she have treated him so cruelly for so long?

But instead she saw her sour, small-featured, beautiful face as if in a mirror. She couldn't see the ghost in back of her beyond the armchair's studded wing. As she stood at the window examining her expression, she smelled the odor of the pig again redoubled—a hot smell of garbage.

She didn't want to turn and look. She saw fear in her own face. She imagined the ghost was changing, and she didn't want to see the pig itself, or some devil, or some rotted corpse. She thought if she didn't look, then she'd protect herself. She was waiting for the ghost to speak.

"Turn around and look at me," he said, and his voice was not the grunting of a pig, the wheezing of a corpse. But it was soft, sweet, and hesitant, a young girl's voice, and maybe that was worst of all. The baroness squeezed her eyelids shut. She dropped the golden ring and put her hands over her ears, but still could hear the words. "Dear, you were always crude, a country girl, a peasant from the mountains. The white tyger? No. Turn around and tell me to my face."

In a moment he went on, "But if you could have seen yourself on the stage of the Ambassadors in that performance of Klaus Israel's *Cleopatra*—do you remember? In the last moment with the snake in your hand, your bosom was entirely uncovered. I went three times a week and von Schenck laughed at me. He said you'd never look twice, a broken-down old soldier.

"Tonight is the night to confess these things. I admire your bravery, as I admired it then—I proved him wrong. I thought you'd look at a deputy prime minister and better things to come. I thought—you see? The court-martial, the testimony against my friend. It was the price I paid. It made a beggar out of me. Look behind you."

She didn't turn around, didn't open her eyes. But she could hear the soft, breathy voice again. "Dear, you have climbed a long stair to this room. But I think there's a short way down."

The lantern blew out, and when she opened her eyes she was in darkness. Save for herself, the room was empty.

THAT NIGHT THE CLOAK OF Saturn, god of death, passed over Germany as well. In the countryside there were some hidden celebrations, seances and family gatherings behind locked doors. As on most of the feast days of the old calenders, the police were in the streets, watching for any public demonstration. In years past the peasants and the townspeople had painted their faces to look like skulls. But this could not be tolerated in wartime. News had just arrived of a bloody battle near the city of Pskov. It was one car in a baggage train of victories, but many men had died.

In Ratisbon, two men drank a toast of Roumanian brandy. They were not believers in the ordinary way. They approached these mysteries with the coldness of scientists, and the service that they paid was an ironic one. Arslan Lubomyr, glass in hand, recited a few lines of an old monastic chant, praising the wines at Saturn's wedding feast.

In the gas-lit chamber at the top of the high house, perched on a cedar bench next to an inlaid table, the elector was in an anxious mood. All evening they had been discussing politics and the elections to the Reichstag. "Humor me tonight," he said. "Let me ask you. Why do nations go to war?"

Then after a pause, "What is there in Russia that is worth these miseries? Already oil and sugar are rationed in the Kirchenstrasse market."

As usual he was dressed in evening clothes. He said, "My friend, I'm glad you've come to visit me at last. Now I can look into your face when I talk to you. It is easier to see if you are telling me the truth. Do you believe the justifications of the foreign minister? I read the transcript of his speech in the *Gazette*. Do you think we have a duty to take over the affairs of these corrupt and backward governments—a moral duty, whatever the cost, as he explains it?"

The lieutenant-major was a handsome man with dark, thin, Asiatic features. He was in uniform—brass buttons, silver braid. He sat in a stuffed armchair, his boots stretched out.

"Humor me," his host continued. "Is there no room in Europe to contain some backwardness? Perhaps the mark of a great nation is to leave others in peace."

Fascinated by the ugliness of his host, Lubomyr sipped the liquor in his glass. He looked away, then back again, studying for an instant the elector's nose. He had his own political opinions, his own fears that Germany's success in battle could be stolen away by cowardly politicians. The war coalition was a fragile one, and it depressed him to think about it.

Instead he saw a way to introduce a subject to the conversation. He'd been looking for the chance since his arrival the night before. "I think those countries have a clearer duty to resist," he said. "I mean whatever the benefit."

It was hard for Lubomyr to judge expressions on his host's ruined face, though he now saw the elector was peering at him keenly. "My friend, I think so, too. So the force comes from our side. Why is it, do you think?"

Lubomyr brought his hand up to hide his eyes. He was irritated by these constant declarations of friendship, the use of the familiar forms of speech—irritated and obscurely touched. Once again he made a motion toward his subject. "I think all nations are like animals. Some are sheep and some are wolves."

He crossed his legs and the elector shook his head. "I have a sympathy for sheep. It's all right for a handsome fellow like yourself. But I've spent a long time in this room. These things are revealed at death and not before. They say Alexander of Macedon was a prong-horned snail. And I believe I have discovered some sheeplike characteristics . . ."

Around them at the borders of the room stood several of the elector's simulacra. They came and went, engaged in unknown tasks. Lubomyr was used to them by now. They were blond, moustached, identical.

"My friend, I see you are surprised. It's because I have depended on the courage of others. Yourself, for instance."

Lubomyr shook his head. "You have defied conventions. That takes bravery."

"Ah, my friend. That is only because I had no choice. Without choices we are all champions."

Lubomyr took another sip of brandy. His subject was close at hand. "I can see you're in a melancholy mood," he said. "And I don't understand. I came here to offer our congratulations, unofficially, of course. You had your part in our success on June the seventh. There are people on the staff who understand our debt to you, and in the highest reaches of the government. I am sure that when the war is over, unofficially—"

"Of course."

The elector sighed. He put his small, elegant hand out to the table in front of them, and almost touched a bronze statue of Tsong Kapa, the Buddhist deity. Several small objects were scattered over the complicated surface. "It's a delusion," he continued, "that cowards have a lot to lose. But I will miss my beautiful things."

"Your grace, this is morbid—"

Ratisbon smiled. "It is the night for truth-telling. And you have made me drunk. I feel it suddenly. But I'm talking about something else—a danger."

There was an empty vase on the table and he reached for it. His expression was difficult to interpret. But his small grasping hands were eloquent.

"There's always danger," said Lubomyr tolerantly. "Our own politicians are a venal lot. If it wasn't for von Stoessel and the ministers—three men! And the Russians!"

"No! Not from that side. But from underneath. You understand?"

He had scarcely tasted from his glass, which he now placed clumsily in the center of the table. He did seem drunk all of a sudden, Lubomyr thought. Perhaps it was for the best, but perhaps it was a complication. "Underneath?"

"My friend, this brandy you have brought has poisoned me. It is too sweet. From Roumania, I think."

Baffled, Lubomyr nodded. "They have signed the treaty of alliance, as you know. They are fighting beside us in the Ukraine."

He took an ostentatious sip from his own glass, and then continued. "But your patriotism is to be commended. As I say, these things have not escaped the notice of the general staff. Let me tell you I am here to welcome you to Berlin or wherever you wish to go. You must keep appearances, of course."

"Of course."

"There is one thing," continued Lubomyr. And now he had arrived. "I don't know how to put it. The office of the foreign minister has given me a message. There is a story that you might be keeping two Roumanian subjects here for patriotic reasons. One is the child of Madame Ceausescu."

Now he sat forward in his armchair, glanced into the elector's face. "The minister believes the time has come to reward her for her change in attitude. He wants to invite her to Berlin and reunite them publicly—you understand. We are signatory to provisions for the ethical treatment of prisoners. With your new passport, I have a letter in my bag that explains the particulars," he said. "Tomorrow . . ."

He let his voice trail away. He found himself watching the elector's hands. There was a bowl of nuts on the Chinese bench next to the man's knee. Lubomyr watched him pick up a macadamia nut, covered with white dust.

"And Clara Brancoveanu?"

"Her, too."

Still chewing on the nut, the elector put his forefinger onto the surface of the table. He stared down at the assortment of objects for a moment, as if contemplating a problem on an invisible chessboard. But when he raised his head, Lubomyr could see the ridges of his smallpox-ravaged face were tinged with sudden color, white and red. His lips were twisted back to reveal pearllike teeth. Only his large eyes were calm, expressionless. He cleared his throat. "Weren't you listening to me? Are you all fools? Roumania, that's where the danger is. Roumania."

When he was talking about cowardice and sheep, Lubomyr had not imagined what a frightening figure the man could make when he was angry, as now.

"You make me want to puke," he said. Around them in the darkened room, four blond, moustached, identical servants paused to listen.

Only the elector's brown eyes were calm while the rest of him twitched and fidgeted. He held his hands above the inlaid surface of the table, which now seemed to reveal a kind of pattern in the marquetry. "Look," he said, "are you insane? Do you think you have the knowledge to protect yourselves without my help?"

He was referring, Lubomyr knew, to the hidden world. This kind of talk was rare in Germany, a shared interest that had brought the men together. After the elector's expulsion from Roumania, Lubomyr had written him a letter from the university. In five years of correspondence he had learned much, benefited much.

"Look around you! Don't you see the beauty of my collection? But you want to take away the prize! You must know how those two wronged me and wronged all of us. Nicola Ceausescu robbed me of the most valuable jewel in Europe, a German national treasure. Clara Brancoveanu betrayed me when she was my guest, when she was twenty-three years old and pregnant, too. There were anti-German riots all over Transylvania, Bucovina, Bucharest itself after the empress had her husband murdered. I offered that girl the hospitality of my house for her sake and for Schenck von Schenck—I didn't turn her away when she was pregnant and without funds. And I thought she'd be happy to learn that we were marching on Roumania to protect her interests and our people. We were going to avenge her husband. But she betrayed us. Six kilometers!"

"And the boy?" asked Lubomyr. He was looking at the man's fingers, which had selected another nut.

"Kepler's Eye! I wanted Kepler's Eye! Is that too much? Isn't that what every man wants—to try to change things for the better? Do you think there'd be a need for all this fighting? Without the stone, what am I? A national scandal and a joke, while Nicola Ceausescu uses it for her own vanity, a mirror for herself. I have heard she gives theatrical performances and the people cheer her idiotic self-indulgence—if there was any doubt of the stone's effect, then that should settle it. But what do you suppose that power would be worth in the hands of a dedicated and serious man?"

Nicola Ceausescu had already been a subject of conversation earlier that night. The two men had already discussed her thwarted attempt to smuggle radium from Abyssinia. They had discussed the tourmaline, and in that context conversed easily and pleasurably about land reform, new rights for citizens, the abolition of hereditary privilege. But the elector was an unstable fellow after all, and with a growing sense of anxiousness, Lubomyr watched the movements of his hands.

In his patent-leather case, as he had said, Lubomyr had brought an offer from the government, a possibility of rehabilitation. Now he wondered why he'd bothered to mention it. Arriving in Ratisbon the day before by train, he had not been prepared for the elector's ugliness. Now, glancing up at the elector's seared and puckered face, he thought a thousand tourmalines, a bath of tourmalines, a purple shower of tourmalines would yield only a minimal effect.

"We are thankful for your patriotism," he repeated blandly.

When he had spoken to his contacts in Berlin, he had not understood how isolated the elector had become, how solitary, how irrelevant—a rich man who lived by himself in a big house on a hill above the old part of the town. Daily his servant, Dr. Theodore, came shopping at the Kirchenstrasse market.

From the squares and street corners you could see the overgrown terraces of the park. The gates were open to the lower garden. Children played and were not chased away. In the afternoon, Arslan Lubomyr had climbed the cobbled drive. The house was not an ancient one. It had a stucco façade. Dr. Theodore had brought him up after he'd rung the bell—the first of many Dr. Theodores. Now in the dark chamber at the top of the house, they clustered around him as the elector raised his hand. Unhinged by loneliness, sucking on a macadamia nut, he gestured over the tabletop. "My friend, this is not your fault, I know. But you must not allow yourself to be the errand boy for fools. If I have taught you anything in these five years, it is to look beneath the surface of the world. You can't doubt the reality of what I say, that after all this time I've still kept watch over my country. For years I have accustomed myself to only a few hours of sleep, so that the shield I have in place cannot be broken or disturbed. I have received no thanks for this, but only ridicule and abuse from those who have no understanding of the world. And now you've come to rob me and insult me at the time when I'm most needed. Do you believe your bombs and guns and your new tanks will be enough to protect you? All these things can be blown away like spiderwebs. Now in the Reichstag they are working to undo all that. And I tell you now I made a terrible mistake when I allowed you to let Miranda Popescu escape that day in the Dobruja forest. You should have shot her through the skull. I was in love with a sense of symmetry, that she would take our forged letter to the Russians. I thought she was a defenseless girl. But now she rises again to challenge us in the heart of Europe—this is the moment you have chosen to insult me. What if I refuse? Are you authorized to have me arrested, take these things of mine away by force? My friend, I wish you luck."

Lubomyr couldn't look at the man's face. He found himself disgusted and repulsed by this long speech, angered by the suggestion that he might have been capable of murdering a beautiful young woman, a civilian—or not beautiful, particularly, as he now remembered her, but fresh and alive; it didn't matter. He passed his hand over his eyes, staring instead at the surface of the table in front of him.

Now he saw a change in it, a pattern in the marquetry he'd not observed before. And the objects he had thought were placed at random, the bud vase, the incense burner, the small statues of Tsong Kapa and Kwan Yin, the ashtray, and the brandy glass now appeared like the counters in a game. And the board they sat on now revealed itself in alternating blocks of color, and stylized patterns that suggested rivers, rocks, mountains, seas—the continent of Europe, Lubomyr now saw. There were the thousand islands and the wreck of Britain, there was the submerged coast of France. There was the enormous white mass of the Pyrenees, six thousand meters tall, and then the verdant Alpine hills. There stood the abandoned ruins of Rome. There were the great capitals: Warsaw, Prague, Bucharest, Berlin, and Petersburg.

Fascinated in spite of himself, Lubomyr leaned forward to look. Was this a pattern that had been there all the time, and now he was only just seeing it? Or was the elector showing him some aspect of the hidden world? As the gaslight dimmed along the sconces in the wall, Lubomyr saw more and more. A new light seemed to rise out of the brandy glass, set in the Hungarian forest. "These are the powers that protect the world," came the elector's voice. "It doesn't matter that the armies fight. We have achieved an equilibrium, though we struggle for advantage. There in Krakow is a professor of philology. There in Bratislava is a milkmaid in a barn. Her name is Zuzana, and she sits upon her stool, smiling and laughing to herself—I have seen her in my glass. There in Mogosoaia is the ghost of Aegypta Schenck—old enemies, she and I. For a long time I had her bottled up, but now she has escaped."

Uncertain, feeling the alcohol that he had drunk, Lubomyr glanced up at the elector's ruined face. He tried to follow the gestures of the man's clean little hands, looking for the conjuring trick: His host was pointing toward the statue of Kwan Yin, slightly to the north and west of the Roumanian capital. The token of Aegypta Schenck, Lubomyr supposed, and now he looked for other tokens. Near at hand, in Germany, on a hill outside of Ratisbon there was a pebble he hadn't seen until that moment. Now it glinted in the light thrown by the brandy glass, diffused through the red dregs of the wine.

"And I will tell you a secret that in time you'd have to know," said the elector. "Each one of us requires a prisoner. For the Baron Ceausescu it was his own son. And when he surrendered his son he lost his power. The milkmaid has a lover whom she tortures. Each of us in different ways has interpreted the texts of Hermes Trismegistus in his lessons to a young conjurer. And you see how effective they have been at least in my case. We feed on our prisoners in ways you cannot guess, and I think I am the honest one because I hold them under lock and key. Do you want to take away my strength, now of all times? You see there is no one to the west," said the elector, gesturing. "You see there is a wave of darkness rising from the west across the sea."

His face, disfigured, hard to read, nevertheless showed traces of a new anxiety, a new weakness. "I need them," he went on. "Aegypta Schenk held her own niece in the palm of her hand. But when she let her go, when she let her escape into the real world, then she was defeated and killed by a minor adept almost the same day! It was because she was a woman, and she did not have the firmness to be cruel. . . ."

All this time, Arslan Lubomyr had felt a mix of competing sensations: curiosity, drunkenness, anxiety, disappointment. This last reaction now was uppermost as he leaned back in his chair. He didn't know whether to interrupt. So that's why the elector had kept his prisoners all these years! For nothing— Lubomyr had read the new edition of the letters to a young conjurer, the annotations that explained the errors in all previous translations. Was it possible the elector was not aware of the ambiguities in the ancient text? Was it possible he had never read the letters in the original hieroglyphs? Or was he was using Trismegistus as a screen to hide some other more malevolent motive—revenge, perhaps, or sadism? If so it was a horrifying disappointment, and Lubomyr would put some version of it in his report, when he left for Berlin the following morning.

As if he sensed some of Lubomyr's disgust, the Elector of Ratisbon paused and stared at him, before he continued with his rant. "My friend, was it foolish for me to think you could learn some of my skills? Can you guess how you have disappointed me? I tell you we are in a delicate position in this country, and everything we've worked for can be stripped away. Yes, we've won a victory, but you must know this war is not popular. Bodies are returning on every train. Many are asking these same questions, now the tsar has offered peace.

Should we press forward? Should we retreat? These things are in a subtle balance in the middle of a parliamentary election. But if von Stoessel fails, or one or two men are defeated, what will happen then?"

Lubomyr stared at the elector's hands. On the smallest finger of his left hand, the man wore a signet with an intricate seal. Between the forefinger and thumb of his right hand, he held a nut. It was odd, strange, almost spherical, covered with white dust. Then it disappeared into his mouth.

The elector coughed and wheezed. "It is up to me to protect these men. If—" and he was silent.

There was a flicker in the lights, a strangled groan. Arslan Lubomyr glanced up, and for a long minute he couldn't guess what had happened. The strangeness of the elector's face made all expressions difficult to interpret. But then he saw the man was choking, gasping for air. His hands rose to his neck, clutched at his throat.

As the light spread out of the inlaid map, Lubomyr had been conscious of the servants gathering around to watch. Now he sat horrified in his chair, his hands squeezing its carved arms, hoping for them to intervene until he saw they couldn't. They were also stricken. Two collapsed onto their knees on the carpet—they were not groaning or scratching at their necks. Instead they settled onto their hands and knees, and as Lubomyr watched they seemed to shrink into themselves, dissolve as the gaslight dimmed, and the darkness grew opaque around him. Still the red light spilled out of the brandy glass, and Lubomyr could see his host, see the left hand gesturing—help me, oh my God. But nauseated by fear, he found he could do nothing except rub the arms of his chair with his greasy palms, while at the same time staring into the elector's limpid eyes, which now were saying, "You are a dead man. I will not forgive you."

But the Elector of Ratisbon was so ugly! How could Lubomyr touch him, touch his flesh? How could he touch this mad, dangerous, misguided man, who had half stood from his chair, and who was rocking back and forth, clutching at his throat—the light flickered and dimmed. The room grew dark. And at the last instant Lubomyr flung himself from his chair and grabbed hold of the man, forcing his face down onto the darkened table. Now it was possible to touch him, now he could no longer see.

The servants had been swallowed up in darkness. The room was completely dark. Lubomyr felt his fear rise up; he could not help himself. In any case the nut wouldn't budge out of the elector's throat. As he squeezed and pressed and flailed, Lubomyr could feel the man's heart racing under his hands. It seemed to shudder in every part of him.

The table was broken, overturned, and the young man staggered up. Stumbling and panicked, he groped his way across the floor, banging into furniture until he reached the stairs.

SEVERAL FLOORS BELOW AT CLOSE to the same moment, Clara Brancoveanu was thinking about cucumber sandwiches, sardines, and a bottle of Riesling—the luncheon she had mentioned to the air that morning, as she imagined it was. She stood in the parlor, waiting for the dumbwaiter's second bell. Already she had drunk a quantity of tea. She leafed impatiently through the afternoon papers, an afternoon five years before. Still she called out brightly, "I see there is a surge upon the stock exchange!" This kind of joke had become a ritual.

Melancholy in her middle age, crazy with fear that she would meet her death in those comfortable rooms, nevertheless she almost missed the opportunity to escape. It was Felix who first noticed the flickering of the lights. It was Felix who first heard the click of the dumbwaiter's lock. He ran to the double doors and opened them; the bell had not rung, and there was no food inside. Nor was the box there. But he could see the double rope and the empty shaft.

"Mother," he said. He reached in and pulled on the counterweight, and the box came up from underneath. Never before had he been able to control it.

"Come," he said. He was a sensitive boy, and in the prickling of his skin he could feel a change. Just a small thing as the lights dimmed and then extinguished themselves one by one. He knew something must be done. The roof of the box was below him.

"Come," he said to the princess. And when she made a motion to resist, he grabbed hold of her arm and bundled her through the doors, onto the top of the dumbwaiter's box.

"What are you doing? Please, let go of me!" Felix Ceausescu had never touched her before. He held the double rope in his other hand, bracing it against her weight.

"Didn't you ask for this one chance?" he said. And the box sagged down to the floor below, as far as he would risk. "Kick open the door. The locks have gone."

What was this energy that possessed him? He was not a powerful boy. But he hung onto the rope as she pushed through into the room below. Then he surrendered it and climbed down, hanging by his fingers from the sill as the light failed completely.

Above him on the staircase, Arslan Lubomyr clattered down the five flights to the entrance hall and groped his way across the marble floor. He was terrified of the pitch-darkness, but even more terrified after a few moments when the lights began to glow again, weakly, fitfully at first. He ran to the great door and fumbled with the bolts and pounded on the oak beams until they surrendered, and he pushed out into the night. But in the yellow gaslight that shone from the pediment, he saw the smiling and officious face of Dr. Theodore, a pair of Dr. Theodores who took him by the arms and brought him back into the hall. Nor did he struggle when they pulled him up the stairs. If he had struggled, if he had taken up any of their time, perhaps Felix Ceausescu and the princess would not have found the front door open and unguarded when they peeked out from the servant's hallway underneath the stairs.

At first they hesitated on the threshold, astonished by the darkness and the open air. Felix wondered if a thunderstorm had come. Princess Clara imagined for a moment that the world had been transformed during her long captivity, the sun darkened in the sky. But when they recognized the night for what it was, they staggered out into the park and hurried down the cobblestones into the town.

18   *Reunions*

ANDROMEDA IN HER DOG shape had disappeared after the derailment. Nor had de Graz bothered to look for her. He'd come to Bucharest, riding in the special horse-drawn coaches sent for passengers of the Hephaestion. He'd been taken to the bureau of railroads to receive a commendation. Later there was a memorial for the mysterious commercial traveler from Abyssinia, the sole casualty from the wreck. There was a reception given by the police commissioner of Bucharest. By that time Pieter had already left the hall. Pleading tiredness, he'd gone to his hotel, paid for by the grateful bureau. And at first in the beautiful summer weather he had thought he would be happy to explore the streets of Bucharest and see what had changed after so long. But after two nights he slipped away to Mogosoaia, his heart in a chaos that he didn't understand.

Peter Gross had understood. Now it was as if his conscious and subconscious selves had been reversed. And de Graz had little interest in self-examination. It was true he'd given his oath to protect Miranda Popescu. He'd promised her father on his deathbed, and there was a cold self-satisfaction in thinking that his word of honor was still good after these years, these complications. But why did his heart thump in his chest as he approached Mogosoaia on the train? Why did stanzas of English poetry come unbidden to his mind? Why did he think often of the girl's face? Or a woman now of course, grown up from the days he'd taken care of her at Mamaia Castle on the beach. Less of her father in her looks now. More of her mother—why did he drum his fingers on the leather seats and on his pants? Though he'd refused all money, he'd allowed some passengers from the Hephaestion to buy him a suit of clothes.

The train emptied at his stop. The platform was full of people. Since the events at the Venus shrine, many had come out to pledge their loyalty, though to whom or what it was not clear. Miranda Popescu had disappeared. Her followers had been arrested. The shrine itself was occupied by the police and there were soldiers in the woods. But curious people came and went. Some had packed chicken or ham sandwiches and come out with their families for the day. The weather had turned after a cold spring, and it was summer after all.

Young men slept out in the fallow fields around the Brancoveanu palace, hoping to be part of something. But de Graz was not like that. He had a plan.

Or else it was half a plan and half a memory. When Frederick Schenck von Schenck had been denounced and arrested, he was staying in the Brancoveanu guesthouse with his pregnant wife. And he was already sick, that was the ironic part. Or not so much ironic—de Graz was an uncomplicated man—but sad. He had a cancer in his bowels. He'd said nothing to the princess for fear of alarming her, but he was already making his arrangements. Later, when the news came that he'd been shot in an escape attempt, people said he had been murdered. De Graz himself had thought so. But Prochenko disagreed. The prince would have had no wish to die in prison.

Pieter thought about these things as he walked up the cinder roadway from the station. The soldiers in the crowd were dressed in green uniforms, and they wore on their shapeless wool berets the insignia of a Targoviste sappers regiment that had fought well at Havsa. At the stone gate of the park they leaned dispiritedly on their rifles, unchanged since the Turkish wars. The guns were older than they were.

Though they had mounted their long bayonets, they made no attempt to stop the people streaming through the gate, even to check their papers, which was a relief. Pieter had none, either in his own name or in the name of his alias, Peter Gross. Andromeda—Prochenko—had purchased a false set in Adrianopole. But Pieter hadn't seen her since the wreck.

It was a lovely summer morning, bright and sunny after an intermittent rain. Shrubs and briars had been allowed to grow under the oak trees, though the paths were clear. Though he was not a romantic person, Pieter rejoiced in the smell of the earth, and he found himself paying attention to the birds and squirrels, even the insects as he walked. And when the great bulk of the Brancoveanu palace came into view, he felt suddenly giddy, not because it was a beautiful building—no one had ever claimed that. Nor had he himself ever been inside it. Already during his service to the prince, it had been abandoned, boarded up.

But in distance in a grove of pines he saw the tiled roof of Sophie's guest-house, built for the prince's grandmother in an Oriental style. There he had stayed once, and there he had promised to defend the prince's child. That promise, sworn on his honor as a patriot, had taken him a long and weary way, first to Mamaia Castle and to Massachusetts, where he'd gone through school and high school in the body of a crippled boy.

Later he had come to Heliopolis with Prochenko. He had lived through many follies and stupidities, but now here he was again, standing in his flesh, the road now looped together under his feet, tied into a knot.

His trail had come full circle here, but where was hers—Miranda's? Days before, she'd been here. It was the talk of Bucharest. Even the director of railroads had mentioned it half wistfully, as if he too had been tempted to give up everything to march under her banner, white-haired and portly as he was, and dressed in a cream-colored waistcoat. "If I didn't have responsibilities, Domnul Gross," he'd said, as they stood together looking at the woodblock caricature that was posted on the wall of his office as on every wall in Bucharest—one thousand marks reward for news leading to capture of the woman who called herself Miranda Popescu. . . . Even then, reading the text, de Graz had imagined that Miranda's army would contain a great many poets, lovers, women, and old men, but few professional soldiers beside himself. It didn't matter. He was enough, if he could only find her.

Some lines of English poetry came into his mind, "Let us be true to one another, for the world which seems . . ." Seems what? What indeed? But she was here somewhere in the forest. He walked through the overgrown gardens, following his nose, understanding only where he would not go. Not to the guesthouse where the path would be muddied with sad memories. Not to the Venus shrine where Radu Luckacz was searching with his men.

Pieter de Graz was a man of impulse. Always he was searching for a sense of rightness that went beyond words. How could that be accomplished except through faith and trust in his own destiny? God spoke to men who did not contradict. Always he had been unpopular in the army, though he'd won more ribbons and medals than he could wear.

Now in his brown coat and trousers, his laced-up leather shoes, he stood at the border of the forest next to the old barn. Though there was a path under the trees, he didn't take it. Instead he struck immediately into the woods, pushing through the undergrowth, stepping over the dead leaves and sometimes finding cart tracks and stone walls. This had been agricultural land two hundred years before.

He pushed northeast through the brambles for many hours. He had no weapons or water or supplies. But in other ways he was prepared. His trail was as straight as if drawn with a rule. In time he came into the older forest, never cut.

Toward evening he crossed some rotten strands of barbed wire and stood beside the ruins of an old tower. Baron Ceausescu had sequestered the entire area in the old days, a circle of ancient trees held in the long curve of the river. Now those laws had been relaxed, more through inattention than design. There were still some notice boards nailed to the trees, but Pieter didn't read them. Instead he peered up at the body of a rat, tacked to the bark of an enormous oak. Its belly had been split and stuffed with fetish objects to guard against bad luck. There were beads, medallions, coins, and other objects wrapped in cloth.

He had stumbled out of the prickers now, his coat covered with green burrs. He plucked them off, looking in both directions down a muddy, leaf-meal path. For the first time he was unsure now how to go. The orientation of the path to the notice boards and tower was unclear.

But one way led deeper into the old forest. Choosing it, Pieter walked for several kilometers without seeing anyone. Moving through his thoughts as if through a sequence of empty rooms, he took a long time to become aware of a creature beside him in the undergrowth, longer still to realize that the creature was staying with him parallel to the path. He heard a crashing in the brambles, stopping when he stopped to look. Nothing was distinct in the low light. But there was some lurking movement that soon disappeared until he saw a figure up ahead. Something or someone was on the path in front of him, and without thinking Pieter thought that if he just broke forward in a run, shouting, shaking his fist, then the animal would blunder away—it seemed timid enough. But when it started coming toward him, he found his pretended anger swelling into something real; he paused to pick up a broken stick. And when the creature leaped at him he jammed the stick into its ribs and twisted it. At first he thought it was a monkey or an ape. It leaped on him and locked its legs around his waist, its arms around his neck. He felt in his body an immediate reaction, as if a child had reached up to hug him. So he dropped the stick and put his hands around the creature's knees, supporting it against his body—it was a female, he imagined.

There still persisted in the Roumanian forest the remnants of an older race of human beings, the original inhabitants of Europe. Displaced in neolithic times by waves of immigrants from Africa, they had retreated to the lonely corners of the continent, where they lived on government preserves. The Chevalier de Graz had not paid much attention to his education, but he remembered a few things.

Now he stood with his legs spread, supporting the woman with his hands under her rear. He had stabbed her with a stick and he could feel the warm blood, but she showed no reaction. Suddenly he felt the heat of the afternoon, and a small sensation on his neck where she was kissing him or maybe licking at the sweat under his ear. He glanced sidelong at her face and got a brief impression of long eyelashes and pale, hairy skin. But he couldn't get much of a sense of her, because she was dressed in strips of cloth wound around her arms and legs and body. The hair was clipped short on the back of her head.

A female, he thought, because he knew the males were shy and large, much stronger than a man. Driven out from the Carpathians, some family groups had been resettled by the Brancoveanus on their private land.

The air was hot and still. Pieter felt the tickling under his ear and listened also to small murmured words in a language he didn't know. The woman was talking to him. Or else she carried on a laughing, whispered, singsong conversation with herself. She couldn't have expected him to understand. She didn't seem embarrassed. In time she released her grip and climbed down. And he could see where she was wounded in the side, though she paid no attention. She took him by the hand and pulled him off the track into the undergrowth, finding a deer path through the brambles, and he followed her.

Pieter de Graz felt none of the aggression that comes from curiosity. As always, the part of him that thought about things was separate from the part that acted. Without thinking he imagined that the woman was taking him to Miranda Popescu. Perhaps she had found refuge in the dangerous small villages of these creatures, or in the caves they once had decorated with painted animals, where the Roumanian police would search for her last of all. The woman was laughing and chattering as she dragged him along, and in the speckled sunlight it was hard to see her face. This was partly because she was in front of him, and partly because he found himself glancing away when she turned back, made uncomfortable by her big eye-ridges and sloping forehead, her big jaw and teeth.

In the woods in front of them he heard a gunshot.

The woman's skin was pale, her hair was gray, not thick enough to be called fur. Though most of her was covered in dirty strips of cloth, her forearms were bare past the elbow. And though she was smiling, Pieter sensed from her an impression of urgency and danger. She had let go of his hand as the land started to rise, and she moved quietly and quickly through the undergrowth, bent almost double. Quietly and quickly Pieter followed her. It was a skill he had from Berkshire County. Was Miranda hurt?

Then suddenly they came onto an outcropping of rocks above a clearing of felled trees. There were thatch-roofed wooden huts below them. Miranda Popescu lay in a circle of trampled earth on a tarpaulin or stretcher—he could just make it out. Dressed in the silver uniforms of the German military police, two men stood upright on either side of her. Two others were kneeling.

Pieter took his jacket off and dropped it on the rocks. The woman who had led him sat and hugged her legs. There was blood on her side, but she took no notice.

For a moment, dully, Pieter wondered what Sasha Prochenko might do now. Perhaps he would call out, wave, climb down slowly through the rocks, approach the policemen smiling with his hands open—whatever he did, it would involve a lot of talking. Pieter crouched behind a rock as one of the kneeling men looked up, stood up, pointed at the woman sitting cross-legged. One of the soldiers raised his rifle, but he didn't fire, and the woman didn't move.

Pieter recognized the man who had pointed, though he was older and white-haired now, a one-eyed man named Ernest Dysart who had fought with Schenck von Schenck. Prochenko would have definitely called out to him. They were old comrades, after all. But de Graz slipped back out of sight over the lip of the hill, then climbed down through the rocks. After circling through the trees, he came to the back of one of the small houses. In the village he could slip from house to house.

Some of these places were ruined or abandoned, and some were simple dirt-floored huts. There were about fifteen houses in all, arranged in two rough circles around the trampled clearing. One was larger than the rest, and its back door was open. Through it he stepped into a room with woven matting on the floor. There was a fireplace, a wood stove, a spinning wheel and treadle loom, some metal pots and even a few books. The house was neat as any peasant's cottage with its high shelf of painted crockery—Pieter de Graz saw none of these things. He was looking for the mark of a struggle, but he didn't find it, though the front door was ajar. And he was looking for a weapon, which he discovered near the household altar of Diana the huntress. It was a thin-bladed knife stuck into the timbers of the wall.

The shutters were closed on the glassless front windows. Pieter looked out through the slits into the trampled yard. The soldiers were close by, and he heard them talking. But it was hard to listen, hard to concentrate—they had put their hands upon the general's daughter. He couldn't see her face, but he could recognize her hair and legs. He found a noise of protest coming out of him, a low coughing noise. At the same time he started to pound his fist against the window frame. He wanted Miranda Popescu to wake up, and he thought surely the soldiers would be frightened of the creatures who lived in these houses. They were fierce, crazy creatures, as the world knew. Then he went and stood next to the doorjamb, next to the wooden lock plate so that he could meet them as they came to look. This was so easy, a child could have done it. He saw the muzzle of the rifle poking open the door, and he studied it as it came through, a fine light weapon from Abyssinia, perhaps.

He kicked the door and the man in the silver uniform staggered forward. He had a big fleshy nose, and Pieter grabbed hold of it. With his knife he sawed off a piece of it, then kicked the gun loose as he jumped across the open doorway and the second soldier fired his gun, fired it again—a high, odd, muffled sound. Pieter imagined he was safe for several seconds at least; the door was flat against the wall, and he had the double thickness of the door and wall. It didn't matter, though. He didn't need the time. The first soldier blocked the threshold. He was rolling on the ground and screaming, his hands over his face. The second soldier must have realized how exposed he was. He scuttled backward when Pieter looked out through the slits of the second window, and Dysart had disappeared.

It was time for talking now or else pretending to talk. Pieter dropped the knife and ripped away the bloody cuff of his sleeve, then pulled out his pocket handkerchief and wiped his hands as he ran through the cottage, slipped out the rear door.

The wounded soldier was still screaming. It was the end of the afternoon, and the sun hung low over the ragged cliffs. Rubbing his hands, Pieter moved away from the sun around the circle of huts. Between two of them he found the body of a little hairy woman dressed in a blue dress and white apron. She was curled up like a dog.

Pieter's right hand wouldn't come clean, and he now saw that he was wounded. A bullet had passed through the middle of his palm. Now when he saw the hole it started to throb, and he tied the handkerchief around it as he left the woman and went on. He flexed his fingers, and his hand hurt, and he wondered if he would meet Dysart circling around, or the German soldier, or the other man he'd scarcely seen except for an impression of drab black clothes and a slouch hat—he was the one, as it turned out. De Graz saw him lurking by the inner house, and so he changed directions and came up behind him, making no effort to be quiet.

The man turned back when he saw him, came toward him with his hands out. "Domnul Gross, where did you come from?" he whispered. "From the reception—heaven be praised. I am happy to see another citizen of Roumania. You are Roumanian?" he asked, speaking in that language but with a harsh, Hungarian accent.

"Oui."

"I am so glad to hear it! Did you see one of those savage men? Are you here for the reward? I am asking you to help me—the hero of the Hephaestion—I am so glad. The Germans have her now."

"Oui."

He was a gaunt little man with a luxurious black moustache. He studied Pieter keenly without seeing him. "We saw him through the door. He bit Lieutenant Schneider's nose completely. Come with me!"

Grabbing Pieter's arm, he led him back the way he'd come. When they passed the curled-up body in its apron and bonnet, he groaned—"But this is terrible! These Germans have no affection for life except their own. Heaven forgive me for coming out with them. And that coward Dysart, where is he?"

He seemed anxious to talk. He kept a long, whispered commentary as he led Pieter back to the big cottage and the sound of muffled screams. "I must tell you this is an enormous creature. I think two meters tall. Did you see him run away? You must be careful."

But Pieter was a brave man, the hero of the Hephaestion disaster. Without hesitation he stepped through the back door of the cottage where the soldier was laid out. The knife, he saw, had fallen behind a chair. In the shadows of the room it was invisible. But it was too close to the severed nose, a gobbet of raw flesh. If the Germans looked for it, then they would find it.

Pieter wondered if he should seize it up and attack the second soldier who now crouched over his comrade, bandaging his head. He spoke to him in German, a language Pieter didn't know. And he had managed to cover his entire face above his mouth with blood-soaked bandages. Even his eyes were covered over.

Pieter's hand throbbed, and the bandage was soaked through. The little man was behind him again and led him through the front door into the yard. There lay the general's daughter on her stretcher. It was put together, Pieter saw, out of a broken canvas cot. "Dysart!" called the man behind him, "Dysart!" Then in a lower tone, "Where is that illegitimate fool?"

Pieter had gone down on his knees beside the cot. He couldn't see the girl's face, but only her black hair and the ridge of her ear poking through. He put his left hand out to touch her and then hesitated, and then moved his open hand above her body, stroking the air a few inches above her flank, cupping her shoulder, her elbow, and her hip. He listened to her breathing and imagined the warmth of her; the sun was down behind the cliff. He smelled the fragrance of dirt and dust, and his mind was full of English words. "Ah love," he thought, "let us be true to one another . . . ," which was stupid nonsense. This was the daughter of General Schenck von Schenck. He had known her since she was in diapers.

"A thousands marks' reward is a beautiful sight," said the drab man with the absurd black moustache. "How did you hurt your hand? You must have hurt it in the wreck!"

Then the soldier came to the doorway and called out in German. The man listened, and then whispered to Pieter, "These men are potato-eaters. He wants us to carry back his friend. It is always the same with them. Heaven forbid that one of them should be getting hurt! In Russia I have heard it is always the Roumanians, always the Hungarians while they hang back. It is because they think we are like nothing or like dirt, perhaps. I tell you, my friend, I am glad to see you. Listen to him—he says Lieutenant Schneider cannot walk. He cares more for his comfort than for our success."

All this time the soldier had been calling out in German, and now he walked over toward them. He had both Abyssinian rifles slung over his back. Without ceremony, with bloody hands, he lifted up one side of the canvas stretcher and dumped out Miranda Popescu. She groaned and rolled over onto her back. Pieter reached his hands out, but he couldn't touch her.

"Qu'est-ce qu'elle a?" he asked.

The little man squatted down and fanned himself with his soft hat. His long gray hair was combed back from his forehead. "No, she's not sick. We found her in the house like this. Wake her up, make her walk, I beg you—try! Otherwise we cannot leave one man to guard her—where is Dysart? I tell you we must not stay here after dark."

Miranda Popescu was wearing a loose cotton shirt and undershirt, a leather belt and riding pants, although her boots were gone. Now he could see her face, her pale cheeks chafed and roughened by the sun. He could see her small chin and dark, heavy eyebrows, her beautiful hair. Around her neck was a silver locket and around her left wrist was the bracelet of the Brancoveanus. "I could carry her," he said in ordinary peasant's language for the first time.

"Yes, you are a powerful man. On your back, perhaps? I think she is drugged or in a trance."

All this time the soldier had been speaking. He had dragged the stretcher closer to the house, and now came back to stand above their heads, cursing and gesturing. He was a big man with a big, fleshy face. The man with the black moustache got up to talk to him, and whatever he had said about potato-eaters, now he seemed anxious to please. Together they went to the house and led out poor Lieutenant Schneider. All his bandages were soaked with blood, as well as the front of his fine uniform. He staggered and fell down. They laid him on the cot.

And he was lucky he was not particularly heavy. Otherwise they'd not have managed it. Even so they had to rest often as they carried the man away, following Pieter under the cliffs and down the track. And at first he would wait for them, perhaps leaning with his back against a tree. But he never put the girl down because of the promise he had made to her father. Nor did he carry her on his back but in his arms, her cheek against his shoulder. She was hot and he was sweating in the cooling dusk, and as the shadows lengthened he walked faster, out of sight of the other two, nor did he pay attention to the drab little man when he cried out, begging, then commanding him to wait. Already they were behind him, and he was thinking about Captain Dysart, Ernest Dysart, who had fought with the general and was a different and more dangerous kind of man. When he got to the deer path that the woman had showed him earlier that day, he ducked down under the brambles and followed it with Miranda Popescu in his arms. As silently as he knew how, he circled back toward the village and the cliff. About dark, he reached where he had left his jacket, and the woman was still sitting, waiting. She was wounded in the side and his hand bothered him.

NOW ALL PIETER'S LIFE, ALL his experiences seemed like a dream to him, a strange, chaotic rush. But because he was a man who'd never fed his own imagination, it was hard for him to understand how powerful a dream could be, how it could form a tunnel to a hidden world, a hole to crawl out through. Once you were out, your life inside seemed fragmentary and confused, remembered only vaguely or in the middle of the night.

This was Miranda's experience when she had drunk the water from the pool and then pushed through the cave's new rocky egress into the bright sun. Now, days later, slumbering in Pieter de Graz's arms, her cheek against his shoulder or else her long neck hanging back, she was alive and wakeful elsewhere. Vaguely and intermittently she was aware of being carried and supported, as Pieter stumbled up the deer path to the ragged clifftop above the town. There the woman was still waiting, and she led him onward into the dark woods until they found a place of shelter in a cottage in the woods. There was Ludu Rat-tooth, who helped him put her down onto a bed of pine needles and old quilts, and took her temperature with a mercury thermometer—she had a fever.

The Gypsy girl and de Graz sat down over her head. And when she struggled sometimes and cried out, the girl said, "Rest now, hush," and other small things. Intermittently she was aware of them as figures in a dream. But in the secret world she saw she'd fallen into a trap.

And the floor of the pit had wooden tyger stakes protruding from the mud, their points reinforced with metal. She had fallen between them and was not hurt, but the pit was a deep one and she couldn't climb up the steep sides. She clawed down dirt upon herself whenever she tried.

Above the circle of the hole it was bright day, a cloudless sky like a disk of painted tin. In her little prison she paced back and forth, back and forth, angry and coughing deep in her chest. How much time did she have? The men would come soon and they would shoot her.

Above her in the side of the pit there protruded the bend of a tree root, and she wondered if she could climb that far. Or if she could scrape down enough dirt to fill the pit entirely. If she undercut the sides, there might be some kind of mudslide and something might change, and so she set to work digging at the soft earth and digging at the rocks.

Then she heard a noise, and when she looked up there were other animals, the ones that sometimes followed her. Grass hung down over the lip of the pit, and she could see the little rat nosing around and hear its screaming. And she could hear the chattering of monkeys in the trees outside the hole. They were excited about something, a new creature who now climbed down onto the exposed root. At first the tyger thought it was a man, but the smell was wrong and she could recognize it now, a larger kind of ape, and tailless. It had brown hair, and it perched above her looking down, not chattering like the others, but staring at her until she stopped her pacing and stretched her body up the pit's steep side, reaching out with her big claws.

The ape had brown eyes, curly fur. And he wasn't telling her to rest quiet and do nothing. Instead, wordlessly, he begged her to exert herself, and he had help for her, too, some tangled strands of vines and creepers that he was bundling over the edge, a net with one edge still caught in tree branches, because she tore at it and found it firm. But she was too heavy to drag herself up, though she was a good climber, lighter and more agile than her Asian cousins, and she would often sleep in trees or drag a meal up there. But in the pit she struggled and fell until another mass of knotted vines came over the edge, a mass that now filled much of the hole, and she pulled herself up a few feet at a time. And when finally she had dragged herself onto the grass, she saw the trees were empty and the ape was gone, and everything was still. Around a tyger in the forest there is always a circle of quiet, and even the birds stop squawking and calling.

When she was safe in the long marshy grass, she pondered what she would do. Because her thoughts were slow and deliberate, she lay until evening in her nest of grass, licking herself and smelling the warm wind. She wasn't hungry, nor did she have an instinct for revenge. But this was her forest, or it had been until men and women had come and settled here in the richest valleys, people with no animal nature, or so they tried to persuade themselves. They had villages now everywhere, even in the forest itself, and more were coming every day.

Toward dusk she got up, stretched, and shook herself. And when the moon came over the hill she started away down the valley over the wet ground. Always she was surrounded by a circle of silence, as if she were the only living creature in this teeming swamp. Once only she heard the high, nervous bark of a dog, one of several that followed her at a respectful distance when she was hunting, as now.

The men had a city. For a long time they had not budged from it because they were afraid. But now they were sustained by a new kind of arrogance that allowed them to move freely.

For many years they had built up the walls of their city so they couldn't be attacked. But the white tyger wondered if they still protected the old wall, or if the thinking that allowed them to venture out had also allowed them to neglect it. She wondered if there was some hole or broken slide of rubble or unguarded watchtower.

Past midnight she came onto the plain and in the distance she saw the place lit up. Now this was dangerous, and she slunk from rock to rock beside the road. But in the silver moonlight she was hard to see, and so she continued mile after mile until she saw the gate of the city in front of her. Four roads came together there, and she had seen no traffic along any of them. But now suddenly she heard a clamor of movement and the blaring of horns, and the gates ground open, and a crowd of men and cars came out, an army of soldiers, tanks, and weapons of all sorts, regiment after regiment, all carrying the eagle flag of Germany, and they marched off to the east.

Curled up behind a boulder on a low ridge half a mile from the road, the tyger watched them for several hours. When the last men were gone, she climbed around the ridge to the west side, and there she saw a different army coming home: ambulance cars, mule-drawn carts, wounded men, an intermittent, oozing stream that trickled through a smaller barbican.

The tyger was able to cross the road quietly, unperceived. Near the junction with the south road, she saw a teenage boy and a gray-haired woman cowering at the bottom of a small ravine. Had she seen the woman before? They were not worth her notice as she circled the walls, and they were gone when she passed the place again. She was looking for weakness and she found it in a tiny portal near the ravine. Perhaps the woman and the boy had escaped that way.

The old stones had tumbled down and had not been repaired. The wooden door was split in half. And in the guardhouse the tyger could see a man sitting in the shadows, staring at the lantern on his desk. He had black hair and a bald spot, and the hair combed over. When he looked up, she saw his face had been much ravaged by disease. The window was unbarred and he saw her, but he raised no alarm when she slunk past him through the broken door.

And maybe the city had been emptied by the emigrants who had left it to settle elsewhere in the tyger's home. Or else it had been emptied by the rush of the departing army. But she saw no one in the darkened street that curled upward in a mounting circle. From the wall, searchlights had shone out in all directions, casting garish shadows on the plain. But once inside the walls, everything was dark and quiet, and the tyger walked along the gutter, up and up into the summit of the town. There she found a little building separate from the rest, an altar or a shrine, she thought, made of white marble. The door was open, and everything was dark. And when she stepped across the threshold, she knew she had come into a place of secret power, and she could smell men sleeping in the little room, a family of brothers perhaps, drugged and unconscious in the hot stinking dark. There were three of them, and one was a little man, a soldier. And there were two others. Dysart had told her about these three men, when he was talking about the new elections in Germany. And as she moved among them she mauled them and bit them and they never cried out.

IN HER BED OF QUILTS and pine needles, in an abandoned and overgrown log cottage in the Mogosoaia woods, Miranda turned and struggled throughout the night. In the morning in her shelter in the mountains, Valeria Dragonesti awoke for the last time. She'd rested badly and her nurse had despaired of her. Sometimes she had not been able to find a pulse or hear a breath. Toward dawn she'd sent for General Antonescu. But he didn't arrive until after nine o'clock.

That year the weather had been cold. Summer had come late to the high mountains. But at dawn there were already swarms of mosquitoes in the meadows. Antonescu had grunted and slapped as he stood watching the sky grow pale. And when he climbed down the rock slope into the valley, he could see butterflies among the empty tents, and he was sweating. His boots were muddy and one leaked, so in the antechamber of the little hut he drew them off, rubbed his bare feet, warmed his toes in the sunlight from the open door. From his pocket he pulled out the long silver canister that he'd received from the wreck of the Hephaestion. It was blackened and burned from the ordnance that had blown up in the fire. The top of it was gone. He had been wrong not to go himself and take charge of the assault on the train, whatever the risks. Stefan had obviously made a balls of it. All he had brought back was this one empty canister.

He heard the nurse call and went in, ducking his head. He sat down on a stool, prepared, as he'd been for weeks, to know the worst. He sat looking at the wasted face, reduced to its essentials, all puffiness gone. He reached his enormous hand, then hesitated as she woke.

Her eyes were watery and blue, her eyelids tinged with red. She smiled at him. "I had such a dream," she murmured, her voice indistinct and hoarse.

Later he would punish himself by remembering these words, the last she ever spoke to him. Knowing she was near death, still he could not gather his attention sufficiently to listen, because he had no interest in dreams. Instead he watched her as she prattled on—her cheeks were flushed. "And then . . . ," she said. "And then . . ."

During his influential days in Bucharest and abroad, it had been the vogue for ladies to write down their dreams and then discuss them in the frankest language, as if they held the key to everything, as if their waking lives had no importance. And maybe he was just a coarse old bumpkin but he couldn't listen to these fairy stories, even when he tried to be polite, even when, as now, he realized he would look back later and reproach himself.

For a moment he forced himself to pay attention. He was glad to hear that she was saying something hopeful, enumerating a list of things that God would say to her or she to God. Her blue eyes shone. "That's good," he murmured, tapping his bare foot on the raw wooden boards—he couldn't stand it. It disgusted him to think of her dying in this humble shed, her only company a rough uncultured soldier and an idiotic nurse who should have called him sooner. He'd been up waiting the entire night, or only dozed off in his armchair once or twice. He'd had no dreams.

Now he allowed his anger to grow strong—he would not weep like a girl. He found himself turning over in his hands the silver canister from Abyssinia, blackened from the explosion, lead-lined, he could see. What had Nicola Ceausescu wanted it for? Was this the terrible weapon that could make Europe tremble? More than ever he regretted leaving the derailment to Stefan, who had blown up the baggage car—what did he think was going to happen? Along with these canisters (were there any that had not burst open?), the car was packed with ammunition, guns.

Maybe if he'd manage to salvage this mysterious weapon, he could have made Roumania regret the day they'd driven their rightful empress into exile. No, it was too late for that. In his indignation and grief, General Antonescu didn't notice the exact moment when Valeria Dragonesti stopped speaking, when she closed her eyes, and when her breathing faltered, then subsided. Nor did he notice a little creature at the corner of her mouth, a silverfish or else a worm.

By himself in the hut, he could not keep from weeping. Grief shook him and then left him, as the wind might shake the branches of a tree. He squeezed his eyes closed, put his fist against his mouth, and tears would still come out.

How repulsive it was for a strong man to sit bawling like a child, his eyes red and his nose running! Surely something could be done—he would ask for a meeting with the German governor. He would ask for his men to be released to their own homes. "Go away," he would tell them. "Get married, go on home." Maybe the Germans would permit it if he surrendered to stand trial.

Maybe they would permit it if he brought them the canister, evidence of—what? Some plan of Nicola Ceausescu's. The ordnance in the baggage car was nothing, a diversion or a ruse. That much was clear. These canisters—Stefan had seen dozens of them scattered about—they were the important cargo. Whatever they contained, it was obvious (wasn't it?) that Ceausescu planned to use it against Germany. Otherwise, why all the secrecy? No doubt she had already cleaned up the site of the accident. Perhaps this was the last canister left.

But Ceausescu was nothing without the Germans. In which case, had she gone mad? It didn't matter. What was important was what the German governor might believe.

Antonescu turned the silver tube between his hands. He rubbed away some of the black ash. There were markings on the base, hieroglyphs and then some European translations—NEPENTHE. He could just make out the letters.

Vaguely he remembered something from his school days, a classical reference. Nepenthe, a medicine administered by gods, a cure for all unhappiness. If the canister had been intact, maybe now he would have broken it open in his hands, sprayed it around the room where the empress lay dead.

But no, he thought as he sat blowing his nose. My miseries are too precious to give up.

MIRANDA STARTED AWAKE. She was lying in a tangle of quilts and blankets in a corner of the floor. Around her stood three sides of a log cabin, and the fourth side was broken in. Most of the roof was still intact above her. There was the ape lying in a corner. There was the rat, curled up in its armpit. The ape was moaning in its sleep and Miranda could see why. It had hurt its paw, wrapped in a bloody bandage.

"Wake up," Miranda said. "Wake up!" and she clapped her hands. She could tell they were in danger. There was a scent of urine around the place, a fox, she thought. It wasn't safe to sleep like that. She picked a stick from the ground and climbed out through the broken wall into the forest light. Above her in the trees some monkeys screamed. They knew a fox had come. They knew he'd walked around the cabin once. With the stick in her hand she followed it, hoping she'd find nothing. The fox might have been scared away by her human smell. The woods were beautiful in the bright summer sunlight.

It was a pine forest. Light sifted through black needles onto the thick ground. Her feet made no noise. In front of her on a fallen log she saw a little bird whose feathers glistened in the sun. When she came close she saw the bird was made of precious stones. Diamonds glinted on its breast, rubies and sapphires on its wings. Its beak was made of gold.

As soon as she had seen this bird, Miranda wanted to touch it and capture it. She thought she'd weave a cage out of willow branches and carry it away. So she came up behind it with the stick. But at the last moment the bird hopped a few feet farther along the fallen trunk, and turned back as if to say, "I know what you are doing!" So Miranda slipped into the shadow at the other side of the tree, and with all her strength and swiftness leaped onto the little creature.

But when she held it cupped between her fingers, she could feel its jeweled heart beat. And when it opened its golden beak, she was astonished to find that it could speak. In a soft, small voice it begged her to let it go. And it had guessed Miranda's plan. "If you put me in a cage I'll die," it said.

So Miranda opened her hands and let the bird fly away. It rose above her to the bough of a tree. There it perched with the sunlight on its throat, whispering and singing, cocking its head, winking its pretty emerald eye.

"You are a soft-hearted girl," it said. "I'll give you anything you want. So have a care!"

Miranda didn't need to think. But when she opened her mouth to say she wanted to go home to her own house in Berkshire County, she saw the bird wink once, and she couldn't make a sound. And when she thought of the two friends she hadn't seen in a long time, she saw the little bird wink two times with its emerald eye, and for the second time she could say nothing.

Furious and impatient, she tried to ask for humbler things, a meat sandwich and a ginger ale. Even this was too much for the bird, who winked at her. Miranda shook her fist, picked up a stone, and only then did she find her mouth unsealed. Only then could she stammer out a wish. "Tell me what to do."

Then the bird said, "For the sake of your kindness I will grant your wish. You must go straight on through this wood, not turning to the right or left. In the evening you'll find what you are looking for."

Even from the inside, Miranda could recognize the language of fairy stories. Stanley had read her fairy stories, and Rachel, too. Naturally, when she looked around, the three-walled cabin was no longer there. The woods had darkened into evening already. The animals had fled away. Because this was a dream and not real life, everything was different in a moment. The trees had lost their leaves. Nor was there a mulch of fallen leaves and needles, but just the hard gray ground. The trees were rootless, angular, and dead—dry sticks pressed into dirt. The air was cold. Miranda looked at her hands and saw they were chapped and red.

And because this was a dream, she had no choice where she went, but found herself walking in the direction the bird had indicated before it flew away. There was a gap in the trees that way. Miranda walked over the level ground and soon noticed a gray expanse of gravel underfoot. In the failing light she came to a small town, a double row of tiny clapboard houses, and she walked between them on a duckboard made of gray planks.

The houses were identical small cubes with high-pitched roofs. No doors were visible. But there was a four-paned window in the narrow wall of each, set so that Miranda could see into each interior. Stripes of colored light shone from the windows, merged on the surface of the duckboard.

There were eight houses on Miranda's left hand, eight on her right. Ahead of her was some kind of broken, indeterminate structure, different from this orderly double row. Standing on the rough planks, Miranda chose the second house on the left. She stepped down onto the gravel and walked over to the windowsill, following a path of amber light. She put her hands on the painted wood, noticing as she did so that there was no glass in the mullioned window. And inside the house, in a single, light-filled room, someone was sitting at a wooden table, it and the chair the only pieces of furniture. The table and she took up most of the space, so the room was like a cage. There was no ceiling above her, but just the open roof where the light was shining. All lines and contours were lost. She seemed to sit under the open sky.

The woman had brown hair streaked with gray. Her hands were clenched into fists on the surface of the table. Her hands and face were molded out of the same chalky substance. Miranda recognized her by her sweater and jeans and hair—her American mother. "Rachel," she said or tried to say.

IN THAT AIRLESS, STERILE PLACE, no sound came out of her. But in the little cottage where Ludu Rat-tooth sat with the Chevalier de Graz, she was able to blurt out a groan, and she rolled onto her side. She was lying in a nest of quilts.

The Gypsy girl, Ludu Rat-tooth, was by the fire, heating a basin of water. Once again she was describing to Pieter how she'd found Miranda in the woods above the cavern of Mary Magdalene. Maybe she'd climbed up through one of the small fissures in the rock. The strain had been too much for her. She hadn't regained consciousness. Then the ape women had carried her into the village under the cliff where the soldiers had come.

"Hush," said Pieter, raising his bandaged hand.

Night was drawing in. The fire burned on a low stone hearth, shedding more comfort than warmth. Already the air was hot and stagnant. But the fire was the source of light in the little room.

Ludu Rat-tooth sat beside it, stirring it with an iron poker, making the sparks crackle and dance. She had a spotted, lumpy face. But she was skillful with her hands and careful with Miranda. She was the one who'd bandaged Pieter's gunshot wound, although it wasn't much. The ball had passed through the center of his palm, and he could bend each finger. But it was sore, infected, he guessed, and she had put some stuff on it and bound it up, for which he was grateful.

Now she looked up, and he could see her narrow eyes. She didn't like the forest people—who could blame her? But once again she told him how she had found this place and fixed it up, and the forest woman had led him there— why was she talking about this over and over? It was because she had to talk to cover her anxiety. She knew Radu Luckacz would come after them again. "Quiet," he said, more urgently, and she was quiet. The sparks crackled in the chimney and on the hearth.

Pieter had heard a noise, a breaking stick. He stood up and took the poker from her. It was time to fight again, and he squeezed the iron bar in his right hand, feeling the protest of the infected flesh. Then he slipped out through the window into the dark.

The cottage was an old wooden structure, long abandoned. Parts of the roof, parts of the wall had fallen in. The forest had grown up around it. Thickets and brambles grew against the outer walls. Crouching underneath their leaves and tangled branches, Pieter moved among the stems, quiet as he could through the dead mulch. The ground was damp.

Below the house there was a small crease in the land, a tiny brook. There was a clearing, too, in a small dell. Some saplings had been cut down. As quietly as he could manage, Pieter circled round until he crossed the stream. There in the mud he found the heavy hoofprints of the horse, the bootprints of the man.

That old fox Dysart was hampered, Pieter guessed, because he needed to bring Miranda out alive. The notice board had specified that she be brought to justice. The reward was offered for her person, not her corpse. He'd have no scruples about the Gypsy, but he didn't want to share a thousand marks with a lot of policemen. He wanted to bring out the white tyger by himself.

And so he'd leave the horse in a clearing out of earshot from the cottage on the hill. Pieter found it there, a beautiful black gelding, standing absolutely quiet in the dark.

For a few moments Pieter kept to the shelter of the large trees. He wanted to lead the gelding away to a different place so Dysart would have to look for it. He must move quickly for Ludu Rat-tooth's sake. Although he didn't think Dysart would shoot her through the window as she sat beside the hearth—he'd want to question her, to find out where the man had gone. Doubtless Luckacz had told him about Peter Gross.

He watched the horse let its head sink down. It was absolutely calm, although it must have known Pieter was there. He squeezed the poker, feeling the hot flesh of his wounded hand under the bandage, and then stepped into the clearing—a mistake. Dysart was there waiting.

"Stop," he said in English. Pieter stopped.

"Put it down," he said, and Pieter let the poker drop.

"Come here," he said, and stepped out from behind a tree. In the half-moon light, in the clearing, Pieter saw a small, bow-legged man with long white hair and a broad-brimmed hat. He was dressed in pale pants and a white shirt. He had a pistol in his left hand.

"Come here," he said again, but Pieter didn't move. He thought if Dysart were going to shoot him, he would shoot him. So he stepped backward toward the horse, who raised its head.

Dysart came toward him. In the moonlight, now, his features became clearer, his seamed, scarred face, his single eye, his white moustache. He had been wounded at Havsa, Pieter had heard. His right eye had been cut out from his head. No trace of it remained.

Past fifty, he was stylishly, even foppishly dressed, Pieter saw when the man paused to light a small cigar. With his right hand he had drawn it from an inside pocket and placed it between his lips. Then from another pocket he had taken his lighter and flicked it open, and had lit the cigar without ever taking his eye from Pieter's face. Nor did the gun in his hand move a millimeter. It was a revolver, and in the small flame Pieter recognized the inlaid metalwork. Once it had belonged to Frederick Schenck von Schenck.

One step, Pieter knew, was all he was allowed. Now he stood still and let the man come closer. Dysart kept the cigar in the corner of his mouth away from his good eye, so the smoke wouldn't bother it. He kept his lighter in his right hand, the gun in his left. Pieter smelled the burning tobacco as he came close.

And as he stepped forward over the uneven ground, the horse grew restive and unquiet. It jerked sideways suddenly and laid its ears back. The reins, which had been looped around a broken branch, came free.

At two meters' distance, Dysart paused again. He held up the lighter, flicked the flame alive. I'm a dead man, thought Pieter, and he wondered what his old friend Sasha Prochenko might have accomplished at that moment, what words he'd have spoken, because this was the time for words.

But he said nothing. If Dysart was surprised to see him, he gave no sign. "The Chevalier de Graz," he said. "Still at his post."

Doubtless some words could be spoken. They were old comrades, after all. At that moment it was a liability. Prochenko would have said something. I'm a dead man, Pieter thought again.

When Dysart fired the gun, Pieter leaped backward and to the right, away from the man's good eye. He tripped and sprawled over the ground. His head fell back, and he felt rather than saw what happened next, the horse surge forward into the line of the second shot, blocking the way. Then without thinking Peter struggled backward, scuttling like a crab through the sapling stumps until he flopped over in the tall weeds and scrambled up the slope. Behind him there were shots and the horse screaming. When Pieter looked back through the trees, he saw the horse was down, kicking and screaming—a terrible sound that Pieter suddenly remembered in his guts, from Nova Zagora and many other places long ago. A circle of furious movement in the high weeds—he hoped Dysart had the decency to put the beast out of its pain. The man stood below him with his feet apart, and a shot rattled through the trees near Pieter's head.

IN THE SECRET WORLD MIRANDA heard the crack of the gun. She thought a branch had snapped in the sterile wood behind her.

She didn't turn around. She stood on the duckboard between the rows of little houses, peering in again at Rachel's image. The creature inside the house was lifeless, motionless, grotesque, yet even so Miranda felt a surge of nostalgic yearning that was like nausea. Was this her private, hidden world, populated with cold, chalk-white figures from her vanished life? Or else some kind of obstacle or test, a scrim she had to tear through to proceed? Or were these warehouse sheds, where Aunt Aegypta kept her broken puppets? She'd come back here after glancing into each small house. Each had contained a frozen figure from Miranda's life—teachers, people she had known; she couldn't stand it. Turning away, she hurried down the long duckboard, desperate to see a living creature.

At the end, she paused. The trees were broken around a strange, ruined structure that seemed to have been excavated from the stony ground—an archeological dig, perhaps. More lifeless ruins: She put her fist against her chest, against her beating heart. But then with a spasm of relief she saw her horse, her own horse, Telemonian Ajax, whom she'd ridden to Braila and across the plain. He pricked his ears forward as he came toward her out of the wood, moving with a smooth, silky gait that was not like him. He made no noise in the undergrowth among those cold trees. But he was happy to see her, she could tell, although he didn't neigh or nicker. He reached out his big head as he walked toward her, and she ran to meet him and put her arms around his neck. "Good boy," she said, "Good boy," and wished there was something to give him, some piece of sugar or an apple in this terrible place. In the real world, she wondered, who was caring for him now? Who was currying him down and combing out his tail? Not that pig Dysart or the man with the black moustache. She had left Ajax in a stable by the Brancoveanu Palace, his first night in a stall.

She burrowed her face into his black coat, hoping to liberate some smell, some rough stink of sweat, but there was nothing. Nor did he make a sound. Miranda knew there was something wrong, knew that the real horse was elsewhere. But even so she took a comfort from his black cold mass, and he was moving forward, urging her forward, so she swung herself up bareback, holding onto his mane. His steps were smooth and noiseless as he carried her up out of that place, and up a long hill in the blue, strange twilight. And she felt she was ascending out of the low, stale air into a more rarefied place: Surely this was the glass hill from the fairy tale. Without the black horse she would never have been able to climb so high. She would have slid down over and over. Surely sparks rang from his hooves.

And at the top stood the castle of the princess in the fairy tale. It was the little town in Massachusetts where the princess had once lived, and she rode silently down Main Street under a black, summer sky. And she saw no one, and there were no lights in the windows until she reached the castle walls, and dismounted in the front yard of her old house near the college green, with gray clapboards and high dormers and bright windows and red shutters, or "raspberry," as her mother had called them. She slid down off the horse, walked forward a few steps, and when she turned around Ajax was gone. He had moved away under the trees. Miranda climbed up the porch steps, and the door was open.

"Rachel," she cried out. "Stanley!" Every light was on, but no one was home. And the house was a terrible mess, she saw as she moved from room to room downstairs. More than any other single thing this was upsetting, because Rachel had always been so fastidious a housekeeper. But maybe no one had lived here for many years; the rugs were stiff with muddy footprints, the upholstery streaked with grime. Windows were broken. And there were vermin in the house, fleas hopping on the cushions, roaches burrowing in the breakfast cereal that was spilled over the kitchen floor. In every corner there were corpses of dead roaches and ladybugs —Rachel always had had a peculiar horror of roaches, which were rare in Berkshire County.

Rats and squirrels scuttled in the walls. Everywhere there were the droppings of small animals. Mice had chewed the old newspapers into shreds. All the kitchen cabinets were open. The cleaning cabinet was open, and Miranda seized one of the brooms. "Rachel," she cried. "Stanley!" No one was home.

Overcome with tears, she started to sweep all the spilled food into the center of the kitchen floor. If Rachel could see me, she thought. But where could she start? Pursued by a sudden loneliness, she ran up the stairs to the third floor, to her room, which was completely trashed. Never had it ever looked like this, Miranda thought, standing on the threshold, even when she had been trying to piss Rachel off. All her clothes were pulled out, flung around. The bed was ripped down to the springs. The books were pulled out of their shelves. They lay in a heap in the middle of the floor. Miranda bent down to pick up one broken-backed volume, *The Essential History.* Some of the pages were ripped out.

But how was it that the book still existed? Kevin Markasev had destroyed it in a fire on Christmas Hill, had burned it up and brought her into the real world, her and Peter and Andromeda. The book had contained a whole false life, and now here it was again, or some version of it. Still, it cheered her to hold it in her hand.

She slid it into her pants pocket. Then with the broom held like a weapon, she descended the stairs again, because she'd heard some movement in the dining room. And on the middle of the table on a filthy doily sat a cat, a big, ripped-up, orange marmalade. Furious suddenly, because she remembered the campaigns Rachel had conducted against her own kitten, Frosty, before she was hit by a car, Miranda struck out with the broom. But the cat raised up its paw to show its claws. It bared its teeth. One incisor had been broken off.

Angry beyond reason, Miranda grabbed the creature up with her bare hands. Its coat was greasy and matted, and it was hard for her to keep her grip because it twisted and scratched and bit. But Miranda had it by the ribs, and she took it to the front door and threw it down the steps. Then she went back to the cleaning cabinet to find some hydrogen peroxide to wash out her cuts; her hands were all scratched up. But when she disturbed the bottles and spray cans at the back of the cabinet, the roaches crawled out and she had to back away.

There, next to the peroxide was a silver canister. Once they'd rented out their house one summer and gone to Colorado. When they returned, they found the place infested with fleas, and Rachel had set off some bombs, one in each room on the first floor. That had done the trick.

Now there was one left at least. Miranda pulled it out and set it upright on the linoleum. The spray nozzle was still intact.

IN HER GARRET IN THE People's Palace, the Baroness Ceausescu was brushing her hair. She was humming softly to herself. For the moment there was nothing to be done. Radu Luckacz would bring the girl to her. He would bring her Miranda Popescu. She glanced into her handheld mirror, frowned, made a face, and put it down. She put down the brush and comb and climbed onto her iron bed where she lay looking up at the ceiling, arms stretched to each side.

SHE TURNED OVER AND was instantly asleep. In Ratisbon the elector was sitting by the window, rubbing at an itch in his sore and swollen throat. He sat looking out over his garden where policemen were digging by torchlight in the rhododendron bed.

He had almost choked to death. But the poisoned nut in his throat had come dislodged when he fell. Or else pounding on his back, Lieutenant-Major Lubomyr had managed to dislodge it. Since yesterday they had been searching for his body.

Soon they would find it, the elector had no doubt. In the meantime there was no reason to be impolite. With him were two detectives from the military police. He had served them coffee with his own hands, and talked to them about political developments as they unfolded. That day the government had suffered losses, preparatory to the general election. There was talk of a vote of no confidence, as several smaller parties were abandoning the coalition. Worst of all, three ministries had been compromised. The foreign secretary had been struck by an automobile while he was crossing the street, and was thought unlikely to recover. The minister for war had shot himself while cleaning his own gun, after a public accusation of corruption—all on the same night. Worst of all, General von Stoessel's body had been discovered in a homosexual brothel in Kaunas, five hundred kilometers from the front line.

"Tell me," murmured the elector. "In what condition was the body found? Had he been mauled or attacked in any way? Perhaps by a wild animal—were there tooth marks or claw marks in his flesh?"

"Please?"

They thought he was insane. How could such fools call themselves detectives? They were handsome, dark young men, and they stood in their overcoats sipping coffee from his beautiful Limoges cups. They had not taken their gloves off. In the afternoon he'd shown them through the house, the princess's apartments, empty now—"You see I have nothing to hide!"

"So you live here by yourself?"

"As you see."

"We had reports of a servant."

"He has left me."

"Ah."

They were idiots, and soon they would be dead. They stood behind him looking out into the garden where it had started to rain. The diggers were close now. Lubomyr was under the pear tree in a dignified spot.

The elector leaned forward, and with his thumb and forefinger he plucked a powdered ball from the bowl on the table. For the tenth time he examined it. He had thought it was a macadamia nut and almost choked on it. But it was larger than a nut, and covered with an anaesthetic powder that had numbed his throat. In other words, a piece of sorcery. Who was responsible? he asked himself for the tenth time. Lubomyr himself, he'd thought as he was gasping for breath, but now he wasn't sure. More likely the ball had come out of Roumania, from one of the three women there who had destroyed his life.

Now he regretted his impulsiveness. But in one way things were better and clearer since Lubomyr's death. His prisoners were gone, and there was nothing now to keep him here where he was not appreciated, where his patriotic contributions were ignored. Behind him the men were discussing the possible cease-fire. "Why not?" one asked. "Now the tsar will give us what we want. We were fighting for the German citizens of Lithuania. Is it not so?"

They disgusted him, their smooth faces and dark sideburns. Doubtless they took him for some strange variety of circus freak. A sick, demented man in an old house, a murderer, perhaps. Well, they would see. Dr. Theodore had done for Lubomyr, but Dr. Theodore had gone away. They'd find the elector was not yet too frail to do his own work.

Near him in the shadows stood a suit of armor. It had belonged to the first Elector of Ratisbon, who had worn it at the siege of Bern. The shield was decorated with the symbol of his house, a coiled serpent. Inlaid in Damascus steel, the figure seemed more like a dragon or a centipede in this incarnation, with numerous small feet and hands. It had a human face.

The policemen had started underneath the pear tree where the dirt had been disturbed. The elector squeezed the soft, white ball between his fingers. It had a poison on it, a salted dust that had numbed his throat and made it impossible for him to swallow, a dust that had almost killed him. Surely it had been reasonable at that moment to convince himself that Lubomyr was an assassin, had been directed by the Office of Domestic Security to dispose of him. And even if before he died, Lubomyr had made a case for his own innocence, still the elector, stung by the ingratitude of his own government, had made no effort to fight against the enemies of Germany as they'd come thieving in the night. Now he was recovered, though.

But he would miss this room! Everything here, every piece of furniture or art, he had chosen for its healing or restorative properties. Each object was a treasure, a source of ongoing delight. But they would be hard to carry with him, impossible to find again. Under his stool he'd put his small valise, packed the night before. Some money, a change of clothes, some books, and of course the passport he had taken from Lubomyr's baggage, filled out in his name and signed by the foreign secretary, now in a coma in a Berlin hospital—it didn't matter. By dawn he'd be across the border, one way or the other. The war was ending here, but he would bring it to Roumania.

One of the policemen in the garden now stood up and laid aside his spade. He turned toward the window, made a sign, and it was time. The Elector of

Ratisbon picked up his demitasse, sipped from it, and laid it down. At the same time he placed the poisoned nut in the pocket of his vest, removing the silver derringer he ordinarily kept there.

PIETER DE GRAZ STOOD UNDER a beech tree, his hand against its silver trunk. Below him in the dell, Captain Dysart stood over the body of the black horse, quiet now at last. He was reloading his revolver. Now he snapped it shut.

For a while he stood peering into the darkness, listening for movement, but Pieter didn't move. He supposed he could have run away into the deeper woods, and Dysart wouldn't even have bothered to shoot. But Pieter wanted to keep the man in the open where he could see him in the half-light, in his white shirt, pale pants. He wanted to be the one who chased him as he moved. And so he waited for Dysart to turn around and climb out of the dell, up the west side toward the cottage in the pine trees where Miranda lay.

Now immediately Pieter realized his mistake. He should have run into the trees, drawn the man away. Once at the cottage there was no predicting what he'd do. He wasn't strong enough to carry Miranda out, not with Pieter waiting. Surely the horse had been valuable to him, vital to his plan. Ludu Rat-tooth's life was not as valuable, nor Miranda's either. Luckacz would pay a thousand marks if she wasn't harmed. But doubtless he'd pay something for her corpse.

Fearing the worst, Pieter blundered through the trees. But as he moved, he remembered some of the habits he had learned in Berkshire County when he was a boy. Soon he was on all fours, pulling himself along under the briars— he could move quicker that way. He climbed over the brook and paused to drink. In three minutes he was at the cottage, but Dysart had preceded him.

He hadn't heard any shots, but as he came to the window, Pieter could see that Ludu Rat-tooth had run away. Dysart was alone in the little house, bending over Miranda where she lay near the hearth. He had the pistol in his left hand. Its octagonal barrel was pointed to the ceiling. The light shone on the intricate pattern of gold and silver briars, chasing each other over the dull, blue, tempered steel. When de Graz had made his oath to Frederick Schenck von Schenck, that same long-barreled revolver had lain on his bedside table.

With his right hand, Captain Dysart was searching in Miranda's shirt, causing her to groan and move. In the darkness outside the hut, Pieter squeezed his wounded hand into a fist, feeling the inflamed flesh under the bandage. What was the man doing? No, he was searching for something.

"Come inside," he said in English. "I know you're there."

Pieter stood outside the wooden wall twenty feet away, near the broken corner of the roof. "Don't worry," Dysart said. "I give you my word. I've never broken it."

In a niche of the stone chimney, serving as a mantel, Pieter saw the Gypsy's images of King Jesus and Queen Mary Magdalene. Traces of oatmeal clung to their painted faces. "She had two purses," Dysart went on. "One was a drawstring leather bag, or cloth, I think. The other was a beaded purse for ladies. One was full of Moldovan double-eagles, the other with thousand-drachma pieces. She didn't even know how much money she had."

He pulled the quilt from Miranda's body. "Damn it, where is it? Have you seen it?"

"No," Pieter said, and took a step beside the wall.

"I looked for it before. Then I found the general's gun. Isn't it a beauty? Don't worry. I give my word."

He had risen now and turned to stand facing the window. Pieter stepped away out of sight and put his back to the bark-covered planks. There was a knothole that gleamed red and yellow near his hand, and he wondered whether it was visible from the inside. He didn't want to get drilled though the eye as he stooped to take a peek.

"See, I'll put it down."

But Pieter couldn't see. He stood beside the knothole with his back against the wall. "Ah," Dysart continued. "Of course. The Gypsy must have taken the money. How stupid of me. She's probably halfway to the coast."

"Probably," Pieter said, and took another step. There were two windows in the wall, two meters or so apart. Pieter stood between them, his shoulders pressed against the dark, rough surface.

"So we're back to the reward," Dysart said. "Luckacz will be here soon. You don't have much luck, I think. Not without a gun. I'll make a bargain. Help me take her out. I'll give you half. And I promise she won't get hurt."

Pieter wondered about this, and turned to press his cheek against the wall.

"For old times' sake," said Captain Dysart. "You remember that time in Thessalonika. Two men with guns and just a handkerchief between them. You know how hard it is to shoot a man."

Pieter had no memory of this, thank God. He listened for Dysart's step on the floorboards. He listened for the movement of his voice. So far as he could tell, the man hadn't budged.

"She'll be all right. They always are. What did you get out of the Havsa campaign? I got seventy-five piastres a month, with one eye and a ruptured ear. It took years for me to learn to shoot again.

"I think a change is coming," Dysart went on. "What do you think? Something has got to break. I think it's time we went beyond these princes and princesses. That's all in the past."

"Yes," Pieter said, in spite of himself. He took a step toward the far window.

"So, what do you think? Do we have a bargain?"

Pieter wondered what Prochenko would have done. His own mind was empty save for physical sensations—his cheek against the bark. The pain in his right hand. A birdcall in the dark, summer woods.

"You can't save her," continued Dysart. "So we might as well . . ."

The important thing, Pieter thought, was to get into the room. "All right," he said and pounded his fist against the wall. Then he stepped back to the knothole. Peering through, he saw Captain Dysart near the opposite wall. He had indeed put up the gun. The plain bone handle stuck out from his belt.

Crouching down, Pieter could see better. The man had his hands held out. In the firelight Pieter could see his fawn-colored trousers and white shirt, smeared now with mud. A twig was tangled in his long white hair. And behind his head there was a hint of motion. Squinting, Pieter could see Ludu Rattooth with a piece of firewood above her head. Maybe she had crept over the windowsill. There was a window in the far wall.

"All right," he said again, and pounded on the bark next to the knothole. Making as much noise as he could, he ran to the door, in time to see Dysart pluck the gun out of his belt and turn. But the girl managed to club him with the stick over his head, and then grab hold of him as he shot once, twice, three, four times. The explosions were deafening in that little space. Pieter leaped in over the threshold just as it seemed Miranda came awake. Her body shook and spasmed, and he jumped past her to where the man was struggling with the girl.

Pieter jumped over the uneven boards, some of which had broken to show the black dirt beneath. Dysart was clumsy, slow. The Gypsy had broken the skin on his pale forehead.

Pieter grabbed him by the arm and twisted his arm up. But there were no more shots. The gun fell to the floor. The girl was free and had collapsed onto Miranda's quilts while Pieter staggered and almost fell. The man had kicked him on the inside of the knee, stomped on his foot.

But he pulled Dysart down and fell on top of him. The white shirt had some perfume in the cloth. Dysart's body was slippery with sweat and slipped away from him. Pieter had him by the shirt, though, and with his left hand he was reaching for the gun, fallen in a gap between the floorboards. He could feel the metal underneath his fingers, and he thought he was going to let go of the shirt as it was ripping now, as Dysart pulled away. Pieter felt a pain in his right hand as he reached out with his left, intent on the gun, and unaware of Dysart's knife until that moment; he'd flailed backward at Pieter but couldn't reach him. But he could reach the hand clutching his shirt, and he slid the blade between Pieter's middle and fourth fingers. He was cutting down between the bones toward the hole in Pieter's palm, and the bandage was giving way.

But Pieter had the gun by the barrel. His arm moved slowly, gathering the strength of his body as he rolled back, as he pulled Dysart down. He hadn't let go with his right hand. And with his left he swung the gun as if through layers of interference, and caught Dysart on his forehead once again, next to the row of tiny blood drops where the girl had marked him. Then he let go with his maimed hand and rolled onto his stomach, holding the gun out in his weak, left hand, where it felt oddly comfortable. It was a six-shooter. He had two shots left, with any luck.

But as Dysart said, it's hard to kill a man. Maybe with his right hand Pieter could have managed it, but not his left.

He lay on his stomach, watching the blood pulse from between his fingers, and the long, smooth cut. Behind him, curled up with Miranda, the girl wept. Leaving his red knife on the floor, Dysart rose from his hands and knees until he stood upright, and Pieter rose with him. Bleeding from his forehead, the man staggered backward toward the door, while Pieter put his right hand into his left armpit. The pain was very bad when he pressed down. He closed his eyes for a moment, hardly more than a blink, and when he opened them Dysart was gone.

THAT NIGHT ALSO, AT 11:29, the Bavarian Hydra Express left Ratisbon Station, en route to Vienna, Belgrade, Bucharest. On it, in an ordinary third-class compartment in the middle of the train, Clara Brancoveanu and the boy sat side by side. On their laps they held some paper boxes of sandwiches and fruit. They planned to sit up all night, playing cards and reading. They had not been able to afford a private compartment, certainly not the luxurious first-class sleeper behind the engine where the elector sat at his table. Keeping inside his hired cab till the last instant, he had not seen them board the train.

In front of him on the small table lay some papers and notebooks, some letters and his letter opener. He had washed his hands before he handled them. But he was soon distracted. Now he lay back in his fauteuil and closed his eyes. His thoughts were far away.

It was only with his eyes closed that he could catch a glimpse of the dark town in the hidden world. And even when he stood as if above it on the slopes of Christmas Hill, he did not recognize the place. Nor could he see Miranda sitting on the porch of her parents' house, after she'd put down the silver canister.

She sat in the front doorway, watching the moon above the mountain peaks. On the surface of the threshold lay the book, *The Essential History*.

Closed inside of it was the small silver letter opener that Stanley had given her one Christmas. When she opened the book to the page that was indicated by the blade, she was discouraged to find there was some damage to it, a place where the onionskin paper had been dug away. No, that wasn't it. There was a bug living in it that had dug a long, meandering wormhole. When she opened the last part of the book she could see the bug itself, a worm or a centipede that now surged out onto the page. It was fully two inches long. "Ugh," said Miranda, and she pressed the point of the letter opener into its thin body, crushing it rather than stabbing it, so that its small guts left a smear.

Disgusted, she threw down the book, threw down the flat silver blade. And then she got up and walked down the porch steps, deciding to take a walk downtown while she waited for the pesticide to work. She knew the houses were all empty. She didn't have to look. Nor were the streetlights on. The whole town was deserted, and she walked down the concrete sidewalks across Main Street to Water Street, and down to the fieldstone gate. Without asking herself why, she wanted to visit once more the places she had visited with Peter Gross. More than that, she wanted to get away from the abandoned buildings. She wanted to walk instead among the maples, birches, and conifers that led down to the little cottage by the brook, the ice house with its broken roof and floor.

But in the darkness she couldn't find the path. Or else she found a path, but it wasn't the right one. It led her west and uphill toward the museum until she stood in a small grove of birches, their trunks gleaming in the moonlight. This was the place where she had found the woodchuck, or whatever it was, nailed to the tree. There was no sign of it now. But then a little way farther was the skull, a skull of a big animal, and there were some bones, too.

This was the lair of the white tyger. Miranda turned around. She felt calm, sleek, satisfied. There was a glint of metal under her feet, and she bent down to draw out of the moss, as if out of a scabbard, a small sword. The knob of the pommel was a curled-up snake. Inlaid snakes chased each other down the blade, which was short and heavy with a single edge.

Turning into the forest again, she saw a cat on a broken log, the same cat that had followed her from her house, mangy and unkempt, but with gleaming eyes—a big, baggy orange marmalade with a broken incisor. As Miranda watched, it jumped down from the log and disappeared.

Miranda was sweating and the wind moved through the trees. She could feel it in her hair. She was in danger, she knew, not from the marmalade cat but from something else, some colder and more subtle thing. As she searched for the trail again back toward the ice house, she was aware of other animals flee-ing and scampering away, not from her, she thought. She pushed her way uphill through a tangle of brambles; no one had kept up the trail, she thought. Peter hadn't kept up the trail. All the undergrowth was higher, and she had to hack at it with the sharp sword. Then for a while it was easier going. The ground was bare. Ahead of her there was an animal that turned now and dragged itself to-ward her on its bottom, a little, naked ape, she saw, wounded in the belly. It sat hugging itself with long, hairless arms.

"Go on, get," she said, but it didn't move. With lidless eyes it stared past her, and she turned to see the land had changed again, opened out, and above her she could see the treeless slope of Christmas Hill. There was a half-moon in the starless sky, and on the crest of the hill a half a mile away she could see something coiling and unwinding down the pasture, while the wind brought to her a small burning stink. It was some kind of a colossal beast, a worm or a snake or a centipede that wound down through the pasture side to side, a shal-low zigzag, and the moon shone on its back. And its eyes were big and shone not with reflected light, like the cat's or the little monkey's. But they were globes like an insect's eyes, and lit with the same fire that was burning the grass behind it as it moved.

AT THAT SAME MOMENT IN the third-class compartment of the Bavarian Hydra Express, a celebration was in progress. Unorganized, spontaneous, it had ignited out of the high spirits of the car, which was full of people: soldiers, tradesmen, and old women. Here as everywhere in Germany there were ru-mors of a cease-fire after the sudden, astonishing victories of the Lithuanian campaign. The war was scarcely two weeks old, but already (it was reported) the Duma had delivered an ultimatum to the tsar. With the vote of no confidence and the deaths of von Stoessel and the ministers, everything had changed. Already (it was reported) the young tsarevich had been released as a gesture of good faith. In return, Kaliningrad was to be reannexed.

Two men in the corner of the car were playing the accordion and fiddle. People stood around them and grabbed hold of each other as the train went round a curve. Men embraced, laughed, slapped each other on the back. They pulled out bottles of schnapps and hard cider. They ate sausage sandwiches. The air was full of tobacco smoke and patriotic songs.

The musicians were at the front next to the washroom, where there was an open space for luggage and freight. Down the center of the car was a wide aisle, crammed now with people. Princess Clara, keeping to herself, conversing softly with the boy, didn't see Dr. Theodore until he was hanging by the strap above them.

This is how they'd come to occupy their seats: They had escaped from the elector's house with their clothes and nothing else. Frightened, terrified by freedom, they'd staggered down into the town. There they'd accosted a professor of religion at the university, walking with his wife, a doctor, and their dogs. These people had taken them in, given them a place to stay, and notified the police who (as it turned out) were already pursuing an investigation.

Herr Professor Wobbe-Heck had urged them to stay, but they'd been too frightened. He had sent telegrams on their behalf to Helena Lupescu, Madame Sebastian, and others—the princess's old friends. He'd bought them a ticket. They had no papers, but Clara Brancoveanu hardly expected to be stopped at the border. Her companion was the son of the white tyger, after all.

Now, sitting on the train two days from their escape, the princess was able to breathe freely. Still, she was terrified by the commotion and loud noises. But in the crowded car, as they climbed up the grade into the mountains, she'd experienced a new kind of sensation—timid hope. As the train had gathered speed, she'd lost some of her worst fears. Though the pressure of the crowd was painful, anonymity was a delight.

Herr Professor Wobbe-Heck had told her of the stories in the press, now several weeks old. Miranda Popescu was alive. "I wonder if it can be so?" she asked herself now.

Felix heard her as he shuffled the cards, though she'd been talking to herself. He looked up with a worried face, which made her smile. "My boy, I'll always care for you," she said.

"And did you tell my mother I was coming?"

"No."

He shuddered. "I scarcely remember her."

"Oh my boy, don't worry. She'll be glad to see you. And for your sake I'll forgive her, though her husband . . ."

The terror on his face had touched her heart. But now she followed his staring eyes, and looked up to see Dr. Theodore hanging by the strap, looming over them as the train went around a curve.

For a moment she didn't recognize him. It had been years, after all, since he had brought her meals with his own hands, ushered in her guests. But now here he was again, unaged, a handsome man with a yellow moustache and blue eyes, a strong, brutal face that was softened now with several days' growth upon his cheeks. But what was wrong with him? He wasn't wearing a necktie, and his shirt collar was open. When he started to speak, she knew he had been drinking.

"Don't be alarmed," he said.

Petrified, she grabbed hold of the arms of her seat. She couldn't speak, though what was there to say? Now she remembered all too well the metallic rasp of the doctor's voice, though it was softened now by alcohol, she had to admit. Oh, but he'd been cruel to her, unfeeling!

"Ma'am, it will be all right," he stammered now. "Today is a great day. You know there are changes. Every one of us. Don't . . . tax yourself—unnecessarily. This train is headed to Roumania. You understand?"

Perhaps she had misjudged him. Certainly in the past he'd brought her medicine for her neuralgia and epsom salts—she had to be fair. But always there had been a hard, inhuman, ageless way with him, which had not disappeared. Through his fumbling reassurances, it was still there. He dropped his right hand from the strap to try to touch Felix's hair, except he shied away.

"I'm sorry," murmured Dr. Theodore. "Don't be afraid."

But every time he said that, she felt more of a threat. "Where is your master?" she asked now. "Is he on this train?"

"I have no master," the fellow answered drunkenly. She could scarcely hear him above the music and the shouting in the car. Then he turned and staggered into the crowded aisle again, and she lost sight of him. She didn't see him cross into the second-class compartment on his way up to the private first-class carriages, at the door of one of which he stopped to knock.

———

AS THE TRAIN APPROACHED THE Austrian frontier, it blew its whistle and slowed down. The elector was in his fauteuil, looking over the notebooks he had taken from his house. Each one was stamped on its leather cover with the token of his family, the silver snake of Ratisbon with its exaggerated eyes. Each page displayed the token of the snake, whose ribs at times resembled the legs of a centipede. In these notebooks his simulacra had compiled their observations of the princess and the boy, or so he'd thought.

But he'd been mistaken. So it was with a kind of bemused trepidation that he watched the man come in, watched him lock the door behind him, watched him stagger drunkenly into the compartment. The train whistled, and the brake came on.

The elector was suffering from one of his migraines. He had been reading:

May the seventeenth—not left his room all day. He has scarcely eaten, only lemon punch and oatmeal bread. I have experimented with different substances without result. He eats nuts, though. These are rare nuts from the spice islands that must be especially ordered. A shipment is due in the Kirchenstrasse, and I think something might be done. . . .

The entry was in his own minute handwriting, beautiful, but difficult to make out. Some lines were illegible. Here was an entry for the first week in June:

He makes the lemon punch himself. But he has asked me to bring from the cellar a bottle of Roumanian brandy. I have heard the cork may be penetrated with a hypodermic syringe. There is at the same time some success with the macadamia nuts. I must be careful, though. I have no wish to harm Lt.-Major Lubomyr when he arrives. . . .

As he read, the elector had been playing with his paper knife, a piece of iron ornamented with the snake of Ratisbon. He pricked the point against his wrist. It was still sharp. Always he had loved the look and feel of polished iron. Now he rubbed along his sleeve, momentarily wiping away fingerprints. "So," he said. "My suspicions were . . . misplaced."

"Yes."

"Often one imagines powerful enemies from far away. One imagines the governments and sorcerers of the world. Sometimes the truth is more . . . pedestrian."

"Yes."

"Sometimes there's a traitor close at hand."

"Yes."

"Tell me, are we coming to the border now? I'm afraid someone has telegraphed ahead."

"It is possible."

"Please, just one more question. What is the mood of the people on the train? I believe I can hear music playing."

Dr. Theodore grabbed hold of the brass rail that closed in the ornate upper bunk. He rubbed his mouth. "They are happy that a larger war has been averted. Our victory came so rapidly because of the attack on June the seventh. We have you to thank."

THEY WERE COMING INTO THE station. The half-moon was behind the mountain peaks. But in the secret world it shone in the cloudless sky above Christmas Hill. The snake was coming, winding down the pasture. Then it slowed as it reached the bottom and moved toward her. Miranda could see the burning fire, smell the stink of it, and she could hear the scream.

She stood in the open with her sword. Moonlight glinted on the snake's silver back. Close at hand, though, she could see it wasn't as big as she had feared. But it was breathing fire from its terrible mouth, and she found herself surrounded by a cloud of burning steam. Its eyes shone out of the fire, but she stood her ground.

In front of her it slowed now, stopped, raised itself up. She felt the burning on her skin. But as the head came swinging toward her, as the beast reached out to touch her with its claws, she saw the unprotected place on its pale belly. As it came down she struck the blade into its flesh, then jumped aside.

It wasn't finished. With a shrill whistle of rage, it raised itself up. So she hacked at it again and again while it poured out its smoke and steam. Blinded, she stabbed at it until the sword fell from her hand.

Then she was alone in the dark wood. The cold silver body lay inert. But she was burned and bleeding. She scarcely had the strength to limp away. Now more than ever it was important to find the ice house where Peter used to wait for her after school. Sometimes she stumbled on the rocks, scratched herself as she pressed through the brambles. But she recognized the contour of the ground, heard the murmur of the stream. She could see the little cottage up ahead, its windows glowing among the pine trees. How comfortable it looked as she crept toward it, holding her side! She felt drained and weak after the long dreaming, but as she came close she could see the glowing of the fire, and Ludu Rat-tooth was there, and Peter Gross, her friend. How strange he looked! How he had changed! He was a man now.

Peeking over the sill, she could just see the bed of quilts and blankets near the fire. She could scarcely hear the Gypsy's voice. "Shh, she's waking up." But she had one more task before she rested.

Inside the cottage, in the glow of the fire, they were trying to rouse her. They didn't know the danger, and so in the gray light of dawn she put out her claws. She moved down the slope toward the little stream. She jumped onto a log. She could still smell the blood of the hurt monkey, and she knew the fox could smell it, too. And so she slipped into a cleft between the branches and waited for him to come. With his bottle-brush tail and his curious, stiff-legged gait he ran up from the stream; his legs were black. He was a fast, vicious little creature, but even hurt she was still faster. She took him behind the head.

The fox was Ernest Dysart. Later the police would find him in the woods, mauled as if by an enormous animal. By that time, hours later, the cottage would be empty. Miranda Popescu and the others would have escaped into the safety of the deeper woods.

But with the sunlight streaking through the straight trunks of the pines, the white tyger crept up toward the house again.

For a while she stood guard under the windowsill, hearing the Gypsy girl inside. Ludu Rat-tooth—the little rat wouldn't dare to show her nose over the threshold. But the ape was there, lying on its back in a pile of black needles, its big eyes closed. It was de Graz's animal, the symbol of his house. Miranda didn't recognize it. But now she found herself overjoyed to see an insect on the monkey's long, pale lip, the prettiest bug in all the universe, she thought. Once she'd had him in a little box in tara mortilor. Now here he was again, with his flame-colored carapace and long head.

She put out her hand. The bug crept into her palm. Never had she felt so pleased to see a bug of any kind. It opened up its wings, revealing the blue shell underneath.

She brought it closer to her face. She yawned, then lay down in the under-brush below the sill. Hurt and exhausted, she closed her eyes, and then she was waking with a pain in her side.

And Peter was there with her, grown into a man—had it been five years for him? She was astonished by how happy she felt to find him sitting next to her among the quilts. Happy, shy, and awkward, because he looked so grown up, and because there was something in his face she didn't recognize. Doubtless he had lived through an ordeal, as she had. He would tell her about all of it. He would have stories to braid together with her story, and braiding them would make them stronger. He and she had come a long way from the woods along the Hoosick River where she'd last seen him in the snow.

Oh, but she was glad to see him, and she scrambled up to put her arms around his neck and hug him. He was about to say something, and she put her fingers to his lips, and at the same time she was squeezing him to see if he was real, squeezing his shoulder and arm until he winced. "Çela fait mal," he said.

His right hand was covered in a mass of bandages, which nevertheless were crusted and leaking. Ludu Rat-tooth was standing in the broken corner where the logs and shakes had fallen in, looking out at the sun in the long trees, the mist rising through the branches.

"Where have you been?" Peter asked in French, and again she put her fingers to his lips—she wanted him to talk to her in English.

She wanted to touch him and squeeze him, though she was exhausted, weak, with scratches and burns on her arms and hands. She pulled herself up so she could whisper in his ear, "I'm glad to see you."

He frowned.

"You know," she said, "it's not what it's cracked up to be, this princess thing."

She said this to let him know nothing had changed, at least as far as she was concerned. "It's amazing what you can tolerate," she said. "It's amazing what you can put up with.

"Especially with friends," she said when he said nothing, to let him know they could continue as before because nothing had changed. But he frowned and pulled his head away. He wasn't happy she had hugged him. He wasn't happy she was touching him now. And so she took her hand away. "How are you feeling?"

He shrugged.

"Where's Andromeda?" she asked.

He shrugged.

And she knew suddenly and with foreboding that it was stupid to imagine even for a moment nothing had changed.

Later, when she'd had time to think, she realized it was stupid to console yourself. Because nothing ever stays the same, and everything is always different, and Peter was different, and she herself was different, and everyone is simultaneously rushing toward someone and rushing away, especially people who care about each other after all. And the past drops away and has no meaning for the future, except for moments we look back and say, "Yes, I remember that." Or, "Yes, I felt that." Or, "I believed that." And those images of ourselves are bound to us as if through secret threads of glass.

But if we could forget our disappointment, and if there were something to shatter those tough, sharp threads, sever them, how happy we would be! And the past would recede from us, and we would turn from the people we have known and stumble forward, and meet them coming the other way.

19 | *The Tourmaline*

IN BUCHAREST, AT TWILIGHT on the day Miranda woke, the Baroness Ceausescu read this opinion column in the *Evenimentul Zilei*:

TRAGEDY ABOARD THE HYDRA—The mystery has deepened surrounding the death of Theodore von Geiss und Ratisbon, the hereditary elector of that town. The facts are not at issue. He was found in his first-class sitting room, and the door was locked on the inside. Rather it is the mystery of what pushed this man, a rising star in German politics at one time, to suicide and despair. Doubtless he was aware that a warrant had been issued for his arrest, and the police were prepared to take him into custody at the frontier. When discovered, he had opened his veins with a brass paper knife and could not be revived. But the deeper mystery remains: What is the identity of the corpse that was discovered in his garden in a shallow grave? And how was he able to slip away from the police, leaving two of them mortally wounded? And most of all: What of the presence of Princess Clara Brancoveanu on the same train, traveling with young Felix Ceausescu? They are expected to be met by cheering crowds, when the train crosses the Hungarian border as early as today. . . .

Since the night when she had seen her husband's ghost, the baroness imagined she had felt the unmediated pressure of the world. She imagined she had made decisions, put in motion chains of consequence whose effects now she was powerless to resist. She had scarcely left the People's Palace except to travel under guard to the National Theatre, where before small audiences she had sung a few songs, practiced a few moments, muttered a few spells. And if she had left her people delirious with rapture, she had not been satisfied—she was too old, too brittle to achieve what she most craved. It is difficult for any artist to survive an absence of twenty years—my dear!

But in her private struggle with the third act of *The Tourmaline* (or *The White Tyger,* as she sometimes called it), the baroness imagined she'd achieved a breakthrough. Of course it is when times are blackest that true worth shines through. Everyone knows that. And if after years of trying she had finally broken her husband's heart, what could it mean? Except that she was able to stand on her own feet for the first time since she'd been a child.

She stood in her husband's laboratory. No, he wouldn't be with her any more, strengthening her hand, showing her what to do. She had lit the lamp on Cleopatra's altar, and by its light she examined the newspaper article, where it continued:

> . . . as early as today. What official reception they can expect from the German Authority, or from the white tyger of Pietrosul, fresh from her triumph on the boards of the National, is unclear. In the meantime there are rumored sightings near the capital of the woman who calls herself Miranda Popescu, and whose claims or pretended claims this paper continues to regard with grave suspicion. . . .

It was the baroness's intention, of course, to meet the train at the station as it steamed in from Germany. Yes, she would see her son again. She burned with anticipation. And she would see Clara Brancoveanu once again. And she would offer her shelter in the palace. A penniless refugee—it was an act of simple charity. And it would give a secret pleasure. When the baroness was a child, homeless in the streets of Bucharest, once she had been taken in by the Brancoveanu orphanage.

What had her dead husband said? For the sake of her own power and strength, it was important to find someone to replace Kevin Markasev. Her husband had always kept her from her own accomplishments, but he was not a fool—it was for this reason, she realized now, that she was attempting to revive her career upon the stage. The baron had stripped her of everything when he had forced her to give that up, as had been doubtless his intention.

Now she would take that power back. And she would hold her son, Felix, and Princess Clara, and maybe even Miranda Popescu too, in time, under her roof. What had Hermes Trismegistus said about the need for hostages? But it was not enough. Now more than ever she needed Kepler's Eye to see her way forward in the struggle against Germany. This was the crisis of the last act of the play. To resolve it she needed the tourmaline, the real one, not the fake. Mlle. Corelli had told her where to look.

All that day she had been reading in her husband's books, trying to find out about the jewel. The language had been difficult, abstruse, and she'd lacked the patience to decipher it entirely. Even so, she had come to the conclusion that the baron hadn't really understood the power of the stone. In love himself, he had thought only about love. Kepler too, and that fool of an elector—the sentimentality of these men had blinded them. It took a woman to use power wisely, not in a frivolous manner, nor for the sake of her own vanity.

She had only a few hours before the train arrived at midnight at the Gara de Nord. She had Captain Corelli's address. Now he was a professor at the university. How had he enjoyed his treasure all these years? Was he a fool like these others? Had he used it to lure prostitutes into his room?

Now she heard the ringing of the bell, which Jean-Baptiste employed to summon her. A guest had come—no, three rings and then silence. It was Radu Luckacz, doubtless with news about the Popescu girl.

She had dressed modestly for her interview with the professor, a waistless gray smock with a Parisian hemline at midcalf. It was a cool night, and she wrapped a gray, fringed shawl around her shoulders as she left the room. She passed through her bedchamber and then into the more public apartments, until she found at last the little sitting room where Radu Luckacz waited for her.

She opened her shawl so he could see the fine bones of her neck. She came close to him so he could smell the fragrance of her perfume, mixed always with her own body's smell—she was careful not to cover it completely. He stood with his hat in his hands, looking more than ever like a rusty old crow.

"Madam," he insisted after an agonized silence. "I have good news. We have surrounded Miranda Popescu in the forest above Mogosoaia. You understand it is in the old preserve where those monkey-faced barbarians are living. You know they were protected by Aegypta Schenck and then forgotten by us, neglected for too long. I have spoken to the German ambassador, who agrees it might be time to harvest those old trees. They will bring a good price in Germany. . . ."

"Surrounded?" murmured the Baroness Ceausescu.

"Yes, ma'am," Luckacz persisted in his shrill, nasal, Hungarian-accented voice, too loud for the little room. "We have her in a circle. She has left all human habitation, and there is only one more place to look. We will take them at Constantin's Ford. She is with that fellow only, and one Gypsy servant. . . ."

"She is not to be harmed," murmured the baroness.

"Ma'am, your compassion is well known. . . ."

She put her hand out toward him, pausing a few centimeters from his coat. The lamps were low. Shadows flickered around them. "I will bring her here. I will reunite her with her mother. Perhaps she and Felix . . ."

"Ma'am, she is a murderess!"

Ah! And is that really such a bar? the baroness thought. Then she spoke wistfully, sadly: "Please, I want you to bring an honor guard to the station. And a brass band. Could you manage a brass band?"

For a moment she felt overcome with sadness, imagining herself in Clara Brancoveanu's place. "My friend, you've helped me," she whispered to Radu Luckacz. "And one more thing—have you found Markasev, the boy who escaped from us? You remember I asked you. . . ."

"Yes. So far I have discovered nothing. We must be discreet. I have people in the hospices and shelters. You know the German government has opened up some houses for the indigent. . . ."

The baroness shrugged her shoulders, wrinkled her nose. "Thank you, my old friend."

She could not bear to think of Kevin Markasev in any of those places. Since her husband had told her how the boy was made, she had felt the attachment even more strongly. Now she regretted her rashness in the house on Spatarul, mourned her lack of foresight. But what use were any of these regrets—Aegypta Schenck's murder, or the lies she had told her husband? Looking backward, you assumed a burden that you couldn't carry, that you must dispose of if you wanted to move forward. Because in another sense these mistakes were part of what made her strong, her passionate, impulsive nature—she could not help herself!

And she need not have worried, because Kevin Markasev was not at that moment in some dismal dormitory for the homeless. As she came out one of the side doors of the palace under the porte-cochère, Kevin Markasev was waiting by the gate. He was in a crowd of people waiting in the cold, misty evening to catch a glimpse of her. As her footman handed her into the carriage, he was one of only a few who did not wave or cry out. Only he stood with his hands in his pockets, a woolen cap pulled low over his forehead; as she scanned the faces of crowd under the streetlight, Nicola Ceausescu didn't recognize him.

Nor was he in her thoughts as she sat back against the leather seats. She was thinking of her interview with Professor Corelli. Maybe she should have walked along the Strada Floreasca in disguise, knocked on his door. Maybe she should have summoned him—no, the jewel was in his secret place. And from his house she had to go directly to the station to meet Radu Luckacz and the train. So she had decided to pay an official visit—unannounced—in her coach and four.

At a corner of the street, she pounded on the window with her gloved hand. The footman saw her and called to the postilion up ahead. The coach slowed, stopped, and at the entrance to an alley between two brick buildings, a woman stepped from the shadows.

A hooded cloak obscured her face. In the deserted street she stepped over the coach and stepped onto the rung. The baroness opened the door for her and she slipped inside.

"Oof," she said, and giggled, turning down her hood to reveal her long nose and big mouth, big teeth. She smelled of liquor. "Ma'am, are you sure this is a good idea?"

AT TWILIGHT PIETER LED THE general's daughter into the old-growth section of the Mogosoaia woods, enormous oaks and beeches that had never been timbered, and they crunched through layers of acorns and beechnuts underfoot. Often he found signs of bears—scratches in the tree bark at about eye level. But of the forest people there was no longer any trace.

"Nous ne pouvons pas rester ici," said de Graz. "Il faut que nous . . ."

They were crossing a little stream. Miranda Popescu sat down to take her boots off. "Mademoiselle," he said. "Je vous en prie. . . ."

"Oh, Peter, I'm so tired. Completement fatiguée. Just let's sit here for five minutes."

"Mademoiselle—"

"Don't call me that. Don't be so formal. Please—there's no need."

The Gypsy, who had been walking behind them, now came up. She spoke the language of the country people. "We can't go on. We'll stop here for the night."

De Graz muttered a curse. Bitterly, as if they were children he explained the facts to them. Their only chance was to slip over the river in the darkness, the Colentina River where it broke at Constantin's Ford. If soldiers and policemen had not already secured it . . .

The light was fading from the trees. "Well, then let's wait for darkness," argued the Gypsy. "Can't you see how tired she is? We'll rest here for a few hours."

How could these women be so headstrong? How could he help them if they would not help themselves? Frustrated, he made his right hand into a fist inside his bandage, squeezing it to feel the puffed-up wound. That was real at least. He would need a surgeon soon.

"It's all right," said Mlle. Popescu. She had stood again to cross the brook. Now she turned around to face them with the water around her bare ankles. "Ludu—he's right. The quicker we are, the more we'll have a chance. Besides, if we reach the river we will have to wait till darkness then. We'll have an hour at least."

This surprised de Graz. He had made the same calculation, more or less. Now on the far bank she was rubbing her feet before she slipped into her socks again—that had to stop. It was nonsense for her to think she could keep her feet dry. So once the stream was past he turned north onto swampier ground just to teach her a lesson. And of course the way was more direct.

The Gypsy cursed him. But now Mlle. Popescu was following him with grim stubbornness as they splashed over the uneven hummocks and through the dead trees. There were mosquitoes. He caught at them with his left hand as he stamped a path through the undergrowth. Sometimes he held aside the brambles for her, turning to watch her flushed, angry face. At Mamaia Castle he had not known much about children, and she had not taught him much. She'd been too proud and too precocious. But he remembered this way of goading her.

Now she was a woman.

And it was true—she must be tired. Two days of wandering in the hidden world—he knew about that. He had been lost in an American boy's body and he still had dreams. But he had woken up, and now she was awake, and he would bring her across the river at Constantin's Ford, the only possibility on foot. Bucharest on the north side had spread beyond its walls, which had been torn down in many places. But his mother had a house near Lake Herastrau. There was a fig tree in the courtyard, he remembered. Seven steps led to the door, which was painted red.

It was strange, he thought, how you could give your life over to other people. But that's what a soldier did, and that's what a soldier's glory meant. Dysart had forgotten that, had gone out for himself. Now he was worse than dead.

Pieter's hand ached where Dysart had cut him. It throbbed and ached. In half an hour they left the wet ground behind—they hadn't lost any time, and might even have gained something. And he could smell the river. In a thicket of pine trees they sat down and waited for the moon to rise. Businesslike, Miranda Popescu stripped off her wet boots. Then she brushed her teeth, wrapped herself up, and in the last light she sat down to read once more the letter that she carried with her money in the beaded purse. The Gypsy had kept it for her after all.

"What is that?" he asked.

Mlle. Popescu looked up at him. And she actually smiled; in her expression there was no trace of any anger. When she was a child, sometimes she'd been cross with him for days.

"Do you remember?" she said. "Please correct me. But was there a time—I must have been about seven—when my aunt and I sat on camp stools in a farmer's field. There was a tent, and lots of food, and bottles of wine in copper tubs, on ice. Some officers gave an exhibition of trick riding and dressage. And I remember you on a big gray horse. Prochenko was there with us in his uniform. I saw him under the torchlight. He promised me a sip of wine!"

Curse his handsome face! "He had hurt himself," murmured de Graz. "Otherwise he would have won as always."

"You see—I remember him saying that! If I read this letter before I fall asleep, then in the morning I remember something like that, some small thing. And of course it's looking at your face that brings it back. Hearing your voice. I think we were friends before. That's not too much to ask!"

Later he went down to the riverbank to reconnoiter. He came out from the trees. Crouching down among some cattails, he surveyed the broad, shallow reach of the Colentina, slow and noiseless here. There were no lights anywhere that he could see, no sign of life on either bank, which proved nothing, obviously.

When he came back, Miranda Popescu was alone. Doubtless the Gypsy had gone out to squat somewhere. Curled up on a bed of pine needles, wrapped in a gray shawl, the general's daughter had fallen asleep. De Graz sat watching her. There was a mist above the trees, and beads of moisture on the surface of the shawl.

Restless, she murmured and rolled over. The letter had fallen from her hand. Inadvertently he caught a glimpse of it as he bent over her. The light was almost gone. "If you are as I think a princess of Roumania . . . ," he read.

Perhaps. He'd sworn his parole to Frederick Schenck von Schenck, and to his sister too, whose handwriting it was. But there's many a slip 'twixt the cup and the lip, as his old nurse used to say in English, he remembered suddenly. Mrs. Abigail. She'd had a wart on her cheek. The wart had had a hair in the middle of it.

The moon was up now, though it was hidden in the mist. But the sky was brighter in the east. Soon he'd wake her, Miranda Popescu, who now turned onto her back. He could see her cheeks and long neck. Her face was beautiful in the soft light. Drops of mist were in her hair.

Nurse Abigail must have taught him some English doggerel, which he now remembered:

They flee from me that sometime did me seek,
With naked foot stalking within my chamber:
Once I have seen them gentle, tame, and meek,
That now are wild, and do not once remember. . . .

What if she was the general's daughter? A man could look, couldn't he?

He stood over her as she awoke and stretched, opened her eyes. He had not been alone with her before. Too soon there was some noise from beyond the thicket. But it was only the Gypsy coming back. She was excited, laughing, and she bent down to grasp Miranda's hands—"Oh, miss, you won't believe it!"

And as Miranda Popescu turned her head, the girl went on—"I saw one! Oh, I'm sure I saw one."

"What?"

"And it was huge! A white tyger, miss. I saw it underneath a tree!"

HAVING REACHED THE UNIVERSITY DISTRICT in the eastern part of Bucharest, the baroness's horses slowed to a walk. The baroness sat forward on the seat. Mlle. Corelli was beside her. A creature of impulse, Nicola Ceausescu had not planned carefully what she would say or do.

But when the carriage stopped outside the narrow stone house, she pushed open the door and stepped onto the rung. She had posted one of Luckacz's men at the corner of the road, who now touched his cap—"He's still inside."

"Thank you." Standing in the unpaved street, looking up at the dark, elegant façade—Professor Corelli, historian and antiquarian, was nevertheless from an important family—the baroness now understood why she had brought the girl. And it was not, as she had first supposed, because she needed her to show her the location of the jewel. But the baroness wanted something to trade. Years before, the Elector of Ratisbon (now deceased!) had proposed a trade: her son for Kepler's Eye.

"Come, my dear," she said to Mlle. Corelli, holding up a gloved hand to help her from the coach.

Oh, but she had been a fool, the baroness thought, not to trade the false stone for the boy—her only son! But how could she have known? It didn't matter. In two hours she would embrace her darling Felix on the station platform in front of the assembled dignitaries, the real jewel in her pocket. That would be the moment of her victory, and the band would play the appropriate motif, mixed inevitably with other, darker themes—she had given Luckacz some sheet music from the third act of her drama to pass on to the musicians. Oh, but her husband had been right! Trismegistus was right! The elector had given up his prisoners. Now he was dead. She felt a thrill of triumph.

"Come on, my dear," she repeated, her fingers clamped around the girl's elbow. "Please don't dawdle. Your father is expecting us."

This was untrue. It was not the baroness's habit to come announced. But even in the dark street, she thought she could detect a wistful kind of apprehension in Mlle. Corelli's painted face—"Ma'am, what did he say?"

"Hush, child. He will be glad to see you."

This proved to be an exaggeration. Fingers clamped under her elbow, she led the girl up the stone steps while one of the footmen rang the bell. Gaslight flickered in the portico. In time they heard the sound of the bolt pulled back. New light spilled out from the hall, and a servant stood with his hand on the doorknob. In back of him a big man with a loud, jovial voice—"Who is it, Gaston, please?"

The servant, who couldn't have been more than twenty, peered out doubtfully. He said nothing, but in time he pulled the door back to reveal his master, a big man dressed in slippers and a smoking jacket. "You!" he said.

Then Gaston was gone, and the man stood alone on the threshold barring their way. He was clean-shaven, with a high, pale face, good features, and gold-rimmed spectacles. "You are not welome here," he said.

The baroness felt the girl cringe under her hand. In what spirit of bravado had she painted her lips and eyes? "Please, father," she said.

Now her cloak had parted, and the baroness could see also that her clothes underneath were far from modest, a low-cut shirt, silk stockings above her knees. And it was just those small, defiant, self-defeating details that touched the baroness in an obscure section of her heart—Mlle. Corelli had prepared herself with some carefulness. And at that moment she reminded the baroness of herself, of errors she had made.

She dismissed her own footman with a nod, a gesture of her head. "Please, sir," she said. "Do you recognize me?"

At receptions and official functions, at all social gatherings, Nicola Ceausescu felt a constant tremor of pride and shame, wondering if each old or middle-aged man remembered seeing her as she'd appeared as Ariadne, or Medea, or Mary Magdalene, or Saint Joan, or Miranda Brancoveanu, or Cleopatra with her breasts uncovered at the end of the last act. As they bent to kiss her hand, she wondered if they were at that moment imagining her in greasepaint as she stood upon the boards of the Ambassadors in Bucharest, or on similar stages in many foreign capitals. Perhaps that was why she felt such sympathy now for Mlle. Corelli, a tiresome girl in many respects—why she felt tears now on her own unpowdered cheek. "You would not turn your own daughter away?"

In spite of the professor's pale complexion, she could tell his nature was choleric—she could see the blood rise to his face. And in spite of his good looks, there was something in him that recalled a gnawing, biting animal, a marmot or a squirrel perhaps—she could see his long fingernails and big front teeth. "Yes, I recognize you," he cried. "You're the start of this."

He had his fingernails on the doorpost, and with his other hand he held onto the knob so that the way was blocked. "That night she sneaked away from home to one of your performances," he chattered angrily. "She came back telling me she'd be an actress, which meant a whore in your case as the old baron found out soon enough. A whore in her case, too; the whole city knows it. Not that I blame her—a nation of whores now, and Germany has hired us by the hour . . . ," on and on.

At every repetition of this ugly word, she felt Mlle. Corelli cringe as if she had been slapped. And the baroness felt also the force of what he said. Was it true she had destroyed this family? She'd heard Corelli's wife had died, though she was not yet old. And the son was now a soldier in the Ukraine.

But surely the professor could have used the power of the tourmaline to save himself, protect himself, protect his home. So he was a coward after all, without the strength to do what's necessary. In her heart the baroness felt a surge of music, and she imagined momentarily how various themes from the overture of the first act would repeat in the third—she had risen from the streets to the top of her profession. And yes, she had betrayed her country to the Germans, but she would rise above them, too, and all Roumania would profit, and all its citizens would thank her, finally.

Now more than ever she had need of the jewel, useless in this coward's hands. "Please," she murmured. "Everything you say is true."

As she spoke, she put a spell into the words, a small piece of conjuring she had learned out of her husband's books. She knew the spell was powerful because of what she was, a beautiful woman who now pulled her gray shawl from her neck. And Corelli was silent, his voice extinguished as she reached out and put her gloved finger to his lips, while at the same time she pushed him backward with the weight of her gloved forefinger. She tightened her grip on the daughter's arm, and pushed her father back against the door. "Please," she said. "May we come in?"

"No," said Mlle Corelli. "He doesn't want me here." But she also was powerless to resist as Nicola Ceausescu pushed her way into the hall. It was a comfortable old place, smelling of smoke, lined with red wallpaper and glass-fronted cabinets. And on the left-hand side, a mirror, in which she caught a glimpse of herself—her helmet of copper-colored hair, her unlined, small-featured face. A beautiful woman, as all the world agreed. And if she couldn't see it, if even momentary, sidelong glances were enough to shake her confidence, that was a tragedy to be explored in the first act of her drama and then again in closing scenes. Now there was no time for it as she felt the small effects of her conjuring begin to dissipate and drift away. Corelli struggled to speak. The girl twisted her arm away and pulled it free.

The baroness slammed the door behind them, and they all stood together in the narrow hall. There were doors with velvet curtains on the right-hand side, a staircase up ahead. On her right a row of cabinets displaying Roman glassware and ceramics and other curiosities, all painstakingly labeled, and among which she searched in vain for mineral samples or uncut jewels. She needed the tourmaline, needed to find it, if only to defeat the self-doubt that now assailed her—"Gaston, Gaston," Corelli managed to say, and for a moment the baroness felt a thrill of fear. What would he do, call the police? But the police were already outside, would arrest him and burn down the house if she gave the order— no, that wasn't the reason she had come. Now she knew: she had come here to rectify the damage she had done to this family, to earn the trust her people had in her, to demonstrate she was the white tyger in more than just a name. What had Corelli called her? The Germans' hired servant? Something uglier than that.

And if she needed a reward for her efforts, a small but valuable token that nevertheless would enable her to achieve more, heal more broken families, who would deny her? Not some nervous professor with a face like a rodent's, who had made no use of it himself. "Come," she said, muttering another small curse under her breath and turning fiercely on the girl, who cowered against the closed door.

In order to heal them, first she must cause pain. "Tell me where it is."

"Ma'am, I . . ."

"Where does he keep it? Tell me quick!"

But the fool wasn't paying enough attention. Instead she was looking toward her father, even reaching out to touch him in spite of the cruel thing he'd said. And she was right to be concerned—the man was flushed and stammering. Still impeded by the fading spell, he touched his throat, and with his other hand gestured toward his servant on the stairs. There the door led to to the servants' quarters. When the baroness glanced that way again, the door stood open and the boy had disappeared.

It didn't matter. If he left the house by the back door, then her policeman would pick him up—she'd given orders to arrest anyone who tried to leave. "The tourmaline—tell me now!" she said, while at the same time she repeated in her mind the formula for squeezing and tightening, which she'd learned in her husband's book. And it was having a renewed effect. Corelli staggered back against one of his cabinets, hands at his throat. He was a coward and a weakling, and the girl, too. "Please, ma'am," she begged, holding her hands out beseechingly—her cloak had slid aside, revealing her whore's clothes, the dark material cut low over her breasts. Still she could not keep herself from looking toward the second pair of velvet curtains and then looking away.

It was enough. And once they had surrendered—father and daughter, both—then the baroness could afford to be generous again. Corelli could breathe easier again, as the baroness reconsidered. Not cowards but lost sheep from a dispersed flock, now reunited at long last.

"Ma'am, he has a weak heart," protested the girl. Nicola Ceausescu seized her by the elbow. Then she was shepherding them both through the curtains, and they came into a drawing room and study. There were bookcases, dark furniture, leather chairs. On the side away from the street Corelli kept his chamber of curiosities, a small area like a stage that was lined with cabinets and shelves. Light came from sconces set into the walls, chimneys of frosted glass with the flames turned low. The baroness had a vague impression of apothecary jars and bones, animal skeletons and stuffed hunting trophies, as she surmised. But on the floor beside an armchair was the safe.

"Tell me," she said to Mlle. Corelli, but the girl was useless now, in tears. Her cloak had fallen back from her shoulders, exposing her bare arms. Her father stood in the light, and any suggestion of a squirrel or a mouse had vanished from his face, ennobled now with suffering and concern. "Natalie," he murmured, wringing his hands, though still he did not dare to approach the girl. "Open it," said Nicola Ceausescu.

But Corelli had recovered his capacity for speech. "You have no right to come in here," he protested. "We are private citizens in our own house. Gaston will tell them at the station house that you are trying to rob us. There are policeman in the next road!"

So it was already "our house"—his and the girl's! In five minutes the baroness had brought them together under one roof. But she could do more. She still had Mlle. Corelli by the arm. She could twist her arm and hurt her, or else more than that. Delighting in the moment, the baroness closed her eyes. And she imagined reaching out with some small spell or conjuring, something that would mar the girl in subtle ways and punish her inside, damage her so that her own father would no longer feel his heart touched in her presence.

It wouldn't take much. The girl was already so close. Smiling, cocking her head, the baroness opened her eyes.

Always her power as an actress—supernatural, some people said—was in the way she could allow her intentions to be read in her expressions and the language of her body. Groaning and defeated now, Corelli went down on his knees to fumble with the combination of the safe. With her hand around his daughter's elbow, the baroness listened to her own harsh, even breath, listened to the sobbing of the girl. What contempt she had for this man who now knelt at her feet, and who all these years had kept in a steel box one of the wonders of the world, a jewel that had grown inside the skull of Johannes Kepler the alchemist, a symbol of his entry into a mystic brotherhood of conjurers.

Click, click, click went the combination dials, spinning under Corelli's thin fingers. No doubt he was a scientist who neither respected nor believed the power of Kepler's Eye. No doubt he conceived of it as just another object in his collection of historical and natural oddities—one with a greater than average intrinsic value, perhaps, and certainly a romantic provenance.

A blinkered academician, he could not have been expected to understand. With his belief in rational categories, he would have had no mental compartment for an object that was described in different documents as a mineral, a bodily organ, and even sometimes as a piece of fruit—a grape, as the baroness had read in one possibly metaphorical poem. Or a berry, as she had read it described in one of Kepler's own journal entries—a pitted fruit that had improved his vision, made him what he was. It had grown inside him from a seed.

Now the door of the safe stood open. Nicola Ceausescu let go of the girl's arm. Hoisting up her skirt, she squatted beside the fumbling Corelli, and with her own hands she drew out the wooden tray of jewels. But there was nothing but garbage—fossils, petrified remains, and in another small box some diamond jewelry, some diamond and platinum trash that had doubtless belonged to the deceased and unlamented Madame Corelli—oh, this was a family of slaves!

Lips curled in disgust, she turned the professor as he labored to stand. She had scattered his wife's jewelry over the carpet, and with a cry he bent to gather them again. Doubtless he had been saving them for his only daughter, and doubtless also it broke his heart whenever he looked at them—there was something like that now in his face.

Enraged, the baroness raised her hand and saw his look of fear—what was wrong with him? Surely he could see that she was just one weak woman, weaker than he. Surely if he chose, he could punish her as she deserved.

But now she realized what he was actually afraid of, and it wasn't her, or at least not entirely. Maybe he'd been counting the minutes since Gaston had left, and maybe now he understood she had the power of the state behind her, and Radu Luckacz's police force, and the German army, all of which allowed her to do whatever she wished, behave like a lunatic inside his house, humiliate him and his daughter, too. They had no recourse. They had no recourse if she struck him across the face, as now, and watched a gash appear over his eye. Even inside her glove, the baron's golden ring must have caught him wrong.

They had no recourse if she batted his spectacles to the corner of the room, as now. "Stop!" cried the girl, tears disfiguring her face. "Stop, you monster!"

Was that the word? the baroness asked herself. Was that what Corelli had called her in the hall? No, it was an uglier word than that. No wonder she was angry now.

And the girl had stumbled across the room to fall over her father, raise him up, cradle him in her arms, blot away the blood on his eyebrow and the bridge of his nose. "Papa," she cried, "papa," and he was weeping, too.

The Baroness Ceausescu rose to her feet. All was quiet now except for their snuffling and the beating of her heart as she studied the room for other hiding places. There was the professor's desk, and on the blotter under the lamp stood a row of photographs in silver frames: a gray-haired woman with a kind, soft face. A boy in military uniform, a row of ribbons on his chest. And an exposure of Mlle. Corelli with flowers in her hair, taken when she was eight or nine.

Nicola Ceausescu turned instead to the collection. It occupied the back end of the room, a small three-sided chamber with a raised floor that separated it from the larger space. The baroness stepped onto the bare boards, stepped into the chamber; again she had the impression she was stepping out onto a stage. She felt the same gooseflesh, the same sense of anticipation and self-consciousness. Corelli and his daughter were her audience. Caught in each other's arms, they stared at her with wet, frightened eyes.

But as always when she'd taken a few steps, she stopped caring about any audience. It was as if the missing fourth wall of the chamber now magically re-formed, and she was there alone. Alone with her art, and with Corelli's strange collection of perplexing or disgusting artifacts—a row of fetuses in cloudy glass jars. Preserved specimens of enormous bugs. Human skeletons, wired together, hanging from hooks, and elsewhere bins of animal bones.

The light flickered from the sconces. Somewhere in here, she knew or thought she knew, was Kepler's Eye, a tourmaline (she knew or thought she knew) with a unique power. Johannes Kepler had a thousand lovers—that was factually correct. But he had also, as the baroness had discovered in last few days, won over a million marks at games of chance. On one occasion he had rolled eleven consecutive double-sixes with eleven sets of dice.

The Elector of Ratisbon, what could he not have accomplished with good luck? Now he was dead. Luck also, the baroness knew, had deserted the Corellis over the past five years—but was it possible the girl had lied to her? Was it possible, finally, the jewel was no longer here? That she had goaded the baroness into throwing it into the fountain—throwing it away!—by claiming it was false. Real or not, it had taken Nicola Ceausescu to the apex of her power.

And if the girl had tricked her, she would pay for it. The baroness now turned back into the room. The light flickered, and she saw the Corellis clutched together, only dimly now, unclearly as if through a scrim. At the same time she noticed on her right-hand side a line of stuffed birds. One of them she recognized, though she'd never been much for natural history. But she remembered the brandywine birds in the low bushes in the early morning when she was just a child.

And she remembered it flitting from Aegypta Schenck's cottage, after she had strangled her by Venus's pool. That was the same night she had found the jewel, taken it from Claude Spitz in the entranceway of her old house in Saltpetre Street—surely all her bad luck since that night had been the result of that double murder. Horrified, she gaped at the bird that stood suddenly lifelike on the shelf, its head cocked as if watching her, a dried berry in its beak.

Slowly, hesitantly, staring at the bird, she murmured a small prayer. It was a nostrum of her mother's, passed down among the villagers of Pietrosul. The baroness had heard her mother say the words, once when she'd lost a copper coin.

Hardly had the words left her mouth when the coin revealed itself in the dirt under a stool. Now, scarcely had the baroness finished when she spied a human skull on a shelf of human remains. It was unusually small, she thought. And there were holes in the cranium as if from a process of trepanning. And the bone gleamed like polished ivory. And there was a discoloration, a broken line over the eye ridge. And a tiny pasteboard placard: I. Kepler.

She struck out with her hand. The cranium separated, bounced away. Disturbed also by the sudden movement, one of the skeletons made a little dance. At the front of the skull there was an empty cradle in the bone—nothing there.

Corelli's murmured voice came from behind her: ". . . my jewel . . ." Slowly, frightened now, a lump in her throat, she turned around. But he wasn't looking at her. He was talking about his daughter, whom he now raised to her feet. He was crooning over her. What now?

Unbidden to her mind came part of another prayer, which she had spoken in the room she'd shared with Kevin Markasev on the night Claude Spitz returned to life. And no sooner had it left her lips than she heard a fluttering and a whirring from behind her. What kind of a sour magic trick was this? When she turned, the stuffed bird had left its perch. It flapped around her in a circle and then out into the room.

Awestruck, she let it go. She stood murmuring her prayer in the little room, the prayer that brings dead things to life. For a moment she blinked stupidly and brought her hands up to her face, unsure of what to do. She was alone. Corelli and his daughter had already stumbled from the room. Should she chase after them? Should she call for the police? Should she send a message to the Ukraine, to the commander of Lieutenant Corelli's regiment? She had power to crush them all. And if she wanted, she could send Radu Luckacz's men to scour the area around Maximillian's fountain. They would question everyone who lived near there. Why had she not thought of this before?

The bird fluttered in a circle around the room. Then it too was out the door and in the chamber there was quiet for the first time, it seemed, in ages. Now the decision was hers, but first she must convince herself. Had the Corellis ever really owned the jewel, or had the baroness possessed it for a while and then lost it? She found herself immobile, balanced between possibilities.

But this she knew, or she suspected with a sudden certainty that was like knowledge: The tourmaline was gone out of her hands. It was gone like a fluttering bird, gone for good; and it was useless to search for it. And her husband had withdrawn his shelter, his protection, and the stone was gone for good.

"Ah, God," she murmured, unable to bear the thought of it. No, she would search at Maximillian's fountain. No, she would press the professor for the truth, even if she had to torture it out of him. She would know the truth.

But after another moment, standing in Corelli's exhibition chamber as if on a stage, she changed her mind. And she remembered standing in the lights at the Ambassadors during the first production of *Cleopatra*—oh, she had begged and pleaded with the director and the costume mistress. In the last act, vulnerable and exposed, alone on stage she had looked out over the audience, feeling her humilation and her shame. Then as her little, croaking voice had started on the final aria, she had imagined something else: a sudden power. That night she'd had no tourmaline. That night she'd seen her husband for the first time, captured him and the whole city of Bucharest.

Now as then she stood on her own feet, feeling a sense of vertigo that was nevertheless exhilarating. What was it the baron had said the last time she had seen him? "It is confidence you lack. Faith in your own power. Faith to see yourself as others see you."

No, she told herself as if aloud, and for a moment she believed it: Everything she had accomplished she had earned and paid for. If men and women hurried to obey her, it was because of what she was and what she'd done. She was the white tyger of Roumania. Who would take that away without a fight?

The Corellis—no—it didn't matter. She would see Radu Luckacz at the station in forty minutes' time. She would feel his love for her, and she would tell him her desires, and together they would plot the third act of her opera, *The White Tyger.* In the meantime, she had a train to meet. And she would see her son!

THE STREET DOOR TO CORELLI'S house stood open and the little bird veered out and up into the sky. She flew in a circle around the chimney, then streaked away north toward Constantin's Ford. She carried something in her beak. It was a fondness for grapes that had given the bird her name.

Earlier that same day, farther south, Andromeda had stood with her hand on the marble counter in a café in the town of Chiselet. She had finished her own cup of brandywine, which she'd had served with a bowl of ice. Once or twice in the past hour she had laid her cheek down on the stone countertop, taking comfort from its coldness. She was wearing the Abyssinian technician's clothes.

This was the town where Andromeda had wandered after the wreck of the Hephaestion. The technician had had money in his trouser pocket. Now, several days later, Andromeda had spent the last of it.

Always when she found her human shape again, she was hectic and hot for a few days. Always she retained some of the dog's temperature. But this time she'd felt something new when she had come to her woman's shape again. Her eyes itched, her cheeks burned, her heart pounded in her chest.

And she was not the only one in Chiselet to feel these indications. The old woman who took her last coin in the café, the boy who wiped the stone-topped counter where she stood, too excited to sit down, looking out into the dusty street—both of them felt much as she did, as if a sickness had spread from her.

In the days that followed, the German health authorities would sequester both the old woman and the young boy, place under quarantine the wreck of the Hephaestion and the entire district of Chiselet. They were monitoring the effects of radiation. They were puzzled by the symptoms they observed. They had little knowledge of the facts, and there was little to be done in any case.

The situation was more serious than they supposed. Nor at first could they rule out the effect of some separate contagion, a sickness spreading everywhere Andromeda had passed those first days of her homecoming, a fever of forgetfulness and change, moving everywhere away from her like a new, blank page.